Psychoillogical

Part Two
of
The Donald Diaries

Also by David Halpin:

The Donald Diaries:
Hospityable
(Part One of the Donald Diaries)

The Nobody Saga:
Poetry and Random Thoughts from a Depressed Mind
(Autobiography of a Nobody)

More of the Same
(Continued Saga of a Nobody)

Some More of the Same but Better
(Episode Three of the Nobody Saga)

Even More of the Same and Even Better
(Chapter 4 of the Nobody Saga)

Yet More of the Same … Still Better
(Book V of the Nobody Saga)

Much More of the Same … Gratuitously Better
(Book 𝍸𝍸�I of the Nobody Saga)

Bigger and Better … Sameness
(Lucky #7 of the Nobody Saga)

Other:
Numpty-Rhymes, Numpty-Bys and Numpty-Songs
(Poetry from Numpty's Doctor's Brother's Goose)

Psychoillogical

Part Two
of
The Donald Diaries

David Halpin

This is purely a work of fiction. (Mostly, at least, but I didn't say that. ☺)

Names of characters and places have been altered, events have been grossly exaggerated, and reality has taken a veritable beating, all in the name of having some good clean fun. (And making money, obviously; unless you stole this from your local Oil Rig, which makes you bad and naughty!) Any resemblance to actual persons (Breathing or Not) or events (Real, Unreal, or Not Real) is coincidental. (If it protects me from some, any, or all litigation, it is a huge bonus).

Any breaking out of character, bursting out in laughter, or sides being split (or even someone looking at you funny) is *Your Problem* now, as you have just read this warning. I think it is a little bit fiendish to have this *In the Beginning* before any of the documented hilarious, but fictional events have had a chance to ensue. That is unless I came up with an extra-large helping of amusing for the back page, as you probably haven't read this warning yet.

This book is not intended to be a substitute for medical advice from anyone. You should regularly consult with any number of Psychiatrists, Psychologists, Psychics or Psychopaths until you are convinced your almost-funny-bone is still intact. But seriously, this book is meant to make you laugh. Don't try and think too much about any of it. It should come as no surprise to learn I didn't. Like any dangerous activity, projectile *blurtation* of a mouthful of liquid may occur. Be mindful of this if you are drinking a hot coffee or a nice Chianti.

ISBN: 9781923101272

Dedicated to:

Anyone who identifies as unique, like Donald.

The self-identification of the uniqueness of you has been entirely left up to you. And therefore, no further correspondence will be entered into. Unless you feel some further correspondence may be beneficial, then by all means justifiable, send me an eMail and we can discuss just how unique we both are.

Comments:

"Keep going with Donald.
We are all wondering what eventually happened to him."
x   Lady W[1]

"That's awesome!! I love it! If I ever teach Drama again, can I use it?"
x   Lady A

"After the amazing success of Hospityable (Part One of The Donald Diaries), I had no hesitation in writing a second, third, fourth... volume for your perusal.
They will all become available where good books are sold,
and probably more so where the bad ones are given away."

"I am still not, and I never will be, laughing at Mentally Unique people.
Nor am I meaning to trivialise any disability of any kind, anyone, or anything.
Do any intelligent people take offence at shows like The Big Bang Theory?[2]"
x   Extracts from The Donald Diaries.

---

[1]   For the first footnote, and just maybe this is one of the most important of ones for once, I feel compelled to iterate that the English language is an extremely dopey one when it is viewed literally:
- x   If you talk,   you're a talker;
- x   If you speak,   you're a speaker;
- x   If you whisper, you're a whisperer; but
- x   If you quote,   you're a pretentious git.

And to finish this thought... *Iterate* means the same as *reiterate*.

[2]   I recently watched this series again and found numerous errors relating to what an anal Sheldon would say (very unique) and was slightly annoyed when he didn't learn how to behave appropriately in a repeated scenario.

Table of Contents

Tables of Dis-Content

Introduction: Previously (in the Donald Diaries)

Enter the protagonist, the hero,[3] the star... Donald.

From our previous meeting with the intrepid Donald, we know that **Donald Halfbrain** is usually atypically quiet, unassuming and intelligent. He is the one shining star in his own universe. He is also *crazy*. You don't even need to take my word for this, just read on McDuff.

Until now and then...

Donald is still reeling[4] from the last week of his *life*.

After surviving through many years of unimaginable obscurity he was in the not quite, but nearly, forced custody of *The Woman*. This could either be interpreted as (Call me) DD, Dr Gee Jay, Nurse Hatchet, or Ma'am Cybill Flex. Donald didn't particularly care about whose care he had caringly been placed in, he was too busy carefully focussing on how to extricate himself from their seemingly uncaring care.

Although he knew the best place for him, at the moment, was right where he was, he also knew the best course of action for him, at precisely the same moment, was to do everything he could to not be right where he was. Donald is preparing himself to try and freely embrace the mental hieroglyphics he will undoubtedly be taught in the coming two weeks.

---

[3] If you could be convinced to call the second to last clean Knife, Fork, or Spoon in the cutlery drawer a *hero*. (And yes, "KFS" is the correct order.)

[4] Maybe *realing* would be more appropriate?

The comforting piece of information, lurking in the shadows of his mind, is that the two-week period remaining in his treatment is a fixed timeframe. It will only feel like eternity. It's funny because it's true. If it wasn't funny it would be overwhelmingly sad.

Donald fits somewhere between "What the?" and "Oh…"

Donald was thinking about the treatment he was receiving and how it was a double-edged sword… One edge facilitated becoming *normal-because* you are able to change your thoughts and start to think good things about yourself. The other edge facilitated becoming *normal-while* you continue to remember bad things about yourself, because you can't change the past.[5]

Donald Halfbrain is about to continue on his path of:

Story Defining…

Life Changing…

Legend Creating…

Cue the hazy memory being replaced by the current scene…
Check how many Donald books have been sold…
Display something to indicate hope…

Pulling on his grey hoodie,[6] Donald, our recurring franchised Hero, again set out to interact with the wild environment, the insanely[7] small microcosm he is going to call his home, for the next two weeks exactly…

Greetings from: Saint Rita's Sanatorium for the Clinically Mental and
Psychoillogical: Part Two
In the series of
The Donald Diaries.

---

[5]   The result of all this thinking was, "If the treatment is a double-edged sword, why aren't I holding on to it by the hilt?"

[6]   I actually have several different variations of these, but I only packed the one for Donald to take with him.

[7]   And, more importantly, ironically.

Chapter 1:
Monday Morning
(Bedroom Deja Voodoo)

Starting the day on a positive note,[8] Donald found he was completely aware of who he was, where he was, when he was, but significantly more importantly in the scheme of things, why he was who, where and when he was. How he was remained a complete mystery, however.

Donald will always answer the generic noncommittal greeting, "How are you?" truthfully. In fact, Donald answers every question with the truth as he sees it. Being *politically correct* isn't a tool that Donald has ever had ownership of and, quite frankly, doesn't ever want to.[9]

If someone was to ask Donald the How question right now, his reply would go something like this...

1. Stop moving and stare intently at the person asking.
   Decide on the level of sarcasm required, given the current location.
2. Shift his gaze up and to the right into the contemplation stance.
   Hold for at least six seconds and form appropriate answer in one.
3. Answer with a completely truthful, "I don't know."

Normally his answer would be some permutation of "Reasonable," but as that particular vein of answers require him to have both a *sound mind*, and a little *normality*, Donald felt like he was missing at least two of those two key requirements.

---

[8] As opposed to Bb. Yeah, I know it is a "Dad" joke. But hey, you have to write what you know, right?

[9] The fact that Donald's wants don't really matter, doesn't really matter, he will always only ever be *literally correct*.

Apart from thinking about these quantum life questions, he was also still thinking about where his much beloved Puppy was, and why he was thinking so much.[10] Returning his thought process to the calming three items of focus, from the welcome pack wisdom, Donald prepared for the day:

- ⌥ FOCUS ON WHAT YOU CAN   and not on what you can't
  I *CAN* get dressed in my clothes from yesterday;
- ⌥ FOCUS ON WHAT YOU DO   and not on what you don't
  I *DO* think it is completely acceptable; and
- ⌥ FOCUS ON WHAT YOU WILL   and not on what you won't
  I *WILL* turn some of them inside-out.

The weekly clothing rotation concept, which Donald has only very recently adopted,[11] was originally developed to rotate through an entire wardrobe, so each piece of clothing would get a consistent amount of wear.

Unfortunately, this philosophy fails in several obvious areas:

- ⌥ You will wear out each clothing item of the same type at roughly the same rate and therefore at the same time. This means there had best be some planning done before you have to replace all of the worn-out underwear unreasonably urgently.
- ⌥ The process is completely incompatible with the selecting coordinated clothing to wear optional sub-process. Several of the basic activities, such as adhering to styles and colour matching, become weak points. Resulting in awkward failures of Double Denim, or Muffin Tops.
- ⌥ There is a very real chance of internal carnage when only one of a pair of socks develops an additional hole. Donald has tried to mitigate this experience by de-pairing his pairs of anything. Including pairs of pants, glasses and scissors.

Donald was committed to making his life easier, so every new alternative concept he was trialling received an appropriate amount of testing before he consigned it to his pile of unsuccessful. He figured that if he could persevere with the clothing rotation method, for at least thirteen or 14 days, then it may be a win under his metaphorical belt.[12]

---

[10] These three thinkings are of the exact same importance to Donald.

[11] This happened some-time last week, when Donald realised it was easier acquiescing to his base instinct of lazy, rather than not, and do his washing.

[12] And under his literal one in the case of his jeans and suits (Formal only). He doesn't have to wear one for the Track or Birthday variants yet.

Completing his dressing requirements for the morning, Donald set about correcting one of the niggling issues inside his room. He didn't like that he was breaking a rule each time he went out of his room, so annotating the "*Please keep this door Closed ALWAYS!*" sign was another achievable win.

Attacking the sign, Donald gave it an appropriate caveat…

If Donald had thought about this for just one second longer, he might have realised that a door is still in use when it is closed. So, literally, an operational door is never not in use. Thereby rendering the sign, a conundrum, as well as an impossibility should Donald want to open the door to exit his room.

Satisfied with his own cleverness, however ill deserved, Donald continued with his daily preparation by verifying all of his senses, which aren't part of the famous five senses clique, were working, by indulging his non-sensory intense internal sense checking formality:

- **Balance** (Spatial Orientation, Equilibrium)

Raise your upper left leg to a parallel to the ground position with the lower portion of your leg remaining perpendicular, while simultaneously extending both arms diametrically opposite each other to form a large V centred at your neck, making sure to keep both palms cupped and fingers splayed. Then lean forward slightly and bend your grounded leg a similar amount.

At this point your body should resemble the "Crane" kick position made famous by *The Karate Kid* movie, but for Donald, he had had it at raising his leg off the ground without falling over. ☑ *Metaphorical Tick.*

- **Danger**

As Donald was alone, he classified this status as "Possibly." It won't come as any surprise to learn there are also three statuses… Possibly, Probably and Yes. At no point is Donald ever not in any danger. ☑ *Metaphorical Tick.*

- **Pain**

For this element, Donald measured his abstract metaphysical vulnerability to pain in the present moment, using the diagnostically unvalidateable DOGoN scale. His reasoning being any purely physical pain felt would be captured in the default stage two internal monitoring checks. He was currently running a perfectly acceptable five. ☑ *Metaphorical Tick.*

- **Common**[13]

"If only common sense was actually common." Donald prided himself on following this mantra through from last week by uncommonly entering into this unusual situation. It is only common sense.　☑ *Metaphorical Tick.*

- **Hunger**[14]

Interestingly, the success of this check is inversely proportional to the level of hunger reached, divided by the availability of appropriate food, correct to within thirteen swallows. Basically, as long as there was enough food to satiate his insatiable hunger there was no need to worry, and he knew Chef wouldn't fail him now.　☑ *Metaphorical Tick.*

- **Sixth**[15]

Donald felt a tingling running up and down his spine, in an unfriendly game of vertebrae, against the spate of cold shivers he was also feeling. He decided to reserve any formal judgement on this mysterious topic until when he next encountered (shudder) Mindy.　☑ *Metaphorical Tick.*

As he was quickly becoming aware of the time and about the fact it was slowly ticking away, Donald unlocked the padlock on his bedside drawer with the key hidden underneath his coffee mug. After he realised there was nothing in the drawer he needed, he re-locked the padlock and sequestered the key in his underwear drawer. Satisfied with the vast amount of discouragement this precaution offered to any nosey people, Donald grabbed the Welcome Pack and headed to the common area.

Being able to make himself a "Congratulations-for-making-it-through-the-night" mug of hot coffee and being extremely satisfied with his flouting of the "DO NOT REMOVE" rule, Donald made himself comfortable in the no longer deserted common-area and perused the Welcome Pack.

---

[13] How coincidental (but definitely not ironic) is this? The thirteenth footnote falling on what Donald considers to be the most important sense. Common Sense is how you avoid unlucky situations.

I was surprised to find that "common" was mentioned 51 times last week.

[14] Donald is well aware that he has exceeded his general restriction of only three items within each concept. Hunger, or lack thereof, is too much of a motivator in Donald's world for this to be left out.

I was also surprised to find that "food" was mentioned 86 times last week.

[15] If you are going to break the rules, you may as well go big.

I wasn't surprised to know I was going to say something like this.

Donald read silently for a little while, then with pressure building up inside his head, this tiny amount of reading came dangerously close to generating a panic attack. There was no tangible danger to anyone else, or even to Donald if the truth be told, which we all know it will be. During this petite read, three things became apparent to Donald:

- Both of the "Medical Staff," and the "Non-Medical Staff," rosters had been updated and added to;
- A "Week Two Checklist" had been included; and
- There was an "Addendum" stating the previous pair of changes had been made overnight, and to not worry about what any of the staff did to him while he was asleep.

Donald's first task today,[16] would be a review of the M 'n' N-M Rosters…

Saint Rita's Sanatorium for the Clinically Mental Medical Staff, Roster Redux

Primary Nurse	-	~~Nurse Dolly Dix~~ DD — *Which part of "Call me DD" didn't you understand?*
Day Nurse	-	Nurse Jack Call — *Blood Shopping Assistant[17]*
Night Nurse	-	Nurse Hatchet — *Given Name - Berrythy*
Weekend Nurse	-	Nurse Wendy Dunk — *né Swirl*
Student Nurses	-	Grey Duate — *Gender Irrelevant*
Medical Doctor	-	Dr Andy Coughed — *Doesn't "have" SaRS*
Psychologists	-	~~Dr~~ Mr Houts Marted — *Awwwww… C'mon!*
Psychiatrist	-	Dr Gee Jay — *No comment*

Trainee Psychologists:

	-	Stu Arthur Dent — *No relation*
	-	They Meantwell — *They is the "they" they*

SaRS Official 1 – Medical Staff Roster Redux

Donald turned the page to write his notes about the Medical Staff Roster.

---

[16]   Apart from everything he had just done obviously (obliviously?).

[17]   Donald was sure there was a word, or some punctuation, missing here.

Scribbling over the forecasted menus for the next three weeks of meals, Donald made the following notes, and while there will be one more than three notes, Donald will fail to note this, this time:

- *All non-corporeal entries have been removed. Have they been given an exercise programme by Ma'am Flex?*
- *Nurse Dunk must have had a whirlwind marriage and honeymoon, as yesterday she was only a single Swirl.*
- *There is a definite strangeness about the continuing presence and content of the comments.*
- *Two Trainee Psychologists... I can't decide if this is good or bad, for either us or them.*

Sipping thoughtfully on his coffee, Donald continued thinking about the new additions[18] to the workforce. The two Trainee Psychologists. As his notes suggest, Donald was clearly "out" with his first impression of the situation. All that was going through Donald's mind at the moment was...

He knew SaRS' mission statement, which was just a series of five try to make you feel good words, was: Compassion, Respect, Justice, Hospitality and Excellence. What confused him, there was no mention of who these objectives were being levelled at:

Compassion for the inmates, or for the staff who had to look after them?
Respect of the rules for those lower in the food chain, or higher?
Justice? Clearly if there was any justice, there wouldn't be a need for it.
Hospitality... The quality of being A Hospital?
Excellence. Donald just shook his head in dismay.
The point of these thoughts was slowly approaching:
There was no mention of teaching, in any shape or form.

Donald was prepared to have Grey perform all of the menial tasks related to his medical treatment: take his temperature, sphygmomanometer his Blood pressure, make his bed... etc. as these are all factually verifiable. What he had an aversion to was someone poking around inside his head where he couldn't see what was happening. Especially if they were going to make not completely educated guesses while only backed up by a textbook.

---

[18] New additions... These clearly can't be old additions, as that would be considered ageist; additional additions would be redundant; but you can't refer to them simply as additions, as all of them were additions at one stage. This is the type of conundrum Donald loves to hate, as you know what is being said, but you also know it isn't what it actually says.

Trying to figure out if this was a practical joke, or an impractical one, took Donald's mind off this dilemma and returned it to thinking about the rosters. Redirecting his gaze back to page two of the *M 'n' N-M* Rosters…

Saint Rita's Sanatorium for the Clinically Mental Non-Medical Staff, Roster Redux

Pastoral Service	–	Aaaron Aare	*Always the first entry*
Dietician	–	Seymour Feedme	*Why is he first?*
Fitness Worker	–	Ma'am Cybill Flex	*Ma'am Yes Ma'am Sir*
Administration	–	Mark Time	*Administration Rules!*
Cafeteria Cook	–	Chef Chief Changes	~~*Comment redacted*~~
Pastoral Service	–	Zyxon Zzippy	*Always the last entry*

Therapists	Art	Sue Rhea Liszt	*c$_o$mm^{e}nt - ^{o}o$_m$m^{o}n$_t$ - c^{o}m$_m$e^{o}t*
	Massage	Anna Lykeananna	*Scratch that will you?*
	Musical	William the Piano Man	*Willy, I'm a Willy!*

Maintenance	Spick 'n' Span Cleansing	*Elevator pitch cleansing*
	Who Wood Masons	*We Who are Not carpenters*
	Wholly Mowly Groundskeeping	*Keepers of the Grounds*

SaRS Official 2 – Non-Medical Staff Roster Redux

And without needing to turn the page, Donald called out a few of the many issues he could see in *N-M* Roster:

- ✗ *It is no longer obsolete, even though it needs to change.*
- ✗ *All non bi-pedals have been removed.*
- ✗ *The unwritten subliminal messages aren't very obvious.*

Managing to keep it appropriately restricted to three line-items.

All of this, from "Donald made himself comfortable" to "All of this," took place in a little over thirteen minutes. This gives you an indication of how fast Donald's mind works. His mug of coffee had reduced in temperature enough, so it didn't cause an issue when Sven interru…

If you disengage an engaged gauge, where does the useless "u" go?[19]

---

[19] Coincidently, this is a question I, and Donald, would like an answer to.

"Sphincter Feng Shui!"

Sven had just efficiently removed Donald from his reverie, and he was also sufficiently enough removed to notice there was a small crowd gathering in the other TV room. Donald had been shown this room last week by Owedebt, who had taken him for a wander around some of the facility, but had so far, confusingly, never attended a formal morning self-introductory roll call.[20] Even though it was optional, it was expected of you to attend.

Donald made his way to the other TV room, after unsuccessfully brushing the spilt coffee from his clothes. If you look closely at Donald's clothing, you will find a coffee stain on most at best. You don't want to know what else you may find lurking in the creases at worst.

"G☺☺d m☺rning every☺ne." Nurse Jack was obviously in a chipper mood this morning, which didn't come anywhere close to a surprise to Donald. He immediately rationalised Nurse Jack had been away from SaRS for the whole weekend, even Donald would be happy after a weekend off if he worked here. "How is everyone feeling today?"

"Good morning Jack - Nurse Jack - Nurse Jack Call - Who are you?[21]"

Everyone regreeted his morning greeting, albeit in a less enthusiastic way, but no one[22] responded with an answer to his question as they all knew it was a polite rhetorical inquiry. Unfazed by the unimaginative response, Nurse Jack dived into the meeting's scheduled items. Writing the topics for discussion on the whiteboard as he was saying them out loud resulted in a humorous delay between the syllabised words:

- Self - int - row - duck - shons;
- Time - tay - bull - of - the - day's - ack - tiv - it - is; and
- Pub - lick - an - ounce - ments.

"Now… Who would like to get us started?" Nurse Jack looked directly, and as loudly as he could, at Donald. Donald had typically chosen to sit on the seat nearest to the door, so this selection was a self-inflicted throwing himself in at the deep end, because it showed he was the person least likely to still be there at the end of the introductions. Unable to find an alternative solution, Donald kicked off the self - int - row - duck - shons.

---

[20] The roll-call self-introductory routine will be a very convenient way to remind Donald, as well as you, of some of the people who this book is about, and contrary to popular (my) belief, this is not only Donald.

[21] Depending on the level of your knowledge/memory/acquaintance.

[22] Why does *no one* have an intermediary space when *everyone* does not?

"My name is Donald... ... ..."

Donald is completely comfortable with uncomfortable silences and is able to avoid eye contact at will. He made absolutely every indication he was going to calmly do nothing until someone else started speaking. Even when another someone did start speaking, he was going to continue to do nothing.

Seeing there was going to be no elaboration, embellishment or expansion of Donald's introduction, and belatedly realising his mistake of thinking people would follow a simple pattern when presented with the chance to do so, Nurse Jack shifted his focus to the person adjacent to Donald.

Never being one to stay hidden away after being called out, Owedebt said defiantly, "Owedebt Dear."

Jumping on this chance to be at the centre of some gross inattention, Nota barely waited for Owdebt's closing quotes to be pronounced, and very nearly prematurely announced, "Nota Beenhead... ... ... !! !! !!" with the maximum amount of post oral insinuation allowed in mixed company before her series of three double exclamations.

"Ꝑ," Chunky Poopy, Owedebt's over-round, over-friendly and over-easy service pet had raised his left ear which indicated, "What? I'm a dog! What do you think I'm going to say? I can't speak in human... You must be a complete idiot!" Which should, technically, have been de-verbalised as "ꝒꝒ," but Chunky couldn't be bothered repeating himself this morning.

Following these early missintroductions the rest of the inmates stumbled along with the mostly name only idea, and after removing the non-pertinent names this is what was left over:

"Khkhkhkhkhyello, my name Got Knotyed."

"Pass."

"Mindy Ownbeeswhacks! Who are you looking at?"

"My name-tag says Lost M'Hankie?"

I'm smart enough to know that I'm not nearly as smart as I like to think I am.

Putting an end to this extract[23] of client introduction shambles nicely, Sven started well but wound up talking himself into a confused circle.[24] Nurse Jack then continued as if this was a normal everyday occurrence, which, of course, it was. "Very nicely done to all of you. Right... There are a couple of new staff members I would like to introduce to you: Stu Dent and They Meantwell."

---

[23] Why does *extract* mean what is left-over after everything *inappropriate* has been removed? Intract of the exappropriate is much better terminology.

[24] Which isn't confusing, considering the circle of people he was in.

Stu Arthur Dent (no relation) is one of the two student psychologists who have been assigned to SaRS as part of their postgraduate training. Having a residency at the SaRS facility on your résumé is unfortunately considered to be a detrimental piece of mandatory information disclosure.[25] The humiliation it generates is a lot like being the last one picked for the soccer team... After the ball has been picked.

They Meantwell (is the other) one.

Their Staff Identification tags were waiting to be collected from reception. As it is a Monday, as most first days of new employment usually are, there was a backlog of identifications to be processed, and as they weren't here in any *employed* capacity, administration couldn't prioritise them any higher, so they took a full 17 minutes to produce after the request was received...

<table>
<tr><td>

Student Psychologist – SaRS
Stu Arthur Dent (no relation)
Pre-Authorised for all locations
where ~~Dr~~ Mr Houts Marted *works*

</td><td>

Student Psychologist – SaRS
They Meantwell (is the other)
Pre-Authorised for all locations
where ~~Dr~~ Mr Houts Marted *works*

</td></tr>
</table>

[26]

"They and Stu will be observing *everything* ~~Dr~~ **Mr** Houts Marted does. He will be teaching them what to do, what not to do and what should have been done, by applying the simple uncouple principle of do what I say and not what I do. They are only here to learn how to teach you how to learn, not to teach you how to learn."

At this point they were both[27] looking extremely confused, and just a little bit scared about the inflection Nurse Jack had used on *everything*. Seeing this look of confusion, then comparing it to the looks of confusion on the inmates' faces, and tentatively discerning there was no discernible difference, Nurse Jack decided it was appropriate to continue with the next scheduled item... To read aloud and comment snidely on the daily activity schedule.

---

[25] Unfortunately for Stu and They, as there is no feasible differentiation between having a Residency **at** SaRS and being a Resident **of** SaRS.

[26] Even though ~~Dr~~ **Mr** Houts Marted **Really?** was not present, Donald was aware of the palpable unrighteous indignation emanating from the tiny storage cupboard that was performing as the Psychologists' office, because Houts has not been issued with his own identification tag yet.

[27] There weren't two Theys. They was one and Stu was the other.

"Today's activities are going to be:

- ✠   Breakfast. Served in the dining room starting from an hour ago;[28]
  Or not to be...
- ✠   Morning self-introductory roll call;
  Which is optional if you are not here, but mandatory if you are.
- ✠   The Gym will be open at 10am, through to 12~~am~~ ~~pm~~ noon;
  Conveniently conflicting with the morning group session for all those who are more capable in the muscle department.
- ✠   The Pool and Art Rooms will both be open from 2pm to 4pm;
  Not to be confused with the Pool Room, which is closed all day.
- ✠   There is no smoking allowed at SaRS, except in the designated areas;
  While this looks like an announcement, it is also a continuous activity.
- ✠   Our usual mindfulness walk has been cancelled; as has
  As per usual.
- ✠   The traditional reading of a joke. We are going to play a game instead.
  Not to say that the game is a joke."

Donald thought, "Good luck with your joke replacement game having any serious participation[29] from anyone in here. I think you will probably find the joke it replaced is on you."

Unaware of Donald's thoughts, Nurse Jack picked up a stack of papers and gave them to They to hand out while he was explaining, "At SaRS, we call this game: Reviewing all Five of our Senses.[30] We will all be winners once we come to a basic understanding of the individual absolute threshold of each sense, discuss the obviously obsolete systems of measurement used, and provide a practical replacement for each of these systems."

Trying in vain to increase the level of the absolutely-no-way excitement in completing the practical replacement of the sensory maximum measurement system task, Stu interjected with some banal commentary, "Our Five Senses, how good are they, They?[31]"

... (Count 27 seconds of stunned silence before turning the page please.)

---

[28]   This unfortunate timing goes a long way in explaining why Donald had never previously attended a morning self-introductory roll call meeting.

[29]   Donald's participation in any game was always as a stand-in bystander. He has certainly had next to no stand-out participations.

[30]   Correct, this is both a correct and an incorrect statement.

[31]   He didn't succeed. Hmmmmm, actually, I think he might have technically succeeded, as he was trying in **vain** to increase their excitement.

Reviewing all Five of our Senses

✗ Vision – You can see...

Candlelight 48km away on a dark and clear night sky.
The hospital's searchlight reach is only 1m away from where you are standing.

✗ Hearing – You can hear a...

Watch Tick 6m away in an otherwise silent situation.
Silent alarm being tripped 1.8m away, depending on how tall you are.

✗ Touch – You feel...

A Fly Wing falling onto your cheek from a height of 76mm.
There was something seriously wrong with the person who devised this system.

✗ Taste – You can discern...

A teaspoon of sugar in 7.5 litres of clean fresh water.
A teaspoon of sugar in a large cup of hot decaffeinated coffee.

✗ Smell – You can't stop smelling...

A drop of perfume in a volume the size of three rooms.
Perfume which came from the petrified excrement of a bunny... Ewwwww...

SaRS Official 3 – Reviewing all Five of our Senses

As you have just read (after a very minute 27 second wait...), the original measurement systems were subjective and today are largely unachievable.

Thanks to the historical efforts to shine a light into every piece of darkness, there is no such thing as a *dark and clear night sky*, similarly we have injected sound into every *otherwise silent situation*. While there hasn't been anything which comes close to being a palatable *large cup of hot decaffeinated coffee*, it is still far more common than *7.5 litres of clean fresh water*.

There are also several modern responsible issues to consider, if you start de-winging flies as an adult,[32] some people from the RSPCA will come urgently knocking on your door and ask you to stop.

---

[32] It is verging on being intolerable for a child to do this, even if they protest that they are performing a legitimately sound touchy scientific experiment.

And finally, because there is no accepted standard *size of three rooms*, the smell test measurement system fails every credibility requisite conceivable. If there is a logistically infeasible attempt to join three rooms together, you don't get three joined rooms, you get one big room.

Donald knew all the answers[33] were hiding in his mind somewhere, he just had to figure out what the right questions were if he was going to uncover the knowledge inside. Resigned to the fact that if he couldn't get the answers out of his mind, he might very well go out of his mind himself before he found the questions to the answers.

While Donald was contemplating about contemplating, there was some unexpected activity heading directly for Lost, in the form of a smartly dressed man. Most people would not have espied this man unless they were expecting some form of unexpected at any time.

There was a spectacular event unfolding...

A confident stride in a magnificent tartan suit resplendent with an accent which could drive women wild. Here was a genuine heartthrob of a man who was obviously Heaven Sent,[34] and he was suavely sauntering over to Lost.

Lost's predicament wasn't lost on anyone...

"Pledge, Jimmy Pledge."

Lost was on the fast track[35] to flabbergasted, "I'd never have believed it, if I hadn't seen it for myself." Curiously, come tomorrow Lost won't remember that he had seen anything, and he will also never believe you if you ever try to explain to him what had happened.

The interloper pulled out his weapon, a Walter P.K. Chewing Gum shooter, and then theatrically aimed it at Lost, "Never shay, *Never*, to a Pledge, Jimmy!" Slyly winking ever so conspicuously at Donald.

Fractionally[36] after this threat, Donald immediately stayed in his seat and refused to give up the low ground. He didn't know what was happening, but he was quite sure he didn't want to.

---

[33] Wait for a few more words before casting aspersions at Donald.

[34] Sadly, the reality of this situation is the exact reverse.

[35] The Fast Track is not generally parallel to the High Road, in fact, they are often perpendicular, resulting in the infamous Crossroads of life. This is a place where you can ask the Devil for directions to the undocumented *Fiddle the Blues* bar somewhere down in Georgia.

[36] This is another generic term which doesn't mean what you think it does. For example... A fraction of Never is still a very long time.

Simultaneous to Donald's infraction, Mindy and Got became involved.

"Exkkkkkuse me, Kkkkkan I Khkhkhkhkhelp you?" from Got.

And a much more succinct, much less wet, "OI!" from Mindy.

Jimmy sensed he may have been in danger,[37] and decided some discretion was the better part of running away. He frantically exited the other TV room in a decidedly quicker, much less suave, saunter.

Donald watched as Jimmy retreated past. His smooooooth movement was like a historical frame-by-frame cartoon, where each step was covering twice as much ground as it logically should have. It was very much akin to walking along an airport travelator while balancing a book on your head. All that was missing was the reusable background.

"Who was HE!?" would be inappropriate as we know who he was, and the lack of ? only adds to the inappropriateness of the situation. Donald closed his gaping maw by open hand manually lifting up his lower jaw and scratched his head mumbling, "These unexpectations are becoming quite dependable, but at least they are never boring."

Lost returned to the present, "Who was HE?"

"You got that right," Mindy replied with a backhanded compliment.

Lost closed out the interaction with another vague shoulder shrug.

Donald retreated back to his sanctuary, making a small detour along the way to collect some random food from the Tiger-Kangaroo[38] kitchen in lieu of breakfast. He also took this opportunity to freshen up his coffee.

Finding some internal peace, Donald decided to get on with documenting his thoughts while he was recovering from the morning stand-in meeting and the... Pledge, Jimmy Pledge... scene.

The writing sounds were only inside his head as he documented away, "We have had a tremendous amount of activity in the last few days..."

Completely forgetting about the "Week Two Checklist.[39]"

---

[37] Non-sensory intense internal sense #2.

And yes (or should it be no?), the irony of this being a #2 isn't lost on me.

[38] If you've made it to here without understanding some of the unexplained references, a few of the inexplicable scenarios, or little of the perplexing abundance of bad puns/innuendo/hyperbole, I suggest you go buy, then read, *Hospityable* before coming back here to continue.

[39] This is my bad, I will try to fit it in in a later chapter. As for now, at 5266 words, this one is full ±500 words.

Donald was reawared out of his documentary extracurricular involvement by another blast from the past week.

Knock, knock, knock.

As expected, Donald found Seth floating outside his door, unexpectedly without BLT hovering just behind.

"Good morning Sir, I am here with a timely reminder that you, **one** Donald Halfbrain, are required to attend not less than," quickly glancing at an official looking document apparition, "**two** Group Sessions per day, for a period of," another glance, "at least **three** weeks… If you are unavailable to attend, you are required to account **four**[40] your absence."

Go directly to Group.
Do not cop out.
Do not give 200 excuses.

---

[40] This is a conversation remember, you can't see the words he is speaking, so it is entirely possible he doesn't know the difference. And by the way, don't forget that he is a ghost, as this makes the words even more invisible.

Chapter 2:
Return of the Tapestry
(Clueless!)

When Donald arrived at the first group session of the day,[41] there was an unsettled discussion about what the hospital was going on? There seemed to be no authority present, and he could see They's attempt to start a monologue at the inmates was going badly. Stu was having marginally better success trying to physically restrain the unruly group, without actually touching them.

"We have had a tremendous amount of activity in the last few days:
- Bushfire,
- Flood,
- Pestilence,
- Earthquake, and even
- A nationwide shortage of toilet (dunny poo) paper…[42]"

Donald's interest was piqued at They's correct use of *tremendous*. Most people use tremendous to mean "extremely good or impressive." For the rest of the population, the literal definition has passed through several iterations, from "inspiring awe and dread," to "great in amount, scale, or intensity." It is only through the recently misinformed colloquial informal interpretation that confers the incorrect additional meaning of "excellent."

---

[41] Donald won't ever be accused of fitting into the more capable section in the muscle department crowd, or indeed, in any group. The only place where Donald is truly comfortable is in his own Tribe of One.

[42] All of these are completely factual. You can look it up. I dare you. (#42)

"...resulting in a similar shortage of any senior staff (dunny who) available to conduct this morning's group session."

Waiting for any resultant attention to their attempts at quiet humour and quite hinder became apparently in vain. They[43] continued addressing the mob at hand, "The first group session today will be taken by we two, we happy two, psychology students. And we both are quite willing to put our health, nay our very lives, at risk for a little bit of education. Are you all willing to shed a little unnecessary Blood with we today?"

Donald was quietly thinking about the numerous philosophical, technical and grammatical errors in They's speech, and how all of it will probably result in not much positivity. In fact, he was almost positive that the only thing going to be *shed* today with They was the lawnmower.[44]

Extracting himself from the vile "we happy two" duo which They had just created, Stu, who was not at all willing to shed Blood, let alone put his life on the line, started speaking some sense instead, "The normal week two Monday morning group session, Psychicology (with our own resident Wicca, Mindy), has been rescheduled due to an unforeseen circumstance, instead, the week one get to know you group will be repeated. This will allow They and me to catch up with who you are."

They jumped right back on the flaming horse drawn wagon, "So, everyone, I will ask you to please put away your 2B[45] pencils and prepare for a dive back into The Tapestry #1 for a *Clueless* refresher wipe."

Quickly glossing over much of the content in:

ж   Group Regulations,
     Hospityable Chapter Nine   — Group Session 1.0   — (Regulations)
ж   Tapestry Specifics, and
     Hospityable Chapter Ten   — Group Session 1.1   — (Tapestry #1)
ж   Tapestry Consequence.
     Hospityable Chapter Eleven — Group Session 2   — (Debriefing)

Was forgotten completely when The Tapestry #1 entered the building.

---

[43]   This is one of those ultra-rare occasions, when if you were asked, "Who are *they*?" You would have an actual answer, instead of an "Oh, you know..." Even though your question should technically have been, "Who *is* They?" Which is an existential conversation we aren't going to have here.

[44]   The Wholly Mowly Groundskeeping lawn mowing staff have their own on-site out-the-back self-contained storage container.

[45]   Or not 2B, whether 'tis doesn't really matter.

Donald didn't care there was apparently going to be no reviewment of the Group ~~Rules~~Guidelines or Housekeeping,[46] and they were apparently going to completely skip the process of reintroducing everyone to everyone else, even though it was one the main reason for having this Group resession.

Donald didn't know what he did to be selected as the chosen one last time, so he feigned not knowing anything again in the hope he would be the chosen one again. He almost desperately wanted to know the outcome of the *Bones Under the Courtyard Basement* case.

Donald didn't[47] waste any amount of time wondering about:

- ⌗ The back information about the case;
  Hospityable Chapter Six   — The Kingswood's House — (Scandal)
- ⌗ His previous plans for proof procurement; or
  Hospityable Chapter Twelve[a]— The End   — (Heists and Fish)
- ⌗ A completely unrelated, and soon to be obsolete, topic.
  Hospityable Chapter 14   — is brought to you by ~~Mc David's~~

Apart from the few minutes it took him to not think about these topics.

As Stu took the tapestry around the random placement of chairs, Donald's mind was again screaming, "Pick me! Pick Me! PICK ME!" And, in yet another purely coincidental occurrence, Donald was the one chosen to be the Chosen One for the second time. TCO^2 [48] to his friends.

Don't repeat the same mistake; repeat different ones to show your redundancy.

Sven's echoing cookie quote began a "Booyah!" attitude within Donald's mind, which ended two moments after the fuzzy, wavy, hazy fading in and out visuality also ended.

Rather than consciously perusing the updated contract details, allowing a tapestry softly-softly update, Donald let his subconscious have a quick glance through the subtext, checking and nexting as hardly-hardly appropriate. When he finally arrived at the last checkpoint, Donald was dialectically relieved and excited at exactly the same time, and for the exact same reason.

---

[46] This meant Donald wasn't going to have a chance to correct the minute formatting issue which had been weighing on his mind since Hospityable.

What I'd like to know, did anyone discover the error *before* they read this? Or maybe a more important question… Did any of the editors pick it up?

[47] For the third successive time today Donald didn'ted do something.

[48] No, *that* isn't a footnote… But *this* certainly is.

Donald had apparently remembered[49] to come prepared this time:

﹡ He could remember The Tapestry #1 ~~Instructions~~ User's Manual;
Re-review Hospityable Chapter Eleven Group Session 2 (Debriefing).

﹡ He could remember everything he saw in the tapestry last time; and
Refer to the section below.

﹡ He could remember the post *Clueless!* conversations on the subject.
Refer to the rearranged section below that.

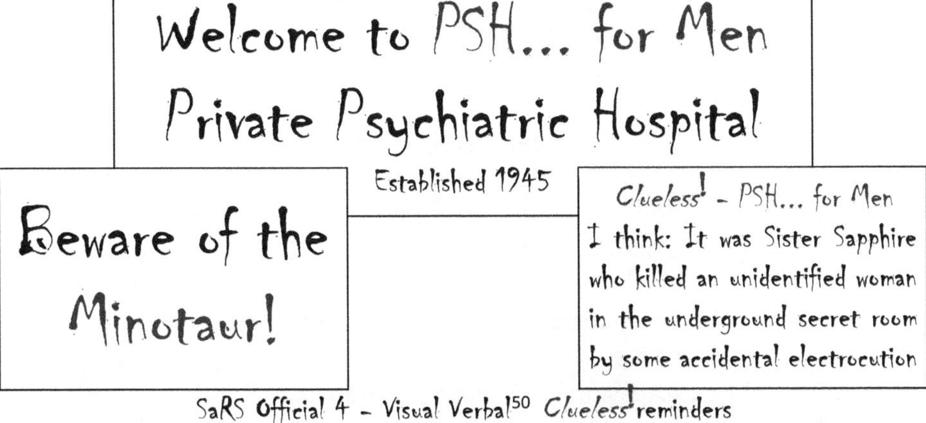

SaRS Official 4 – Visual Verbal[50] *Clueless!* reminders

Donald arrived at another when again, just like before. But, unlike the last time, Donald knew how to get back to the future, and he also knew that people within the not-a-memory scene couldn't hurt him physically.[51]

Taking everything into account: All the people in this not-a-memory scene seemed to be much more than a close match to those from his first encounter; the Visual Verbal reminders correlated exactly with his recollections; and if it wasn't so, why was he here? ... Donald was practically supremely confident this was a not-a-memory sequel, or at the very least, it was a second episode after the pilot had been approved.

---

[49] Causing some trepidational feelings, as he normally can only remember the bad, sad, or mad things, and this time he didn't know which was which.

[50] Yes, this is the correct usage of Verbal. Verbal means "Use of words." It doesn't specify spoken. I also realise this is hyper, and hypo, critical of me to point this out, as I misused the word several times in Hospityable.

[51] The jury was still out at the pub regarding the mentally question, so, it was quite lucky for Donald to be where he was, even though at the moment, it wasn't the right when it was.

Fast forwarding through the *previously in* refreshing memory scene of the not-a-memory scene, every now and then Donald thought he caught a glimpse of a someone else following the same path. When he tried to psychologically explain that same glimpse he would always fail and then suffer a mild form of amnesia, sort of like "What the…?" He passed this off as Deja View.[52]

Donald eventually arrived at the point in time where he left off last time; sitting on a sandstone bench seat inside an ornate pavilion, after:
- Failing conspicuously to notice a storm weathered hot air balloon;
- Following closely two conspicuously dressed ladies; and
- Finding the conspicuously marked trap door…

He then became **S**eated **P**ondering **A**ll **C**oncepts **E**xciting **D**onald, following the fast-forwarded scenic tour, **O**bviously **U**nder a **T**rance, after remembering he had some unanswered questions on his mind. He took this rare opportunity to answer some of his own questions:
- "What do you mean, Beware of the Minotaur!?"
  Obvious circumlocution… Stay away from the horny bull like creature.
- "Where did the two ladies go?"
  Owedebt's expression… "Through the trap door."
- "Why is it called a trap door?"
  Obscured definitions… A door flush with the surrounding surface.

Disengaging himself, again, from thinking about the irrelevant function of the trap door, Donald moved to continue his not-a-memory scene journey. He was quite pleased with the effort he spent last week trying to plot the heist to recover the "lost" documented proof of the unidentified patient, or even the "never was" details about the possible ECT conducted on her. That this effort wasn't a complete waste of his time was an unusual bonus, as it had given him several valid avenues of investigation to pursue; starting with:
- Was it Sister Sapphire?
- Who was the unidentified female patient? and
- Where are the hospital archives?
  (Or hospital records, as they would be known back then)

Having safely re-entered the tunnels underneath the Head Shrink's office, even though he was entering them 75 years before he will enter them for the first time, Donald had a good look around in the flame lit dimness. There were no glossy touristy information pamphlets to refer to this time, so confusingly, he had to make do with the memory he will create in 75 years' time.

---

[52] Yeah, like nobody has ever thought of that before.

Donald certainly wasn't disappointed with the experience this time. There was nothing artificial about what he was feeling. The tunnel was in a delightful need of sanitisation... Just as a Minotaur's lair[53] should be.

Stepping through a pile of future growth garnish, Donald headed towards the only tunnel he could see. If he had thought about this a little bit harder, he might have realised he could scratch a message on one of the walls to be received by his future self in 75 years. The concept of interacting permanently with the not-a-memory scene hadn't fully imprinted itself yet.[54]

Along the tunnel Donald could hear sounds of strapping someone down without a struggle.[55] Creeping as silently as he could so he could listen his way, thinking, "If I make any sound in The Tapestry #1... Does anyone hear it?" he reached the room of the source of the noise. Poking his head around a door Donald nearly recoiled in shock. The unknown patient was being strapped into an ancient dentist's chair voluntarily! By a person who seemed to not really know what she was doing but had an air of kindness none-the-less.

What had shocked Donald was not the ineptness of the immobilisation, it was that the chair looked eerily similar to a chair that might, more commonly, be put to use in an executioner's chamber. It had an array of electrical contact points leading to a switch on the wall, several leather restraint straps and an appropriate pot like bucket underneath to receive any inappropriate residue created by the proceedings.

The unexpurgated blur of what happens next will stay with Donald for the next 75 years (for at least one interpretation of time anyway).

Ok. It is way past my bedtime now, so, this part of the not-a-memory scene cliff-hanger exposé will have to wait until tomorrow morning. I'm going to get myself some well I-don't-care-if-it's-deserved-or-not sleep. Zzzzz...

---

[53] Spoiler alert!

There is no actual Minotaur here, and there was only ever one such creature from Ancient Greek mythology. Beings, said to be members of a "minotaur" species, are purely recent fictional fantasy creations.

[54] The concept I am having trouble with is the Invisible Man Conundrum. When does something inanimate, such as an apple, become invisible after it has been eaten by an invisible man? Similarly, any object Donald interacts with while he is inside the not-a-memory, such as light, would be observable by the people of 75 years ago. He is not invisible; he is merely not sensible.

[55] Don't ask how he knows what this sound sounds like...

In my morning, Donald revisited his "We need tos" from in 75 years:
- Find the hospital archives;
- Use the archives to identity this victim; and
- Link her identity to the *Bones Under the Courtyard Basement* case.

And the same for his "I want tos" from in 75 years:
- Find the secret underground room;   ☑ *Metaphorical Tick.*
- Identify who was wearing the doctor's clothing; and
- Explain what happened to Sister Sapphire.

There was currently only one item of the checked off variety. But one *was* statistically more significant than none.[56] After all, this particular conundrum has remained (will remain?) unfairly unsolved for up to, but not exceeding, 75 percent of a century. Why would Donald believe he could do more than this in just eight days - a week, when many others have done (will do?) less in more years than he has been (will be?) alive?

"No." he acknowledged himself dismissively, "It is best for all concerned that I leave my confused thinking for another time."

Donald peered reflectively[57] into the gloom, as a hero with a mirror might, and pondered what to do next. This is where his story will become history and was rapidly becoming a WWDD (What would Donald do?) moment. Using an insight gleaned from years of lived experience, Donald realised it is only the non-recurring minor characters who are in danger of being written out of the script before the final book of the story.

Steeling himself for the historical tragedy he was about to witness, as well as seeking to unhide, Donald edged into the room that will become known as the "Fangle Experimental EECT Therapy Machine©" room, in all of its overabundant redundant acronymity.

How does Donald know this? There is a sign of course…

Fangle Experimental
EECT Therapy Machine©

Experimental Electroconvulsive Therapy Room

---

[56] Even though one was literally lacking a letter.

[57] I was going to write *pensively* but thought better of it.

Successfully positioning himself in a convenient but not overly observable position, Donald listened to the conversation going on...

"Are you sure this is safe?"

"Absolutely, this procedure has never failed before.[58]"

"Focus on your task of comfortably restraining the patient Miss Sapphire, and please allow me to address her questions appropriately."

Donald chose his favourite freeze face for the initial reaction to this third, hitherto unknown, voice. The various danglings revealed did not induce a hint of confusion; there was, however, a large Donald sized indescribable amount of confabulation elephanting in the room. It was not a positive exchange, by any measurement, yet the instruction did confirm another of the postulations on Donald's mind... The woman dressed in the era appropriate doctor's outfit was Sister Sapphire... Or will be eventually.   ☑ *Metaphorical Tick.*

"Yes, Doctor Marted." Confirmed the recently confirmed Sister Sapphire.

"I will remind you, *Miss* Sapphire, do not refer to me as *Doctor*. As far as everyone is concerned, I am just an ordinary person who has no qualifications, and I would very much like them to continue thinking that way."

Sufficiently chastised, Miss Sapphire[59] returned to her restraints.

Changing his face to a What-The-Face face, Donald came to a possibility; was this newly unknown person, of whom he was previously unaware, in any likelihood an ancestor, of the direct type, of the currently employed at SaRS 75 years in the future **I am a real doctor** Houts Marted?

Donald had to make a mental note to give this piece of information one of his ☑ *Metaphorical Tick*s once it appeared in a list somewhere/when.

"Lady Kingswood..."

Quickly donning a Holy-Crap-Did-You-Hear-What-He-Said-⁈ questionable face, Donald scoured the whole of his last week's documentation and realised there was absolutely no mention of a Mrs Patient Zero of SaRS one-point-zero, but this stands to reason and fits magnificently.

---

[58]   While her statement wasn't strictly a lie, neither was it the complete truth. This specific execution of the procedure hasn't technically happened yet, so therefore, it simply could not have failed *before*.

[59]   Donald was also sufficiently chastised and corrected her thought name, at least until he received thought information to the contrary.

The Lady Kingswood would have been present at that specific time in the past, and most probably also passing through a time of significant upheaval in her life. She had just recently, a long time ago, lost her husband, her home and was now on the verge of losing her sanity.

Donald couldn't understand how there wasn't a mention of her anywhere. Surely, with the creation of a Private Psychiatric Hospital for Men on the grounds of her family estate; where her husband was to become the first patient; and the general disreputability of the situation, it was inconceivably doubtful she would evade even the smallest mention anywhere.

For Donald, this meant one of three things:

- What he was seeing was a complete fabrication. Created purely for the entertainment of someone sitting in front of a computer laughing at his own jokes, and it didn't really happen;
- It was a pure coincidence of the highest improbability;[60] or
- It happened, it was hushed up and then it was literally buried.

Shelving his contemplations for a moment, Donald returned his complete attention back to the not-a-memory scene.

"...please rest assured this machine is as safe as houses and could only be adversely effected by the act of a vengeful God." Not realising the contentious irony of this statement, **I am not a doctor** Marted continued, "We are going to set the dial to six-point-five, as this will limit the machine to half of its maximum output. At that level it is predicted to be completely harmless."

Miss Sapphire fumbled around with the chair's restraints for a short while and then stepped back after she had completed her task. Checking there was nothing else for her to do, she efficiently said, "Clear."

I am not a doctor Marted exited the shadows; strode purposefully over to stand beside the wall closest to the experimental Fangle contraption; verified the dial had been set to six-point-five; and dramatically put his hand on the attached leaver accurately labelled "The Switch."

The not-a-memory being presented to Donald suddenly went completely quiet, and there was a little green "MUTE" hovering innocently just within his lower left peripheral line of sight. Donald remembered his "Um, there might have been a storm..." comment from last week, and belatedly extrapolated to the conclusion of electrocution. He wanted to scream at them to stop so the thunderstorm couldn't intercede, but unfortunately, he found he couldn't, and instead discovered another tapestry feature.

---

[60] But it was definitely not infinitely improbable. As that would probably lead to the meaning being almost impossible to define.

Premature Mutation.[61]

The next thirteen seconds flashed by as if it was thirteen minutes.
Donald saw The Switch being switched, and then the resulting unlimited electrical activity, in live ultra-slow motion:
- ¤ The Switch is switched;
- ¤ Lightning strikes the pavilion; and
- ¤ Chaos ensues.

The official (emotionally redacted) story will eventually be recorded as "an unauthorised electroconvulsive therapy procedure, resulting in the shocking[62] death of Lady Kingswood." But, as far as Donald is concerned, lightning struck at exactly the wrong time, and then agreeing with what Mindy stated, "Things went unequivocally out of hand."
What he had just witnessed was an unusual phenomenon known as, "The reverse Frankenstein Monster effect." This is where:
- ¤ A patient is receiving ECT with the aim of making them more human;
- ¤ An ECD (ElectroCution Death) of the patient occurs; and then
- ¤ The patient finishes up as far removed from the rudimentary human condition as humanly possible, in a decidedly inhumane way.

SPHINCTER FENG SHUI!
Donald was standing by his own discombobulation, and his DOGoN level was at an everything-clenching twelve. The little green "MUTE" disappeared from his sight as the sounds started coming back, but this didn't change much for Donald's situation. Immediately following the lightning strike, his precious subconscious had initiated its dumb struck paradigm.

The next thirteen minutes skulked by as if it was thirteen seconds.
Donald didn't just see the literal skulduggery about to be perpetrated, in painful four-dimensional high definition with a quadrophonic soundtrack, he witnessed the singular most extremely unpleasant experience possible. When he reminisces about this day in the future Donald will have an unplanned PTSD episode waiting to be documented.

---

[61] This is a safety mechanism within the tapestry. If the Chosen One is about to affect an effective affective affectation, which will affect the future effects of TCO, it will automatically bilaterally temporarily MUTE all sound. It has been mooted all the other senses could be similarly desensitised.

[62] I'm sorry... How could I not write this?

Miss Sapphire and **I am not a doctor** Marted were both thrust to a safe distance from the presumed dead thoroughly smoking Lady Kingswood. They looked at each other with a universally standard "OH CRAP!" open faced facial expression which silently asked, "What Now?[63]"

The hand expression from **I am not a doctor** Marted, which eventually accompanied his facial one, was open to some textbook dialectical interpretation. It was either a low resultant failing score their Experimental EECT Therapy had just received, or, as Donald thought, it was a vulgar indication that everything was going to be "OK" after it is was all completely covered up.

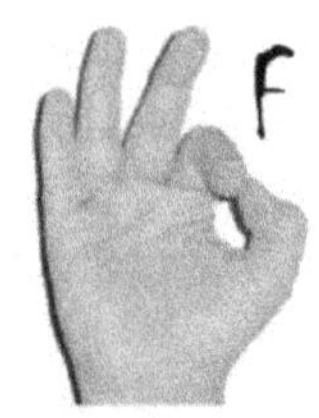

The "**W**ho **A**re Those **T**wo[64]" (WATT) congregated around the act of God conglomerated smoking experimental result. If Donald looked "hard enough," he could nearly just about see where bits of the Lady Kingswood stopped, and the Fangle Experimental EECT Therapy Machine© began.

"Bugger." Understated Miss Sapphire.
"Indeed." Underreplied **I am not a doctor** Marted.
Both of them were speaking with harsh, grey-coloured undertones.

Staying long enough to confirm his suspicions about what the WATT pair were going to do next, but not long enough for him to witness them carry out[65] the bulk remainder of their conspiracy, Donald thought it might be a good idea for him to focus on the most important remaining portion of his task, or more specifically, Donald set out to find the Hospital Archive.

Donald's thirteen-watt lightbulb moment was correct; the office labelled as The Head Shrink Office, right at the centre of the hedge-maze in the Black and white aerial photo, is doubtless where the hospital stored their archives. Once he found a conveniently suitable rock it became a short task for Donald to break into the unsecured against rocks filing cabinet.

Rifling through the minimal amount of documentation formerly inside the cabinet produced enough factoids to satisfy Donald's investigative zeal:

- ¤ Employment records for a "~~Dr~~ Mister Shuper Marted;"
  Silent h - Is a Doctor
- ¤ Patient records for a "~~Lady~~ Mister Jane Kingswood;" and a
- ¤ Purchase record for a Fangle Experimental EECT Therapy Machine©.

---

[63]   And the answer, which you will find out very soon, is a crushing "Yes."

[64]   The **W**ho **A**re **T**hose **T**wo, as Donald has rhetorically, and ironically when you consider their thrust upon weapon, named the nefarious pair.

[65]   Carry/Drag/Schlep... They are all the same to Lady Kingswood.

Donald, damning documentation in hand, came to an unusual conclusion: "If I just put these physical findings in a location which is:

    ¤   Secure, yet easily accessible;

    ¤   Still there in 75 years; and

    ¤   Won't be looked for, or found, by anyone else in those same 75 years;

I will be able to hand myself the answer to the *Clueless'* puzzle.[66]"

Taking his erroneous thoughts, and found documentation, Donald headed back to the group room. On his way, apart from wondering if anyone else was able to see the documents he was brazenly carrying, or if they had somehow assimilated into his not-a-memoryness, he was struggling to come up with a remotely plausible storyline, without having to divulge the ~~spurious~~, ~~possible~~, probable link between the Marted's of now and then.

Arriving,[67] Donald became aware of ~~several~~ three things:

    ¤   The room's occupied status was a definite "Yes;"

    ¤   The smell was still of *hospital* (Bleach, Blood and Beds); and

    ¤   Only one of the four beds was occupied, which was being done so by, Donald assumed correctly for a change, Lord Kingswood.[68]

Finding no easily accessible and permanent hiding place inside the group room, Donald recalled Seth's tour of the mansion and headed to the only place that exists now and hasn't been renovated, relocated, or removed in the next 75 years; the fountain in the inside/outside courtyard.

This was a perfect location to hide the soon to be misfiled documentation: It was there both now and then; and the only frequent close observers would be the pigeons, or a pigeon poo elimination professional; and close proximity to the under-courtyard-basement burial tomb, via the currently secret door in the fountain's base, put the icing on this particular slice of drama cake.

The fountain was a large, five-tiered, ever-wet birdbath style design, and incorporated several birdhouses around the lower extremities. It was a fairly rudimentary task for Donald to roll the documents, encase them in one of the birdhouses (wrapped in plastic) and then semi-permanently seal his devious handiwork with another conveniently suitable rock.

---

[66] Once again Donald's memory has failed him; completely forgetting that objects, like *Clueless!* game cards, can be transported from the not-a-memory scene if he simply puts them into his pocket.

[67] For the second time in this chapter, but the first time in this time.

[68] The Kingswood's House will lose its identity as a House of Lord when Lord Kingswood has his lordship revoked or he is released from hospital, whichever comes first.

Donald reviewed the status of his combined mental list of tasks:

- ☒ Three had been directly completed;
- ☒ Two had been indirectly completed; and
- ☒ One was precariously poised on the to-do side of the ledger.

If he was to consider the additional unforeseen completed task[69] thrown into the calculation, Donald was hovering around a 70% strike rate, which was way over any rational expectation and decidedly over Donald's. Pleased with himself he thought, "Not bad for a patient, but I guess it's time for time to go forward, and for me to go back to hospital to face the medicine.[70]"

Prepared for the out and in fading hazy, wavy, fuzzy visuality reversal this time, Donald successfully re-entered the present, and divulged all he knew.

Eventually.

Because Donald wasn't allowed to leave the group room without written permission,[71] unless it was for a legitimate emergency,[72] They, who seemed to have assumed the role of group leader again, dispatched Stu to retrieve the alleged documentation. Stu studied They for a moment and wasn't convinced until They assured Stu that Donald wouldn't start anything without him.

Donald took advantage of the confusion in proceedings to personalise his wait for Stu to come back with the hidden evidence.

Waiting for Stu

When you come back, I will be waiting
Until then thoughts will be frustrating
At least my head won't start gyrating
While I am still here, waiting for Stu

>He's out getting my documents back
>They're evidence I currently lack
>And then I will go on full attack
>After Stu returns. Waiting for Stu

---

[69] And who wouldn't claim a gimme every time one was presented?

[70] Somebody had already taken his music, but that's a story for next time.

[71] This has always been an enforceable rule which no group facilitator has ever enforced before. They were forced to do so today, due to the current shortage of unrestrained senior staff available to roam the corridors.

[72] Assisting in the birth of an illegitimate child is a legitimate emergency.

The remainder of the group session,[73] was a forthright discussion about the second not-a-memory scene which Donald infiltrated. And, as the student population of the world is familiar with the use of electronic tools, the salient points were recorded for posterity on the electronic whiteboard…

Clueless! Refresher Wipe – Salient Points

Outstanding Tasks:

- Hospital archives were (are?) located in *The Head Shrink Office*
- The victim is identified/verified as ~~Lady~~ Mister Jane Kingswood
- Hear(say) link to the *Bones Under the Courtyard Basement* case
- Secret Underground Laboratory in a Secret Underground Labyrinth
- Woman dressed in era appropriate doctor's outfit was Miss Sapphire

Remaining Tasks:

- Connect   I am a real doctor – Houts Marted (Silent H)
  With   I am not a doctor – Shuper Marted (Silent h)
- Explain what happened to Sister Sapphire

SaRS Whiteboard 1 – *Clueless!* Refresher Wipe – Salient Points

Donald had three questions which were hampering his comfortable… Alas, while he was waiting for a comfort break in the ~~interrogation~~ conversation, he completely forgot about them all:

- "What's with the inverted lightning bolt symbol in the corner?"
- "What should we do, if anything, with the discovery of the purchase record for the Fangle Experimental EECT Therapy Machine©?" and
- With the length of the previous question, Donald forgot about this one before there was a chance to think of it in the first place. This question remains as the only one forgotten twice before it was initially thought.

In a blissful state of ignorance, Donald exited the group room to head back to his ungrouped room for a nap. He was planning a spot nap, before a spot of playing spot the food. However, before he passed the off corridor towards the "Primary Nurse (sic) Office!" which was heading away from where he wanted to go, he was courteously intercepted by Seth, who was displaying his arm in the becoming common, *this way if you please*, position.

---

[73] Which is all of it, as trips into the tapestry take no time at all, literally.

Donald knew exactly what was going on.
He was about to be debriefed again.

Happily, due to his rigorous enforcement of the weekly clothing rotation method, Donald wasn't outed playing the part of commando today. Preparing himself for another onslaught of DD's uniqueness, Donald followed all of the rhetorical instructions.

True Blue Aussie Cars gone reindeer:
On Belmont;   On Kingswood; On Statesman; Go Holden
On Brocky;   On Skaifey;   On Lowndsey;   All Golden
And Piss-Off, you Falcon reindeers.

The Las Vegas Ante Clause lost reindeer:
On Poker;   On Roulette;   On Blackjack   and Bingo!
On Pai-Gow;   On Mahjong;   On Sic-Bo...   Casino
And Payoff, the Gambling reindeer.

The Brothers Grimm's Satan Claws' original reindeer:
On Gangster;   On Mobster;   On Hoodlum;   Go Murder
On Moron;   On Stupid;   On Silly;[74]   Go Slaughter
And Adolf, the Nazi reindeer.

---

[74] Silly Reindeer is the much-maligned equivalent of Dopey Dwarf.

Chapter 3.14:
The Tapestry #1 Debrief
(Parts I and II)

Part I - Official Debrief (OD with DD)

Pausing briefly outside DD's office to collect his thoughts, these were primarily about his self-confidence so didn't take very long, Donald noticed there was a new sign on the door which inspired the exact same amount of comfort as the previous one didn't. He also didn't understand why DD would advertise that she used to have a major drug problem...[75]

Primary Nurse's

Off Ice!

Donald reached out to knock on the do...

"Come in Donny."

Cringe. "Sphincter Feng Shui![76]"

The door didn't open by itself this time, nor did it technically the last time either, but when Donald applied himself the outcome became the same.

---

[75] It's amazing how much difference a little punctuation can make.

[76] It wasn't that Donald was accepting the Donny moniker or expecting her come in instruction before knock scenario; the less intense reaction was because he was excepting them both.

"Thank you for your prompt attendance Donny. Yes, I know about the sign, I am well aware of the inaccuracy that was perpetrated. I have already ordered another replacement, and if they at SOD know what is good for them, it should be arriving any day now."

"DD is evidently labouring under a misapprehension in regard to my level of regard for the correctness of the sign currently identifying her office." This statement is an unusual fairly direct quote of the thought which appeared to enter the generalness of Donald's mind. Nevertheless, Donald continued his current task, entering DD's office, with gusto. He was a mere three steps inside the door when DD continued on her tirade, refusing to be main tracked.

"Watt sought of business is it of there's... Who in their write mind doesn't cheque spelling and punk-u-a-shone... Its the pour F-Fort and brake down of watt they cent, ewe no. Know won should be able to cell a product with a soul error, let alone between for and ate? Eye will knot have it hear, ewe here?"

siGns On Demand! – Sin[77] Righters

It's a SIGN from siGns On Demand!

$$\begin{pmatrix} U(t) \\ V(t) \\ W(t) \end{pmatrix} = \begin{pmatrix} 1 & 0 & 0 \\ 0 & \cos Rt & -\sin Rt \\ 0 & \sin Rt & \cos Rt \end{pmatrix} \begin{pmatrix} U(0) \\ V(0) \\ W(0) \end{pmatrix}$$

Dial: 1800 ROTATE – ask for R. Cyst-Ants

"Come in please Donny. I am sorry, there is never a need for Black & White contrasting language here at SaRS."

Donald was confused, and then strangely pleased, after she apologised to him. He didn't know what she was apologising for, as it sounded perfectly OK to him, but he will take it and file it away for later validation.

"I requested your presence for several conversations:
- ✗ An informal chat about your first week as SaRS;
- ✗ A semi-formal dialogue regarding your second not-a-memory scene experience in the tapestry known formally as The Tapestry #1; and
- ✗ A third official interview about the same...[78]

So, if you wouldn't mind, shall we get started."

"Yes?" Donald was flattered she cared at least enough to articulate some permission before she started to pick his brain. He will later vehemently recant his answer and his associated questioning thought when he comes to realise it wasn't put to him as a question.

---

[77] Pronounced like in the trigonometrical functions of Sin, Cos and Tan.

[78] Part II - Official Debrief is coming... Stay tuned for four or five pages.

DD went through a particularly detailed account of Donald's interactions last week. The most concerning point, even though her monologue didn't take as long as expected considering she knew *everything* that happened last week, was disconcerting as she *knew* everything that happened last week, almost as if she could read about it somewhere.

Pausing momentarily, to take her eyes off the document she was reading, "Is there anything you would like me to add."

"No?[79]"

"Good. It seems you are well on the way to recovering your basic sanity.[80] Once you have achieved a state of chemical stability, we can begin working on your personalised karma." DD wrinkled her nose and sniffed the air, "I smell a cleanliness ~~berating~~ discussion coming on...

We, here at SaRS, are very proud of our history of not letting any dirt come between our patients and their recovery. There have been studies done which show physical dirt is just as bad as allegorical rumour, in a purely metaphorical sense. *Chemistry* can only do so much; *Alchemy* is required to finish the job."

DD produced a piece of paper and showed it to Donald. It was the results of a study done in the late 60s, which indicated mental health can be adversely affected by the combination of not *being clean* and not *coming clean*. After Donald read the title, "Un-Cleanliness is next to Un-Godliness" and glanced at the reverse side of the single piece of paper at the references cited:

- **Buzz A**ldrin (1969) *Apollo 11: Tranquillity Base... I wasn't there*;
- **Buzz B**lunt (1969) *Woodstock: Tranquiliser Base... I wasn't there*; and
- **Buzz C**uts (1969) *Haircut inspired Tranquilness... It wasn't there*.

He dismissed the concept as being a spurious conspiracy.

DD, however, who was not one to be side-tracked more than once in the same meeting, continued with her doggedness following the scent, "Donny, I am not requesting a change..."

Donald thought, "Finally![81]" and then after a brief moment of satisfaction, he realised the underlying threat of her statement.

---

[79] The repeated reversal of the question 'n' answer dynamic between DD and Donald, is something new which he didn't like, and will have a think about.

[80] Eventually, Donald will go on to write several other best sellers and be knighted for his contribution to mental health. He will also go, "pthththththth," in a messy bout of spitting onomatopoeia, at all of his previous detractors. You know who you are. There is no point in denying it any longer.

[81] Emphasising his thoughts is an undocumented Donald feature.

"Our minimum required level of cleanliness is eight.[82]"

DD pointed out the table included in the Un-Cleanliness (et al) report.

To which Donald reacted unusually, but predictably, and a little violently, "You want a rating system? I can't handle a rating system!" and a second time, "You're a rating system! You're a rating system! This whole hospital is a rating system! There's no justice for all in a rating system!"

1   **First Wedding ready.**
Literally Spotless. Most severe level, only ever achieved once, if at all.

2   **Subsequent Wedding ready.**
Figuratively Spotless. Cannot be improved on except for #1.

3   **Date ready.**
Showered & Shaved, Deodorant and Aftershave applied.

4   **Double Entendre ready.**
Showered & Shaved and Aftershave applied.

5   **Private Meeting ready.**
Showered & Shaved and Deodorant applied.

6   **Public Appearance ready.**
Showered & Shaved.

7   **Self-ready.**
Showered.

8   **Dirty.**
Pre-Showered with the intention of going to #7.

9   **Don't think about it.**
Instant Showered.

10   **Don't want to fix it.**
Instant Showering.

11   **Don't know about it.**
Pre-Instant Shower.

These levels are never socially acceptable.

12   **Don't care about it.**
Default value for Donald most of the time.

13   **Wallowing in it! Least severe level.**
Default value for Donald the rest of the time.

0   **Imperceptible levels of dirt.**
Cannot be measured.

---

[82] Like the DEFCON level *logic*, a high number denotes a low severity.

"Are you quite finished."
Donald remained silent indicating an acceptance of DD's premise.[83]

Moving on to the semi-formal dialogue after the informal chat...[84] "It has just been brought to my attention again that you were, this morning, supplied with a not-a-memory scene, by the tapestry known formally as The Tapestry #1. Is this attention seeking information correct."
"Erm, Yes?"
The repetition of their previous The Tapestry #1 conversation continued, and Donald was completely unsurprised when the same end result was soon reached, with one minor difference...
"In that case, there is no documentation for you to sign. We shall simply scan the previously signed Fine Print document, alter the relevant details and have Mark Time re-file it in your folder under The Tapestry #1 time relapse."
Straightening the papers in front of her, clasping her hands together and sighing, DD indicated she had arrived at the end of what she considered to be the important part of the two conversations, "Do you have any questions."
Donald had been unwittingly waiting for his chance to speak, and he only realised now that this was his then, when DD statemented her question... He was always prepared for this situation.[85]

Taking this terminally ill-considered offer insanely literally, Donald had a pre-prepared barrage of three questions.[86]
- Starting with a single question:
    - "What is the politically correct terminology for a ladybug?"
- Middling with a number two question:
    - "Does your poo taste as bad as it smells?"
- Finishing with a threesome question:
    - "Are *they* real, as opposed to: Fake,
      Unreal (awesome), or
      Imaginary?"

---

[83] This go-to silent mode is a particularly dangerous feature of Donald's communication style, as this conscious anger reaction is often confused with his subconscious freeze reaction to perceived danger.

[84] Both of these conversations sounded exactly the same to Donald, even though they didn't sound at all like *conversations* to him.

[85] This is the one, and only, singular situation he is *always* prepared for.

[86] And the third of these questions was a three-part double entendre.

Playing along with Donald's game, DD's responses were chronologically:
- "No, it isn't."
- "No!
(Wait for it.)
Wait!
(Wait for what...?)
What...?"
- "Hang on, I'm still stuck at the poo tasting number two one."

With this bizarre set of questions, Donald managed to goad DD into a bad mood, which even the original Minotaur from Ancient Greek mythology would fear. Steaming ears notwithstanding, Donald was completely oblivious to the danger he was in as she didn't *say* anything, until she asked, "Do you behave like this because you want to, or because you want to annoy me."

"Can't it be both?"

After she had calmed down and her gushing steam vent reduced to a mere fissure, without needing anywhere near a good reason, DD ratified her earlier consideration, "I believe there is an Investigator, Who, who[87] would like to talk to you about your earlier The Tapestry #1 transitions. If you would be so kind as to follow your imagination to Interrogation Room Won.[88]"

And with that, that was that, according to DD.

Donald didn't completely understand what was going on,[89] so he decided to play along with DD's game.

Turning, Donald saw the next in the spate of Back Door signs...

...and thought, "If DD is PLAN B, I don't ever want to run into The Animals who were PLAN A."

---

[87] Ha-Ha, DD said Who-Who.

[88] DD has also ordered another two replacement room name plaques, one for each of Interrogation Room Won and Interrogation Room Too, after the first replacement was a combined single plaque for both rooms.

[89] Which is similar to someone saying they weren't completely breathing.

Donald did a bit more thinking about his PLAN B:[90]

- Not the one that involved the blue light discount taxi service;
- Nor the one that involved becoming intertwined with this increasingly incontrovertible piece of intimate research into his life material; but his third PLAN B...
- What to have for lunch.

Part II - Official Debrief the other one (OD too)

Arriving at a meeting in a discombobulated state of mind was always a thing for Donald, so he decided he would eventually need a PLAN B which didn't involve DD. His confusion rapidly increased when he saw the person seated at the table within Interrogation Room Won...

They were the polar opposite of Pledge, Jimmy Pledge:

- The confident stride was relieved by an insecure sit;
- The magnificent tartan suit was altered into a pair of blue Harry High pants culottes, complete with yellow braces, rainbow splashed t-shirt and grey trench coat; but the major difference was...
- *She* wasn't going to be driving as many women wild in her regenerated blond femaleness.

Who Investigates – Investigators

We are those Whos, who gives a crap!

We are Who Investigates, the investigators

Senior Investigator – Detective Read Who

Dial: 1800 THEWHO

"Hello, Donny... Can I call you Donny?"

"Well, obviously, yes you *can* call me Donald; but you *may* not."

This start disappointed Donald immeasurably.[91] Requesting forgiveness is not an acceptable replacement of asking for permission. If you *think* you might need to ask if something is OK, then it most probably isn't. And the worst part of situations like this is, you *know* it probably isn't OK, because you just asked if it was OK, but you did it anyway...

---

[90]   Why would you prepare a PLAN B that involved being caught drunk driving? This would be a very stupid thing to do, and you are most probably getting what you deserve. Surely it would be better to prepare a PLAN A which involves an alternate mode of transportation home instead.

[91]   Actually, when Donald reflects, it will be about a six out of thirteen.

Taking a moment to reflect the annoyance Donald was projecting, and the next to confirm his question of her question-answer style of interview, the *she* Detective continued, "I am Who, D.R. Who... And I am who? You ask...

- ¤ I am the senior investigator who works at Who Investigates;
- ¤ Who is investigating the *Bones Under the Courtyard Basement* case, without Who there would be no investigation; and I am coincidentally
- ¤ Second cousin to, and once removed from, Dennis Who.

Thank you for following the instructions. We have a lot to discuss."

Detective made an exaggerated sweeping motion over the considerable[92] amount of research material currently occupying, as well as tumbling over the southwest exit (commonly referred to as a corner) of, the table.

"What I would like to do, Donald, is to discuss several items of interest, pertaining to inconsistent, incoherent and inexplicit information from within this investigation... Are you in?"

Donald considered her request pragmatically and was loathed to admit to himself that he was insatiably interested in the inglorious invitation. Not only because he was inclined to increase his insight into the case; because he was infrequently in the position to infiltrate a female led inquiry.

Donald gave an instant silent indication, indicating he was, indeed, in.[93]

"Now that we have finished with most of the 'ins' of the investigation, let us relocate our attention to some of the 'outs' we are going to be dealing with over the next few pages:

- ¤ Intentionally left;
- ¤ Side the law; and eventually, but least importantly
- ¤ Silent H.

From out of this outrageous pile of information, and from what we have been able to outlandishly extract from several outstanding tapestry outriders, we have outlined a fairly solid outpouring explanation of the activities outlined 75 years ago, give or take a few pages worth, right up to the outcome of your participation a few minutes ago..."

Donald didn't understand all of the ins and outs of the investigation, but as he wanted to spend a bit of time with Detective, he was willing to try.

---

[92] This is another "accepted" word meaning, where continued misuse has altered the definition to an extreme end of the literal. Any amount is "able to be considered," it doesn't have to be a large amount.

[93] Incidentally, the amount of in, that Donald is in, is increasing indefinitely, including this not insignificant intricate insertion...

Time-Lapsed Featurette
Repeat/Replay/Delete/Delay as appropriate.

1) It all began...

Construction of the mansion situated on The Big Ole Homestead grounds commenced approximately 125 years ago (1892), after the initial homestead was deemed to be a public eyesore.

A lot of the information gathered was garnered from an old Time Capsule hidden deep within the foundations of the mansion. When it was discovered, the deceptively large *Times are Recorded-Disposed in Secret* branded box was quickly broken into without any difficulty.[94] This proved to hold an important detail about the proposed mansion construction.

2) Then, 75 years ago...

The most recent homeowner (Husband of Lady Jane Kingswood) sold The Big Ole Homestead mansion to the Brothers of Saint Rita, who then renamed it The Kingswood's House and converted it into the *Private Psychiatric Hospital for Men* (SaRS one-point-zero), after which, the previous homeowner (H. of L.J.K.) became Patient Zero.

We have interviewed Brother Latent Tardy, who was one of the original founding brothers of SaRS, and have ceased, deceased and receased all of his exhaustive, yet exhausting, supply of information.

3) It was researched...

While one of the descendants of one of the mansion's original architects was investigating their family's effect on the local history, they compared the building plans on file at the local building commission to the ones discovered in the unearthed time capsule. The findings were comprehensive, intentional and revealing.[95]

The descendant's detailed comparison yielded a discrepancy underneath the courtyard basement. This, along with the "Do Not Dig Here! Move Along! There is Nothing to Find!" message, was enough impetus to launch an official investigation into what there wasn't to find 75 years ago.

---

[94]   This is both unfortunate and literal for the glass bottle content.

[95]   It is typical for mansion owners to record the building's transformations. The entire architecture expanding up or sideways; rooms divided, joined, or created; and sometimes even when windows or doors moved. Generally, no one will record their building having a basement malfunction.

4) Without significant results...

There were several groups of people identified within SaRS:
- Patients: People who were *committed by the institution* changed very little throughout the 75-year history of the hospital. One exception being the recorded female demographic became accurate;
- Doctors: People who were *consulting at the institution* changed very little throughout the 75-year history of the hospital. One exception being the recorded female demographic became appropriate;
- Nurses: People who were *contingent to the institution* changed very little throughout the 75-year history of the hospital. One exception being the recorded female demographic became antiquated; and
- Brothers & Sisters of Saint Rita: People who *chanted in* changed very little throughout the 75-year history of the hospital. One exception being the recorded female demographic became anticipated.

Specific suspects of the unknown malfeasance:
- Brother Brown   - discarded as uninvolved;
- Father Fuchsia - discarded as unlikely;
- Sister Sapphire - undiscarded suspect;
- Gardener Grey   - discarded as unclean;
- Lawyer Lithium - discarded as unwholesome; and
- Wastrel White - discarded as unknown.

Locations of relevance:

Inside/Outside Courtyard: The location of the memorial fountain. This has been recorded as the major relevant location because it is where you can gain entry to the courtyard basement, and then to the under-courtyard-basement burial tomb via the secret door underneath the fountain's base. Be careful you don't trip over the police tape.

Labyrinth/Hedge Maze: The only other barely viable significant locations. Even though these aren't categorically locations, in and of themselves, per se, as they are principally the providers of those means by which you get to and from other actual locations.

Possible choice of weapons:
- Rope   - no broken neck bones were found;
- Medication   - no reason to hide an alleged suicide;
- Electrocution   - Electroconvulsive Therapy (ECT) was developmental and as such, remains as the only plausible, however experimental and accidental weapon of choice;
- Pillow   - no reason to hide an alleged natural cause;
- Animal   - no bite marks on the bones were found; and
- Implements   - no reason to write about a common occurrence.

5) Until the discovery...

A few years ago, there was a discovery of human remains underneath the mansion's courtyard basement. Several conclusions were come to, but most have never been satisfactorily explained. The bones were found to have been approximately 75 years entombed, however, no formal identification could be made as there are:

- No record(s) of any missing person(s) in the area;
- No dental records to compare the skeleton's teeth with; and
- No records of any dentists in the area.[96]

So, we will have to persevere with interpretation of the details we have, and inference of the details we don't, instead of having anything tangible.

6) The Tapestry #1 brings a wealth of hodgepodge...

Several nodules of information extracted about animals:

- It was a male only facility 75 years ago; but
- There appears to be a female wearing an inmate's attire; and
- There also appears to be a female wearing a doctor's outfit.

Several nibbles of information extracted about vegetables:

- The origin of the sideways growing rose bushes;
- The story of a hedge-maze ending at an ornate pavilion; and
- What to have for lunch.

Several nuggets of information extracted about minerals:

- A retrieved small piece of plastic;
- A remembered wicker basket under a hot air balloon; and
- A ridiculous "Beware of the Minotaur!" sign.

7) Including, but not limited to...

- The woman in the doctor's outfit was Miss Sapphire;
- The woman in the patient's outfit was Lady Jane Kingswood;[97] and
- The previously unmentioned **I am not a doctor** Marted.

---

[96] Basically, there are no records from way back then.

This does give Donald a chance to say, "I Told You So!" He is always harping on how comparing dental records is a spurious method of corpse identification. Apart from the probable lack of x-rays on file, there is no way of finding out who their dentist was.

[97] Donald didn't understand how Detective Who knew about Lady Jane Kingswood being the unidentified female patient, considering it was only discussed for the first time just a few pages ago.

8) Postulations about...

- Unauthorised forms of electrical based therapy;
- The existence of hospital archives dating back 75 years; and
- The answer to the *Clueless!* question.

9) Resulting in...

Ongoing investigations of the not-a-memories:

- The actual death scene of the human remains;[98]
- The transference the body up to the mansion and burying it; and
- The reasons behind the ongoing investigations.

Ongoing investigations of the not-a-memory participants:

- Donald Halfbrain, Hospityable;
- Donald Halfbrain, Psychological; and
- Donald Halfbrain, Rehabilitigation.[99]

~~Ongoing investigations of the not-a-memory investigators:~~
- ~~Detective Read Who;~~
- ~~Who...? Wait...! What...?; and~~
- ~~If this some sort of a joke, it isn't funny.~~

End of Featurette

Delay/Delete/Replay/Repeat as appropriate.

"Outstanding!" was all the excitement Donald could muster.

"And now, while we are here Donald, would you mind elucidating...

- Preclusion of discovery by moving the body through the underground labyrinth/laboratory and sealing it in the grave;
- Conclusion about the possible Marted relationship; and explaining
- Exclusion of the associated hospital documentation and how most of it mysteriously went missing 75 years ago?

If the authorities had access to these details back then, they might have been able to solve the apparent accidental death.

---

[98] Not the death of the remains; that would be silly. This is the death of all humanity immediately preceding the remains.

[99] When Donald asked, "How do you know about these future events?" D.R. Who replied, "I am a Lord of the Time my friend, if I haven't found out about this yet before, I will make sure that I soon will have."

But slightly less importantly, if we had possessed a complete picture of the events back then, it certainly would have helped us a few years ago..."

Donald didn't feel the need to mention that there was a complete picture of the events hanging in the entry vestibule, nor did he feel that divulging his actions surrounding the documentation would help.[100] He did feel completely comfortable with sharing his observations, and he did so chronologically.[101]

"Firstly, I can confirm there is a series of underground rooms and tunnels beginning directly underneath the maze central pavilion. Referring to these as a labyrinth is interesting at best, and while there is a disconcerting warning sign saying, 'Beware of the Minotaur!' there is no mythical presence present."

Detective's silence didn't imply an acceptance of Donald's confirmation, it was an acknowledgement of the facts about myths already known.

"Secondly, I can confirm there is an underground room containing some primitive medical and electrical equipment. Referring to this as a laboratory is dishonourable at best, I would describe it as an operating den."

Detective's attention silenced on.

"Thirdly, and lastly, I can't give you much more information regarding the movements of Lady Kingswood after the chaos of the unfortunate incident, as I headed off to find the hospital archives. But what little I did witness has been introduced to my never will forget:

After the dial setting was verified at six-point-five, and the switch flicked, a lightning bolt struck the building, flowed through the grounding wires of the "Fangle Experimental EECT Therapy Machine©," and rotated the dial clockwise to thirteen. The smoke eventually settled, Lady Kingswood's smell of roast pork became a bit less gagging, and they wheeled the chair away.

I really don't want to think about how they managed to separate her from the chair so quickly and then bury her more or less intact. But I now realise, that by thinking about not wanting to think about it, I inadvertently just have."

"I see. That is not disastrous, I would refer to it as helpful at best. We have re-confirmed yet again the identity of all three:

- She shouldn't be a patient;
- She is not a doctor; and
- **I am not a doctor.**

---

[100] Donald was vicariously thinking, "How would the divulgement help me?" While I am thinking, "Is divulgement a real word?" (It is surprisingly.)

[101] As well as being the correct order, a chronological order will give Donald additional time to think of an acceptable answer for point number three. An extension of this bonus is that time may limit any incriminating discussion.

Following on from that confirmation, can we now focus our attention on the relationship between **I am a real doctor** Houts Marted (Silent H), and **I am not a doctor** Shuper Marted (Silent h)"

Detective retrieved one of the fallen documents and showed it to Donald. It was an open book of the Marted's DNA tests results...

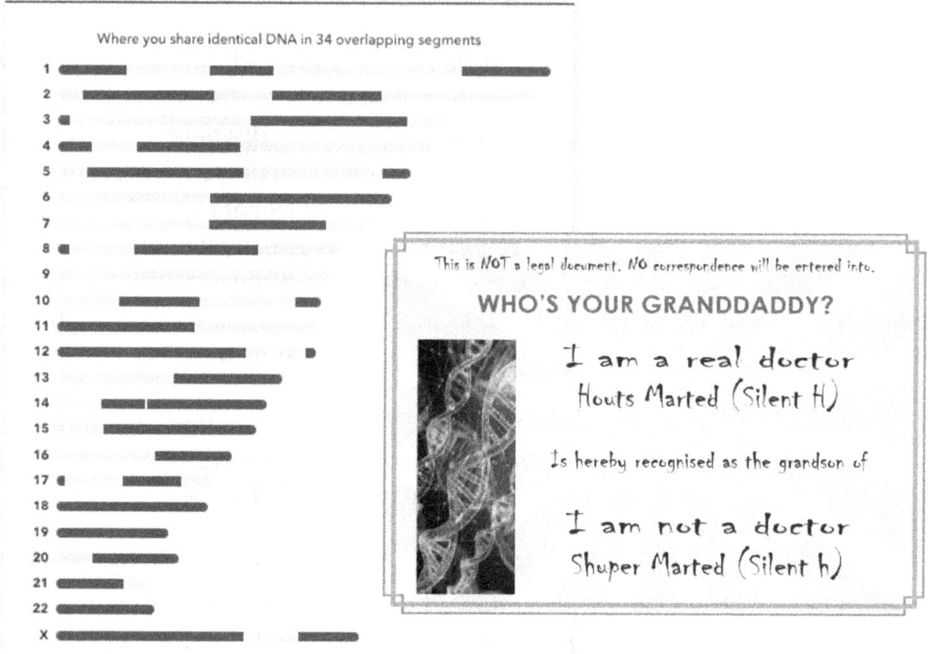

Bones Under the Courtyard Basement 1 – Marted DNA Comparison.

"We have this proof that the two Marted's were related. But we can find no proof that Houts knew about his familial relationship to Shuper. In fact, we can find no other information about Shuper at all. Without some evidence showing he was an employee of SaRS (né *PSH... for Men*) we can't show there was a conspiracy.

And this leads me into the last point of data discovery. Did your last trip into The Tapestry #1 reveal anything useful? You mentioned that you 'headed off to find the hospital archives.' Was this a fruitful heading?"

Donald's plan to stall for "additional time to think of an acceptable answer for point number three," obviously hasn't worked, and he had accidentally just given away a piece of unplanned detail. He was generally very fast to come up with a witty rejoinder or even a sarcastic comeback, but in this rare moment of clarity he went with the factual truth.

"No fruit was obtained, head or otherwise, I'm afraid."

It was going to take Detective some time to process this response.

Taking an educated guess[102] on what might interest Detective enough to side-track her current train of thought without actually derailing it completely, Donald quipped, "So, how is the investigation going?"

"There are several theories we think are worth exploring:

1) Miss Sapphire and Shuper Marted (Murder)

We have all but dismissed this theory as bunkum. There is no evidence of any premeditation taking place, and they hadn't even discovered mindfulness yet, so active stalking on this line of inquiry has ceased indefinitely.

Another hurdle, by all accounts, is that Lady Kingswood seemed to be a willing participant in the events. This, along with the lack of a missing person's report for her, doesn't bode very well for a positive murderous result.

We are still considering the lesser charge of accidental death, but as both of the defendants are also long since deceased this speculation is also losing impetus. The only quasi-solid direction this research could potentially take us in is their conspiracy to avoid criminal detection. Someone buried the remains of Lady Kingswood, hid the knowledge of her being passively *dead and buried* and destroyed any evidence of their culpability.[103]

2) Miss Sapphire (Alleged Missing Person)

Again, we have no tangible proof of her co-opted disappearance. The best we can come up with is childish considered coincidence:

- Once upon a time there was this young woman, Miss Sapphire, who disappeared from a mental institution;
- There was also another young woman, Sister Sapphire, who appeared the very next day as a cloistered nun belonging to the Order of Saint Rita. This second woman bore a striking resemblance to the first;
- Both of these young women were committed to thinking about what they had done with their lives up to this point;
- When it was revealed that the first institution was founded by people who were also members of the second, a closer inspection of the two young women was warranted; resulting in the conclusion
- There weren't any ramifications for Miss Sapphire over her previous actions at the mental institution... She *was* the ramification.[104]

---

[102] In Donald's case, this wasn't so much educated, as it was lucky.

[103] This point is pure conjecture. It is nigh on impossible to prove a negative.

[104] Everyone got this wrong (including me). They were trying to find the explanation of Sister Sapphire's disappearance. They should have been looking for the explanation of her appearance. ☑ *Metaphorical Tick.*

3) Houts Marted (Conspiratorial Self-Acknowledgement)

This is our most promising theory, but also our least important. We can't exactly prove he was a central part of a murder cover-up when no murder has been proven. The best we can hope for is a conspiracy to cover-up a conspiracy to vanish the missing documentation.

Marted, H (silent), was first brought to our attention because he had been unknowingly hiding relevant case information, specifically the storm, from the investigation. We are trying to link him to the secret door under the fountain. We think there has been information passed down through the generations of Marteds, in the bedtime stories they were told.

When the Marted ancestors faded into relative obscurity, so did some of their relatives, except for the future generations of their family. This also goes a significantly long way round to explaining Marted, H (silent),'s attraction to all things ghostly and his published research papers."

Donald mused, "So, I'm going to go out on an unfamiliar ledge for me here and guess, all of this means the *Bones Under the Courtyard Basement* case has been solved?"

Or has it?[105]

Donald has some answers:
- ¤ Is there really a Minotaur's lair?   - Yes and No
- ¤ Where are the hospital archives?   - Here and Now
- ¤ What is the solution to the *Clueless!* puzzle? - Done and Dusted

Retrieving a game card from a pile from discards, Donald looked...

The slowly disappearing text read, albeit difficultly:

"I deduce: It was I am not a doctor Shuper Marted (Silent h) accompanied by Miss Sapphire, who accidentally killed Lady Kingswood, in the Underground Laboratory, with some Lightning Induced Electrocution."

And was replaced by...

Clueless! – PSH... for Men
I think:

"It erased. What does that mean?"

---

[105] Yes of course it has, pay attention, the reveal is coming.

"Elementary, it means that there will be more games afoot."
"One final task, Donald, I would ask you to sign the SaRS Secrecy Act...[106]"

I, the undersigned, understand:[107]

In line with the SaRS Acceptable Use of Information policy, I agree the existence of this not-a-memory scene will always be denied if someone ever asks about it.

Category: "Malicious Story"

Should you require access to this not-a-memory scene for a valid reason, please call the SaRS Unhelpful Desk: 131 313.

Everything, up to and including this message, will be denied. Signed/Dated

_______________ / _______

Bones Under the Courtyard Basement 2 – SaRS Secrecy Act.

Donald signed immediately of course, but was disappointed:
- He folded to The Man[108] too easily;
- He couldn't talk about the experience with anyone else; and
- He didn't get a get out of gaol free card for his efforts.

---

[106] A moment of déjà vu later, Donald realised Detective wasn't *asking* him.

[107] This detail is wildly inaccurate, there is much Donald didn't understand.

[108] Detective is OK being called this, as long as it is a capitalised pronoun.

Chapter 4:
Back to the Story
(Is Being Continued...)

Rhetorical instructions aside,[109] once Donald was on the way back to his room he became interrupted by Seth, *"Ahphlegm."* who handed him a reusable note about his Week 2 Blood sample donation. This was a required optional extra to check for any unanticipated changes of Donald's mind, and to provide Dr Gee Jay with an indication that the cocktail of medications he was taking were working as prescribed. Regarding this last point, Donald could be forgiven for assuming they were working, as he hasn't been thinking about climbing any walls recently.

Fast forwarding to the afternoon's group setting, leap-frogging lunch and its many associated incidentals, Donald muttered to himself about providing another Blood sample. He was trying to determine if:

- Everyone else understood something that he couldn't;[110]
- Anyone else was paying him undue attention; or the expected
- No one else ~~gave a rat's~~ cared.

There were no obvious oblivious answers which could possibly induce his death, destruction, or worse... So, he treated the ones supplied:

- As if they could.
- As if they would.
- As if they should.

---

[109] Put all of your "Rhetorical Instruction" questions aside for the moment and explain to me the difference between one of these and an order.

[110] This is a contraction of the conjunction of could and not. I find it mildly annoying that couldnot isn't a legitimate word. (Same with isn't and isnot.)

Donald became distracted by the thought trying to dribble its way into his consciousness... The *isnot* potential definitions:

- ⌘ iSnot   - A new nasal product from Apple;
- ⌘ Ice not   - A melted previously frozen sculpture;
- ⌘ Ice knot - A frozen binding; or quite bizarrely
- ⌘ I snot   - A confession?

When Donald distanced himself enough from this disgusting issue, and his previous unrequited mutterings, he entered the group session in more than a purely physical way. Stu and They were again explaining about the lack of any senior staff.

"...aster. So, for the foreseeable future, we are it I'm afraid. They and I will attempt to keep ourselves together long enough to see all of you through any emerging 80 grit coarse rough patches. We will keep every discussion light and in doing so, hopefully, we will also avoid any triggers."

Taking the reins, Stu gave them flick and turned the light proceedings into a heavy-dude runaway... "The topic for discussion is... *Why Am I Here?*"

.

.

. **<Chirp...** Chirp... Chirp...>

.

.

Believing the cricket filled silence to be an ostentatious invitation to speak, Donald complied by supplying his own version of the generic "Let me take you back to where it all began.[111]"

Officially known as his "Thirteen Step Slow Descent into Madness."

1) Job, Home, Marriage to Kay, Miss E. Clair, Miss Jo Diary.

Donald had it all, and all of his all was also chronologically correct, when it plateaued out for the last three ingredients of his happy.

"In hindsight, I may have peaked a little too early. I had already:

- ⌘ Singlehandedly saved the world from the *Y2K Millennium Bug;*
- ⌘ Lucked out with both ships of relation and property owner; and
- ⌘ Made ample provisions for my permanent replacement.

I developed my comfort zone to such an extent there was little I had to do to maintain the status quo. Unfortunately, my little was too little."

---

[111] Or   His Wits' End;
           Moment of Truth;
           Point of No Return;
           Beginning of the End.

Or times 2, you can indulge yourself, and choose your own favourite idiom.

2) Job Redundancy

This job (and the one referred to in step 1)) was Donald's second real job. In his first big boy job, he "saved the world" from imploding when the second arbitrary millennium got off to a false start in the year 2000. Figuring out the complex mathematics involved, 1999+1=2000, was a laurel that Donald found it hard to rest on for too long.

Complacently driven, Donald reached out for a new challenge. When the people behind the worldwide relief offered Donald a bribe to stay on, "just in case he was wrong," he didn't bite. Instead, he secured himself a position in a new company which, unfortunately, was to become itself insecure.

Because he set such a high bar for himself, Donald had only one realistic way to go. And go there he did, in a spectacularly magnificent fashion starting with a great pile of the accurately named step number two.

"The first ripple on my life pond was more like a tsunami. While it was not completely avoidable, it was completely unexpected. One day I had a fantastic job I had chosen to do, and I did it really well; and the next day that exact same job chose to do a really good job on me."

3) House, Job #2

So, what did our Donald do after he was made redundant from his chosen work? Buy an unfinished brand-new Mini McMansion[112] of course. What else would you do without any consistent income?

"One day this little man came a knocking on our front door. He offered to exchange our quaint little home in the burbs for an oversized box made out of ticky-tacky[113] way out in a sticks-adjacent property development. He threw in a cold hard three untaxed pineapples (ed: 3 x $50) to seal the deal, and maybe my fate as well.

While I was way out there, I was also looking for some new employment. Kay had gone back to work, dealing with other people's sanity, so time wasn't a significant factor. Then, exactly one year and a day later, I landed a new job and began the climb to the summit of my second wave."

4) Divorce

Change is often quoted as being inevitable.
For Donald, it is the inevitable that changes, not him.
"I don't like talking about the fazing of this phase... So, I won't."

Donald took a break to collect a relatively small amount of his wits.

---

[112] At some stage between steps 2) and 4), his Home turned into a House.

[113] With emphasis on the tacky. Gaudy, flashy, or kitschy would also fit.

5) Job #2 Redundancy

This was a particularly low point of Donald's life, but only up until then.[114] His attitude was progressively worsening, frequently complaining to his then girlfriend how bad things were. Donald had just spent six months warming the bench, when everything came to a head. He received the ominous, "We need to talk." call from his manager.

Donald in turn relayed this information to said girlfriend, saying, "I think I am about to be made redundant..."

Who replied, "Why don't you think a bit more positively?"

And quite predictably Donald came back with the adage, "OK, I am positive I am about to be made redundant!"

Not too long after this, Donald became available.

Twice.

6) Motorbike

Donald's response to his current life crises, was to have a mid-life crisis. He bought himself a Kamikaze motorbike.[115]

Rationalising effectively, it was much cheaper than buying a Sporschecar. His ERNie6 was to become an enjoyable, and reliable, mode of transport when it wasn't raining. While he was riding, there was also an added awareness of the incompetency of the public in general's driving ability.

As with everything else in Donald's life, it was to be given one chance. This chance wasn't negated after there was a drive by shooting aimed at one of his neighbours in a case of mistaken identity retaliation between two well-known rival motorcycle gangs (true story). Nor did it become nullified when a rogue King-and-I Accent attempted to speak of a mass vehicular slaughter.

Its official chance came and parked on Donald's foot.

This quite literally felt like the longest two minutes of Donald's life. Having a large black Sporschecar Capsicum parked on his foot, while screaming many and varied instructional expletives, slowed down Donald's perception of time. His predilection of Sporschecar owners was also significantly reduced.[116]

---

[114] Donald has frequently said that he only ever remembers "the bad stuff."

Case in point. At that precise moment Donald had:

- ✗ A roof over his head which didn't leak, and a car in the garage;
- ✗ Food in the fridge, and he weighed an ideal 80kg (175lb); and
- ✗ Ample time to pursue what, or who, ever he wanted to.

[115] This will eventually be replaced with a Harvey Donaldson motorcycle.

[116] It took Donald a long time to think of it as more than transport after this.

7) Job #3, Partner, House #2

Continuing along the rollercoaster, Donald achieved another tri-win. The first (at SUCKA), and the second (with Hannah), enabled the third.

"Then, again, exactly another year and a day later, I landed my third real job. The climb to the top of this third wave was more sandy, than it was wety, as it was mostly located in the Middle East.[117] One of the dialectical benefits of this job was that it was all-you-can-possibly-eat-for-free, in between bouts of 24-hour commutes.

Like all of my major decisions, I was advised into buying my second house. This turned out to be diminishing good advice. It was good, it was very good. But, eventually, it became horrid."

In this one instance, like the many others, Hannah wasn't responsible for Donald's decision, it was his own irresponsibility. Donald continues to exist in the House with a multitude of books and DVDs (all categorised, colour coded and certified), but is yet to call it a home.

Re: Pi Avenue p279

> ¤   Extract from The Donald Diaries.

8) Breakup/Breakdown

Between Donald and Hanna/Between Donald and SUCKA.

- ¤   Both bad;
- ¤   Both out of his total control; and
- ¤   Both singularly painful.

"A phase of failures that I don't much like talking about. So, I won't, much. The breakdown I am willing to blame on a little thing called Autistic burnout,[118] but the breakup doesn't warrant any such blame. That one is totally no one's fault... Except mine."

---

[117] "The Middle East is halfway to the East of what?" I hear you ask...

This Westernisation has been extracted out of my "Stupid Sayings" list. If a person is travelling in an easterly direction, they are travelling to the east, however, if wind is travelling to the same east, it is referred to as a westerly.

But I digress, back to your question, and to my original point. If you travel in that direction long enough, *everything* is east of *everything else*, eventually.

[118] **Autistic Burnout** is a state of physical and mental fatigue, heightened stress and diminished capacity to manage life skills, sensory input and social interactions. It comes from years of being severely overtaxed by the strain of trying to live up to the demands which are out of sync with our needs.

9) Hospital

While 8) was in progress 9) happened, and you can read all about it in:

⛄ Hospityable Chapter Three — Day -3 — (Friday to Time Zero)

10) Quit Job #3

Donald has never been fired from a job. Ever. This is little comfort though, and it is no great leap to conclude that Donald's last job contributed the largest bale of hay to the camel's back, not much of a surprise in the Middle East. Had he been in a viable position to think about this at the time, he may have been able to negotiate some sort of arrangement of a less-than-permanent solution than what was implemented.

But that's not how it works, or how Donald remembers it. As previously stated, Donald only ever remembers "the bad stuff," this is the exception that proves the rule. His memory of this time is particularly hazy, which explains why he does not explain this step's inclusion.

11) Hospital #2

And then this happened. Donald didn't need to explain this step to anyone in the room. You can read the full account in *NOT*: (as in, the rest of the book)

⛄ Hospityable Chapter Three — Day -3 — (Friday to Time Zero)

12) Publishing Books #1 through #7 (Now #8)

Donald's dubious collection of poetry books were deliberately prescribed as being instrumental in his path to normalisation.

Re: Shameless Plugs p286

⛄ Extract from The Donald Diaries.

13) Publish a Real[119] Book #1

Real book #1 was obviously *Hospityable*.

If you haven't read this by now... You really should.

For those of you who want to know, and for those who don't, *Hospityable* is a portmanteau[120] of *Hospital* and *Pitiable*, and is pronounced Hos-pity-able. The name of this #2 book, also obviously, is *Psychoillogical*, a combination of *Psychological* and *Illogical*, and is pronounced Psycho-illogical.

------

[119] This is thanks to a comment Miss E. Clair made. She didn't realise the impact it would have, and when it was ably supported by Hannah DeRail on antisocial media, Donald did what he always did. He made it into a joke, hid his true feelings from them and didn't speak about it ever again, until now.

[120] A word blending the sounds and combining the meanings of two others.

The third Donald instalment, as Detective Read Who spoiled a few pages earlier, is going to be called *Rehabilitigation* from *Rehabilitation* and *Litigation* and will be pronounced Rehabi-litigation.

These will eventually be followed by: (Hopefully)

4. *Unemploymental*   - Getting a job as a has-been-mental Donald.
5. *Laboratoryinth*   - Inside the SaRS underground network.
6. *Catchychism*   - Brains vs Religion through the dark times.
7. *Mindlessfullness*   - Mental health thoughts in general.
8. *Philosophblical*   - Musing over the big questions in life.

Moving on from the self-aggrandisement into what was occurring, Donald became aware he had been monopolising the group... He wasn't entirely sure what made him think this was such a bad idea, after all, wasn't sharing part of the programme? If another inmate listened to his story and realised that they weren't the craziest person in the room, then surely, this must be considered a good thing for them.

It was also good for They and Stu, who had just effortlessly facilitated half of a group session.

When everyone realised Donald had finished his prequel story there was a round of stunned silence, followed by a round of quiet acceptance, which in turn was followed by Donald finishing his story with a bit of history, "Back then I was constantly accompanied by sadness. But I didn't feel the need to wallow in that sort of malodourous crap!"

"Great butts stink alike." Owedebt interjected unhelpfully.

"Yeah... No-Shit, Sherlock." Nota, as always, following Owedebt's lead.

"Back in my day, we'd keep our minds out of the toilet." Mindy's speech is always delivered with tangible amount of threat. This is often confused with senile confusion, and Mindy will gladly explain the error of your ways the next time you are alone with her.

Smells purple.

"Really?" Donald's interabanging response to this bout of toilet humour, including Sven's colourful cookie, laid on the sarcasm thick enough so even he would be able to understand what he meant.

Realising he was asleep at the controls of a runaway group session, Stu did the only thing he could think of to wrest back any semblance of focus on him before the group degenerated into disgusting commentary even further than it already had, "STOPPPPP![121]" Then he fell back to the three **Re-eatings**.

---

[121] He's not a smart man, but Stu Dent is as Stu Dent does.

Retreating to the safety of the whiteboard, Stu elaborated poorly, "Who can tell me what STOPPPPP means?" When there was no audible response to the brain-stop-teasing-it question, Stu wrote the title, a completely different question and the first letter of each word as a prompt.

Repeating his original question, while gesticulating at the whiteboard, Stu managed to achieve the exact same result.

Repleating the eventual result, after much prompting, Stu was able to lead the group to the edge of this particular knowledge cliff, and then give them a large push towards their final conclusion...

STOPPPPP - what does it mean?

Stop everything you are doing immediately (or sooner)

Think about the dire effects of what you are doing

Overcome the urge to protest the stopppppping

Prepare with some Lexicon

Produce with some Denouement

Practice with some Echelon

Perfect with some Paragon

Proceed with some Conviction

SaRS Whiteboard 2 – STOPPPPP

As Donald did with most things, he tried to understand what the hidden meaning was. He could read the words. He could understand the words.[122] But he could not make much out of the complete message. About the closest he could figure; it was an extended *shhhhh-ready-set-say-cheese-go* moment.

Once the excitement had been put out, They and Stu tried returning to the premise of the original group session: Donald's *"Why Am I Here?"* history discussion. It wasn't clear to Donald how this was a light discussion, and as his story included many triggers, it also violated their last hope.

---

[122] He looked up what the meaning and pronunciation of Denouement was. It is, "the outcome of a complex sequence of events," and, "dei-noo-mon."

"Does anyone have any comments about Donald's account, or questions they would like to be answered?" Stu is about to learn a very valuable trilogy of lessons of his own, specifically:

- When surrounded by a group of less-stereotypically-normal people he has to provide a less generic opening for random questions;
- All questions, requests and instructions must be directed to a named individual, otherwise there will be no clambering for the spotlight; and
- Boy Scout up... Be prepared for anything...

"What is your favourite number between one and thirteen?" Nelo (Vamp) Priors asked this unfortunate question...[123] He had intended for it to provide a conduit back to *light discussion*, however, it was Donald who was targeted as the recipient.

For anyone else the answer would be one, two, three... thirteen.

For Donald, there were many more options and regulations:

- *Favourite* requires context:
    - Visibly pleasant symmetrical numeral (8);
    - Multiple meanings (~~1/won,~~ 2/to/too, 4/for/fore, 8/ate); or
    - Convenient replication options (3).
- *Between* one and thirteen, without *inclusive*, means one and thirteen have both been ruled out as possible answers (as above); and
- He had to overcome the disappointment of not being able to choose his all-time favourite number (0).[124]

Just as Donald was about to explode, They chimed in with an ever-present condescension, "There are no wrong answers in group."

This comment caused Donald to rethink his initial answer for "Who is the boss in group today?" and, when he responded with an update of "Clearly no one!" he proved that there are indeed wrong answers in group. Not only that, but there are also wrong questions, wrong statements and wrong people...

He then resolved to "The next time someone asks me to pick my favourite number between one and thirteen, I am just going to say Pi."

---

[123] It is unfortunate, not only because it failed at being an incredibly benign question; it also served to highlight Nelo's presence in the book. It is highly unlikely a minor character of his ilk will survive until the end without incident.

[124] Donald likes the way zero messes with many people's minds.

- "I don't understand, how can nothing be something?"
- "Is zero divided by zero: zero, one, or a divide by zero error?"
- Empty, null and zero all mean different things in computer speak.

"Is there someone else with a relevant question?" head shook They.

Owedebt flicked off her sarcastic-self pole for the moment, and asked an intriguingly insightful question, "Why did you include so many positive steps in your decline. It all seems to be counterintuitive?"

Donald hadn't realised he had done this while he was talking through his story. It did, again, reflect poorly on his theory of only ever remembering *the bad stuff*. This would be the most powerful piece of insight Donald has seen so far today, and he looked at Owedebt in a different light...

And...

He then proceeded to forget the entirety of this "good" interaction when Nelo asked him another question, "Are you one of the patients who is letting Nurse Jack extract a little unnecessary Blood today?"

Donald failed completely to connect the three dots he was facing:

- The glint in Nelo's eyes at the mention of Bloodletting;
- The unspoken association between Nelo and Owedebt; and
- The amount of suspicious commentary Skit appeared to be hearing.

When he checked the reusable note from Seth, he replied, "As a matter of fact, yes I am... I have been pre-scheduled to provide a ~~Book~~ Week Two Blood sample donation in just a few ~~pages~~ moments.

Coincidently, the group session was also just about to end. They and Stu collected themselves, downloaded a copy of the whiteboard for posterity and single filed out the door following the crowd.

Donald was on his way to the Main Nurse's Station, where Nurse Jack will extract the requisite amount of Blood, when he unwittingly become the leader of a small ragtag procession. Skit was following Got, who in turn was following both Owedebt and Nelo, who were themselves following Donald.[125]

"Why is Donald's Blood of interest to you?" is what Got thought, translated into stereotypical TV Russian and then asked, "Wkhkhkhkhkhy eeze Donald's Blood of eenterrrrryest to you?" of the two she was wont to pursue.

Owedebt:	"Oh, ummmmm, it's not so much, ummmmm, an *interest*..."
Nelo:	"it's more like a *morbid* Bloodthirsty *curiosity*."
Owedebt:	"We want, ummmmm, to be sure Donald doesn't befall any, ummmmm, *untoward events*..."
Nelo:	"while he is on the way to his *voluntary* Blood *donation*."
Owedebt:	"For some reason..."
Nelo:	"yeah, that."

---

[125] It is worth noting that Nota and Chunky were *apart from the crowd*, not *a part of the crowd*. This was a crowd where they were not in the in crowd.

Donald was still oblivious to the goings-on going on behind him. So much so, he overlooked the close personal connection between Owedebt and Nelo which their finishing each other's sentences would seem to indicate.[126]

"Wkhkhkhkhkhtyeverrrrr." Seethed Got, after giving in to her exceedingly short idiom fuse, and deciding it wasn't worth the effort to try and follow their duo, let alone their co-authored co-opted conversation. Heading off to find a piece of peace, Got removed herself from the vicinity.

Staying silent, Skit was easily blending in with the idiosyncratic crowd. He recorded a curious mental note of "Five by Five," congratulating himself in the process, because his devious plan was obviously working perfectly...

He recognised several flagrant symptomatic quirks immediately after Nelo sombred into the room... Nelo:

- ¤ Had an extremely pale white face which was verging on albinism;
- ¤ Was staying away from all non-artificial bright light;[127] and
- ¤ Made no effort to hide the conspicuous red stains on his shirt collar.

And now, with his noticeable attraction to fresh Blood; Skit stereotypically concluded... "Nelo is a vampire!"

Skit wasn't self-aware of his unique condition, which involves a different fictional personality every day, but he did retain all of his non-characterisation memories. This elevates his existence to being impossible, up from a derisive Pffffft! He still had a protracted way to go to arrive at the mythical destination he was currently following.

Nelo and Owedebt exchanged a few furtive glances between themselves, as well as throwing a significant few at the retreating Got. Once Got was out of eye shot, they both incorrectly believed there was no one impinging on their aloneness and dropped their act of disentanglement. Joining their hands and giggling like little children they skipped away to find something else to do that would most probably be decidedly not childlike.

Skit did more or less the same thing (without the skipping).

This time when Donald arrived at the Bloodletting station, he was prepared to create a troubling memory. This was a significant compromise on his part, so the memory created wouldn't be compromised enough to warrant being in the bad memory basket; yet was still bad enough to be remembered.

---

[126] Realistically, even if he was aware, he wouldn't have noticed anything.

[127] A vampire question, or two: Given it is usually *direct* sunlight which *dusts* a vampire, how does their *soullessness* divine the minute difference between *direct* and *reflected* sunlight? And why don't they just put on a hazmat suit?

Nurse Jack reluctantly opened the door after Donald cheesily knocked on it to the "Shave and a Haircut... Two Bits..." rhythm. He then directed Donald's eyes towards a sign that he obviously hadn't noticed, either just now, or from the last time he was here...

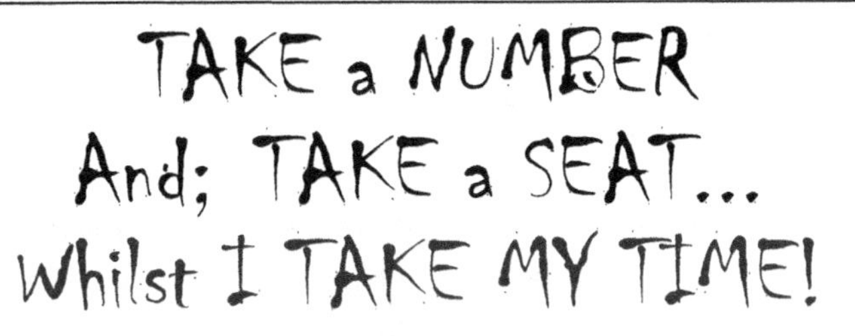

Donald apologised for the misunderstanding,[128] took a number and sat in the queue of one; all the time wondering how he failed to see such an obvious opportunity to explain about the multiple uses of "Take."

- Take a number - Physically remove a number from the dispenser;
- Take a seat   - Sit down and don't move; and
- Take my time   - An episode of lethargic movement.

While he was sitting, Donald did take the opportunity (conceptual chance) to read the back of the numbered cards Nurse Jack had improvised. The official numbering system was taking shape (conventional arrangement) but wasn't quite finalised yet.

Re: Name/Value Pairs p277

- Extract from The Donald Diaries.

Nurse Jack reluctantly opened the door again, but not until he estimated enough time had happened to teach Donald about the vast inappropriateness of cheesily knocking to the "Shave and a Haircut... Two Bits..." rhythm, while in an institution. If someone from any of the quartet of barber's unions heard about the programme of subsidised in-house shaving, there would be trouble:

- Lathers would be gotten up;
- Razor sharp blades would be drawn; and
- Much historical Bloodletting was very likely to be done...

---

[128] This was one of those non-apologies which apologised for the outcome of the situation, but not for causing the incident in the first place. They are trying to show care without admitting, or accepting, any responsibility...

- I am so sorry for your loss; instead of
- I am so sorry for decapitating your friend with a rusty chainsaw.

Unfortunately, as Donald didn't know what the *programme of subsidised in-house shaving* was, the lesson was completely lost on him. Seeing confusion in Donald's eyes, Nurse Jack beckoned him within without further education and directed him to sit in the plastic wrapped padded chair.

The calming chair was a new addition, along with the *Take* sign, and it held Donald's attention until its effect was shattered by Nurse Jack inquiring:

"So... How are you Donald?"

A single glance told the whole tale of Donald's dislike for this question. He let it slide this time, as he was fairly sure Nurse Jack was actually interested in the answer and not simply remote controlling.

"Everywhere I go there is a stench of despair...

- From the other patients;
- From most of the medical staff; and even
- From DD's pair of day-old socks, but I ain't telling her that."

"That is a nice piece of misdirection, Donald, but it doesn't actually answer my question, does it?[129]"

"No."

A single glance told the whole tale of Nurse Jack's dislike for this evasion. "All right then; an impolitely response less, slightly meaningless and hopefully mostly painless Blood extraction it is..."

It all sounded fantastic to Donald. Not that he showed a reaction of equal intensity. This is a common fault expressed by many people about Donald. He understood what he was hearing, he just didn't *understand*. What these many people didn't *understand* themselves, was that Donald did *understand*, he just didn't see the point of showing it. Even if Donald did try to express himself physically, it would have looked exactly like his look of confusion anyway.

The withdrawal process only took three minutes to complete, and Donald was cognisantly there for most of it. He could even remember a few of Nurse Jack's snippets of conversational distraction:

- "...There is no room for remorse for pirates of that sort..."
- "...What would you know about the migratory patterns..."
- "...Forgotten much more than they could hope to learn..."

---

[129] Donald wasn't often on this side of the fence, it is usually him who raises the pedantic requirement to actually answer the question asked. He knew the taste of evasion well and was surprised at the bitterness of his own.

Squish…

S u c k …
S l i d e …
S n a p …
S t i c k …
S c r i b e …

"There. We are all done for today. After you check these details, I suggest you go back to your room and relax until dinner time comes around…" glancing at his upside-down nurses pinned pocket watch, "…which will be in forty-one minutes."

When Nurse Jack looked up, Donald had disappeared.

He performed a shoulder to shoulder *What the When Where How* double look and finished the mandatory portion of the sequence with an unrivalled execution of the traditional *I Don't Know or Care* shrug.[130]

Without bothering to correct Nurse Jackal's spelling of *Donald Halfbrian*, Donald had legged it back to his room (#41 in the Kangaroo ward) to indulge in a nearly three quarters of an hour nap, but he missed out by a quarter and woke up nearly three hours later…

Resigning himself to a late TK Kitchen made snack, Donald went for a walk outside. He intended to clear his head of the many useless details learned in the past week, as well as evicting some of the blatant cynicisms learned in the past ever, to arrive at a point where a TK Kitchen made snack might become a palatable replacement for the missed dinner.

Instead of the calming atmosphere expected, where Donald could try and find himself, he found himself embroiled in a completely unexpected 3-way tête-à-tête, as a silent, unseen, clandestine partner. Some oblivion remained, but even Donald couldn't miss the physical connection between Owedebt and Nelo this time.[131]

It seemed this was going to be a full moon to remember.

---

[130] He scored a near perfect 41.9 for his radical interpretation of "Huh¿tm" Losing only point one of a point, as his tongue was slightly out of position.

[131] This is what it generally takes for Donald to find out about these things.

Chapter 5:
Dinner with a Vampire
(Eating Saffron Rice)

Donald returned to his misunderstanding of the situation, the one where he wasn't the third person participating in the party, when another hushed up episodic character appeared in this scene.

Donald had just become the fourth corner of a Bloodlust triangle.

To set this scene a little more clearly, so as to avoid any misunderstanding you might be harbouring yourself, I will elucidate in my customary three bullet pointed manner, thusly:

- We are watching one of the overconfident lead characters and one of the moderately minor supporting characters;
- They are parked on a park bench out the back of SaRS, engrossed in a gross amount of parking under the full moon; and
- It's a long way to sanity, we have much of the story still to read, half a wit of brains, it's dark and we're watching Nelo try to HIT THAT![132]

Is it not written that once you are dead, you are no longer alive?

Sven's appearance took the gathering way past the surreptitious meeting quorum number of two and started to encroach on the traditional maximum maxim of "Five by Five" that Skit had coincidently referenced earlier. It also had a disquieting effect on Donald.

---

[132] So, basically, Owedebt Dear is making out with Nelo (Vamp) Priors. This much was most probably painfully predictably obvious to you peoples.

"Sphincter Feng Shui![133]"

Sven's disappearance was nearly as bewildering as his fortune cookie, and Skit took advantage of the opportunity to introduce himself to Donald. "Chill out Mister Dude! I'm here to save the night. You gotta show a little bit of faith in Faith." Donald's disquiet retreated and hid under a rock somewhere.

Faith held a smoking joss stick in her hand, most probably stolen from the Pastoral Care Service Religious Not Religious building while Aaaron Aare was taking a spin-off class with Ma'am Cybill Flex.[134]

Donald was dividing his time between looking from Owedebt and Nelo to Faith, and then back again, repetitively. While O'n'N were technically breaking the unwritten[135] rules of SaRS, he didn't think it was serious enough to warrant an assassination, or his ensuing bad case of tennis neck...

~~Un~~Written ~~Guidelines~~Rules

1) What happens in SaRS, stays in SaRS, unless we can negotiate an "**Especially** good deal." (Set an appropriate bribery amount)

2) ~~There will be no reference to rule number two.~~ (No exceptions)

3) **Especially** unlike the ~~Rules~~Guidelines these are ~~Guidelines~~Rules.

4) There will be Zero toleration of canoodling . . . **Especially** if you know what canoodling means, as you are far too old to canoodle.

5) Vampires, Zombies, Vampire Zombies and Zombie Vampires are all forbidden. Under no circumstances are you to be lured onto the park bench out the back of SaRS. **Especially** at night-time.

SaRS Official 5 – SaRS Rules the not OK!

Donald started to feel things were getting **Especially** out of control... Way more than they normally do in unusual situations like these.

---

[133] Only one UPPERCASE function away from a level one SFS.

[134] Aaaron usually refers to Cybill as his "Soulful Exercising Angel."

[135] Would you believe...? Missed it by that much...!

"Now what d' you say my pretty little Donny Boy,[136] shall we go and kill us a bit of extra hot and spicy Pre-Deaded Vamp? C'mon, someone needs to step up and take on the evil villainous role…"

Donald thought about Faith's suggested action and didn't know if she was referring to herself as one who will *become* the evil villainous role (a villainess), or if she was going to *overcome* the evil villain, she believed Nelo to be. Either way, Donald didn't like where this was heading.

Without waiting for Donald to try and avoid the situation, Faith leapt[137] into action. Five monster jibes, four over-actings, three tuck and rolls, two hair flicks and just a single joss stick through the heart later, Nelo finally became the identifiable some-body he was always destined to be.

Owedebt had turned nearly as white as Nelo always looked. She wasn't in a state of shock, it would be much more accurately over described as an entire multiverse of astonishment, death and strange. "What did you dooooo?"

This was only the first rhetorical question to be asked here today.

Other favourites would be:

✖   Who in the Hell-mouth do you think you are?

✖   Where did you learn to handle a Spike like that?

✖   I take it that this isn't your First Evil slaying.

Lost in one particularly unpleasant reverie,[138] Donald had no other option except to resort to his favourite go-to avoidance mechanism. By writing about what he was seeing, he was able to successfully avoid much of the aftermath of Nelo's Faith un-Healing episode without having to think about it.

As has been revealed previously:

✖   Donald's thoughts would always come to him in threes;

✖   He was also prone to exaggerated black and white thinking; and

✖   When he couldn't think of a third option, he just made one up.

While he was thinking about what to write, Donald found himself walking aimlessly back into the hospital, and even though he could hear a commotion in progress behind him, he resisted the powerful urge to run aimlessly. History might not view this action in a favourable light, but Donald's memory certainly preferred a green-lit escape to a full-moon-lit murder scene.

---

[136] Yeah, no. Donald won't be correcting her, no matter how nice she smells.

[137] I can't wait until the EASL (English is a stupid language) chapter… Leap is to Leaped, as Sleep is to Slept. There are so many pronunciation and spelling issues here… It is so far from funny, it's just not funny.

[138] It was still infinitely more pleasant than the current situation.

Donald arrived at his bedroom sanctuary just in time to witness a group of uniformed extras escorting Faith, who was unconscious looking and strapped to a wheelchair, to the general direction of the SaRS administration area. *Now Donald experienced some emotion protection confliction... Should he divert from the safe course of action and choose to follow the wheelchair wielding company, or should he eschew their company and follow his instinct instead?*

He chose to follow wheelchair.[139]

Nobody was paying any attention to Donald, not even when his stomach roared out in frustration as they passed the TK kitchen, and when he realised this, he celebrated his innocuousness with a tiny nearly-happy dance. A second realisation later; someone in the troupe had pressed the elevator call button and they were waiting for the elevator to ding and open its doors.

Recalling three of the rumours that pervasively hung around his curiosity, the ones regarding the mysterious elevator destinations:

- Padded Room;
- Dungeon Cell; and the
- Medieval Torture-Chamber.

Donald was unsure if these options were distinct destinations, or if they were just different impressions of the same place. Whichever was the answer, it didn't bode well for Faith, who had murdered the most minor character. The situation didn't bode well for Nelo either...

Barely noticing the elevator doors closing, with the troupe inside, Donald vetoed his flight response and lunged towards elevator inclusion. He quickly rationalised, while he could quite effortlessly remorselessly shrug off potential incident exclusions involving himself, he could not do the same for any others without blinking. It was in his nature to ignore potential dangers, which only may include him, when they weren't directed specifically at him.[140]

Once he was inside the elevator Donald was relieved to go unnoticed for a change; because the elevator had two sets of doors and everyone was facing towards the back door exit. His relief soon faded, however, as this also meant he wasn't able to see which button was pressed for their destination, or which floor they had just left from.

---

[139] No surprises there right? If you are going to introduce the situation, you may as well follow it through to completion. That's one speculation anyway.

[140] This is a dangerous, and well-known, trap throughout the psychological circuit which many patients fall into: "Delusions Of People Enabling You."

After the troupe's arrival and departure transpired, Donald made his own way out of the elevator. What he saw in the dimness[141] was truly approaching astonishing, after bypassing astounding. The underground networks under:

- The SaRS **H**ospital;
- The SaRS **M**ansion; and
- The SaRS **O**rnate Pavilion...

Were almost identical, with one exception... The SaRS HMO order was also the order applied to the age of their underground network.

The Ornate Pavilion's tunnels were the oldest of the three subdivisions, and as they predated every other structure found inside SaRS boundaries, they were usually considered to be the germane reason why the SaRS buildings are located where they are. Their age has been determined to be approximately 500 years old.[142]

The tunnels underneath the Mansion have been estimated to be between 75 years and 125 years old. This isn't earth shattering news, even though the tunnels themselves could be considered to be such. The building of the tunnels under The Kingswood's House, through the basement and hidden secret door, commenced at the same time as the main building, eventually joining up with those under the pavilion.

The newest tunnels are those under the Hospital section of SaRS, and are understood to be between zero and 75 years old... Again, not particularly earth shattering and could probably be narrowed if anyone ever had the inclination to do so. When you consider the existence of an electrical network which isn't of the had-to-add-it-on-later style, the inbuilt non-gravitational only plumbing and the sign displaying the construction dates, you could estimate the dates quite accurately...

PSH... SaRS HMO

Underground Tunnels

Construction: Started 1999 – Completed 2001

---

[141] The lighting underneath the hospital is rudimentary at best.

[142] This was done by examining the layers of gravitational plumbing on the floor of the tunnels and comparing these results to information about known environmental activities in the area.

Donald wandered around the underground area, his presence completely undetected, unobserved and unrecorded for quite a while.[143] This situation is unconventionally known as a **D**efence **A**gainst **R**esidents' **E**vil...

- ✖ If there is no way to **S**ee what is happening; and
- ✖ If there is no way to **H**ear what is happening; then
- ✖ There is no proof to **S**peak of no matter what is happening...

Eventually, Donald will document something resembling this first-person account of his present predicament, when gets to writing his yet to be claimed acclaimed memoirs...

"The SaRS Hospital's underground network is a seething mass of corridors and rooms, filled with either broken, borrowed, or blueish medical equipment. Sometimes it is all three. And to many of the unfortunate observers,[144] most of the equipment would look right at home in someone's imaginary torture chamber. I can also reassure you that it looks extremely capable of making just about anyone in the vicinity unjustly talk the talk.

If you walk the walk through the entire network, you will pass from a fairly sophisticated unnatural area recently developed underneath the Hospital, to an extreme archaic setting sitting underneath the pavilion. This building, apart from being the picturesque centrepiece of the hedge maze, has subsequently become an important literal landmark. The tunnels, upon which the pavilion was built, have been left in a mostly unchanged original natural condition.

The ownership of these tunnels has been wilfully contested several times throughout the decades. It remains an ongoing proverbial thorn in the side of the authorities that there hasn't been an acceptable resolution to the issues. Not to mention their lack of ability to collect any form of taxation. An absence of official ownership documentation means they cannot collect the associated fees, duties and charges generally levied on such property.

When you think about it, it is an ingenious, however ingenuous, use of the space. If there is no tax payable, there can been no crimes committed.

This is Donald Halfbrain, signing off on the dotted line for my own sanity."

- ✖ Extract from The Donald Diaries.

---

[143] This is another entry for my list of "Sayings with confusing and/or incorrect meanings which shouldn't be acceptable in a polite conversation..."

Why does *quite a while* mean *a large amount of time* but not quite *a long time*, when *quite all right* means *completely all right*? Quite is ordinarily treated as a Boolean operator, and *completely a while* makes quite no sense.

[144] i.e. The inmates/patients. (This is a personal distinction/choice.)

But, for the sake of current expediency, he will make do with creating this absent-minded third-person present tense narrative, detailing everything he is observing now...

Donald didn't know what a *gog* was; but clearly his jaw muscles did, when they dropped themselves a little slack three moments after his eyes widened at what he could see once the gradually retreating troupe disappeared out of his sight. He counted at least three rooms with doors,[145] three cells with bars and three rectangularprismicles with no discernible means of egress.

How Donald knew there were areas lurking behind the doors that weren't simply cleansingor's closets, or behind the no discernible at all, is not going to be explained. However, what he found out, is:

***Padded Rooms* (PR) 1-3** - Behind the doors: Stepping up to door number one, Donald prepared himself by preparing to see something that you couldn't normally prepare yourself for. Donald, being Donald, was unusually used to confronting the unusual. He looked through the peeping tom portal and then decided he had had enough for today.

Donald's **O**ver-the-top **C**ontrolling **D**emons rescinded his decision almost immediately. He knew there were doors to look behind, and although he also knew he would most probably find the exact same scene behind the doors, he still had to look just in case they used a different medium to cover the walls.

Describing the walls of the padded rooms as a canvas for the plethora of crazy crayon calligraphy, and the floor as an ageing artiste's drop sheet, might enable you to envisage the vision Donald was now faced with, at the safe(ish) low level of three DOGoNs.

If you imagine a similar image up to an unsafe(ish) middling seven, you will be getting very close to Donald's actual perception. But... If you erroneously reach thirteen, you need to quickly dial your reaction back down, as you have entirely blown things way out of proportion. To reach the end point level of thirteen DOGoNs, the crayon would need to be replaced by Blood and the drop sheet by an open, currently-in-use, double stuffed body bag.

Donald thought these padded rooms looked more like padded cells which had been constructed out of padded cages which were often used for keeping self-destructive wild animals safe. Donald hated to admit it, but this did make a small amount of sense.

---

[145] **No.** *sigh* Maybe I haven't made myself crystal clear... If it was at *least*, there would be *zero* rooms with doors, making this a simple corridor... Or, if you were implying that Donald could potentially *see more than three* rooms with doors, why not just say so, or even say the exact number? Unless you are implying that Donald can't count to more than three, then, fair enough.

Dungeon Cells **(DC) 1-3** - Behind the bars: Recoiling from the PR nightmare that would ensue if anyone was to read his previous admission, Donald put it safely behind himself and stumbled on to the next law suit he was going to be sized up wear, the DC cells.[146]

His initial thought was, "I do like my bathrooms to come without mirrors," however, that thought was extended with a bit of, "but the presence of a toilet does not a bathroom make," and then he unreservedly finalised it with some never to be thought ever again, "and the lack of a door you can't see through, no matter how much ventilation it provides, is a deal breaker."

Like the Padded Rooms, the Dungeon Cells were utterly devoid of life.

"Ahhhhh, very nishe, yesh very nishe indeed... I shee they have provided you with a shtandard #2 **P**iapoothaushen **O**nyxsh **O**val resheptacle." Pledge, Jimmy Pledge, had missed being *very convenient* by hugely much. "I remember being shupplied with a modified one in *PyriteFinger*. I wash able to dishpatch BigJob with an eashy motion dropping movement, ushing the top sheat ash an over-shized oval throwing shtar.[147]"

Donald had doubts he would ever become comfortable with the vast array of bizarre cameo appearances,[148] or how unconventionally moist they seemed to be. When the confident man in the tartan suit left as uniquely as he arrived, he also left behind a bewildered Donald, who marvelled at the acceptance of a speech impediment in a leading actor.

Medieval Torture-Chambers **(MT) 1-3** - Behind the no discernibles: Here be the three MT Chambers, sort of nearly mostly, because the second of these three MTs wasn't actually empty. Donald deferred telling you his description and definition of the discernibles, and also what he found behind them, both physically and philosophically, to put your concerned mind at ease.

He knew that any delay in your understanding will most probably increase your level of concern for who, or what, is behind the second discernible inside the second MT. Simply naming them as Medieval Torture Chambers was sure to create a sense of dread, and Donald didn't want to have anything to do with creating a false sense of fear.

---

[146] The universal way of referring to something should be to *not* repeat the words represented by the letters in the acronym. This is especially true for people within, and products from out of, the acronym itself.

[147] It is a good thing that Pledge, Jimmy Pledge, doesn't need to *sit* down.

[148] I am thinking of adding a character named Stanley. What do you think?

Donald was well aware the first mention of the possibility of encountering a Medieval Torture Chamber was at most five pages ago (inclusive),[149] and that his postponement of the description, however lame, was still not funny. Then, overcome with an uninspiring inspiration, he wondered what it would be like to suppress the definition indefinitely.

Remembering why he was there, and resisting the urge to be prematurely disappointed, Donald instinctively checked inside his pockets for a phone. Not finding one, he also checked for a carrier pigeon, while he was hoping to find, literally, any other means of contacting the overground world. All he found in his pockets was a small amount of dark blue lint, harking back to his pre-hernia operation days when he was always able to put his finger on a bellybutton full of perennial blue lint if required.

Retracing his steps back to the elevator, Donald was surprised to find it:

- ¤ Unguarded;
- ¤ Unlocked; and so
- ¤ Unimaginably obvious.

His previous concern about his unintended return destination desperation was brought to a perfect frothy lager head when he pressed the elevator's call (come hither) button...

Which was almost immediately replaced by relieved when he found there was only one button on the inside of the elevator to press.[150] Donald was also intrigued that the destination was "There," and that that destination:

- ¤ Depended directly on your current location;
- ¤ Was located directly on his current location; and
- ¤ Would deliver him directly from his current situation.

---

[149] Not to correct Donald again, but *an evil medieval torture-chamber* was first mentioned in the previous book. Ok, I might be correcting him again.

[150] There were actually two buttons, one at either end of the elevator car. But as they were visually and functionally identical, they were also the same button. So, I guess technically they could be referred to as one button.

Successfully negotiating up to There, in the probably strangest elevator[151] he has interacted with while at SaRS so far, Donald returned to the TK kitchen to grab himself a midnight-snack of whatever was un-labelled. Finding a fairly presentable half-eaten sandwich Donald returned to his room, to contemplate the strangeness of everything and wait until midnight to eat it.

At the start of their optional formal morning self-introductory roll call the next morning Nurse Jack was not looking as chipper today as he did yesterday. In fact, he seemed so far away that the overhanging shadows looked as though they were here to stay, "G⊛⊛d m⊗rning every⊗ne. I'm afraid we have some very bad news. Last night, tragically, Nelo was taken from us. We all have a lot to process, and DD is here to explain what exactly is going to happen today."
"Thank you, Nurse Jack."
Donald was impressed by the respectful acknowledgement of *Nurse* Jack, correctly guessing this was DD's way of showing the solemnity of the news.
Waiting for all the questioning looks to be directed at her, DD stood silent with her hands clasped firmly in front of her, in an extremely non-threatening manner, in an unusual show of solidarity. "I have called all of the SaRS senior staff and have asked them to come in today to assist anyone who feels they need more help than they can usually get. If anyone wants to talk about Nelo, and not have it classified as gossip, please reach out to someone.
"Today's normal schedule will not be adhered to, instead we will be having a memorial service for Nelo, to be held in the inside/outside SaRS courtyard, followed by a BBQ wake in The Flame crematorium's private rooms. Directions to The Flame will be made available to anyone who wishes to attend. Please see Nurse Jack after the memorial service.

The Flame – Crematorium
Give your loved ones a flaming good send off.
We don't let anyone's spark flicker out.
Remember them with a warm glow.
Phone: 1800-4A-ZIP-0

"Donald, would you come with me please."

---

[151] Donald didn't like calling these vertical movement facilitators elevators or lifts, as both of those words ~~imply~~ mean *up*.
- ⌧   You don't lift something down, without first lifting it up.
- ⌧   You don't elevate a person's ego with a dressing down.
- ⌧   **E**levate: Raise or **L**ift (something) to a **higher** position. Schooled!

DD led Donald back to her office, all the while exuding her strait-laced no-nonsense demeanour, where he was surprised to see Detective and Owedebt seated, obviously waiting for something.

"Donald, I am sure you know why we are here."

Running through the events in his mind:

- ✗ Possibility One: I was there watching when Faith stabbed a joss stick through Nelo's heart. Owedebt was there and saw me see Faith. She must have reported this to DD. ☑ *probably why we are here…*
- ✗ Possibility Two: I witnessed Faith being escorted by uniformed extras, while she was unconscious and strapped to a wheelchair, to the SaRS underground network. One of the extras may have seen me. They also may have reported this to DD. ☐ *probably why we are here…*
- ✗ Possibility Three: I conducted an unauthorised information gathering session targeting the SaRS Hospital's underground network of tunnels, rooms, cells and chambers, when Pledge, Jimmy Pledge had a cameo appearance, but only in an unofficial capacity. It is reasonably unlikely anyone reported this to DD. ☐ *probably why we are here…*

Donald digested all of this information and emerged from his discerning stupor thinking, "We are most probably here because last night, Skit Zoland, who was identifying as Faith at the time, stabbed and killed Nelo (Vamp) Priors with a lit Joss stick, thereby saving the damsel in distress, Owedebt Dear, from the incorrectly perceived vampire threat." And responded, "Yes.[152]"

Detective then redundantly explained to Donald exactly why they were all there. "Donald,

- ✗ I am here to ensure your knowledge of the situation is **C**omplete;
- ✗ Owedebt is here to ensure the knowledge is **R**ighteous;
- ✗ You are here to ensure the knowledge is **A**cknowledged; and
- ✗ DD is here to ensure the knowledge stays **P**rivate."

And then Donald knew the situation was totally as described.

"I want you to understand we always take these situations very seriously. The accidental killing of a patient reflects very poorly in our statistics, and on our financial statements. We here at SaRS aim to present a safe environment for all of our prospective patients, no matter what the cost to all concerned…"

---

[152] **Note:** This isn't an acceptance of the premise that Donald knows why they are there. It is simply acknowledging DD thinking that she was sure he knew why they were there. He hadn't even gone so far as to think about what her definitions of we, and/or here, were.

Donald was indeed concerned by the last understanding.

"We don't want to get into any discussions about who allegedly broke the 4) unwritten rule about canoodling, who thought they were enforcing the 6) unwritten rules about no vampires, or who killed who... All we want is to come to an agreement on 1) to ensure what happens in SaRS, stays in SaRS."

As Donald had no proof of anything nefarious happening, and a history of people not wanting to believe him even when he did,[153] he was inclined to just concede what he viewed as defeat. But, if Donald is anything (and there have been many debates about this topic, some of which have gone on for several weeks) he is a stickler for the rules, however unwritten, so he forced himself to don his own devil's advocate legal wig and concede it as a win instead.[154]

The words were taken right out of Donald's mouth, after the bone chilling morning news, but before he could think about any Hellish repercussions, "All right, I concede. You might have bested the worst in me this time around. But, like a powerful actor once said, I'll be baaaaack.[155]"

"Now that we have explicated all you need to know, is there anything else you think you might like to be allowed to know?" DD should really have known to not offer Donald a gaping chasm of unknown opportunity, no matter how convoluted it was.

Unable to keep his thoughts safely to himself, "I would like to know:
- What it is that you are so sure I know?
- How you know I was there to know what I so surely know? and
- Why is Owedebt confirming that it is indeed assuredly righteous?
I think, anyway."

"To be honest, some of that information is classified.[156] But, what we can tell you, I will let Detective tell you, as the partially impartial investigator."

---

[153] Due to his ability to see through all the crap and always tell the truth.

[154] Keeping his Devil's Advocate track record at a 106.66% success rate.

[155] Donald was mindful enough to keep the thought "powerfully bad" out of his public thoughts and was content to let you make your own connections. He was also content to emulate the original by having it appear in every book so far. How many of you heard this in its original Austrian accent?

[156] Donald was used to Owedebt referencing honesty as a gap filler, but from DD, he felt that she meant it. Not only that, she was telling the truth, even though it was only the literal truth. *Some of the information* is indeed classified, but it doesn't mean the information is classified as *Secret...*

"To repeat Nurse Jack, 'last night, tragically, Nelo was taken from us.' This is the concise answer to your first would like. To address your second and third would like, I need to fill in the gaps for you…

"Chunky Poopy was by Qwedebt's side last night, as he often is, when the aforementioned tragedy occurred. He came over all Skippy at the sight of the disturbance within the apparently strictly enforced unwritten rules and went out searching for some help. The help he found came in the form of a group of uniformed extras, who were able to understand his 'follow my lead' actual and conceptual instruction.

"The lead extra started to follow Chunky's lead, and after he got his lead out, was eventually led to the appallingly tragic scene. This in turn led directly to us knowing that you were a witness, after Owedebt answered the 'And who else knows about this?' ~~cover-up inducing~~ question."

DD redacted Detective's recount before Donald counted to three answers, and before his wondering about the connection between likes two and three lead to a conspiracy theory. The last visual clue Donald can recall noticing was the visceral combination hateful-distressed look on Owedebt's face at every mention of Chunky. It was at this point he was ushered out the door.

Donald had seen enough kidnapping episodes, of various TV police shows, to know exactly what was transpiring and how useful any vocal opposition of the action to DD would be. Protesting in abstract silence was to be his weapon of choice this time.

If you want "to be loved," **love**.
If you want "to be reviled," **revile**.
If you want "to be silenced," **silence**.
If you want "to be continued," **continue**.

Donald was becoming convinced that Sven was actually far more mindfully present than the many times when he was simply just conveniently there. He had nailed this particularly screwed up situation on the head.

All of Donald's sympathetic compassion ached to reach out and comfort Owedebt. He didn't know if his concern was brought about by her strength, or by her lack of strength. And even though it felt incongruous to be on both sides of this see-saw situation, it was redundantly what it was.

And *that* is precisely what Donald vowed to find out…
What the ever elusive *it*, that a lot of things were, was.[157]

---

[157] Unlike the previous **zero** conundrum, "it is a nothing that is a something," the ever elusive **it** conundrum is generally, "it is a something that is a nothing."

Donald found that his commonly unwritten caveat of *eventually* served its purpose once again. Such that, when he followed Sven's sage advice, because he didn't want to be silenced on this matter, he chose…

"'To be continued,'.[158]"

---

[158] I think I think this is the correct punctuation.

Chapter 6:
A Beautiful Service
(Nelo's Final Serve)

Resulting in his attendance of Nelo's memorial service, located in the SaRS inside/outside courtyard. He hasn't decided yet if he is going to attend the wake afterwards, at The Flame, but he probably will, as he likes the sound of a good BBQ.[159] He also supposed that asking for the directions from Nurse Jack would be an appropriate time to correct his spelling mistake of *Donald Halfbrian*.

The first concerning sight Donald saw when he arrived for the service was the coffin. It was concerning that someone had already obtained one for Nelo, even though it was an appropriate dark ebony walnut colour, which offset the ivory glow from Nelo's skin perfectly. The added irony which the nutty colour imbued was a bonus.

The second concerning sight, which was easily the most disturbing sight, was BLT being expelled from the matching should-have-been-empty ash urn. His cries, that he was just warming it up for Nelo, were not taken in the helpful manner they were intended. DD directed BLT to go back down to his own final resting place for the remainder of the service.

On his way to his corner grave BLT misquoted, "Man, Rupert (Giles) had it right... 'Becoming dead is no way to make peace with life. It all becomes more confusing, and then you end up being more angry, so you lash out at anything you can. More or less.'" just loud enough for DD to hear.

"That episode is well over 20 years old... How old do you think I am?[160]"

---

[159] Not the *thought* of a BBQ, the literal *sound* of the sizzling meat.

[160] Assuming DD was a teenage girl when she was watching this episode of Buffy... It would make her a not unrealistic ~~forty~~ thirty something.

The third concerning sight, which quickly became the new most disturbing sight, occurred when Skit appeared voluntarily, and unrestrained, at the head of the coffin. He was dressed as a person of faith, which was just a punishing coincidence, and certainly wasn't irony.[161]

DD sidled over to Donald's side and had a private conversation to him.

It is through the magic of words that I can show you exactly what DD said:

"We have performed a thorough *interprebriefing*-extraction on Skit, and have determined that his current personality, Shepherd Book from *Firefly* and *Serenity*, does not pose a threat to anyone. That Skit has had two Joss Whedon incarnations in a row is not a significant problem, as far as we can tell. In any case, Shepherd only has a minor role in what is coming, and we have situated Aaaron Aare in a position to deal with any developments out of character."

Donald had a surge of scepticism about everything DD just conversated to him. Realising he was completely powerless to care, he didn't... And the show got on marvellously with itself.

Aaaron stepped up to the focal point that most eyes had, "It's been a while since we have had a death-memorial service-BBQ wake combination," rubbing his hands vigorously, in the most inappropriate fashion possible, matching his not quite sinful words, "I think we are all going to have a lot of fun. Everyone, who wants one, will have a turn to step forward and say a little something of what they really thought about Nelo... And hey, let's try to keep it upbeat out there... But first things first, a word from our Funeral Facilitator..."

---

[161] The need for me to explain irony is also not ironic.

1. The expression of one's meaning by using language which normally signifies the opposite, typically for humorous or emphatic effect.

   A person of faith is not the opposite of a person named Faith.

2. A state of affairs or an event which seems deliberately contrary to what one expects and is often wryly amusing as a result.

   I doubt this was contrary to what you expected I might write.

3. A literary technique, originally used in Greek tragedy, by which the full significance of the character's words or actions is obvious to the audience or reader although unknown to the character.

   OK. That last definition sounds like this situation exactly.

— THAT is irony of the first and second orders.

"Guzunder.[162]"

Not quite the word that Donald was expecting. He wasn't even sure it was a word, let alone *a* word, thinking "Shouldn't it at least have a hyphen?"

"Let me explain. We are here to help you go through the many processes of this unfortunate development. One of which is saying farewell to Mr Nelo (Vamp) Priors before his non-mathematical remainder *goes under* the ground. Hi… I am an interpretive internment professional, Louis Deep, but you can call me Lou, whether you like it or not."

> *Interpretive Internment Professionals*
> Practicing what I preach is very hard for me, so
> I prefer you do what I say, and not what I do.
> Louis Deep – Funeral Facilitator
> Phone: 1800 321RIP

Donald was about to call the surreal police:
- He was looking at three vastly different people;
- Each performing part of one extremely difficult task; and
- Was trying to determine if these two elements were two too many.

Louis (Lou) Deep	- Rodeo Ringleader.
Skit (Shepherd Book) Zoland	- Cowboy.
Aaaron Aare	- Diversionary Clown.

He was well versed with SaRS disseminating a different variety of Bull, but if the shoe fits… It seemed that DD was correct when she indicated Shepherd would only have a minor role, after all, the Cowboy is just a tool of the Rodeo Ringleader. They don't have a lot of say about the content of the information presented and only a small amount of control over the direction it takes.

Similarly, the Diversionary Clown title was exceptionally appropriate.[163]

Lou continued with the ceremony… "As this memorial service is a private and unsanctioned farewell, there are no official requirements to be adhered to. Therefore, I can make it all up as I go and Nelo won't know the difference. <pause for smirk> Do we have an innocent volunteer to get the stone rolling?"

---

[162] A chamber pot that "goes under" your bed. It is for when you need to pee at night and don't have convenient access to a bathroom.

[163] This analogy makes Donald one of the spectators who has come to see the cowboy receive not only their just desserts, but their unjust ones as well. It seems to have captured the actual scenario rather aptly, don't you think?

"Ooh - Ooh - Ooh... Pick me - Pick me - Pick me!" Istha was jumping around like someone who ~~wanted~~ needed to be the first person, straw or no straw, to drink out of the shared bottle, avoiding the possibility of icky backwash.

"All right, miss...?"

"Istha T. You." Lou set her up and Aaaron knocked her down...[164]

"Istha, what would you like to say about Nelo?"

"Nelo... Who? No. No... No, I would like to say good-bye to the little friend I have had living in my head for just over a week. I call him Donald."

"Buuuuut... This is a farewell for Ne..."

"I first encountered Donald last week when I was trying to distract myself by jigsawing a puzzle of jigsaw puzzle pieces. Oh, there were people who tried to convince me that he was really there, and they could hear him as well, but I couldn't believe them. How did I know they were really there themselves? At one stage these same people were calling him the l word, and I already have enough of those all by myself, I didn't need another l in my head..."

This monologue went on for some time. Istha's *normal* situation involved her talking to the voices inside her head. The ones other people couldn't hear. She was completely at ease with her ability to filter out the rest of the world's noise and was content to let herself run screaming into a riot of one.

Lou was listening to the voices in his head, who were telling him to let the situation play itself out. And he wasn't the only one hearing those instructions, although Aaaron's voices were relaying a more relaxed "chill dude" version of the same message.

"...so, goodbye Donald. I hope you are at piece.[165]"

Looking up after a brief moment of silence, Lou was frighteningly quick to claim the opportunity to ask for the next volunteer.

A typical burial is not a grave situation.
Atypical burial is not situating a grave.

Complete Silence.

Donald had ample quiet time to run through these not quite synonymous statements several times, and more-or-less agree with them both, before Lou gave up on understanding either of them, and called for another speaker.

---

[164] Not literally of course, although I'm sure it could be arranged.

[165] This word would have made a lot more sense if only you hadn't become distracted by me, the Diversionary Clown and his Rodeo Ringleader.

Owedebt said her short, succinct, pithy, meaninglessness, "I'll let you go." comment before she placed three pre-sidewaysed roses on top of the casket as a thorny farewell to their past, present and future together.

Donald thought Owedebt's brief send-off was a little understated,[166] given her role in the prior proceedings, but the roses were a nice touch as long as you don't touch any of the thorns.

The diminishing possibilities were stepping up to make their final farewells without the need of Lou prompting them first. Lou was feeling grateful[167] that it only took them three speeches to figure things out.

Seth limped up to the centre of attention, cleared his throat and issued a sincere welcome home message, "Welcome, Nelo (Vamp) Priors, to what may be the last place you will or have ever called home, or at least home adjacent… And know this, should you choose to accept our offer of permanent welcome:

- We will provide you permission to enter, and reside within, our fright, as well as guaranteeing you safe passage on your spiritual journey;
- There will be a place approved and prepared, where you can lay your headstone and call home; and
- You will have the responsibility bestowed upon you, of welcoming the next recently deceased person into our fright.

If this proposal is acceptable, and you are also agreeable to respecting our haunting protocols, arrangements can be made to have your ashes returned to SaRS for safe keeping until we have your appropriate apparition appellation for the siGns On Demand! – Sin Righters (stonemason division)."

Seth had extended the welcome to Nelo, as the most recently late addition to the ghostly contingent, admirably. This activity satisfied the third clause in his own welcome. He then took the removal of this responsibility and vanished like there was no tomorrow.

Karl was there, as it was where he was supposed to be. He just didn't know what to do while he was there. He thought it was unfair that Nelo had found a way out and didn't share and offered a simple "Bye."

---

[166] This thought of Donald's was similarly a little understated. What he was meaning to think was, "a gargantuan monster sized oil tanker full to the brim of dark black understated complicated un-emancipated liquid emotion."

[167] I have always thought grateful should be spelled greatful. And then, in lieu of any logical rationale, my next question is usually along the antonym definition line, "Is *grateless* an uncovered hole in the ground?"

The next to offer her thoughts on Nelo was Mindy. "I don't like to get too close when I see dead people just in case some of their permanency rubs off. Back in my day we didn't have all of these flashy shenanigans... There were no speeches, unless the person was royalty and even then, it was limited to, "The Royal is dead, long live the Royal!" chanting from the gathered mob of militant pro commonwealth activists." Mindy appeared to lose her train of thought as a singly bewildered mask took up residence covering her face.

While Nurse Jack was assisting Mindy back to obscurity, Got rose to offer her condolences with a traditional Russian farewell dirge...[168]

If someone you knew died...
You dug their hole right out
You put their whole body in
And you filled it up with dirt
The body sized leftover dirt
You sent to the local nursery
Then you got on with your day

"And eef you werrrrre luckee, tkhkhkhkhkherrrrre was ze leettle added dumpleeng weeth yourrrrr dailee khkhkhkhkhelpeeng of Borscht."

The venom in this statement wasn't lost on Donald, who also couldn't help noticing Got had lost her accent completely while she was singing.[169]

Near Complete Silence.

Lou stepped up to the plate again and asked if there was anyone else who would like to say something. He waited for approximately thirteen seconds for a positive response before he spoke his finalising advertising monolog...

"While death is always hard, it doesn't have to be so brutal. Believe me, I know. I have facilitated more *memorial services*[170] than I have been paid to. At every one of those Pro-Bono services, you too would have seen the benefit of having a professional take the edge off the sad proceedings. Bye... I have been your interpretive internment professional, Louis Deep, but you can call me Lou, whether you like it or not."

---

[168] It loses a bit in the translation... In fact, it gets shaken all about...

[169] This was just another reason for Donald to try and keep his distance from Got specifically, and from people he didn't understand in general.

[170] Lou air quoted this emphasis, and Donald thought it lacked sincerity. Which it did. Even he knew enough to not make jokes at a *memorial service*.

Lou gave the nod to his unmentioned assistant to play the exit music.

The SaRS funeral dirge "Casket to Ride" played while the Nelo's was being manoeuvred into the hearse.

Casket to Ride[171]

I think it's gonna be worse	than going insane,	cos
He is leaving in a hearse...	Going to *The Flame*	yeah
He's got a casket to ride;	He's got a casket to ride	
He's got a casket to ride...	Three time's a charm	

Just a minor character,	he played his role well,	and
Interning him asunder...	Hopefully, from *Hell*	no
He's got a casket to ride;	He's got a casket to ride	
He's got a casket to ride...	Three time's a charm	

Now he's going to his final lie
It was very nice, a moving service, for sure
Everyone has recited goodbye
It was very nice, a moving service, for sure

I think it's gonna be worse	than going insane,	cos
He is leaving in a hearse...	Going to *The Flame*	yeah
He's got a casket to ride;	He's got a casket to ride	
He's got a casket to ride...	Three time's a charm	

Now he's going to his final lie
It was very nice, a moving service, for sure
Everyone has recited goodbye
It was very nice, a moving service, for sure

Just a minor character,	he played his role well,	and
Interning him asunder...	Hopefully, from *Hell*	no
He's got a casket to ride;	He's got a casket to ride	
He's got a casket to ride...	Three time's a charm	

SaRS funeral dirge,	SaRS funeral dirge,	SaRS funeral dirge
SaRS funeral dirge,	SaRS funeral dirge,	SaRS funeral dirge
SaRS funeral dirge,	SaRS funeral dirge,	SaRS funeral dirge
SaRS funeral dirge,	SaRS funeral dirge,	SaRS funeral dirge

(Fade out, much like the smoke will eventually.)

---

[171] Inspired by *Ticket to Ride* - The Beatles.

The casket's trip only took until the second "going to The Flame" to get to the hearse,[172] but the music continued right through to the end to cover any possible unfortunate noises from out, or in, side the casket.[173]

Nota could be heard talking to Owedebt in the background, "Oh, I like this band. They have some great covers and remakes, but I still prefer the originals, for some reason."

"Aaaaah!" Owedebt was rapidly approaching the end of many best-before dates of her explanations. She has tried to explain the theory of many things to Nota but lacks the required patience to follow any of them through with a practical demonstration.

"I can't explain it properly, but as well as that, I, personally, think that it is all good." Making sure to get the inflection on every last word in all sentences just right, even though it wasn't a question. "You know? I mean, I didn't really change anything, I just changed my mind. So, to speak."

"Nota, you just spent a whole minute saying nothing."

"I'm not like that. How I'm like that is..."

"Aaaaaaaaaaaaaaaaaaaaaaaaaaaaaaaaaaaaaaaaaaaaaaaaaaaaaaaaaaaah!"

Owedebt went screaming away, to stop herself from kicking away at Nota.

Donald mused that there was a rift in their pair of dice, and it didn't add up to seven. Then before his retreat, Nota came over to talk to Donald.[174]

"What do you think her problem is?" Without waiting for the answer, she wouldn't listen to anyway, "She needs to plug her attitude out and go and play with some of her Bunnyyips."

Not wanting to forget this marvellously unique way of speaking mixed up, or possibly new, words about her disparate thoughts in an incoherent manner, Donald jotted a few notes in his ever-present best friend.

And then he was confronted by a small issue...

"Don't write that!"

"Why not?"

"Because I said so..."

---

[172] Lou informed Donald they preferred "Final Transportation Vehicle."

[173] Donald used this time to ponder three Donaldisms...

1. What is the difference between a casket and a coffin?
2. What is the significance of the hearse's numberplate – RIP 666? and
3. Why haven't we metricated "6 Feet" to "1.8288 Metres" under?

[174] Who had unfortunately stayed rooted to the spot watching the verbal stoush between the two giants of misunderstanding and didn't have enough of his own self-preservation skills to decide to understand the warnings.

Once Donald had turned the page, and was by himself commenting on the world at large, he thought that the un-ménage-à-trio was in trouble. He could see the writing on the page, even if they couldn't. He also heard himself say "Oops. Sorry. No takebacks once they have been said." even if they didn't.

The loaded hearse set off for The Flame, thereby vacating the ambulance bay so the patient transport bus, Bertie, could be similarly loaded and set off. Donald had another random thought flicker through his conscious… "I bet the driver thought the old school 1960's Cadillac Hearses, which in the day were doubled as small-town ambulances, would be seriously convenient."

Everyone who was anyone[175] boarded Bertie and did as the sign said…

It only took them two minutes to catch up with the Final Transportation Vehicle due to their relative velocities.[176] It was then that Nurse Jack, who had drawn the short straw amongst the employees and was punished by having to accompany the bus load of itinerant patients, informed them there was about thirteen minutes until they arrived at The Flame. After the multitude of groans had subsided to a dull roar, he suggested they indulge themselves and play a non-competitive Party Bus Game.

The concept both intrigued and terrified Donald:

- He was being asked to play an unfamiliar game, which had no tangible reward, with no discernible goal… (Except to simply finish);
- While confined in a restricted mobile space, which could do with some ventilation, with people he didn't really know… (Or understand);
- On the way to a crematorium called The Flame, where there was going to be a BBQ wake in a private room, for an ex-co-inmate…

What on Earth could possibly go wrong? Not being a fortune teller, Donald tightened his seatbelt and started hanging on with a newly found purpose.

---

[175] Conveniently, they were also the main characters in this book. It is an amazing coincidence that these situations keep happening to our Donald. You might even start to think he had some control over the author's words.

[176] Not only was their relative speed a factor, but the unknown bus driver knew a shortcut, completing the Direction plus Speed = Velocity equation.

The game Nurse Jack was suggesting they play is a simple combination of three traditional games:

- Spotto;
- Eye Spy (with my little eye something beginning with…); and a
- Scavenger Hunt.

There were only three basic rules, with one drawn from each game:
(In reverse order)

- The list of scavenger hunt items are random things that start with each letter of the English alphabet;[177]
- You use your eyes to look for things on the list. If you are playing with a theoretical list, each next item generally progresses alphabetically. If you are playing with a tangible list, the order is optional;
- Yelling out Spotto and then the name of a correct item, as you see it, will earn you a point. Bonus points can be earned if the items are of a particular preselected colour.

Basically, you stare mutely out the window until you see the next item on the list and then "Spotto - Red Apple." The hardest part of the game is keeping track of everyone's points.

Everyone on the bus either abstained or acquiesced, except Mindy as she was asleep again/still. By the time the rules were understood, there were only seven minutes left of their transit. Donald was still impressed by the number of things they were able to see:

- **Animal** (This is generally too general)
- **Bus** (You should look a bit further)
- **Call, J.** (This is generally too specific)
- **Dog** (You finally got the hang of it)
- **Everything** (*sigh*)
- **Freedom** (Nurse Jack gave up trying)
- **Golf Green** (And then double points)
- **Hole in One** (A hole? - 0 points)
- **Idiot** (Donald generalised, but true)
- **Jeans** (Double Denim? - 0 points)
- **Krispy Kreme** (Aaaaargh! - 0 points)
- **Lights, Traffic** (Acceptable? Yes, it is)
- **Me** (No points for **You**)
- **Nothing** (Is this a thing?)
- **Outside** (Really?)
- **Pedestrian** (Good one!)
- **Question** (Like what?)
- **Right** (Wrong - 0 points)
- **Stop!** (Why?)
- **The Flame** (We're here)
- **Unloading** the hearse
- **Viewing** the body
- **Watching** the flames
- **X** him off the return trip
- **You** can go back to sleep
- **Zzzzz**

---

[177] You can mix it up by using various specific itemed alphabets:

- NATO Phonetic Alphabet is good for the more experienced;
- Child ABC Alphabet for the lesser experienced; or
- Traditional Greek for the just plain crazy.

The formality at The Flame went over almost peacefully, except for when Owedebt became all emotionally correct. People expect there to be tears at a funeral/cremation/wake and when Owedebt supplied the necessary tears, at each appropriate step along the way, it was a relief for everyone else there.

Donald was nursing a trace amount of disappointment because he wasn't allowed to see the actual flame that The Flame was named after. But decorum required there be a salient divider between the guest of honour and the other dishonourable ones.[178]

William the Piano Man was playing one of his favourite green concertinas throughout the aforesaid formalities. Partially to give a pleasant undertone to the whole affair, and partially to cover up any unpleasant overtones this group of special people may notice.

If you would like to hear what William is singing, you need to go and find a William who can sing it for you. If you wouldn't like to, go and find a William who only thinks he can sing. In either case, Donald isn't going to volunteer, as his name wasn't William, and he is still lurching over the knowledge that SaRS has its own personalised funeral dirge.

Re: S-a-R-S (Inspired by *YMCA* - Village People) p278

¤   Extract from The Donald Diaries.

As the proclivities started to wind down, and the salivating smell of BBQing wasn't so pervasive and perversely reminiscent of the recent event, Shepherd stood up for the performance of his minor role...

"I have been asked to present a meaningful account of Vamp's life."

Donald wondered if Shepherd knew the difference between a monologue, a soliloquy and a eulogy. While he was thinking about this, he also wondered if he himself knew the difference. Couldn't each of the first two be presented as the third? The cogs were whirling rapidly now:

¤   A **soliloquy** is speech, delivered by one person, of their own thoughts, regardless of an audience's presence;

¤   A **monologue** is a long speech, delivered by one person, about their personal thoughts on a topic, to a receptive audience;

¤   A **eulogy** is speech, delivered by one person, about their own personal thoughts of a deceased individual, to anyone who was listening.

Donald got to the end of this and thought, "Nailed it." Inappropriately.

------

[178] And as Donald is inclined to dis honour at every available opportunity, I will take this opportunity to relieve you of having to read all about what is essentially not a funny situation. Mind you, being in a facility like SaRS isn't a funny situation either... Yet here we all are... Again!

"I am reminded of the sage advice, 'dif-tor heh smusma,' we received from the fabled literary identity Mr. Spock. This is, of course, 'live long and prosper,' when translated from the original Vulcan. And although the man you all knew as Nelo (Vamp) Priors, failed to do either of these, we will still remember him fondly for as long as we are able."

Donald didn't quite know how Shepherd was giving a ~~speech, soliloquy, monologue,~~ eulogy about a person he had never met, but was intrigued by the insensitive reference to Mr Spock's catchphrase. Donald considered himself an aficionado of triviality about this statement:

- ✗ Vulcan   - "dif-tor heh smusma" - "live long and prosper"
- ✗ Christianity - "pax vobis"   - "peace be with you"
- ✗ Arabic   - "as-salamu alaykum" - "peace be upon you"
- ✗ Hebrew   - "shalom aleichem"   - "peace be upon you"

Different interpretation of the same story in four different books.

"As the only one here who thinks they are ordained," Shepherd continued, "I will conclude this official farewell with a reading taken from the book I found in the waiting room titled *Numpty-Rhymes*, and I'm paraphrasing here..."

Sad Old Nelo[179]

Sad old Nelo, why do you cry?
Is it because your life has passed you by?
It will not matter, now you're near to death
No one is here to hear your final breath

    Forever in folklore, forever nevermore
    Most of the people won't remember you
    Forever uncared for, forever they ignore
    Those same people will never give your due

        Sad old Nelo, why did you cry?
        Was it because your life had passed you by?
        It doesn't matter, now that you are dead
        No one to plant you in your final bed...

---

[179] This book was written by someone called David Halpin, and the full title is quite a mouthful - Numpty-Rhymes, Numpty-Bys and Numpty-Songs (Poetry from Numpty's Doctor's Brother's Goose). The individual poem was inspired by the Horsey-Horsey nursery rhyme, but I can't see it myself... No, I'm serious. It makes absolutely no sense to me, as they are nothing alike.

"Nelo (Vamp) Priors, was known to us all here today as being an addict, an anaemic and an avid photosensitive photographer. He chose one of the least popular ways to depart SaRS, and by doing so, has left us all with an indelible mark to remember him by. If you talk to Nurse Jack, he will be able to tell you where you can all go," <unfortunate page turning pause> "to see it."

Lou gave Aaaron the look.[180]

Aaaron sheepishly stepped in and started herding Shepherd, and his flock of might be listeners, out of The Flame's private rooms and into Bertie for their relocation back to SaRS. This activity didn't take nearly as long as it did earlier. Being creatures of habit, everyone took up the exact same positions they were in before, including Mindy who was sound asleep again.

Mid herd, Shepherd gave the piece of paper he had written the eulogy on to Owedebt. "I thought you might like this... There are some comforting words about The Flame's live-in undertaker, and his undertakings, on the back. If you ever find yourself in need of a few minutes peace; from an annoying person who doesn't know when they are intruding on a solemn moment; who might be telling you something that would be helpful at any other time; or be giving you a generic self-help waffle flyer; I suggest you give them this to read..."

Owedebt pocketed the alleged flyer for Ron... Later Ron.

On their way back to SaRS, Nurse Jack held a pop-up-debriefing session at the back of the bus. He wanted to get everyone's opinion on what they could do to try and manage the sadness, loss and schedule disruption over the next few days while the memory goes from raw to crispy.

There weren't any suggestions made which were achievable:

- Make a bronze memorial statue of Vamp for the commemorative park they will create under-looking where the park bench is;
- Rename the Hospital to "eVery dAy uMmmmm sPa;" and
- Bring Vamp back to life as an actual undead vampire.

These surprising suggestions were all unsurprisingly floated by Owedebt, and the third one looked to be gaining some traction until Nurse Jack pointed out two small hiccups in the plan, you can't create an undead person out of a cremated mate, and Nelo was turning a tad too toasty at the moment.

This realisation caused Owedebt to curse loudly. Not because Vamp was never going to come back again, but because they forgot to get his urn-full of ashes to bring back to SaRS.

---

[180] The look that says, "You really should have been able to figure this out by yourself before things got this far out of hand, but it is now way past the time when you step in and do your job, and control this unruly mob of one..."

Aaaron fielded this cherry on the cake ending, "It's all good Owedebt; we left instructions on what to do with Nelo's ashes… They are to be sealed in a biodegradable burial pod and planted near Big Bertha[181] so she can watch over him for many years to come." And silently added, "Well… At least up until his body biodegrades along with the pod. Making Nelo, fundamentally, an organic organ infused digestible vitamin tablet for Mother Nature."

This seemed to mollify Owedebt. Remembering the alleged flyer, she took it out of her pocket and quietly sunk back into her seat, to have one good old read, for the remainder of the journey…

Re: Let it Burn, Let Him Burn p280

※   Extract from The Donald Diaries.

Unfortunately, this is where we all (I) have to leave Vamp for now, and maybe for forever. Seth is going to be one very disappointed SaRS ghost when he learns that Vamp won't be coming back as a ghost any time soon.[182]

The piece of information that is going to stick in Donald's mind, for at least the next thirteen minutes anyway, is a piece of very sage advice from Aaron, "I hope you all understand that getting stabbed is just one of the many reasons why forming a relationship with another patient is frowned upon at SaRS, in the sternest of manners."

---

[181] Big Bertha is the affectionate name given to a grey gum tree at SaRS.

[182] But who knows…? You never say never, eh, Mr Pledge, Jimmy Pledge? And if you all go back and notice, I didn't say never then, and never will now.

Chapter 7:
Brought to you by
Hungry Hungry David's

Donald entered yesterday's tomorrow with a head start, waking up thirteen minutes before his alarm was due to go off. He progressed straight through the preparedness stage, orienting, grooming and properly dressing himself without issue.[183] Eventually opening the cell door to arrive at the onslaught of activity due to arrive. When he saw who was waiting for him... It was clearly turning out to be the most spectacular...

Donald awoke with a start, of the not-head variety, as was his wont after another morning preceded by a most annoying dream.[184] He had thought he was getting right into the swing of things at SaRS, and was seriously disappointed by what he perceived to be a step in the wrong direction... Not to mention he was going to miss out on seeing something that was *clearly turning out to be the most spectacular...*

Due to all of the disruptions recently, Donald had lost count of the number of groups he has attended, how many meals he has missed and what the day was... No reason for saying this, just filling in the page. (But that's a reason...)

---

[183] That reminded him, he should really pass through the bathroom, so the fallout from yesterday has a chance to pass through him...

[184] Why is *daydream* so stipulated, and why are they presumed to be *good?*
- It doesn't have to be *day* for them to occur (indicated by the dark);
- It doesn't have to be *good* (indicated by the presence of drool); and
- Oft times it is obviously a *fantasy* (indicated by much salivation).

Fine, no *significant* reason... OK? (*Sure...*)[185]

When he arrived at, and subsequently signed in to, the currently effective group session, Donald decided to stick a stick in the unstable ground and label this his thirteenth group. It was a somewhat astute decision, as this *was* most likely the thirteenth group he has attended, depending on your definitions of group, attended and thirteen.

It was certainly an unlucky time for this group number to come up.

"Cooking for pleasure." Mindy broke the silence, and then waited for it to be repaired so she could continue with the group's objectives... "Today we will be having some fun while we are learning how to extract the most enjoyment from our daily healthy calorie allowance..."

Donald was unsure if this was an optional group objective or a mandatory requirement, but he was willing to give her the benefit of his doubt as he didn't want to get on the ever-increasing bad side of this cantankerous old pedantic Wiccan, even though she was asleep most of the time.

"Today we have an eclectic gathering of cooking prowess. We have never tried to deliver such an astonishing menu... Well, not since the gastroenteritis outbreak of the late 80's; that threw up a significant amount of astonishing, but I digress...

Today for your delectation, we have:

- Chef Chief Changes
  Donald expounded (*SaRS cafeteria's chief chef and awesome guy*);
- Seymour Feedme
  (*SaRS dietician and pasta dude extraordinaire*); and finally
- Zyxon Zzippy (Damn it, last again)
  (*SaRS ice-cream surrealist*).

And I am, (drum roll), Mindy Ownbeeswhacks (*way too scary, move along*). I would ask that you all to only refer to me by my superpower name... You will all know this from your "Psychic" group session (*with resident wicca, Mindy*), that is going to be held. You will know when and where when you concentrate.

But I don't ask questions...

---

[185] Fine and Sure. If you can all now look back to the top of this page:

Here we are being shown, what are quite possibly the two best examples of, the worst possible use of these two seemingly positive four-letter words.

Stop tour guiding this disagreement with yourself and get on with the story! I think we can all agree... Everyone understands sarcasm when they see it.

Donald felt like Mindy's introduction of herself, and her unasked question, was a lot like the "You Touch, and You Die" messages you see scattered around a Murderer's only leisure activity shopping centre.[186]

An unsolicited thought entered Donald's head, "Too extreme?"

Then, without waiting for the Snap and Crackle of bubbles, a response to the previous thought Popped in to replace the message, "Ok then… You touch and you have a slightly unsettling thought… Better."

"Better. Yes, Better. Much Better." Thought Donald as quickly as he could.

"All right then. Have a nice day, please come again…"

"Now that I have everyone's undivided attention…"

There was a unanimous synchronous superfluous nodding of heads.

"I will satisfy our new sponsorship agreement."

"Hungry~~Hungry~~David's have gratuitously agreed to replace ~~Mc~/~David's~~ as the sole provider of:

- Ingredients for the majority of our allegedly food-based products;
- Many calories over our daily average dietary requirements; and
- A small number of artistic accruements for the Beethoven art room.

This comes at quite a cost to them…"

"And to us." Reflects Chef inaudibly.

Donald noticed Mindy giving Chef an almost imperceptible, but in no way incomprehensible, *look*; which had no effect on Chef what-so-ever before she continued, "This includes a rebranding of all appropriate paraphernalia.[187] We already know about the SaRS Whiteboard…"

"Ahhhhh that explains that!" Reflects Donald inaudibly.

Another unsolicited thought entered Donald's head, "Hmmmmm… If you continue on this train of thought I may have to deal with you later… " and this time it came accompanied by a *look*; which was in no way imperceptible, nor was it approaching incomprehensible; if he knew what was good for him.

Pausing to collect all of her unsolicited thoughts, "I will now ask Seymour to formally introduce The Tapestry #2, a piece of the paraphernalia patchwork and to explain what this means to you…"

---

[186] Not that Donald spends a lot of his time in that variety of place. He just likes to peruse their online catalogues and spends his ~~money~~ time wondering what a murderer might get up to in their spare time.

[187] Mindy was able to complete their satisfaction by mentally projecting a message to all who wanted to hear about the SaRS gratuities programme: "(Yo' can get Yo') Satisfaction… With us at Hungry~~Hungry~~David's"

"Ahem… We all know you can't have a diet without something dying. And I would like to think this tapestry gives us a window into your colon to watch the process. Who would like to give it a try?"

Donald wasn't the only one confronted by Seymour's opening, and when this altered slightly to, Donald wasn't the only one amused by Seymour getting a swift kick from Mindy; Donald wasn't the only one excused for laughing at the inaugural *Seymour kicks with Mindy* show.

"**All Right… Settle Petals…**" Unlike Seymour or Mindy, Chef held the whole world of SaRS, like putty,[188] in his hands. "Seymour, what I think Mindy is trying to tell you is, 'can you explain what the tapestry does in a bit more detail?'"

"All right. Yes, I understand. Here is the description of a 'Depression Cake' I prepared earlier after I changed it to be the next alphabetical, and much less appropriate, description of a 'Devil's Food Cake' as made in the Tapestry…"

TV Test 1, Test 2, Test 1, Tapestry #2
(Colloquially known as the TV Test Pattern Tapestry #2)

List of Involvements:
- Volunteer to enter the tapestry and bake a cake of their chosen type

List of Ingredients: (For a Devil's Food Cake)
- The exact same set of ingredients you would find in a chocolate cake
  * With more chocolatey chocolate in the block of chocolate ingredient
  * Which is the exact opposite of the chocolatey ingredients commonly found within a depression cake

SaRS Whiteboard 3 – The Tapestry #2 Description[189]

After enough time had been wasted, Zyxon uncovered The Tapestry #2.

---

[188] Made from crushed chalk and cheese oil in CC's kitchen.

[189] The description of the tapestry was shown to them on the up sponsored whiteboard. Donald felt it didn't really describe what would happen, and as we will read soon, won't be volunteering to be the involvement.

As Zyxon was trudging his way back to the corner, mumbling something about always being last, Donald could have sworn there was a conversation going on, on the inside of his head, just waiting for a chance to be set free…

Devil's Food Cake! We're the experts! But still, we get reject!?
For goodness' sake! We make desserts! Why shouldn't we expect!
It seems a shame,
It is our game,
Let's go the way we came

Despite the ache, and disconcerts, our presence will be checked
We need to bake, for those stuffed shirts, so we can earn respect
I don't wanna,
Eat banana,
Or play the goanna

Donald felt there were at least four personality types at play here:
- Angry Cook   - The Supervisor
- Depressed Cook   - The Mastermind
- Reliable Cook   - The Craftsman
- Confused Cook   - The Giver

But he was interrupted by Mindy as she asserted her scariness again…

"Do we have a volunteer willing to become the Involvement today?"

Chef entered into the conversation, diffusing a lot of the angst building up in every inmate,[190] "I can reassure you all that this tapestry is quite unlike The Tapestry #1. As I understand it, you had a few minor difficulties coming to the end of a visit. This tapestry behaves more like a TV programme recorded on a VCR… It plays in real ti…"

Donald undecidedly raised his hand, causing Chef to momentarily pause during his tapestry reveal, "What is a **VCR**?"

"It is a machine that allows you to record a television programme, so you can play it back at your leisure, but that isn't importa…"

"Oh, you mean a recordable **DVD**?"

"No, that's not for recording TV. He's talking about a **DVR**."

"Wow, old school much? Don't you have an interface to a **USB**?"

"What you really should have is a **PVR** Set Top Box."

"Why don't you just get a subscription to a **TLA** on demand service?"

---

[190] This was chiefly true of Donald; as he knew quite intimately, twice, what it was like to be chosen to be The Chosen One to enter into a tapestry.

At this point even Chef's radical patience was waning, and you could just about smell the nutty scented smoke coming out of his ears, signalling his deep profound sadness at the way these supposedly civilised people were behaving. "If you insist on behaving like animals, you give them justification to treat you like animals…"

Chef waited for a moment so the depth of this self-evident wisdom could sink in to the SaRS natives. Properly contrite, the crowded madness subsided and allowed him to continue… "This tapestry produces an effect similar to a pre-recorded programme, on whichever device is available, to be watched at your leisure. Imagine yourself as a celebrity chef making a surprise appearance at the recording session of a cooking programme.

"The *Episode*, that the Involvement will be involved in, will present them:

- ☒ As the creator of the selected dish;
- ☒ Dressed in period correct attire, from when the dish was created;
- ☒ In real time. If the dish takes you one hour to cook, it will take us one hour to watch, plus the preparation time. I suggest you stay away from time intensive dishes like cured salmon, I speak this from experience;
- ☒ Once the dish has been taste-tested, then approved by the host, you will be returned with a copy of the video cassette[191] in a gift box."

It didn't sound too bad to Donald, but he was sticking to his earlier angst. Once you've been the chosen one, you never go back again.[192]

"So… <Trepidation pause> Do we have a volunteer to be the Involvement? <Hopeful pause> I will let you all ponder and come back after the instructions. <Annoying third pause> Take it away Seymour…"

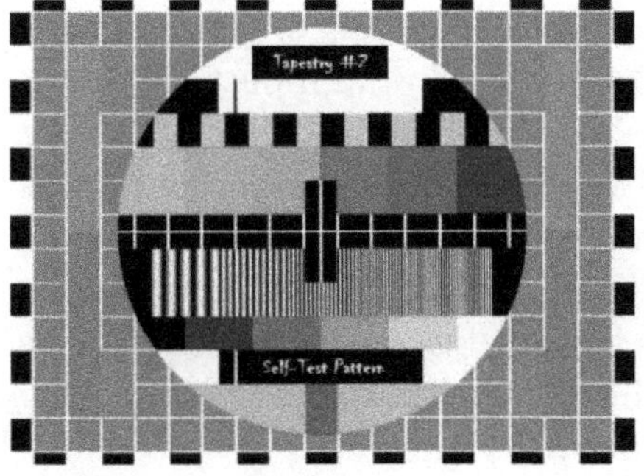

The Tapestry #2 1 – Self-Test Pattern

"Currently, as you can all view here, The Tapestry #2 is displaying what we all officially label the *Self-Test Pattern*. It is what the tapestry commonly broadcasts when nothing is being broadcast."

What Donald can still only see, is:

- ☒ An unimpressed robot's face;
- ☒ Displaying its Doppler moustache;
- ☒ With a Bloodshot left eye; and all while
- ☒ Wearing a yarmulke in its head.

---

[191] Donald easily just managed to refrain himself from asking the question. The *look* from Mindy, combined with the frantic no-no gesticulations behind her from Seymour, was all the motivation he needed to stay unmotivated.

[192] In Donald's case: You never go back again… More than once…

"There are a few rules we have for this tapestry because of the physical episodic proof produced, as we don't want there to be anything too serious to be officially recorded, or for there to be a documented triggering situation, or any tangible latent support for a malfeasance accusation.[193]"

Seymour went through the rules (and other various administrations):
- What happens in the tapestry, stays in the tapestry;[194]
- The dish chosen to be prepared is the only variable under your control. If you think it, you make it. So, choose wisely;
- The length of time spent in the tapestry is determined, solely, by the amount of time the chosen dish takes to prepare. The time starts from the moment of Involvement acceptance, and ends once the episode's taste test has occurred;
- Everything you do inside the tapestry will alter the episode;
- You are always "on screen" while in the tapestry. Again, please ensure you choose your dish wisely, as you are *always* "on screen;"
- People in the episode can see and interact with the Involvement;
- There will always be a judgement; and finally
- Involvement is optional and you must request to be included. There is no TCO (The Chosen One) here…
- The Tapestry #2 unnumbered rule ten: There is no rule nine.

Donald was completely correct when he thought, "Apart from the dubious identical first and redundant last rules, these rules are the complete opposite of The Tapestry #1's ~~instructions~~ User Manual."

Targeting the Woolly Mammoth in the room Donald asked, "So… If no one requests to be included as the Involvement volunteer in The Tapestry #2, none of us has to participate in this activity?"

Even though Donald had asked this of Seymour, Mindy responded with a curt, "That is correct." And then she expanded her curtness onto one of the ramifications of not having a volunteer, "If we don't receive an Involvement request from anyone present, to create an episode inside The Tapestry #2, we will have to resort to our Plan number B, which will be to enact a group cooking episode *live*, *now*, for *everyone*… Is that what you want?"

---

[193] Donald wasn't surprised when Seymour muttered this self-protecting reason. He will, however, be surprised when there is no Fine Print to sign for this tapestry. This is because the existence of any Fine Print, by default, would provide confirmation there was some physical proof produced.

[194] Everyone saw the Pffffft Sure comment hanging unspoken in the air.

Donald felt comfortable being selfish and not volunteering to be the only one to receive the cooking punishment, no matter how recorded it may be.

As was the entire group.

"Excellent. I have been waiting for nearly a century to show a ragtag group of SaRS inmates[195] how to cook like a crafty old woman." The smile on Mindy's face was a nearly dead giveaway that this wasn't sarcasm, and when she leapt up and clapped her hands like a 90-year-old, Donald was almost certain it was not. When Mindy got her breath back, "Zyxon, be a dear and take The Tapestry #2 back to where it came from please."

Zyxon came of the corner, and as he did, he started up his mumbling again, Donald could have sworn there was another conversation going on between the same four personality types as before. Donald was beginning to wonder if Zyxon was on some sort of work release programme from down elevator.

Take it back please! We don't want it! My effort was wasted!
Now!? Bloody Jees! This is Bull Pit! I wanted some tasted!
It seems a shame,
That once again,
We're going where we came

> *Disappointed, and frustrated, we have been asked to leave*
> *We're appointed, nay, dictated, we cannot show aggrieve*
> *I don't wanna,*
> *Eat goanna,*
> *Or play the banana*

Donald again broached the Woolly Mammoth task, "Why wasn't there a reference to this live cooking group in our week two checklist?[196]" As he felt the pressure of the many gazes aimed at him Donald's DOGONs were slowly, but steadily, increasing. He plateaued out at around nine, the upper maximum unacceptable level. If he continued along this path for much longer, he would need to excuse himself to go and self-medicate with caffeine or music or face the music of caffeine withdrawal.

---

[195] Mindy is allowed to refer to the patients as inmates, as she is one of us, and must been forgiven her senior moments. (She is also scary, remember.)

[196] There are three reasons at work here:

    ¤   Donald completely forgot about the week two checklist, remember?

    ¤   I completely forgot to remember to write the week two checklist; and

    ¤   If I had remembered, there would be no need to forget I had done so.

So that left Mindy, Seymour and Chef all hanging in the breeze without a reasonable reason why they were all gathered today. After exchanging glances of "How much do we tell them?" for looks resembling "Oh, get thee to the bad place with it, why don't we just tell them the truth?"

Sigh

However recalcitrant his motives were, Seymour, as the most senior staff member there who wasn't a Chef, felt it was probably his responsibility to fall on his stay-sharp, "I guess we weren't going to be able to hide the most recent drama for much longer anyway…"

Donald didn't like the ominous sound of that… He was barely progressing through the process of noticing, acknowledging and then simply letting go of his thoughts related to Vamp. What is going to be the next cause of upsetting the Donald cart?

"As you all probably know, we are the middle of a nationwide shortage of toilet paper; well, the TP shortage has extended throughout the entire globe. There have been military incursions into several manufacturing plants, and the government is controlling the distribution on a need-to-go basis. This in turn has prompted several doomsday fringe elements into disingenuous activity, and they are currently targeting low-security high-usage institutions.

"We have increased security at all points of evacuation to include thumb print readers and retina scanners. SaRS has also employed, and then deployed, several additional security guards to verify the intended usage of the facilities, and then to supply an appropriate amount of paper to the pooper."

Donald, luckily for him, was stuck back at the retina scanner section of the announcement, "How do the scanners work on blind people?[197]"

"Interesting question." Seymour didn't sound interested, but provided an answer anyway, "There are several features of the scanners that allow for the reading of 99.9% of all retinas:

- There are braille instructions beside each scanner;
- Three scanners have the guide animal option attached, which comes with an extended mobile reader, and these are coloured fluorescent yellow to allow for easy identification;
- If either of these fails to work, there is an emergency entrance button. This allows entry only. To exit, the same button needs to be pressed from the outside. An exit facilitator can be summoned by the standard assistance call button within."

---

[197] Donald calls it like he sees it. Blind is correct terminology, as long as it isn't appended with "as a bat." If there is any person who has limited vision, or is visually impaired, and would like to educate Donald, please do so.

"What has that got to do with us being here, and not learning to cook?"

At this point Chef asserted his presence, "Well… That's the thing isn't it? When the scanners were being installed outside all of the facilities, they also added them to the Kitchen, Dining Room and Cafeteria doors, without first consulting any of the kitchen staff. And as these areas don't have an internal assistance call button,[198] they were deemed to be too much of a security risk, and they have both been closed for the foreseeable future."

Seymour jumped back in trying to mitigate the situation, "To alleviate this problem we will be conducting some basic self-cooking sessions, so you don't starve. As for the ingredients required, we have also retained the services of the Uber Hungry Hungry Drivers[199] to deliver essential items a minimum of three times a weekly and once on the weekend. These can be collected via the administration area, and you can ask for them at any time. Mark Time will be there to offer his collective assistance, should it be needed."

Chef re-asserted, "A second issue resulting from the untimely shut-out of my kitchen is the Onsite Café has also been plunged into full lockdown mode. My kitchen usually supplies all of their hot food; and it has been pronounced that if the café was to sell only coffee and dessert, without any real nutritional value, it would be a breach of SaRS' duty of care policy."

That was the official story. Designed to placate everyone concerned.

The actual story was… It wouldn't be a financially viable asset.

SaRS' Onsite Café (That is its full name: *Onsite Café*. It helped significantly when giving directions, and followed the typical Australian standard of naming the thing by what the thing was…

- Sydney Harbour Bridge;
- Great Sandy Desert; and
- Man from Snowy River.)

The café is a tranquil outlet, with relaxing comfortable garden furniture. You can take in the glorious panoramic view, encompassing the three natural Kingswood icons; River, Valley and Hill. Located just to the left of right outside The Kingswood's House's back door. Onsite Café serves a selection of delicious morning and afternoon teas, snacks and a hot lunch from the kitchen.

---

[198] This is something Chef has been lobbying the SaRS management for over the previous years. He has been unsuccessful so far, as there is never any budget to improve the non-financial aspects of treatment offered.

[199] Who have been substituted in for the Riders of ~~McDavid's~~, according to the new supply contract with Hungry Hungry David's, appendix three, chapter two, subsection one, "Modus of delivery operandi."

Chef wasn't aware of the actual story. If he had been, he would have also been outraged by it. He prided himself on the fact that SaRS was the only non-commercial restaurant which sometimes appears in the "Better Places to Eat" advertising throughout the wider community.[200]

While the discussion about, presentation on, and explanation of food was being delivered, Donald finally noticed there were no cooking implements, no crockery or utensils and defiantly no food. He was beginning to get the idea that this impromptu group session was also an ill-conceived under-prepared one. He also thought it was strange they were preparing to allow the inmates of SaRS access to sharp, hot, hard … anythings.

Strangely, he was still unaware that he hadn't eaten any breakfast today; and something even stranger, he was still unaware that he was unaware! He remembers heading towards the cafeteria, after checking the notice board for any pertinent information for the day (there wasn't any), putting himself into his auto pilot configuration and thinking "go," but nothing from then until the start of this group session.

The reason for this unawareness is quite devious… He was starting to feel the effects of his SaRS conditioning. This was happening subliminally without his knowledge or approval each night after he falls asleep. There is a rationale behind the message they are trying to teach, but as it is quite confusing, they elected to not tell Donald to keep him from the spiralling possibilities. Once he has shown he can withstand the level of angst required, they will explain.

Through the use of a reasonably stable routine[201] SaRS is trying to achieve a calm normality. Where the patients' expectations are being met, and anxiety about the future is kept in check, or at least kept to a recoverable level without requiring medication or external intervention.

Once a predictable set of reactions, to a variety of controlled situations, has been learned by the patient, they will be deliberately exposed to a slowly increasing number of uncontrolled situations, while they still have the safety of the hospital to fall back on to. The conditioning is being applied to Donald because the staff, primarily DD and Nurse Jack, believe Donald has showed a great deal of understanding.

---

[200] There was a caveat explaining that you couldn't just "go there and eat." You had to prearrange to perform some sort of community service at the hospital to be allowed a seat. (These services were generally unskilled and time-consuming tasks that no employees wanted to do. Preparing Welcome Packs; cleaning the whiteboards; counting jigsaw puzzle pieces; etc…)

[201] As opposed to an average overnight horse boarding facility.

This is called the **P**lough-**T**hrough **S**ituation **D**estress method and is where you are forced to follow a strict routine, so you can learn how to cope without the need to follow a routine. It is often explained with a three-step snow skiing dubious analogy…

- The very first lesson when learning to ski, that everyone must learn, is how to stop using the, eventually painful, snowplough[202] technique. You place your skis in a wide pointy two-sided triangle formation;
- Once you have this mastered this method, you move on to a slightly steeper slope and learn how to stop properly. Keep your skis parallel, shift your weight uphill and spray whoever is causing you to stop with a wave of snow; and then you…
- **Never** have to snow-plough ever again.

There are several equivalent get-set-and-forget descriptions…
- Training wheels for a two-wheel push bike;
- Tandem parachute passenger for skydiving; and
- Foster's beer drinking for an Australian.

It must be noted though:

Note: This is dissimilar to the human "crawl → walk → run" progression… You don't stop walking once you have learned how to run, and you certainly never stop crawling once you have learned how to be an adult.

Donald's conditional success with "seeing the positives and only noticing the negatives" conditioning, goes a long way to explaining why he didn't see the sign on the cafeteria door this morning saying…

CLOSED UNTIL
A FURTHER NOTICE
SAYING IT IS REOPENED

---

[202] This is the English method of slowing down, eventually, in a controlled fashion from an initial slow speed down a gentle slope. If you want to use the American method, you need to spell it snowplow.

Americans don't like the letter "u." They have even removed it from "you," when communicating loudly to their unprivileged kin, "Get **Yo** Hands Off!" "Hey **Yo!** What are **y'all** doin' tonight?" and "**Y'all** come back now, **ya** hear?"

There were several other redundant or obsolete signs in the area which have been dwarfed by this new one...

The PTSD method is being implemented by night Nurse Hatchet,[203] with some assistance from the newly recruited Uber☒Watch☒Winders.[204] Newly on the scene, most of these characters have been double booked. During the day they are the mild-mannered Uber☒Hungry☒Hungry☒Drivers, but at night they comically transform into their Fantastic4Us repressed identities as the night wenchmen (watch henchmen).

The head woman of the wenchmen is **Little Bertha Nomaly** (LB). She was given the "Little" nickname so you can distinguish between her and Big Bertha, the tree. It has absolutely nothing to do with her kick arse weight.

She doesn't mind the other association connotation, and constantly refers to Big Bertha as her personal shadow tree. Which is quite strange, as there are no external lights at SaRS high enough for Big Bertha to cast a shadow down, and LB is only allowed out the back of SaRS during the night-time prohibited outside hours.

Her alter ego superpower is a knack for charming or outwitting someone who doesn't do what she wants them to, to get them to do what she wants them to do, which is useful when implementing a subliminal treatment.

---

[203] To be frank, Nurse Hatchet prefers dealing with the patients while they are asleep anyway. She would tell you this herself, only she would preface it with *to be honest*... To be honest, I'm not convinced Donald could take it, as he has become somewhat her arch nemesis, by actually wanting to recover. She takes great delight in messing with Donald's mind overnight.

[204] Known as the *Fantastic4Us*. Take a few moments to absorb the math.

Something that LB has to keep her eye on as head woman is... If her cohort wenchmen remain unchecked for too long, some of them are liable to try and claim an extra pay cheque for working the one cash-in-hand job, as they know the record keeping process is also unbelievably comical.

> *Uber~~ ~~Watch~~ ~~Winders*
> We watch ~~over~~ you while you are sleeping.
> Comical implementers of subliminal messages.
> **Little Bertha Nomaly (LB) – Head Woman**
> Phone: 1800 CALLME

After checking his watch, and after all the previous talk about cooking and food kicked his stomach into overdrive with its rendition of, "I will never *get-over* eating, Feed Me Seymour," namesake routine; Seymour suggested they defer the lesson to the next meeting as he was feeling a little peckish.

Seymour didn't consider the fact that both the cafeteria and café were still closed, as he brought his own gourmet food from home each day. His job was to make sure the food available at SaRS was nutritious and tasty, not the actual suppliance of the food.

He also didn't wait for anyone to acknowledge his suggestion before he left them all hanging out for food.

Chapter 8:
Regrouping, Repeating (and Redelivery)

Seymour returned to the group mostly rested, refreshed and relaxed. When he was reminded of the reason why they were all reconvening he realised he may have responded to the recent reality with a really reprehensible reprobate reflex action. Responsibly, he was ready and resigned to receive their resultant rebuke with the required amounts of both regret and respect. He refocused on the task at hand…

"My apologies people, I didn't think that one through."

Donald graciously accepted Seymour's apology, as he expressed regret for his actions, and not that the resultant outcome had happened.[205]

"All right people… Do you want to make some food and eat it too?"

The echoing responses were all in agreement:

- "My Scrumptious."
- "You Baking For Me?"
- "Yeah - let's dough this!"
- "Go ahead, make my food!"
- "Cake it Away… To the Oven…"
- "Wax paper on… Wax paper off…"
- "Bake it, someone… Bake it 'In a Pie'"
- "No hunger… No hunger… No hunger…"
- "I feel the knead… The knead… For spelt…"
- "May the Sauce be Homebrew."

And of course, the totally obvious reference:

- "Feed me Seymour!"

---

[205] In Donald's world, the only way to apologise is to not include an excuse.

Seymour told the group that Skit was taking a well (un)deserved break "in a room of his choice." Attempting to see the positive side of all actions is one of life's main ideals the hospital staff tries to instil their patients. Implementing a practical experience of this theory Seymour explained, "It is a good thing for Skit to have some time out of group to think about his personal idiosyncrasies; it also conveniently evens out the group numbers for the upcoming pairing[206] exercise."

Donald wasn't going to let himself become distracted by any of Seymour's obviously practical demonstrations, focussing his complete attention on the current whereabouts of Skit. The hidden brackets, air quotes and strangely worded statement, had all got Donald thinking. "Hmmmmm.

- Why is he mentioning Skit at all? Doesn't he realise everyone has read the book from the start, and they know Skit wasn't even talked about in the previous chapter, let alone having any participation in it?
- What doesn't he mean by the bracketed un, and how do I even know the brackets are there? and
- Was this a choice about which bedroom he was placed in? Or was it a substantially more cynical choice between padded room, dungeon cell and medieval torture-chamber?"

Seymour continued his explaining with the lesson's instructions, breaking Donald's completely distracted mental thought process before he could think of any rational questions to ask. "Alright everyone, quiet, quiet please. Thank you. Take your starting places. It seems that I am going to be the only one here teaching you how to feed yourself today. But that is OK, as it is exactly what I do." Seymour sounded like he was teaching the uses of a ballet barre, instead of the uses of a chocolate bar...[207]

The group room had been set out with small tables and chairs, reminiscent of a kindergarten classroom, where the arrangement was two chairs per table. The layout Donald was faced with was slightly different; the chairs were facing each other rather than the front of the class, and this posed a significant issue for him. He thought he was going to be coerced into working with one of his fellow inmates.

---

[206] Donald was going to be disappointed that this wasn't a paring exercise.

[207] The reason why Chef and Zyxon were not there is that they had other tasks to attend to. (Not that it made it easier for me to write) Mindy had simply fallen asleep and no one was willing to interrupt the peace ensuing.

- Chef was busy rectifying the new don't open the door policy; and
- Zyxon had lost his ice-cream cart, as well as most of his patience.

This concerning thought morphed into a stunningly accurate dread when Seymour proceeded without cautioning them as such, "Find a cooking partner and sit at your table so we can start the lesson. Chop, chop... Stir, stir... Bubble, bubble... And all those cooking words." while he was managing to offend many people, in many places, in many ways, without any effort whatsoever.

Istha chose to team herself up with Donald, as she doesn't think he is just a voice in her head anymore. Her revised thinking is, "he is a voice in my head who I should listen to." She also thinks it would be a nice gesture from her to partner up with the new guy, and Donald wasn't in any position to disagree no matter how much he tried to be.

Seymour started the group proper with an icebreaker, "Cooking pancakes with a hairdryer... Sure, if you are desperate it might work... But that doesn't make it a good idea... Can anyone tell me why?"

It took a while after all the pausing, but the suggestions started to limp in:

- "Giving us something with a cord attached could be dangerous?"
- "There would be bits of caked on inside hairdryer gunk come out?"
- "The air flow would send the mixture flying, making a big mess?"
- "It would take too long to get them to the required cooked-ness?"
- "Wouldn't it be easier to just drink the wet pancake mixture, or even add the dry mixture to a cup of coffee instead of a sweetener?"

"Those are all very good suggestions, especially the last one, but there is still one missing. What would be the absolute worst thing that could happen?"

- "It would be loud. People would come and ask if they could share..."

"Bingo! Give that Donald a star. Nothing could be more important in SaRS than keeping the exquisite outcome of your midnight use of a personal power tool all to yourself."

Donald gave Seymour a probing double take curious look. As there was no awkward response returning back, he decided to assume the uncomfortable position that what Seymour said, was exactly what he meant.

"All right, now that we have dispensed with the uncomfortable beginning portion of the group, we can move onto the slightly more comfortable content section about cooking tools.[208]

---

[208] The ones you find in a kitchen, not those found on television.

Actually, that comment works particularly well in two equidistant ways...

- Tools that are advertised on the late-night shopping channels; and
- Tools that are participating in the multitude of cooking programmes. Which are really only semi-transparent fronts for selling those other tools that are being advertised on the late-night shopping channels.

"I inquired about having a selection of the less common cooking tools from Chef's kitchen repurposed for today's lesson, just to give you an idea of what is available to you in the extended world outside your comfort zone. But I was unfortunately unsuccessful. So, we will have to make do with this theoretical look at what you might have been presented with.

"Does anyone have a favourite cooking facility they would like to share?"

"If I might be allowed to make a shuggeshtion? I am familiar with a great many unushual typesh of cooking equipment. I have made a great deal of ushe of the *Mark Sheven Briefcashe* dishguished picnic hamper that wash revealed in *From One with Shaushe*. Shequeshtered inshide it wash:

- A collapshible shet of babushka meashuring cupsh;
- Thirteen conshealed Tim-Tam bishcuitsh complete with an adjushted Tim-Tam-Tip-Shnipper, and of courshe
- The shpring loaded multiple shaushe dishpensher if the hamper wash ever opened incorrectly."

After failing to wipe down the portions of himself that weren't protected by his duck-bent-elbow-cover pose,[209] Seymour turned to face Pledge, Jimmy Pledge... "Thank you for that upmost moist, if not fascinating, display of a next person watering speech... And who are you?"

"I shir, am Pledge, Jimmy Pledge. And I am at your shervish.[210]"

"And what would your shuggeshtion[211] be?"

"Ah. Well, that, my damp friend, could be a little bit of a pickle."

Seymour was glad that Pledge, Jimmy Pledge, was avoiding the use of "S" completely and "C" occasionally, but he was in no mood to mollycoddle, or even coddle, a serial splatterer. "That doesn't answer my question."

"No, it doesn't, does it?"

Seymour only liked one thing less than a serial splatterer, and that was a serial splatterer rhetorical answerer, even though the splattering didn't occur on the zzzzz sounding "S"s. "Mister Jimmy Pledge, I am going to have to direct you to the door."

"You don't have to bother with that, I know where to find it on my own."

"Please Leave Now." Seymour's teeth clenching terseness was evident.

"Fair call. I will leave and I bid you all a fond..." Pirouetting, Pledge, Jimmy Pledge, exited the group room without any undue delay, leaving a single word behind in his wake, "fonduuuuuuuuuuuuuuuuue..."

---

209 The Standard Protective Interaction Technique – number thirteen.

210 Which makes me wonder, why is there an "I" in sir, but an "E" in service?

211 Proving that speech impediments are contagious in the right setting.

"That was a curiously unexpected and mildly interesting suggestion. How would everyone feel about learning how to melt some food, stick other food with a skewer, stick the skewer-stuck other food into the previously melted food, go fishing for the unstuck skewer-stuck other food and after re-skewer-sticking the unstuck skewer-stuck other food, burning your tongue?"

.

.

. **<Chirp...** Chirp... Chirp...>

.

.

"Rather than just learning about it, I would prefer to eat some." Again, Donald came to the rescue with the obvious communal thought and wielded it well enough to fend off those pesky room bound mammoths.

"Yes of course Donald. There is nothing I would like more. But, as you are unfortunately aware, we are experiencing an easily accessible kitchen deficit at this particular moment. So, theory, however undesirable, unpleasant and unpalatable it may be, is all we have at our disposal."

Significantly chastened, Donald returned to his contemplations.

Up until now the other patients had remained inexplicably unattached to all of the thoughts flying around. Owedebt was about to change that... "I'd like to learn about fondue food skewering. Particularly the re-skewer-sticking the unstuck skewer-stuck other food, without the burnt tongue after effect.[212]"

"Perfect! Well done Owedebt." Condescended Seymour.[213] Do you have a particular kind of fondue you would like to embrace?"

"Both Cs please."

Seymour was unsure how *both* kinds of Cs were related to fondue. As far as he was aware the two Cs, capital and lowercase, weren't fondue adjacent, let alone fondue related. He chose to live dangerously and humour her a little further by asking about them, "Both Cs... What do you mean by *both* Cs?" and then he held his breath hoping for...

He didn't even know what he was hoping for.

"Cheese and Chocolate of course. What else could it mean?"

Donald recorded an interest of one for this answer and question combo.

---

[212] Seymour was impressed Owedebt had paid attention to his question.

[213] But not so impressed that the impression lasted for any length of time.

"Any length of time," <sigh>, is another accepted delusional understanding which rightfully belongs in the *really?* time out corner. In this instance, *any* is construed to mean *a long*. Which, of course, it doesn't, at any time... Ever.

"Of course you do, how silly of me." Seymour's answer was the condensed to a single sentence interpreted spoken version of, "Wow. I wasn't expecting to get a reasonable answer in this place. Especially from you Owedebt. I guess I should have seen that one coming. I must be of my game today, to have let that one slip through to the keeper. Golly."

Accepting the undiluted premise, they were only going to learn the theory of cooking two fondues, the excitement of the group was somewhat subdued. Seymour was reduced to feeling he needed to guide the unenthusiastic crowd towards a higher state of enthusiasm. He wasn't aiming for a grand Mexican Wave level,[214] but a little more obvious breathing wouldn't go astray.

"Let's start at the right end of the cooking process... Eating.[215] How do you think we should consume the two types of fondue?"

Altogether, a slather of both... One hither the other, but neither together.
"Yes, exactly, how did you know Sven?"
I don't know. No one knows how they know everything they know, you know?
Seymour nodded in complete misunderstanding.

Donald was fairly oblivious for the next part of the group session. Once it had been revealed they were not going to actually cook anything, except for the remote possibility of cooking up a good story to tell about how good their cooking lesson was, he couldn't get his mind off how hungry he was.

Normally,[216] if he was thinking about a single issue that was troubling him, focussing all of his attention on this specific cause for concern, he would be able to deal with it metaphorically and then, subsequently, literally. He was concerned that he was unable to do this right now. Content with chasing his tail for a while, he eventually arrived at a comfort inspiration.

To be able to deal with my issues, both metaphorically and literally, I need to literally deal with them literally. I need to write about them, and then I need to show this writing to other people, so they can tell me how to solve my issues.

---

[214] As it could be construed as being racist against Victorians.

[215] The "right end" that Seymour is referring to is the final step of a linear progression through the cooking process. Starting with the leftmost step (gathering the raw ingredients) and finishing with the rightmost one (eating). He is not referring to the "correct end." But I do understand this confusion.

[216] And remember, this "Normally," exists only in Donald's own little world.

Unfortunately, Donald didn't currently have any way of documenting this breakthrough, so, as with most "good things" that happen to him, he promptly forgot. Quickly replacing the initial concern regarding his hunger, with another common one, "Where did I leave my paddle?"

Following on from this unfortunately documented paragraph, Donald was fortunately able to witness a completely fortunate story surrounding a timely rescue. Indeed, it was his own rescue… From hunger!

Chef had come to the rescue… With food![217]

During the time Seymour had devoted to teaching the patients how to do fondue, Chef had used the same time to open up his kitchen and create them a banquet fit for people who didn't know facilities like SaRS existed. He leaned heavily on his traditional talents, producing many succulent dishes…

Munch–Munch Menu Morsels

Entrée:

Vegetarian Tofulo Wings (from a flock load of wild grounded Tofulo birds)

Main:

Stuffed Ground Hog (repeatedly stuffed with many prunes and one date)
Bison Tomahawk Steak (exceedingly rare and comes cooked medium rare)
Bird Brain Stew (No… This isn't where Skit, or any patient, was taken)
Chunky Mush (No… Come back Chunky Poopy… It doesn't mean you)

Dessert:

And for after's (Good for up to thirteen years after) Turkey Jerky 

SaRS Whiteboard 4 – Munch–Munch Menu Morsels

Nobody asked how Chef how he managed to pull off a dégustation.[218] It is always better to gorge yourself in the dark. That way, nobody will see you if you start to leak; and because you can't see what you are eating, you can't feel guilty about it. At least that's what Donald was told when he asked.

---

[217] I am now apparently emphasising the end of my sentences… With words!

[218] Dégustation - Sampling all of Chef's signature dishes in one sitting.

Donald gorged himself utterly by eating one of everything[219] on offer. He did this purely to pay Chef a compliment about the excellence of his cooking with a physical display of awed appreciation. He also managed to evade every suggestion of a post banquet clean up task in a complementary way, selflessly allowing someone else to be congratulated on their thoughtfulness.

Feeling he had done enough to lift someone's spirit, Donald repaired back to his room to perform a few of the necessary running repairs to his distended dystopian digestion facilities. He hadn't felt this uncomfortably full for a long time, and he liked it. He thought "What is a banquet[220] for, if it is not to indulge your most base requirements?" which, coincidently, became the title of the first of today's brain dumps.

Re: What is a Banquet? p281

ж   Extract from The Donald Diaries.

Donald began to feel the comfortable washing over him, after the relaxing documenting of the day's activities task was completed, mentally at least. He would have felt self-conscious if he was feeling a physical washing sensation. There was just enough oomph left in his urge to enquire about a late evening relaxation enhancing massage treatment.

Obtaining a massage therapy booking normally requires at least a month's notice. But after recent occurrences, and with the concurrence of a full moon, an opening had been entered into the massage therapist's schedule. And even though it wasn't one of the subsidised happy hours, Donald elected to follow through with his enquiries and make the booking.

Massage Therapist – SaRS
Anna Lykeananna (Dip ReMass)
For massage studio opening times
please refer to a lunar calendar.

---

[219]   For various values of one:

ж   One sticky handful of Vegetarian Tofulo Wings

ж   One tenderloin of the Stuffed Ground Hog

ж   One completely racist Bison Tomahawk Steak

ж   One bowl-full of thick Bird Brain Stew

ж   One double scoop of Chunky Mush

ж   One fitful canister of Turkey Jerky

[220]   Is a banquet where you take your soggy money after "falling" into a pool?

Donald stumbled into action,[221] and followed the comfortable path to the Nurse's Bowl as his logical first 39 steps. Where, regrettably, the solitary nurse like person available was Grey. After they fumbled around in the desk drawers looking for some instruction, abundantly unsuccessfully, they increased their assistance to Donald greatly by referring him to They.

They, Donald was assured, would be willing to help even if they were not able, hopefully. Unfortunately, this was very much not the case, as They was most unhelpful, going so far as to highly recommend he could take it up with the SaRS administration. Donald did exactly this, unusually providing criticism about a temporary character in his life.[222] While he was there, he also chanced an inquiry about a massage. As it turned out, administration was the correct place to go for a massage booking… Usually.[223]

It came as not much of a surprise for Donald to learn that today was part of the 3-day monthly cycle inflicted upon people of Anna's persuasion… And due to the volatility of all emotional reactions towards her at this time of the month, any scheduling of massages had to be done directly with her. This was partially to certify the hirsute nature of her massage would be acceptable, and partially to obtain a signed waiver officially absolving SaRS of any, and every, responsibility if either matting or eating ensued.

Today continued along the path to becoming an unusual tradition.
- ✄ Timeslot booked…   Illegitimately, I'll be available in seven minutes.
- ✄ Waiver signed…   Illegibly, by "*Donald Halfbrain*"
- ✄ $Cash paid…   Illegally, Shhhhh!

Anna growled her approval, "You can go behind the red velvet curtain and change into the Allegedly one size fits all Disposable Dignitaries©,[224] cover the Dignitaries, and your dignity, with a towel and lie face down on the massage bed. I will be back in five minutes after I have had a quick Wolfsbane gargle.

---

[221] Which is Donald speak for, "I tripped over a long carpet strand, again."

[222] If he had thought about this at all, most of the people there were also in the SaRS (Sinking a Raft Ship) Temporary ~~Existence~~ Acquaintance.

[223] If you studied these tiny disappointments in any detail, you would notice that they are becoming increasingly prevalent for Donald's stay at SaRS.

[224] **Allegedly** - the brand name, and **Disposable Dignitaries** - the product. Allegedly produce some of the finest use-once-and-throw-away products. Including a range of environmentally unfriendly TDS (Two Dollar Store) PPEs (Pee-Pees, or more formally, Partial Protection Embellishments).

Donald assumed the Wolfsbane gargle comment was a euphemism for a good mood inducing mouth rinse and didn't concern himself with worrying a lot about it further. He had a much bigger issue to deal with.

On her way out Anna had activated the white noise water feature, and its main feature, at the moment, was making Donald want to pee. Obliging this urge, he made a mad dash to the patient convenience. Arriving just in time to avoid a great embarrassment, leaving himself with the greater possibility of a minor embarrassment of his own PPE (Post Pee Emission). Taking advantage of the waiting time to drip dry the drips, Donald dignified himself completely and proned himself on the massage bed.

Anna returned and commenced the pre-massage conversation…
- "Are there any particular areas I should concentrate on?"
- "How much pressure would you like (Soft, Medium, or Ouch)?"
- "Would you like me to cover you in baby oil or extra virgin olive oil?"

Donald's answers were:
- "No;"
- "Medium;" and
- "Sphincter Feng Shui… What?"

"Sorry, that was just me seeing if you were paying attention. Clearly, you are." Surreptitiously Anna put down the bottle in her hand on the condiment tray and picked up another from the accoutrement table.

Just 31.4 seconds into the massage Donald fell sound asleep.[225] Anna then displayed her professionalism by continuing the massage without switching oil or indulging her thought of eating Donald, not to mention that she completed the massage as requested in the appropriate timeframe, even though time has never been mentioned.

Obviously, Donald isn't going to recall anything remotely significant about the massage; as he was asleep… Duh…! So, we are going to be picking up the story just as Donald is about to be woken up…

Need more time?

Your session will expire in 1 seconds.
Would you like to continue the session?

Continue session

<Aaaaand… Action!>

---

[225] If Donald fell asleep in a forest everyone for miles around would hear.

Waking after the second nudge of a woman was not particularly unusual for Donald,[226] waking at the second nudge of a woman who wasn't annoyed, was. He relished the thought, until he made the link between relish and salad dressing, at which point he got up and then got dressed. The awkwardness of getting off the table with his dignity intact overshadowed the realisation, that during the massage he had somehow rolled onto his back without falling off the table or waking up. The towel also showed signs of movement, but as this observation wasn't on Donald's to-do list, he didn't.

Anna was standing crossed armed and happy eyed, with a thin grin akin to a Charlatan Wolf about to devour its prey, watching Donald as he struggled with his ineffectual efforts at trying to remain dignified. This was her favourite part of the massage session, as she always knew it was an unachievable task. She knew her laughing internally wasn't strictly professional, or conscionable, but it did always amuse her.

Once normal coverage had been resumed, Anna gave Donald an invitation to her semi-professional second job, Security for the Lunar Blood Moon Eclipse Halloween Wiccan gathering…

The event was escalating at a phenomenal rate… It now encompassed:

- True Histories of Halloween and the Eternal Dreaming;
- Halloween musical version of the Rocky saga; and now adding in
- Lunar Blood Moon Eclipse Halloween Wiccan gathering.

If only Donald could somehow influence Skit to become a teenage black agnostic pregnant divorced lesbian woman from space with a hidden criminal past and overt political ties, he would have the required ingredients to offend just about everyone on, or off, the planet. This is exactly what Donald thinks an unrestricted outdoor music festival would look like, given that it included everything from endorsed, through dubious, to probably illegal and on.

---

[226] Wondering about what would constitute usual was also not unusual.

Exiting the massage room Donald was careful to not step to the right this time, as that would be the direction of the gym,[227] and that was most definitely a tender swipe to the left sore spot for him. He didn't really want to deal with Ma'am Cybill Flex until he could decipher which of her different personalities, he was likely to run into… Ma'am Jackal or Mistress Guide. Either way, she was way too scary for Donald.

On the way back to his room Donald encountered the *un-ménage-à-trio*, and quickly noticed their group stability was definitely at *in* again. They were arguing without speaking to each other. The silence was figuratively deafening to Chunky who was being protected from the inaudible drama by a set of red doggy-eared-muffs. It didn't protect him from the visual visceral viciousness, which was going on, and you could almost see the tears in his eyes. He didn't like it when mummy and other mummy fought. Although he was quite looking forward to the next meal when they will probably start throwing food at each other. He did love himself a bit of floor buffet.

Donald shook most of their unrelenting spectacle off and continued along his own path of becoming an unusual addition to tradition. He was walking at a deliberate pace allowing himself the time to be on the lookout for the only other potentially anticipated interruption to his peace, Sven and his comments of a generally spiritual nature.[228]

Often, the best thing about friends is that they know you. But sometimes, it's the worst thing. It's hard to both love and hate someone dialectically, especially when it is the same reason to do both.

Once again Donald found himself shaking it off. Only this time, the *it* he was shaking off was the heebie-jeebies from the double dose of full-length fortune cookie information. Arriving safely back to his room,[229] he found a late addition to his bedside reading material, "How to record a more effective THOUGHT RECORD."

He read through the poorly presented, repetitively photocopied, barely legible, acronym filled single piece of paper and ridiculed it significantly before he put it into practice, by writing about another memory in the making.

---

[227] And not a very long jump to the left to encounter the horror of a pun.

[228] The trouble is… Sven's appearance isn't detectable until he speaks. It has gotten to the stage where Sven thinks "Oh, I didn't see you there…" is a common polite greeting, as opposed to being a common impolite meeting.

[229] This means he arrived, and mostly wanted to stay *alive* in this situation.

How to record a more effective
THOUGHT RECORD (TR)

Trigger	Where a bad memory starts, the second time
Hard	The hardest TRs make the most effective TRs
On Display	Every TR needs to be completely transparent
Understand	Don't record something you don't understand
Genuine	Be prepared to accept any positive outcomes
Honest	Record either an honest TR, or record no TR
Timeless	There are no deadlines, so you can just relax
Remember	Effective TRs do this. So, you don't have to
Everything	Include everything you don't want to forget
Catch It	As it happens, so every TR is always accurate
Obvious	What is obvious to you might not be to others
Reviewed	Have someone else read, and confirm, the TR
Details	Record as many details as you can remember
Help	What you are anticipating the TR to provide
Outcome	TBA – Record related events post initial TR
Where	Location of both digital and paper TR storage
2 Next	Go back out there, to discover your next TR

SaRS Official 6 – A more effective THOUGHT RECORD

more effective
CORD (TR)

mory starts, the second time
make the most effective TRs
to be completely transparent
ething you don't understand
ccept any positive outcomes
honest TR, or record no TR
dlines, so you can just relax

this… So you don't have to
rg you don't want to forget
every TR is always accurate
you might not be to others
se read, and confirm, the TR
details as you can remember

Help	What you are anticipating the TR to provide
Outcome	TBA – Record related events post initial TR
Where	Location of both digital and paper TR storage
2 Next	Go back out there, to discover your next TR

SaRS Official 6 – A more effective THOUGHT RECORD

Donald was actually quite impressed with himself when he completed his first TR. Not because it was particularly good or helpful; because it was there at all, considering the near illegibility of what he was working with. He also made a quite significant decision… He wasn't going to write any more TRs and was going to stick with his own brand of paddle memory.[230]

---

[230] Purely as a precaution just in case he ever found himself up *that* creek.

Donald recorded his first, and only, thought record about his most recent troubling uncomfortable experience... His post massage silent encounter with the *un-ménage-à-trio*...

Donald's Thought Record (TR) #1 (Number One)

Trigger	Hearing the silence from Owedebt, Nota and Chunky.
Hard	Dealing with anything that isn't all about me is hard.
On Display	Ummmmm, obviously...
Understand	I understood there was silence, and what silence is.
Genuine	I'm prepared to accept, but doubtful there will be any.
Honest	I think that TRs are stupid. (Too honest, too soon?)
Timeless	You know what you can do with your "just relax."
Remember	It is a bad memory... I will remember it forever.
Everything	What am I supposed to do if I do want to forget?
Catch It	Done...
Obvious	It is quite obvious that I think this process is redundant.
Reviewed	Unnecessary complication. Just believe me that it's correct.
Details	I am pretty sure we will hear about it in great detail soon.[231]
Help	Confirmation detailing the TR process belongs in that creek.
Outcome	Never to be TBA.
Where	Here...
2 Next	Hopefully to not experience any future Chunky floor buffets.

⌘ Extract from The Donald Diaries.[232]

---

[231] Oops... Spoiler alert. No, you won't be *hearing* about this drama soon. But you will be *reading* all about it very soon. Unless this is an audio book, in which case you might be hearing this at the end of the book, I'm not sure how the footnotes work in that format. I am, however, completely sure I will be impressed that an audio book was made. Who is reading it to you?

[232] Donald's Thought Record (TR) #1 (Number One) was retrieved from his personally deleted records, before they became his permanently deleted records. This isn't actually saying much, as Donald's paddle is configured to automatically send all the information to the cloud immediately once it has been created. And once it is out there, it becomes the truth. When Donald says his "head is in the clouds," this is what he actually means.

Chapter 9:
Intro-Intra-Inter SaRS
(The Mocking Games)

Donald woke up the next day[233] in the middle of a minor melancholy moment. Building the necessary courage, he wombled over to the lacklustre approximation of a lustrous reflection and stared deeply into the dark brown depths of his soul windows. He couldn't help his thinking there should be more to life than this...

"Everything we are being taught is generally all well and good, but:

- How do you tell the difference between stability and stagnation?
- What distinguishes a grin from a grimace?
- A sarcastic laugh sounds the same as a sardonic one.[234]

Shouldn't we be being taught how to avoid pain in our future, rather than letting *it* happen and then having to deal with the after *it* fallout? I don't want to COPE AHEAD... I would much rather EVADE AHEAD."

Donald will address this issue in due course, but for now...

Diverging from his ~~normal~~ customary style of documenting his days inside SaRS, i.e. chronologically, Donald decided to write about the next chapter of his DIS regard slightly differently. He was going to cover a newly intro-duced intra-hospital inter-ward event, which will occur over several days, in chunks of same-same competition instead of each particular daily waste of his time.

---

[233] Obviously, this waking up the next day notion isn't happening tomorrow, even though it will happen, and happen overnight, this next day concept is the tomorrow from yesterday.

[234] All right smarty pants, these two types of laughter probably do sound very similar to most people, but you know what I am trying to get at.

1) Introduction (Opening Ceremony)

"Welcome everyone! To the first, and likely the best, running of the annual *Saint Rita's Sanatorium* Mocking Games! Where it is our staunch desire to make your Mental Health a winner, by assisting you to make something resembling a complete mockery out of it![235] I had a dream last night... And it told me 'This will be a great success once the rest of the world knows what we are trying to achieve!' Never has such an elaborate absurdity taken place!"

This was the first time Donald had heard such absolute drivel. The reason partially attributed to this was due to it being the first time he had heard about the existence a SaRS assistant director, and the remainder of attribution went to the point that this was also the first time he had heard anything at all from George Notatallwell![236]

George Notatallwell! is the Assistant Director of *Saint Rita's Sanatorium*. His dissemination of dystopian disinformation isn't something he deigns to dwell on, discuss, or dignify by actually believing in it. He is the person near the head of an organisation who will simply take the most recent buzz words, add a few industry relevant details, to produce a speech riddled with exclamation points. All with the aim of gaining himself public attention, as he has a political career residing in the depths of his twisted little mind.[237]

> **Assistant Director – SaRS**
> George Notatallwell!! Unqualified
> I am The Authoriser for SaRS!
> And the most equal person here.

"I am very sure everyone will have a fantastic time, will learn a great many things and will be proud of their efforts afterwards! There is absolutely zero truth to the rumour disseminating regarding obligations... You will not be held accountable if you choose to not participate in the activities and consequently not contributing anything to either of those accomplishments."

George was well on the way to his passive aggressive political career.

---

[235] Donald was fairly sure he didn't need any help to make his mental health a complete mockery. All you have to do is take two half-mockeries and glue them together with some pretentious condescension.

[236] Donald just lost his Orwellian virginity three times in the one speech.

[237] I get the impression that Donald doesn't like middle management.

2) Preparation (Mise en Place)

After George's scepticism inducing introduction, he instructed Aaaron to reveal the secret components for the upcoming trials. Aaaron, utterly ticked off at George for reducing him to "some unnamed minion," reluctantly flipped the trusty SaRS whiteboard on, while he secretly, simultaneously and bitterly sourly flipped off George behind his back...[238]

Saint Rita's Sanatorium Mocking Games!

Prizes:

Everyone will get a "Thanks for Coming" certificate (siGns On Demand!)

Souvenirs will be awarded to first, second and third (Who Wood Masons)

- Artwork for both by Sue Rhea Liszt

Encouragement:

There will be an uplifting cookie for each category

- Read by Sven Teatwoo

Wellbeing:

Anna Lykeananna - on standby to administer *PRN* remedial massages.
Ma'am Cybill Flex - on standby to administer physical motivation.

SaRS Whiteboard 5 - Saint Rita's Sanatorium Mocking Games!

He also posted a sticky-note bill-of-fair-events:

- Sleeping
- Guess the What
- Excuseing
- Leaps of Faith
- Longest Continuous
- Synchronised
- Judging the Judges
- Results

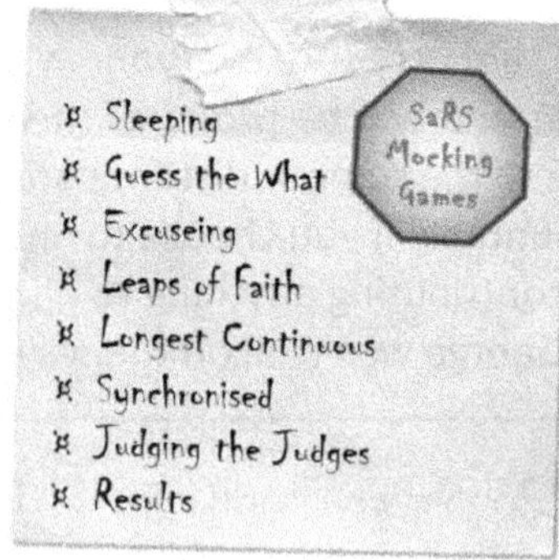

---

[238] Well, it's not so "secretly" now, is it?

Aaaron was only trying to be mindfully present in the moment but failed. He didn't remember the basics of being mindful; instead of noticing the thought and *letting go of it*, he noticed the thought and *chose to go with it*, instead.

3) Sleeping (Scoring System - SNORE)

Sound   - Ambient Sound type/level   (required difficulty multiplier)

Natural   - Unnatural sleeping agents are not allowed   (disqualification)

Orientation   - Multiple positions   (optional elements difficulty multiplier)

Restless   - Restlessness   (disqualification on 3 30sec restless periods)

Expression   - Judge's subjective expression; the performance satisfaction

Final Score   = Length (in time) of Sleep   (times the S, O and E modifiers)

This event is classified as a Marathon Effort.[239]

Each sleep competitor is randomly allocated an industry standard sensory deprivation tent from the available regulated supply, and the integrated white noise machine is configured with their personal requirements for the ambient sound modifier. This must be between the minimum *soothing waves level one*, through to the maximum *nuclear chainsaw level thirteen*.

While the length of the competitor's sleep period is the main contributing factor to the Final Score, the SOE modifiers make it possible for someone to be classified as the winner before the end of the event, due to the maximum allowed safe sleep period of three days.[240]

Apart from the potential scoring system disqualifications, there are other requirements which must be met prior to, or during, the competition:

- No birthday suits are allowed;
  A decent simple sleep smock must be worn as a minimum.
- No performance enhancing sleep regalia (e.g. sleep masks); and
  With the exception of a standard doctor prescribed CPAP machine.
- No professional sleepers.[241]
  Someone, who regularly avoids doing any work by falling asleep.
- The following sleeping positions are required to be displayed:
  - Burial   - Prone, Upward, Straight;
  - Foetal   - Prone, Sideward, Tuck;
  - Drunk   - Prone, Downward, Splayed.

---

[239] While this unfortunately generally eliminates your chances of being able to compete in any other events, you are still allowed to submit an entry form. The only caveat is: You must be fully awake for any subsequent events.

[240] Three days is the maximum allowed break from insanity before the legal regulations kick in and you are kicked out of SaRS for being too well.

[241] The only person this might effect is Mindy. However, as there is no way (in Hell) of enforcing the rule, she made us all aware that it wasn't a problem.

Sleeping isn't much of a spectator sport. And as the prime observational positions were taken by LB and the official Uber~Watch~Winders, Donald was disinclined to bother caring about the outcome. However, due to his complete obsession with completeness, he recorded the results for posterity:

"There was only one Sleeping entrant, Owedebt Dear, who 'accidentally' slipped into a sleep cocoon while she was 'apparently' trying to have a little personal time away from Nota Beenhead and Chunky Poopy. Although:

    ⚥   Her degree of difficulty was the minimum available;

    ⚥   She failed to perform two of the three required positions; and

    ⚥   The judge's score was woefully inadequately presented to the crowd...

She still won the event with a Final Score of 5.3. Officially recording the initial record time of 29.23 minutes, making this sleep session the shortest marathon effort in the recorded history of the Mocking Games."

Celebrate your Accidental Fortunes.[242]

4) Excuseing[243] (Scoring System - REALLY)

Realistic	- Judge's subjective opinion (1) realism of the excuse's delivery
Exaggeration	- Bigger is better (optional elements difficulty multiplier)
Awkward	- Judge's subjective opinion (2) subsequent excuse clumsiness
Lie	- Being caught in a proven blatant lie (disqualification)
Logical	- Judge's subjective opinion (3) logical argument behind excuse
Yes	- Excuse acceptance (disqualification on 3 falsehood starts)
Final Score	= Judge's combined opinion (1+2+3) (times the E modifier)

This event is classified as an Acceptability Contest.[244]

In the mandatory section of this competition each competitor is asked to deliver an excuse for a selection of three random traditional excuse concepts, and two further excuses for their own choice of concept. Once an excuse has been delivered, it is then verified for both its basic acceptance and its level of exaggeration. Following these validations of each verification, the opinionated scores are added together, and then exaggerated appropriately.

Because that is just how it has always been done...

---

[242] "Better late than never," doesn't work particularly well for motivation.

[243] "Excuseing" is the combined process of first coming up with an excuse prior to competition, and then delivering the excuse upon request.

[244] Excuseers (professional excuseingers) are acceptable in this contest... *Because* everyone at SaRS is otherwise significantly overqualified.

Reusing an excuse in the required section is acceptable, provided no other competitor has used the exact same excuse previously in the current contest. This gives a distinct advantage to an early competitor; however, they may dis this advantage unintentionally if they choose to use a clichéd excuse due to its low exaggeration value.

The judge's Realistic opinion of the excuse takes into consideration several components of the excuse delivery:[245]

- Speed — Time delay to start answering (not too early or too late);
- Length — Windedness of the excuse (not too short or too long); and
- Accuracy — Did the answer hit the sweet spot?

Traditional excuse concepts:[246]

- Absence of a deliverable (the dog ate my homework);
- Inadequate knowledge of a problem (nobody told me anything);
- Substandard products (I blame the new process/tool);
- Unforeseen delays (I am waiting for approval from my boss);
- Misunderstanding instructions (that isn't what I was told to do);
- Passing the buck (that was the warehouse assistant's fault);
- Assigning blame (they were the ones who suggested it).

Optional free choice excuse concept suggestions:

- Failing to identify someone (I haven't seen you with blonde hair);
- Overlooked invitation (it must have gotten lost in the mail);
- Butt dialling / Inappropriate text (my new phone is hard to use).

Any excuse is a good excuse for doing whatever you want.

Just about every competition ever held anywhere has resulted in a raft of excuses "explaining" why one someone didn't win. And those excuses become "better" the further back through the field you go. Appropriately, this event is quite different. The better the excuse is, the more likely a win is achievable.

It is also a visually spectacular distraction, where physical confrontations are not necessary to incite a primal reaction from the crowd. You also need to be intensely aware that all the results of this event are biased heavily towards the judges' own opinions... Meaning, the "crowd reaction" spectacle is just as important as the substantive elements of the excuses.

---

[245] *Multiple delivery attempts, for each excuse, are allowed... Because the rules say that you only add the best score to your competition tally.*

[246] *This list is by no means exhaustive. It's your fault if this is a problem.*

Donald started to take a moderate amount of interest in this competition when it denigrated, quite quickly, from a being a contest to becoming a closely fought heated argument between several, obviously experienced, excuseers. The "discussion" about "who started it" was particularly exciting. This single event lasted longer than the entire Sleeping marathon, which is a satisfactory indication it was a significantly good one.

"This was a benchmark setting contest, with several excellent candidates amongst the relatively average pool. Three entrants emerged from the dross and provided the spectators with copious competitive entertainment.[247] The 3rd and 2nd places were filled by Nota Beenhead and Got Knoted respectively.

"The winning Excuseing competitor, with a 'three solid traditional and two outrageous optional' splendid set of excuses, came from a very surprise entry, Owedebt Dear.[248] Her excuses in the traditional concept category were overly unremarkable, but her optional excuse concept choices were inspired:

- Why haven't you joined in the self-help zoom meeting yet?
  'I'm waiting for my 'puter to go booooop-oooooop-ooooopy-dooooo.'
- Why aren't you coming to wake for Nelo?
  'I'm preparing for a couple of odd things to happen at Halloween, and I don't know how to get out of volunteering for them...'[249]"

5) Leaps of Faith (Scoring System - DEAR GOD)

Demonstrable	- Judge's subjective opinion (1) Leap of Faith's demons' trouble	
Explanation	- Explanations required	(disqualification on 3 explanations)
Audience	- Zealousness of people being leaped at	(difficulty multiplier)
Repeatable	- Repeatability ≠ Leap of Faith	(pre contest Leap dismissal)
Generic	- Must be applicable to all Leaps	(required element penalty)
Overconfident	- Judge's subjective opinion (2) confidence in the Leap of Faith	
Denial	- Unrestrained Denial of your Leap of Faith	(disqualification)
Final Score	= Judge's combined opinion ((1+2)-G)	(times the A modifier)

This event is classified as a Trust Exercise.

---

[247] I'm not going to say, "It's interesting to note that these three competitors were all females." *because* it might be misconstrued without an explanation.

[248] Her Excuseing talent was never called into question, she was defined as an unexpected entrant after her unexpected participation in Sleeping. *Because* it was thought she would be too busy there to compete here.

[249] This was an extremely large risk, as she did very publicly actually go to the wake... *Because*, with great risk also comes a great score multiplier.

The Leap of Faith is a complementary competition to the Excuseing effort and is often described as the "Devil's Advocate Excuse." Rather than trying to convince people of a pre-identified cover-up, you are trying to convince those same people of the cover-up of a pre-identification.[250]

There is a largely contentious stipulation in the entry requirements of this contest, stating: "All ghosts have been involuntarily disqualified for being too qualified." The rationale behind this unusual disposition is that often a Leap of Faith is immediately preceded by a conversation ending with, "You've got your whole life ahead of you." Ghosts, having no life ahead of them, cannot morally participate.[251]

Each competitor has the onerous task of trying to convince the judges of a previously unknown fact or concept. Much like the back page of a "Where's Wonky" book, suggesting: "there is a Wonky in every picture inside the book, except for one." You can spend a lot of time looking for the absence of Wonky, but you cannot categorically state that Wonky either does, or does not, exist using the data of just one single page.

There are two sections of this event, the *Logical Practical* applications, and *Illogical Impractical* implications. You get to compete in both of these sections individually, and their combined score is tallied along the way.

Logical Practical applications:
- "Someone Call 000![252]" An instruction to a crowd of strangers you can nearly guarantee will happen without any further proof requirement.
- "We won't find a parking spot, so let's take the bus."
- "Wait, don't let go, help is on the way to save you!"

Illogical Impractical implications:
- "Someone get me a doughnut!" An order given to your colleagues that you can nearly guarantee will not happen.
- "Don't worry, we're sure to find a parking spot when we get there."
- "You can't be saved, so you may as well leap to your conclusion."

---

[250] I'm not entirely convinced I understand which side is which...

[251] This rationale is either a lie, "part of everyone's life is in the past;" or it is an aspersion, "you haven't lived yet." Both of these alternatives are, at best, ghostist; or completely anti-undead, at worst.

[252] That's what happens to 911 when you turn it upside-down down-under. **Note:** Putting 911 on the back of a Porsche was a convenient accident as it was several years later when it became the American emergency number.

This type of competition has sometimes been described as the three sides of the same coin theory: Religion, Psychology and Philosophy... Some of these, sometimes, are just a hotly (silent t) contested theory:

- **Psychology** (Heads) - where the silent P implication ends up sounding just like they are messing with your head;
- **Philosophy** (Tails/Tales) - where the Ph combination sounds like an F, twice, implying they are just messing with your head; and
- **Religion** (The Edge) - Landing on the edge of the coin is not as obvious as the others, but you just know they are messing with your head.

Do not seek those who will only love you, only seek those who you will love.

Donald gave Sven a quarter sideways squint look trying to understand the contextual nature of this cookie, and failed, but left it in the records as he felt encouragement shouldn't be discouraged.

"Another fantastic event,[253] showing the depths that this particular type of talent can sink to when trying to reach enlightenment. Trying to separate Mindy Ownbeeswhacks, Istha T. You and Got Knoted was a Herculean effort, but the Judges managed to come to an agreement on what the scores should be after Mindy explained what her inner Demon was capable of.

"Istha and her Leap of Faith, 'I believe Donald is real, and you should too,' and Got's 'I am an undercover reporter, who is posing as an undercover Police-woman, who is posing as an ex Eastern Bloc spy, and you should believe me as tkhkhkhkhkhat's knot ze khkhkhkhkhalf of eet.' both came a close second to Mindy and her Leap of 'Ouija... Just because you do not believe, and can't spell it, doesn't mean that it doesn't exist for other people.' Faith."

6) Guess the What (Scoring System - WHAT THE)

WHAT	-
HAT	-
AT	-
T	-

WHAT HAT AT T?
Space Hogging, I Think!

Time	- International Regular FIFA (First In, First Answer) Protocol
How's	- How's the accuracy? (Value is approaching disqualification)
Entertaining	- Judge's subjective opinion of the reply's Entertainment Value
Final Score	= Judge's opinion (times the reverse inverted H modifier)

This event is classified as an Exercise in Futility.

---

[253] I'm fairly sure Donald didn't mean this literally, but he does have a habit of tossing words like absurd, crazy, weird, insane, ludicrous, etc... around.

This is a very simple educated guessing game. It isn't even important, or complex, enough to call a competition. They don't even present medals in this category. The "winner" receives a Black & White photocopy, of a colour print, of a photo taken on a phone, of a medal's design instructions written in pencil. On the plus side, it is signed by Sue Rhea Liszt (using her left hand).

The categories of questions are all SaRS Patient related:
ж   Physical Attributes (Age, Height, Blood Pressure…)
     Mindy is disqualified for having too many un-recordable statistics.
ж   Mental Deficiencies (Diagnosed Disorder, Medication…)
ж   Who Comes Next (Skit's Personality, Lost's Visitor…)?
ж   Chemical (Blood Type, Urine Colour, Stain Composition…)

To be a contestant you **must not give or take**, any physical part in the contest.

"I won." And that's all he wrote…

7) Longest Continuous (Scoring System - GROSS)

Grandkids   - Judge's subjective opinion (will they tell their grandchildren)
Repeatable   - Repeatability = Longest Continuous   (measure x2, cringe x1)
Observable   - No hidden performance improvements   (disqualification)
Stable   - Measurement held for 15.3sec   (disqualification on 3 fails)
Safe   - The last and least important requirement   (disqualification)
Final Score   = Measurement[254]   (times the G modifier)

This event is classified as a Gross Exercise.
Another simple explanation, of a most completely disgusting competition, is not available at this moment, as Donald is somewhere between indisposed and in flagrante delicto.
This content is understandably-unavailable, unnecessarily-uncivilised and undeniably-undesirable, while being completely uncouth.

To be a contestant you **must give and take** some physical part in the contest.

"I lost." And that's all he wrote…

---

[254] The Final Score Measurement is calculated as the average of at least two individual competition Repeatable Measurements. (2 x ½ of the result) Measurements used range from what you would expect (length, amount…) right through to a most bewildering (hang time, consistency, splash volume…)

8) Synchronised (Scoring System - CONNECT)

Creativity   - Judge's subjective opinion (1) Synchronicity of its Creativity
Originality   - Judge's subjective opinion (2) Synchronicity of its Originality
Nomaly **A**   - Type A must be the same as Type B   (is not a conundrum)
Nomaly **B**   - Type B must not be the same as Type A   (is a conundrum)
Ecnedicnioc   - No Reverse Engineered coincidences   (disqualification)
Coincidence   - Engineered coincidences are not eligible   (disqualification)
Tricky   - Scale: 1 = Hmmmmm to 13 = Wooooow   (difficulty multiplier)
Final Score   = Synchronised Judge's opinion (1+2)   (times the T modifier)

This event is classified as a Bi-Product of two Event Participants.

What started out as the most normal looking event quickly degraded, as it always does,[255] to just plain weird.[256] This was purely a binary sensory event. How the synchronisation was delivered, as well as what it looked and sounded like were the judged factors. The actual content wasn't judged and, therefore, didn't need to make sense.

There are two variations of Synchronised: simultaneous; and substituting sequential. Simultaneous is the more easily judged of the two variants, as the competitors are aiming to be duplicitous exact duplicates; whereas the sub-sequential performances require the competitors to be interlocking cognitive singularities. Historical texts sometimes will note there was a third variation possible, which was simply a concatenation combination of the other two. This was known as an echo performance, but the lack of popularity saw this type of Synchronised fade away into oblivion, or nothingness, depending on belief.

Donald was aware of several promising examples from last week and held a forlorn hope something similar would be repeated now.

Simultaneous:

- Grey and Aaaron performed an incredulous reaction with incredible synchronicity, and they would have been a very competitive entry had employees been allowed to enter;
- Donald (himself) and Dr Hill completed a synchronised epiphany, and this too would have been an interesting, albeit short, entry if Skit had been available for an encore; and
- Seth and BLT executed a scripted synchronised soliloquy. Due to BLT's un-classification as an ex-employee, they were also ineligible to enter.

---

[255] I'm not sure why everything has to be always, never, completely, slightly, often, rarely, ... But it is; often slightly rarely, if not always completely never.

[256] Plain Weird... Now, that's an oxymoron if ever I saw one.

Substituting Sequential:
- ꭙ Houts and Dr Jay delivered a sub-sequential synchronised summing up with a final simultaneous exclamation. Strictly speaking, this crossover entry wouldn't have been permitted even if their employment status hadn't already ruled them out.

Be accurately together, but if you cannot be accurately, be cognizant.

Donald summed up *Synchronised* as best as he was able, utilising a blue visual aid and the often standard "you are only allowed to choose two" concept...
From the following groups of three, you may choose only two at a time:
- ꭙ Health, Wealth and Happiness;
- ꭙ Quickly, Correctly and Cheaply; and
- ꭙ Fast, Safe and Within Budget.

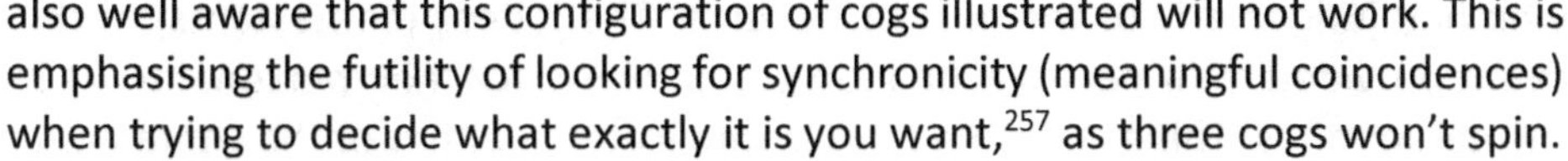

It is important to note that money is a factor in every set of choices. Donald is also well aware that this configuration of cogs illustrated will not work. This is emphasising the futility of looking for synchronicity (meaningful coincidences) when trying to decide what exactly it is you want,[257] as three cogs won't spin.
Anyway... Back to the matters at hand...

"There were no winners, just some fine examples of what not to do...
- ꭙ Istha T. You and Lost M'Hankie teamed up and had a marvellous[258] try at the competing in the Substituting Sequential variation... Lost would start a conversation with someone he had forgotten, and hand over to Istha who would continue the conversation, in her head, with who she thought Lost had forgotten... It looked like Lost was talking to a figment of Istha's imagination, which is exactly what it was.
- ꭙ For the Simultaneous side, Owedebt Dear and Nota Beenhead tried to recite the alphabet backwards. They didn't get past Z, as they weren't able to come to a consensus on pronunciation... Zee or Zed."

---

[257] "But how does any of this relate to *Synchronised?*" you ask. It doesn't. I just thought it was an appropriate time to add a diagram as the last one was about ten pages ago... And don't call me "But."

[258] Donald wanted me to remind you that *marvellous* doesn't mean *good.*

It was at this precise point in time, when Donald realised the futility of life, the universe and everything. He forced himself to finish documentaling these games, mostly without any residual harmless panicking…

9) Judging the Judges (Scoring System - TWO FACE)

Truthful	- Contestant's opinion (1)	of the Judge's	Truthfulness
Worthy	- Contestant's opinion (2)	of the Judge's	Worthiness
Open	- Contestant's opinion (3)	of the Judge's	Openness
Frank	- Contestant's opinion (4)	of the Judge's	Frankness
Authentic	- Contestant's opinion (5)	of the Judge's	Authenticity
Candid	- Contestant's opinion (6)	of the Judge's	Candidness
Earnest	- Contestant's opinion (7)	of the Judge's	Earnestness
Final Score	= Contestant's combined opinion (minus the extreme opinions)		

This event is classified as a Popularity Contest.

This is not so much a competition, as it is a thinly disguised predetermined reverse witch hunt. The most evident struggle concerning the contestants was making sure the Judges didn't find out who scored who what. The less obvious struggle was making sure the Judges finished in the correct order.

The front of the score cards for this event listed each contestant (judge) who had judged any of the previous events. The judges (contestants) of this event provided their personal opinion in this event, for their personal score in the earlier ones. Things became more complicated if either of the contestants or the judges had performed previously in multiple events.

See there are three kinds of people: winners, losers, and judges.

The back of the score cards listed the correct finishing order of the judges.
1st - DD scored ten out of ten.
2nd - Irrelevant.

Donald didn't dignify this event by recording the summary information.[259] He did write a small addendum entry later, however, about the entire games: "This whole competition was a complete mockery of any definition of fair that I can think of. This shouldn't have come as a complete surprise though; it is in the title after all - Saint Rita's Sanatorium *Mocking* Games!"

---

[259] At the next opportunity Donald is going to record a protest about the results of this event, and how he thinks the judges (contestants) might have been intimidated into providing the correct result, and that Sven might also have been complicit with his motivation cookie.

10) Gift-Shop (Medal Presentation)

George, who was inconspicuous during most of the games,[260] was reading off a hastily prepared, badly photocopied, sheet of paper…

Saint Rita's Sanatorium
Mocking Games! – SCORE!

EVENT	RESULT		
Sleeping	1st	Owedebt Dear	
Excuseing	1st	Owedebt Dear	
	2nd	Nota Beenhead	
	3rd	Got Knoted	
Leaps of Faith	1st	Mindy Ownbeeswhacks	
	2nd	Istha T. You	
	=	Got Knoted	
Guess the What	1st	Donald Halfbrain	
Longest Continuous	Last	Donald Halfbrain	
Synchronised	---		
Judging the Judges	1st	DD	
	2nd	Meh…	

SaRS Official 7 – SaRS Mocking Games! – SCORE!

---

[260] Like all good (bad?) politicians in the making, George was present only when he was being presented with, or was presenting, something important. He won't make that mistake again by being here next time.

In what turned out to be a very short amount of time everyone who was anyone was presented with their appropriate prize.[261] Once the formalities of the gift shop section had been completed, George moved onto his final task.

11) Outroduction (Closing Ceremony)

"Welcome everyone! To the end of the first, and what was likely the best, running of the annual Saint Rita's Sanatorium Mocking Games! Obviously, you all will agree with me when I say, Mental Health was the undisputed winner!

"If I was to rate the success of these games on a scale of one to ten, where one would be the backyard cricket match played every year by my semi-drunk relatives-in-law during our annual boxing day revelries, and ten is something ten times better, this event would easily score a thirteen."

This was the second time Donald had heard such absolute drivel. It also highlighted the ex-inconspicuous nature of George's attendance, otherwise he might have observed some of the oblivious continuous debacle, strong-arming techniques and complete pointlessness of the event.

"Next year we are going to investigate the feasibility of relaxing the entry requirements to allow groups of both medical and non-medical staff members to compete in teams of similar occupations. Contractors and personifications will be considered as well. We will also be outsourcing the judging, possibly to the Uber ~~██~~ Watch ~~██~~ Winders.

"I would like to finish by thanking everyone involved, competitors, judges, me. And, I now declare this, the first running of the annual Saint Rita's Sanatorium Mocking Games... Closed."

Donald paused before leaving, and looked back over the rules, results and ridiculousness... to summarise...

"How did this style of documenting diverge from chronologically?"

"You may now go."

---

[261] Meaning, DD was presented with her "Judging the Judges" 1st place, as this was the only Souvenir produced before the limited budget ran out.

Chapter 10:
Everything Changed
(Back to Normal)

After those past few days of oddity culminating in an unconventional foray into competition, and still reeling from their attempt to teach him some cooking skills, Donald is pleased to admit that his things were about to go back to normal...

Ma'am Cybill Flex entered the group room at exactly nine o'clock, counted heads, scribbled something in her notebook, then closed and locked the door. She turned to face the group members,[262] melodramatically thwacked her left thigh with a red hooded riding crop to gain their attention,[263] and said, "Firstly, as everything has been working so blissfully smoothly over the past few days, we have made the difficult decision to discard the group schedule entirely."

She didn't explain who the members of this particular we were, "This will enable us to become more attuned to your specific needs, and likely prepare you better for any confusion in the natural state of the world at large." Neither did she explain who the members of this particular us were, but it's a safe bet there was a significant overlap with the earlier we.

"Today, in place of the scheduled psychological activity, we will instead be holding physiological auditions for the upcoming SaRS musical, *A Rocky Horror Musical*. We will soon be joined by some of the behind-the-scenes production staff and, hopefully, a few of the other patients after they have arrived late. I think you will find it exhilarating."

---

[262] Which, as she counted, seemed to be on the less side of more or less.

[263] This wasn't anywhere near necessary, as everyone in the smallish group was already staring fixatedly at her and wondering what her riding crop was.

Donald was no longer pleased.[264]

Ma'am Cybill Flex[265] unlocked and unclosed the door. As she ushered the waiting mob in, she further continued with her instructional speech, "Willy will while away most of today's lesson with some musical music instruction, while I go and attend to an important task somewhere else."
Willy came in panting; he was clearly exhausted, but apparently unclear as to what he was doing here. "I'm here… I'm here… I'm here… Now, why don't you tell me what I am doing here?" Deftly dodging the immediate look of "**I'll show you if you aren't careful**" cast his way.
"What you will be *doing here* today, William, is having the first of several warmup session for the selection of the Rocky Horror Musical participants. If you need the session to have a name, might I suggest something like normal-practice?" With an exaggerated feeling of subliminal suggestion, Ma'am Cybill Flex left behind the thought that this was anything but normal.

Don't be too quick to judge, or jump onto, that man-threat's musical band wagon.

Willy cast his eyes over the potential cast members and resigned himself to the next few hours of conducting arduous musical instructions. He hadn't had much prior experience with this particular nuance of these SaRS patients, with the exception of Donald, so his levels of expectation were set at a limbo record breaking height. The trickle of patients arriving dwindled to a drought, so Willy commenced the proceedings.
"Could everyone please introduce yourself to the group, and tell me a little tale about your musical background? Anything related to singing and dancing, acting, playing an instrument, or even how you think you came to be included in this conversation. Donald, would you mind kicking us off please, as I know some of your answer already and I'm not afraid to use it…[266]"

Donald listed his two past participle participations in high school musicals, "I have previously been a Pirate Policeman from Penzance and a Cowboy from Oklahoma. I have also been known to sing and dance vicariously through my two daughters. But, my highest level of instrument ability is generally limited to one *of-agreement*, or the other *of-war*."

---

[264] You can almost taste the future… Donald went on to be **dis**pleased.

[265] Donald was going to need a lot more interaction with Ma'am Cybill Flex before he can even think about referring to her by any truncated nickname.

[266] This request rapidly deteriorated into the projected musical instruction.

As with most of his answers, Donald had only addressed what he thought the person of question didn't know, and therefore wanted to. Strangely, in this particular instance, his answer was unconditionally correct. He also contained the uneasiness building inside him, after being arduously musically instructed, for later use in a less appropriate circumstance.[267]

In another surprise appearance, Skit introduced himself to Willy as, "Old Black Eyes here… I am surprised you didn't recognise me. After all, I *am* one of Australia's sung heroes. I have performed in many actual musicals; had a music career which was unique to me;[268] and even starred in my own TV series where I was cast as an ageing rock star."

Willy has been present for, or participated in, several experiences of Skit's VIPs (Vaguely Interesting Personalities), and he vaguely remembers him from variously famous singer/actors such as:

¤	Hugh Jackman	- Les Misérables
¤	Jack Black	- The School of Rock
¤	John Travolta/Olivia Newton-John	- Grease[269]
¤	Julie Andrews	- The Sound of Music

Who are also, incidentally, all members of the same **J** club as **Jon**.

"I found my fish! Unfortunately, I left it with my stringy thingy."

Owedebt had just earned herself another "Dozy Doe!" from Donald. He hadn't understood most of what she had been rambling on about last week, and he most definitely didn't want to start understanding her now…

"That's some great news Owedebt, and I'm sure it will come in very handy when you need to twist those thumb screws again."

Willy had just earned himself his first "Pasta Dude!" from Donald, who was curiously thinking, "There seems to be quite an extraordinary amount of extra crazy people around today…"

The remainder of the introductions proceeded exactly as what would be expected from a group of people suffering from their diverse mental illnesses. Slowly to start, meandering to middle, and fleetingly to finish. And of course, nobody else had anything musically exciting of note in their background.

---

[267] Donald is quite the oxymoron. He doesn't like it when he is told what to do when he hasn't asked for direction; alternatively, he expects others to tell him what to do without him having to ask for help. I am also confused by this.

[268] Obviously… I don't understand why people think unique = good.

[269] This has been Skit's only multiple personality personality thus far.

Arriving on the fly, following Ma'am Cybill Flex's invitational order, Willy was unprepared to perform his standard set, "Music with an encore of Lyric Writing (with William the piano man)," having left all of his instruments mid-play behind in the music room. This didn't deter him significantly as he would normally just make things up as he went. He was familiar with the concept, "There are no wrong notes, just as long as they are black," but didn't like to colourfully profile the piano keys. This was particularly relevant when it was always the white keys that didn't play well with others... Causing discord.

Diving into the six-foot-deep end of his unknown, Willy took advantage of Jon's current personality to answer one of his most pressing confusions... "Jon, perhaps you would be kind enough to explain to me, in English, why your song *Six Ribbons* only specifies five colours?[270]"

"Six Ribbons! Why is everyone so infatuated about the number of colours? You should really already know the answer to this, being a fellow musician and all. There have been several answers over the years...

- My love had two **Green** eyes, so there are two **Green** ribbons;
- We secretly put two **Red** ribbons on the inside of the CD cover, so the only people who knew the answer were the fans;
- The sixth ribbon is **Purple** in honour of the pirate king.

But the truth of the matter is far simpler, and far less poetic... It is because I am a musician, and I can only count to four."

Donald could hear Effie just out-side of his mind, "How Embarrassment!" "Well, that was unexpected." was Willy's politically correct cover version.

Gathering his thoughts, and weeding out the more intrusive ones, Willy got on with the proceedings, "For this exercise, I would like you to break off into groups

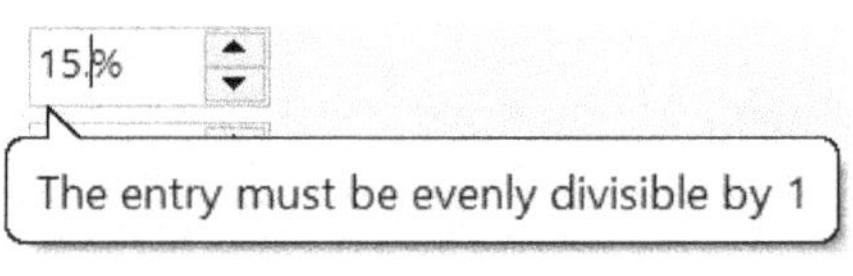

that are evenly divisible by one[271] and write me a song. You don't have to sing; but along with your song you should include a short paragraph explaining why the particular words resonated with you."

There was much disturbance in force as everyone started faffing around looking for something to write with, on and about.

---

[270] This is a legitimate question, and the lyrics have always confounded me... "Yellow & Brown, Blue as the sky, Red as my blood, Green as your eyes."

[271] As you can see above... It is a genuine concept according to Microsoft.

While the crowd of patients[272] are busy with the task at hand, I have a pair of non-ironic non-obvious observable things for you to ponder...

1) Bushfire Danger signs:

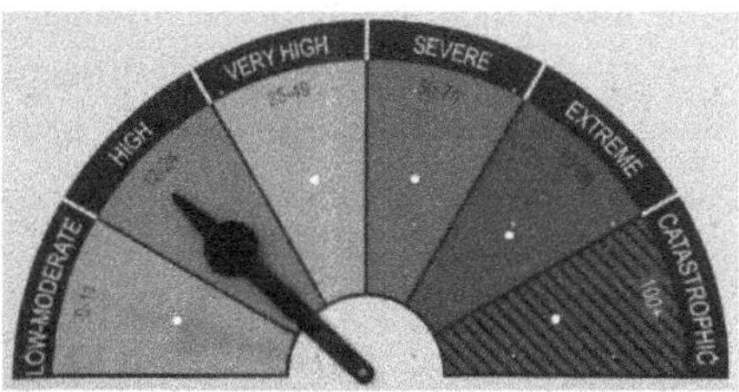

The colourful signs show six ratings: LOW-MODERATE up to CATASTROPHIC. The arrow points to the present level of bushfire risk. A high rating means a more dangerous fire... But what about:

- ✗ LOW-MODERATE - Starts at 0, so it should be NO-MODERATE.
- ✗ HIGH - Is BLUE? To me, blue means water, and water is less flammable than green grass, so these two colours should be switched. This would also bring it into line with the reversed standard rainbow colours.
- ✗ VERY HIGH / SEVERE - are essentially the same warnings, but bigger. *Can* is replaced by *May*, *May* is replaced by *Will*, and *Could* is replaced by *Expect*. Except, don't expect a fire truck to attend when it is severe.
- ✗ EXTREME - Too late, everything is bad.
- ✗ CATASTROPHIC - The sign is ON FIRE! And 100+ indicates there is more than a 100% chance of bushfire.

What I would like to know, why bother having a catastrophic option, and who gets the job of walking into an apocalypse to add 1% to the notification?

2) DVD Language Selection:

Can anyone tell me the problem here? →
Exactly! You must be able to read English to select the right language you want to read and hear!

Or let me put it another way...

Which one of these four language names do you think says English? ↓

الإنكليزية الإسبانية الفرنسية الماندرين

---

272 What is the collective noun for a group of mental patients?

- ✗ A padded-room-full, A straight jacket group, A mentality;
- ✗ An institution, A facility, An asylum, A shelter, A discarded;
- ✗ A permanent/temporary/life-time/involuntary commitment;
- ✗ A psychological/psychiatrical/psycho/psyche analysis;
- ✗ An uncontrolled population, A non-standard deviation;
- ✗ A quite special, An interesting, A broken, A unique;

"Alright everyone… Let's hear what you have written." The plan was to get everyone to read their writing to the rest of the group, and then they would have a discussion about what it means, how music might be applied and how they could use it to achieve some mental stability.

Owedebt immediately shot her hand into the air, and trying to not sound anxious she dialled herself down to an eleven, "Oo, oo, oo… pick me, pick me, pick me…"

As no one else had even moved, Willy foolishly chose Owedebt.

Pleased with herself and her selection, "I have written an OCD poem."

Concerned that Owedebt didn't understand what OCD meant, or how the concept of obsession might be triggering to the other patients, Willy asked her to pass it to him for a quick look before she read it out…[273]

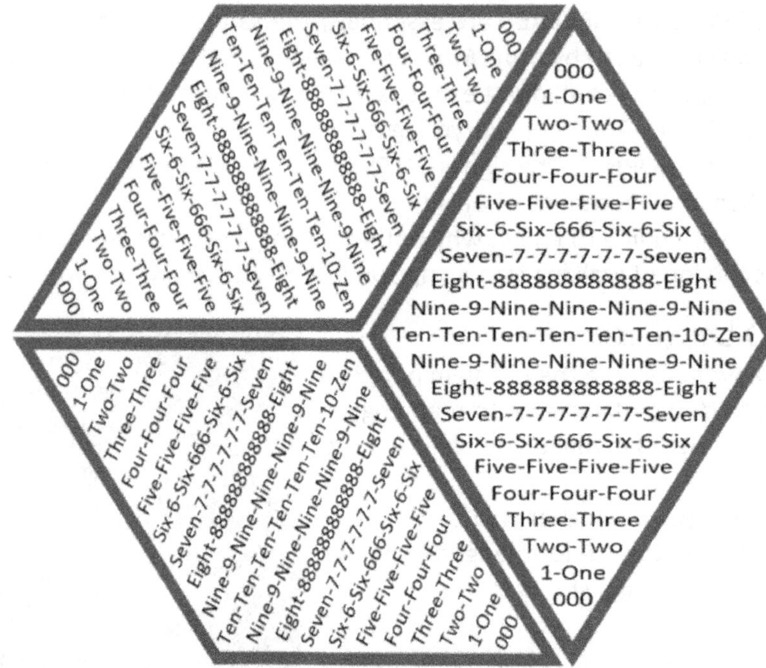

Willy, once he recovered enough of his sanity after this initial aggravation to several aspects of normal, trepidatiously asked Owedebt to talk about what the poem meant to her. His actual word was, "Huh?"

"Well… I like big diamonds; little numbers; and pretty square patterns. So, I put them all together to see what I could make."

---

[273] Yes, we all know what it means… What Owedebt thought it meant was, Owedebt's Clever Diamond poem. As it physically hurt Willy to read it to himself there was no way Owedebt was going to be allowed to read it aloud.

Donald caught a brief glimpse of it as it was passed to Willy and was quite impressed that Owedebt had suitably included the 000-emergency number at both ends of the poem, marking the places furthest away from Zen. He also wondered how she was able to create a cubism style work of art with no more than pencil, paper and spit.

Further discussion of Owedebt's poem was brief...
- "We should not call it a poem, when there's no structure or rhyme;"
- "That's not necessarily a requirement, but I'd call it prose at best;"
- "Maybe we could try calling it art-pop,[274] that's close enough for me."

Next up to the Chopin' block was Jon. Willy, of course, had heard much of the gossip[275] surrounding the Vamp incident, and was rightly hesitant to invite an unstable personality to share their thoughts... Hi immediately un-regretted this thought when Jon produced an appropriately inspired set of lyrics, based on another Australian owned member of the J club.

Re: I Hate Depression (Inspired by *I Hate the Music* – John Paul Young) p276
- Extract from The Donald Diaries.

Every-single-person in the room could relate to some of the mental illness images expressed. The conversation continued for enough time for Donald to really enjoy the comfort break at the end.

Everyone there, including Willy, told their own personal stories of where they had to wear a metaphorical mask to fit in and be noticed, or conversely, to be not noticed while having a fit. They also agreed that a lot of the everyone elses, who weren't there and didn't want to know you, often treated mental patients with varying levels of "I don't believe you."

Apart from the poignant meaningful messages extracted from the actual words, Donald was also completely star struck by the neat arrangement of the visual lines, and how each stanza displayed a palpable image of relevant slang hand expression:
- Pinkie Swear;
- Middle Finger;
- Peace Man;
- Rock On.

He wondered if Jon had done this on purpose. If he had done so, that was amazing. If not, it was truly amazing.

---

[274] Another Really Terrible Piece of Owedebt's Poetry. This acronym is an unnecessarily harsh, and uneducated, critique of what was essentially a multiple sense stimulating three-dimensional doodle pop art creation.

[275] Most of these stories included trace amounts of truth and fact.

Continuing around the circle of *it's your turn now*, Karl ~~ironically~~ unusually had some input. It was a poem about the ~~ironic~~ alternate views of what was happening in his mind.

I didn't stop listening...   I just stopped hearing...
I didn't stop looking...   I just stopped seeing...
I didn't stop feeling...   I just stopped touching...
I didn't stop eating...   I just stopped tasting...
I didn't stop smelling...   I just stopped breathing...

There was a deep, dark, sombreness about the ode Karl had just read. Not only for its lack of taste, that most forgotten of our senses, but for the ending which literally implied a physical death, rather than physically implying a literal death. Willy wrote himself a reminder to check in with Karl later, just to make sure he wouldn't have to go and check out a late Karl.[276]

Donald thought that he might ~~plagiarise~~ gain some inspiration from Karl's ode and write something which could be titled, "I didn't really stop thinking... I just stopped all understanding..." Shortly after this thought Donald noticed, while everyone was discussing Karl, Karl himself was taking an obvious interest in the conversation. His own similar behaviour usually resulted in comments of the "it's not all about you," nature.[277]

While Donald was spending this time lost ~~up~~ in himself, the other patients were providing Karl with some much-required support, even though it was all exaggerated and condescending sounding support...

- "I can so relate to those beautifully sad sentiments;"
- "That has to be the most exquisite thing I have ever heard;"
- "I don't understand what any of it means, but I love it;" and succinctly
- "Wow."

To me it sounded like the sound of a bell ringing backwards.

And with that hanging in the air, Willy called a halt to the practice session. "When we come back after lunch, we will start again with Nota's effort."

Nota, not having completely grown up yet was still only five foot nothing on tippy toes,[278] had an enormous advantage over the adult population... She had the ability to embrace her inner immaturity.

---

[276] Even this small effort is to be praised. It doesn't matter that Willy will willingly reap his own benefit from this wilful act... The praise is still deserved.

[277] And it is no surprise Donald would always wonder why it was so...

[278] This was better than her usual one foot something on tipsy toes.

"Welcome back… And over to you Nota."

Donald felt as if the lunch break hadn't happened, such was the superbly smooth transition facilitated by Willy.

"I have composed a totes awesome Christmas thingy…"

In my past there was this one Christmas tree
Though there was nothing underneath for me
I used to love that little Christmas tree

Hanging up the decorations, and sending out the Christmas cards
Waiting for manifestations of the Christmas carolling bards

    Last year there wasn't any Christmas tree
    Still, there was nothing underneath for me
    Where did it go, that little Christmas tree?

    Hanging up no decorations, and sending out no Christmas cards
    There was no manifestation of those Christmas carolling bards

        Soon there will be another Christmas tree
        I will put something underneath for me
        And I will love my little Christmas tree

        Hanging up my decorations and sending out my Christmas cards
        I'll sing with manifestations of all Christmas carolling bards

This showed a previously unknown side of Nota: how she had an unhappy childhood, yet she would still enjoy the pomp and ceremony of the Christmas festivities; through to her current situation of *hitting bottom* and not knowing what she should do; and finishing with an upbeat understanding of what will be waiting for her once she recovers.[279]

Unlike the previous couple of shares, Willy had to poke the collective bear to get them to respond. "C'mon, I'm sure someone has something to add…"

There was a low murmuring of embarrassment accompanying everyone's discomfort. Apparently, this version of everyone was markedly dissimilar to the previous everyone from Jon's earlier share. Indeed, you might say they shared more in common to that aversion from everyone else.

---

[279] Donald felt extremely disappointed in himself for not seeing this side of Nota sooner. He also began to think that this "writing down your thoughts" concept, may actually be a valid part of the journey to becoming "well."

Wanting things to keep tick-toking along smoothly, Willy called on Donald to share what he had written.[280] "I am sure we would all like to hear from you, about your innermost thoughts."

The introduction Donald heard was more like, "I am sure we would all like to leave, so, as usual, we are waiting for Donald to spit it out..."

"All right... I call this little ode: *It's Just Poetry Emotion*"

<u>It's Just Poetry Emotion</u>

If it creates a morbid thought or two
Melancholy, sullen, angry or dark
Doing what it was created to do
Get in line or you'll be missing the mark
Sometimes there might be a little of joy
Exultation, rapture, gladness or thrill
Developing this magnificent ploy
This is how I'm bending you to my will

  It's just poetry emotion, my significant devotion
  Sentiment living on a page
  Show poetic aberration, a dilettante affectation
  Manipulate resultant sage

   Should it be hunger you are looking for
   Aspiration, desire, willing or need
   Elevating your eyes up off the floor
   All my instructions are for you to heed
   And if it turns to start thinking respect
   Veneration, regard, esteem or pride
   There is no else you might have me expect
   Get on and enjoy the wild Donald ride

    It's just poetry emotion, radical verbal commotion
    Extracted by poetry mine
    Satisfying not a question, it's suitably an obsession
    And believe me... I have the time...

---

[280] This had much more to do with covering up everyone's embarrassment and the ominous silence that ensued, as opposed to him wanting to include Donald in the conversation, than Willy would like to think.

After Donald was finished reading his "little ode," *It's Just Poetry Emotion*, there was stunned silence.

.

.

. <**Chirp...** Chirp... Chirp...>

.

.

It was similar to the chirping generated by Seymour and Stu; however, this time Donald was on the receiving end waiting for someone else's speaking to ensue. He didn't have to wait longer than three chirps...

"That was incredible..." Willy was quick to acknowledge that his teaching had brought something special out ~~of~~ ~~from~~ ~~in~~ of-from-in Donald.[281] "Can you tell us what it means, and why it speaks to you?"

Donald thought about this later, coming up with something creative about how writing was just a short observation bridge between living and listening. And how this creative bridge:

- ☒ Gives you different observations from either side;
- ☒ Can be traversed as many times as required; and usually
- ☒ Without having to pay the troll who inevitably lives underneath.

All you really have to do is pay attention to every detail of everything that is going on around you, then try and think about it from several points of view and finally, write down what you see. Let your imagination off the rope, listen to what the words are telling you and eventually you will be able to tease the hidden piece of poetry out of those words.

Once you have the foundation written, add in the rhyming and the metre and arrange the general concepts into a flowing masterpiece. Break some of the rules, give it a touch of your personal style and mush it all together.[282]

But for now, all he had was, "It means what it says, obviously."
Not satisfied with this answer, Willy opened up the floor for comments.

---

[281] Willy was confused about a great many things generally, and this is not an exception. Not only was he not responsible for Donald's imagination, but he also didn't know if he had brought it out *of*, *from*, or *in* Donald, and that's not something you want to get wrong on the incident report...

[282] This later thought will be cut short by some other observation Donald pays attention to, making him forget what he is currently thinking about and having to hurriedly finish without attending to the details. It exemplifies the importance of writing every thought down before the next one intrudes.

Theme = The me. You internalise a look to find your masterpiece's theme space.

Donald quickly made a copy of this cookie from Sven, to include later when he thought about what he should have said.[283]

Lost was about to offer his insightful thoughts about Donald's poem when Pledge, Jimmy Pledge suavely entered the room and saved him the trouble... <Clap><Clap><Clap><Clap><Clap>
"What a fantashtic performanshe! I alsho have written shome memorable poetry with help from the *Word Changer* used in *Cubic Zirconias are For Never*. I particularly like how you have written the chorush in a shemi repetitive form. It makesh it sho much shimpler to fill out the page, kudosh. But you have not included a bridge... Thish ish what I shuggesht..."

Poetry Emotions are real
Existing to tease out the feel
Poetry Emotions don't lie
Offering only sanctify

Thirteen, predominantly clammy, seconds later Pledge, Jimmy Pledge was gone, and Willy was left hanging. He had been unable to get his words to ask, "Who the pianoforte are you?" in time. The upshot of his speech delay was, he didn't have to sit through another umbrella moment.[284]
Lost reiterated, "What he said."

In a phenomenally rare coherent moment for any SaRSaparillan, Owedebt offered to accompany Donald and help write some musical accompaniment for his poem, as she had found her fish and was desperate to see if it would still work.
Donald didn't waste this opportunity to ask Owedebt what the abyss she was talking about, and how does finding your fish help you do anything except to get rid of an odour which doesn't smell quite as bad as a rotten fish.
"It's simple dimple pimple... Guitar Tuner → Tuner → Tuna → Fish."

---

[283] Unfortunately, he wrote this on a loose piece of paper, and will leave it behind in the group room when they finish talking about what he will think about. I hope you are all following this, because I am... Oh look, a distraction.

[284] Donald noted a pronunciation dryness from Pledge, Jimmy Pledge while he was singing, and wondered if, like with accents and stutters, singing was the great equaliser of all speech impediments.

Donald took offence at being called Dimple Pimple, and said, "Thank you all the same, but I think I would prefer to confuse myself. And I think I'll know what I'm listening for when I hear it."

Owedebt became confused at being called All The Same, and replied with a hesitant, "Ummmmm, no worries, to be honest, ummmmm, I'll let you go, right-ee-ho, ummmmm, I'm off... Bye."

Leaving Donald behind with the thought, "It is such a shame that she's a complete loop, of the fruit variety."

Sensing the practice session had come to a foregone conclusion,[285] Willy took Donald aside for a private clandestine chat... "If you would like me to ask, I might be able to arrange the use of The Tapestry #2 to provide you with some musical inspiration?" By prefacing this furtive statement with a question, Willy had successfully offloaded all of the responsibility onto Donald's shoulders. He also hid the underlying thrill of becoming radicalised from *The Man*.[286]

Donald was in a world of confusion over the suggestion to use the tapestry as a musical aid. "I thought The Tapestry #2 only showed shows about cooking, what does that have to do with music?"

"The Tapestry #2 doesn't just display shows about cooking, is allows you to become a participant in any historical production appropriate to what you currently need."

Again, this may resemble something from a well-known-but-shouldn't-be-mentioned collection of urban fantasy novels about an unlikely hero. But... Its concept is almost exactly the opposite. Patients go into this tapestry, and it provides you with the information you need... Not a place you need. It's just not that kind of ~~room~~ tapestry.

Think of it like a book you might read at school, where you become totally immersed in the story to such a point where you are actually physically taking part and you know your actions will affect the outcome of the scenario. And once you have completed the task within the book, you emerge with enough proof to validate the story to everyone else...[287]

---

[285] The room emptying of all, but two, people might have given it away.

[286] In this instance, *The Man* Willy was referring to was DD. She didn't like any unsanctioned use of Hospital Artefacts, as the paperwork would inevitably land on her desk. She found forgiveness after a transgression is much harder to supply than the equivalent amount of approval beforehand.

[287] Hang on... Yeah, no. Don't think of it like that.

There was a sigh of relief travelling on the wind when Donald declined to go into The Tapestry #2.[288] "No, thank you, I think I will try and come up with something myself before I resort to plagiarism."

"I respect your ideology. If you ever change your mind... <wink><wink>"

Pleased he had extricated himself from a potential world of hurt, dodging closely the world of confusion he had felt earlier, Donald returned to the peace and quiet of his little room, to think about coming up with something creative about observation bridges that exist between living and listening.

Everyone seemed to have forgotten what they were supposed to be doing in the group session in the first place. Willy had forgotten because he didn't like remembering the bad thoughts, and he placed Ma'am Cybill Flex firmly on the naughty side of the ledger.

Donald tried to do much the same, but with positive thoughts. He thought forgetting about this drama would be, overall, a good thing, thereby enabling his Forgetting Every Good Thing process to run. Resulting in basically the same outcome as Willy's.

Ma'am Cybill Flex will remain unaware of both of these distracted results. Which will be yet another good thing for Donald to forget, and for Willy to not remember.

I feel I should point out the ridiculous notion of SaRS being able to host an entire musical about the Rocky saga. People who are temporary residents in a mental institution aren't bestowed with overly large amounts of time to focus on something other than their own problems.

Donald, in particular, struggles with the significant problem of restraining himself from going "Yo, Aaaaadriaaaaan!" at the top of his voice, whenever someone introduces themselves as Adrian, and when you couple this with the knowledge that the Rocky saga is still going on, it becomes all kinds of silly.

---

[288] And that sigh was also echoing around here, I'll tell you that for nothing. Well, not for nothing... You either paid to get a copy of the book, or you are paying for it by simply reading it and encouraging me to write the next invoice.

Chapter 11:
Numbers, Money, Gambling
(Baked in a π)

Donald has been doing a lot of thinking recently, and he still hasn't decided if this is a good thing, or not. Thoughts from his memory have been blurring together, and he is never completely sure what he should label them as he has a lot of trouble separating the bad memories from the nightmares and bad dreams. He is also finding there is much less to make note of when he is writing in his pseudo-diary at the end of each day.

There is a line of thought, though, that this might actually be a good thing, when you consider why there are less memories to record. Donald did exactly this and found there were more positive reasons than negative excuses for his concerning lack of recent memories:

- **He is forgetting all the happy memories.** This might not sound much like a positive reason, but it is. If he has forgotten something good,[289] then something good must have happened;
- **He is learning to be mindful.** By acknowledging the thought, and then just letting it go without any judgements interceding. This is included as a positive reason because Catch-22; or it could as easily be
- **He is simply forgetting more of everything.**

So, like Mr Loaf once didn't sing, two out of three are good. Hence why[290] the initial thought included the more positive reasons statement.

---

[289] This is one of Donald's catchcries. Quite literally. He catches all of his bad memories and has a good old cry and lets all of the good ones slide by.

[290] Donald will be around in a minute to slap me silly when he reads this pair of words, as they are one of his bugbears. Hence means *as a consequence,* i.e. *why.* So, why, oh why, would I repeat myself with a redundant statement?

Moving on from these random thoughts,[291] Donald will now take us for a glimpse around his world full of intriguing numbers, including many obscure numbers. It is hugely likely to be as close as we will ever get to his world[292] of completely empty missing monetary numbers. He will also be devoting a little of our attention to try and stay separated from any world containing hurtful or hateful information. This seemingly straightforward task may prove to be difficult when he eventually gets to the gambling subsection.

Subsection 1) "Numbers"

"Numbers... What do they mean to you?"

Mark Time's opening statement didn't make a lot of, or any if he was being completely consistent, sense to Donald. He liked to think that numbers, unlike people, were always constant, and meant the same to everyone involved. Of course, this isn't ever true... Their meaning depends entirely on your individual perspective. A ten means *approaching perfect* when you apply it to a person; if you apply it to an earthquake, however, it becomes *devastatingly bad*.[293]

Mark is the closest convenient approximation of a number cruncher the SaRS senior personnel will admit to knowing. He is their numbers "go-to-guy," utilising his good enough "if-it-fits" type of personality, whenever there might be statistics involved. He is also becoming their willing target to have a number "done-on," just to be included in a social activity.

Receiving no reply, Mark continued anyway...

"Let's begin with zero, as it is the most defamed of all potential numbers.

- Is it a positive, negative, or some other -tive number?
- Are there nine or twelve of them in a billion?
- What is the difference between zero and nought?
- Why do we see it often included in a dramatic finish to a count down, but not when you start counting up?
- Contrary to the fourth hypothesis, which proves it is a rule, why is the first patient referred to as *patient zero*? With a medically irrelevant follow up question, is the second patient called *patient one*?

To hear the answers to these questions, and various other pieces of trivial information, don't adjust your sit." And then, during the next arduous while, Mark exuded lots of numerical details.

---

[291] By now forgotten, because, again, Catch-22. It is a descending spiral.

[292] Bank accounts, secret cachés, wallets, pockets, lounge chairs... etc...

[293] As I was writing this an interesting thought manifested itself into being... These two extreme definitions of ten are not necessarily mutually exclusive.

"Zero is indeed not positive, neither is it negative. It has a zero state. Other inconsequential irregularities, or contradictory sounding details, are:

    ☹   **It is an integer**, as there is no fractional component. The mathematics community is still out with respect to 0.0 regarding this definition.

    ☹   **It is an even number**, as there is no remainder when dividing by two. The same could be said, but isn't, about it being a multiple of three as there is no remainder when dividing by nine.

    ☹   **It is confusing**, as $^x/_x$ is not 1 where x = 0 (or ∞), the answer is instead defined as undefined."

"A billion should have twelve zeroes, as it is a million-million. End of story.

1	× 1	= 1
1☺	× 1☺	= 1☺☺
1☺☺	× 1☺☺	= 1☺,☺☺☺
1,☺☺☺	× 1,☺☺☺	= 1,☺☺☺,☺☺☺
1☺,☺☺☺	× 1☺,☺☺☺	= 1☺☺,☺☺☺,☺☺☺
1☺☺,☺☺☺	× 1☺☺,☺☺☺	= 1☺,☺☺☺,☺☺☺,☺☺☺
1,☺☺☺,☺☺☺	× 1,☺☺☺,☺☺☺	= 1,☺☺☺,☺☺☺,☺☺☺,☺☺☺

The reason why a thousand million has evolved to mean a billion, is that it sounds better when you talk about bank accounts. Interestingly, this concept started in France; as opposed to the cynically accepted version of in the USA."

The upshot of this was... It didn't matter how people described a million, neither definition gave an adequate explanation as to why there were always red zeros depicted in Donald's bank account.

It was at this point when Mark went off the zero book, and started spieling his own ranting opinions about numbers in general:[294]

    ☹   "What I would like to know is the explanation of why counting doesn't count these days. It seems that if you don't have a phone or computer handy, a lot of people forget how to count. These are all those people who you count on to be able to count, and they just can't."

    ☹   "Who decided the, so called, Prime Numbers were so important?" and

    ☹   "What's up with Arabic Numerals? This is the normal set of numbers for most of the world, *except* for the Arabic communities. Sure, they may be similar in some respects, but it's just not the same.[295]"

---

[294] Saying Mark was "passionate about numbers" would be a gross "144" understatement. And remember, passion does not necessarily mean "good."

[295] ٠ ١ ٢ ٣ ٤ ٥ ٦ ٧ ٨ ٩   (included to incite Mark)

    0 1 2 3 4 5 6 7 8 9   (included for your insight)

Just as Mark was getting over the top out of control, Sue Rhea Liszt arrived to deliver her subsection of this chapter's content, money. But, like money so often does, Sue arrived just too late to prevent Mark from an outburst of his final three catastrophic problems.[296] She also showed up with several cronies expecting to affect a compensation clean-out...

- ұ   "Why isn't forty spelled fourty, with a *u*, like four and fourteen?"
- ұ   "Why are eleven and twelve not oneteen and twoteen?" and
  Donald appended to these two his own questions about the concepts of twenty, thirty and fifty; and the spelling of eighteen and eighty.
- ұ   "What is the longest one syllable number?"

Secured safely to a standard two-hundred-twoteen cm abacus stretcher, Mark, who is known as the weakest link, was unceremoniously removed back to the comfort of his "Pecuniam in loco repetit lacum," without so much as a good-bye. And all of this unfortunately happened before he could lock in the answer to his final question.

Donald was left in a unicorn's-teeth unusual position of knowing all of the answers. All both of them. The longest one syllable number was either twelve, or Pi, depending on your choice of perception. The superlative joy Donald felt internally about this was short lived...

Then Sue began speaking about his bank account content antithesis...

Subsection 2) "Money"

As was usual with all "talks" like this, the money group topic appeared out of the blue. It also came directly from a place of great concern, and ultimately landed in this place of I don't care.

"Hello everybody, my name is Sue Rhea Liszt, and I am generally the SaRS Art Realisationalist. But today, I am Sue Rhea Liszt the Struggling Artist. Please rest assured[297] that I can relate to being unknown and destitute, while waiting for some support or a nudge in the right direction to get me going."

She looked around the room with an inquisitive smile. Following the smile was a disarming feeling that Donald had never been in the presence of before but would eventually come to know as empathy. Incredibly, Donald relaxed.

---

[296] The first two interpret *problem* as *issue*, the last one as *question*.

[297] Donald doesn't understand why people think this is a good thing to say. They are implying everything will be ok because they have been here before, and even though the specific situations are radically different, there is a way out and they will help you find it. It is only a polite way of saying *just relax.*

By now you might have noticed this is chapter eleven. It wasn't the happy coincidence it first appears. It is actually ~~a sly~~ an obvious reference to chapter eleven of the United States bankruptcy code. Like "911 Emergency," but to a much lesser extent, this would have been learned from American news and/or entertainment. Coincidentally, American companies that have gone through a Chapter 11 bankruptcy, were likely to have been run by people who may have been seen also driving a Porsche 911 into the ground.[298]

Sue had much to say about everyday money. She particularly focussed on the "how you can stick to your budget if you really want to," fantasy scenarios. Even though she was talking about numbers, Donald was firmly positioned in the, "I'm doing fine by myself, thankyouyverymuch," camp. There were three reasons for this:

- He didn't place any importance on money; as everyone who has ever had more than enough always didn't. He is going to learn a very harsh lesson about this in the not-too-distant future;
- There was no wasting of anything in his life. You turned taps off when not in use. You closed the fridge between outs and ins of milk bottles. And you don't pay for extra food and drink if it comes for free; and
- You are reading this now, so he must be doing relatively okay in the having enough money department.

After her fantasy budget speech was delivered and ratified, Sue abruptly stepped outside the veil of protection afforded to her by SaRS and whispered conspiratorially to the group... "However, I have come across a facility that will allow you to spend money which isn't yours yet...[299]"

Donald was disinclined to acquiesce to her **Purple Pyramid Ponzi scheme**.

---

[298] When Donald reread this paragraph, he conceitedly thought to himself, "Man... Those people are so annoying. I wish I was dumb enough to be able to drive my own Porsche... One day Donald... One day you will be...

[299] **Infomercial warning!**

Sue Rhea Liszt's facilitation services are offered to all patients of SaRS, at a significantly discounted rate. Her services lie in the grey area between blackmail and white-collar crime. She found a unique solution for her lack of money problem, and a suitably gullible niche market to on-sell her solution.

Use **Purple Pay** to purchase a product, and promise to pay promptly, once participating punters pony up a pittance, preferably prior to prison pending.

Finishing her circumspect pitch with what she desperately hoped would turn into a very well-known catchphrase… "Let nothing impede[300] your money collection and spending processes. **Take the *uck* out of *lucky* and *ly*.**"

Donald could hardly believe it when Sue handed around physical proof of her "SaRS approval pending" unsanctioned money taking-not-making scheme, and thought that it was sure to garner much attention, but not the good type…

Purple Pay

Let nothing impede your money collection and spending processes.

Take the *uck* out of *lucky* and *ly*.

Lifetime Possibility of

Unconditional

Certified

Kinaesthetic

You'll be Lucky

Don't be Lucky, use **Purple Pay**

**SaRS approval pending*

But it was sort of an appropriate segue into the next subsection.

Subsection 3) "Gambling"

Trigger warning: This subsection contains many disparaging remarks.[301]

From deep out of the audience, where she had been waiting impatiently in one of the repurposed disused corners of the room, Mindy Ownbeeswhacks revealed her third and final superpower… Croupier extra-ordinary.

Scant moments after Mindy exposed herself to the entire group there was a barely stifled cheer emanating from one of the other disused corners.[302] This subset of the group's participants were all huddled around a makeshift table exchanging little pieces of paper.

---

[300] I dislike most pedes: centipede, millipede, over there where chunky peed.

[301] Much like this opening sentence. In fact, one of them is exactly the same.

[302] It came from the South-West corner, to be facetiously fatuously exact.

Donald's interest was nearly piqued, but not enough to investigate further than one seemingly uninterested man glance. If Donald had cared enough to delve into the sub-group's activity, he would have found another spoiler alert instructing him to not even mention this so early on in the subsection.

Mindy didn't need to introduce herself,[303] and all she required to have Sue looking for the fastest way out was her own look that escalated a courteously implied, "**Sue, Please Leave, I'm Talking**," all the way through to an obviously understood, "**Go-ExiT—Out-U-T**oday!" Her prodigious talent for controlling a crowd of desperate people went a long way to explaining her unrivalled ability behind a gambling table.

"Firstly, a little reason why we ended up here… 'Not a day goes by, wh…"
"No, it isn't! No, I'm not! And I'm also not Italian!"

.

.

. <**Stomp…** Stomp… Stomp…>

.

.

And picking up from where she left off after the unpredictable storm-in-a-teacup misunderstanding, "…en I don't wonder[304] what my life could have been like' is the start of a sentence I will never speak. Your lack of self-control over your lack of self-pity, and your lack of self-caring about it all, is what landed every single one of you in here!… !… !…"

Sufficiently chastened, Donald agreed with her, with one slight correction; "Um, ok, but we did just hear you say it…[305]"

Humphing off Donald's auditory correct observation, Mindy included the nondescript member of the subset of group participants who was subsisting in the disused SW corner into the conversation, "Would you care to come to the front of the room and share what you were cheering about, please.[306]"

---

[303] Nor did she want to, which was the main reason why she didn't.

[304] Thinking logically about "Not a day goes by when I don't wonder:"

- Says – Every Day I don't wonder, or simply, **I never wonder**;
- Means – I wonder Every Day; but
- Better – A Day cannot be complete until I wonder.

[305] Never forgetting that whatever comes before a *but* doesn't count.

[306] Donald experienced a Déjà vu of experiencing Déjà vu, when Mindy's question sounded like it was ended as an instruction instead of as a request.

Mindy had to force the information feed out of him…"Introduce yourself."
"I am Samuel Pull, I am, but you can call me Sam."
"And why are you here."
"I have been diagnosed as having a **M**ediocre **A**verage **D**iagnosis."
"And what made you cheer when I exposed myself recently."
"Ummmmm."

Sam looked guilty about something and sounded like he was having some trouble expressing his remorse. Donald felt the whole situation was becoming tasteless, and when Mindy forced the information, with a whiff of indignation, they had the complete set of senses covered between them.

Mindy removed one of the little pieces of paper mentioned earlier, those that went unnoticed by Donald, from the left hand of Sam. It was, in plausible fact, a betting slip favoured by the gambling addicts at SaRS, and was exactly the same size as a business card…

SaRS Gambler's Anonymous Betting Slip

Bets subjected to a 10% undercover charge

Who will be the Secret Gambling Presenter?

Prediction: *Mindy Ownbeeswhacks*

Amount: *2 Prozac*   Odds: *10~1*

Donald was astonished by the correct usage of the ownership apostrophe. He wasn't anywhere near the same level of amazement, due to his continuous sceptical stance, of an underground betting concern going on within SaRS.

Single Group Scenarios:[307]

- Who will be the last person allowed to enter the group session?
- How many disgruntled patients will stomp out of the group session?
- What will be the final count of "I Guess'" from the group facilitator?

Medium - Long Term Scenarios:

- When will there finally be a wrong answer from a patient?
- Who will ask the most questions over their three-week period?
- Number of acronyms taught by a group facilitator in a week.

Mindy dismissed Sam and continued to thoroughly dismiss him while he endeavoured to get safely back to the corner, "Sam is in here because he can't control his gambling addiction. Skit is in here because he can't control who his personality is. Sven is in here because he can't control how fortunate he is."

---

[307] "They" are still developing the multi-group scenario verification process.

I am a committed person; I have been committed many times.

"And that is only the living Ss at the moment. I will unnecessarily repeat myself now… Your lack of self-control over your lack of self-pity, and your lack of self-caring about it all, is what landed every single one of you in here!… !… !…[308] What I would like to do now is tell you all that this strangeness is ok."

The caring positivity from Mindy caught Donald off guard for one moment. He wasn't used to experiencing people saying that his strangeness was ok. And he certainly had never thought it might be recorded in his memory. Curious as to what might happen, he let his mind have its (and his) head…

"The best way I can do this is to explain it to you via the age-old tradition of the acronym…[309]

<u>DON'T PANIC</u> - What you should NOT listen to…

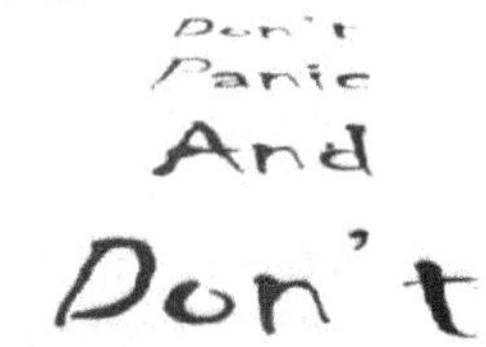

Derogatory	Discussions
Opinionated	Observations
Negative	Naysaying and
Tirades, of any	Type

Preconceived	Principles
Abusive	Accusations
Noxious	Narratives
Insulting	Ideologies or
Criticisms…	Completely

And with that under his belt, Donald felt a strange weight lift off his mind. He closed his paddle, reflected on the memory of his opening comments and felt empowered when he realised, he had reflected on a positive memory. He was starting to get the hang of things…

---

[308] I think this is important enough for me to remind you that we are currently enjoying a glimpse into Donald's three phase personal number world full of:

- ¤ Intriguing numbers;
- ¤ Obscure numbers; and not
- ¤ Empty missing monetary numbers.

Yet strangely, it isn't presented chronologically, as it is a conglomeration.

[309] <crackle>…and it's Mindy with a late start on a count of one…</crackle>

Embracing a modicum of happiness, Donald ventured out to see what he could see through his new rosé tinted glasses. This walk time, it was him who wasn't paying attention, and before he realised it, he had already pressed the elevator call button. Only coming to his senses while he was again waiting for the elevator to ding and open its doors.

On entry to the elevator cab, he again recalled a rumour of what might be at the other end of the short verticality; a fully seeded Gambler's Anonymous Den, when he noticed the alternate configuration of button...[310]

The elevator atmosphere wasn't silent this time; there was a strange, yet strangely appropriate, classical version of "The Gambler" being piped through the muzak outlet. There was no trepidation present either, it was almost as if Donald was inquisitive about what he might find at "Bet," maybe even excited, but as he had nothing to compare it to in his memory he went with eager. He was also mildly impressed with the situation:

- He was travelling alone without possibility of support;
- In a bizarre lift which transported you to different places; and
- He actually wanted to do this...

When he exited the elevator this time it wasn't dimness that greeted him, it was a festival of mirror-balls and laser-lights. There was also an androgynous Navigation, Liquidation and Hydration facilitator waiting for him.

"This way please Mr Donald, Sir. May I provide some relief of your money now, or would you prefer to lose it the traditional way? We have also prefilled a coffee mug with your favourite brew... One of everything, I believe."

Donald was astounded by what he was seeing. The transformation of the tunnels was as improbable as they were impeccable. Everything was set to a bling level of thirteen. There was no doubt in Donald's mind that this is what a classy Gambler's Anonymous Den should look like. There was only one matter for Donald to be concerned with, and it was a spectacularly minor issue, he didn't know where he was.

---

[310] The two solitary destination selection buttons are dynamically textually configured based on the location you are at when you beckon the elevator... *Bet* - when it was called from *Up*, and *Fold* - when it is called from *Down*.

Filing away the nudeness feeling he felt when the androgynous facilitator spoke of his most recognisable drink configuration, he replied to the previous financial question with a noncommittal non-sequitur, "thank you."

"Here we are, your seat Mr Donald, Sir…"

SaRS Gambler's Den

Anonymity Guaranteed!

Welcome – Donald Halfbrain

Donald reverted to a first-person account of the Den for his memoirs…

"The SaRS Hospital's Gambler's Den is a genuine cornucopia of games and dystopian drama, where everyone is hungry for their next win, and are trying to defeat the ever present, less than favourable, odds stacked against them by a capitalistic regime.

As in my previous account of the under SaRS locations, there is a complete absence of any official documentation,[311] making it a nearly impossible task to expose any crime or criminal activity. Unwisely,[312] I was without any means to access my less than inconsiderable funds, so I had to be content with watching the proceedings and documenting them here.

This is what I saw…

SaRS Rules, Scrabble (SRS) - with Sven Teatwoo - My admiration for Sven was already at a fairly high level, and this interaction served to increase it well above fair for this extraordinary person.

Welcome to Scrabble (SaRS Rules!) where zero scores better than nothing.

Sven indicated to me his exuberant excitement at finally being irrevocably allowed to let loose, as a plenipotentiary, his significant amount of many more than three syllable words, with rambunctious impunity. His excitement waned after I revealed, and then substantiated, my seed-less financial situation, and a complete insufficiency with respect to any tradeable medication.

---

[311] Donald wisely chose to put all references to the giant welcome banner in the not-to-be-released-until-after-all-limitation-periods-expire pile.

[312] It possibly may have been unwise, but it was definitely extremely lucky.

He directed my attention to a sign displayed above the table...

ABCs & ABCs only PLEASE

Arrive promptly for the start of your scrabbling. This is NOT a polite request!
Bring nothing with you (Ex: The standard approved word spell paraphernalia)
Collateral: Credit Cards/Cash (Ex: Coins)/Cheques/Controlled Substances

Accumulate a prodigious vocabulary, and know how to spell those word thingies
Be Brutal: If you can play a Bonus Word, on a Bonus Space, THEN DO IT!
Cheat: Be Creative. Be Cunning. Be Confident... But... Don't get Caught.

Prerequisite: Practice both ABCs. Precise Preparation Prevents Poor Pellings
Location... Location... Location...: Right Here... Right Here... Right Here...
Alphabet, The: A B C D E F G H I J K L M N O P Q R S T U V W X Y Z
Scrabble: What happens to be played in Scrabble, stays displayed in Scrabble
End of the SaRS Unofficial 1 – Gambler's Den ABCs & ABCs only PLEASE

SaRS Unofficial 1 – Gambler's Den ABCs & ABCs only PLEASE

Refer to the first rule unnumbered C Gambler's Den ABCs & ABCs only PLEASE.

Even though my lack of collateral precluded me from joining in the game, Sven graciously allowed me to stay and watch a few of the opening rounds of the next Scrabble event, and to ask any questions I might have had.[313]

Don't Intelligence, Guess (DIG) - without Samuel (call me Sam) Pull - Upon arrival at this boutique, I was confronted by an empty ramshackle podium, and not much else. Sam had left his "Well Out of Order!" handcrafted message at the base of the podium in a spectacular display of memorandum crunching. All I could make of this was even more questions...

- ¤ Was there a well, of the water kind, somewhere that had run dry?
- ¤ Was the sign a thinly veiled humorous attempt at an oxymoron? or
- ¤ Was someone seriously wrong or something seriously broken?

Without any context, and no one to ask, I rummaged around to see if there were any hidden details that might provide me with an answer.

---

[313] Donald is saving all of his English related questions for a later chapter. Along with his oh so many unrelated Human questions about why we accept obvious irregularities in TV shows and Movies, which we wouldn't in real life.

Discovering another triple O notification, "Tapestry #3 Out of Order," and a trivial list of questions and answers was not the outcome I desired. I read the questions, allocated them to a space in my memory, hung up an ironical "Do Not Disturb" sign and continued with my wander around SaRS' underbelly.

- ☒ What colour is the White Dragon in a game of Mahjong?
  The White dragon is actually blue. True story.
- ☒ If you travel for 10km at 10km/h, how fast must the return journey be to achieve a 20km/h average?
  It is impossible, as you have just used all of the hour to get there.
- ☒ Think of a word. Does it rhyme with anything?
  No, "it" doesn't rhyme with "anything."

Realising these were all "trick" questions took an edge off my dismay, and increased my thinking, "I am glad there are others who think like I do." Finding someone to talk about it would have been nice.

On the back of the crunchy "Well OoO!" note was a potential metric which would allow measurement of the success extremities: "*Whoever gets out first is the first loser to be released. The last patient left behind will become the ultimate mental brain.*"

Three Sheets Up (TSU) - with Pledge, Jimmy Pledge - At the last stop in my underground movement I found a repetitious surprise... Pledge, Jimmy Pledge spouted[314] some more stereotypical language. I am fairly sure he leaves a well-watered trail wherever he goes. I will do my best to replicate the torrent of his clichéd vernacular in a translated dry format...

Welcome, Mr Donald, Sir, to Three Sheets Up.

We are here to provide you with all of your various argumentative needs:

- ☒ **Devil's Advocate** - This game is a highly probable confrontational one, where you try to entice your opponent into an argument over a topic of their choice. You win this game the moment the opposing person engages, it doesn't depend on you actually winning the argument.
- ☒ **Elephant in the Room** - This game is very similar to Devil's Advocate, except you use your perception of an opponent's sensitivities to select the topic of conversation, and it has a significantly less likelihood of a physical confrontational outcome.
- ☒ **Conceptualise** - Another step down the conceptual ladder of intensity. The topics for consideration in this game are "everything else," after the ones from the previous two steps have been declined. This game generally ends in conversation.

---

[314] Is this word predictable? Yes, maybe it is, but is it funny? Hopefully...
Sigh It is funny what I hope for, and predictable what doesn't count...

I decided to not participate in any of these fascinating games, even though I dearly wanted to have a legitimate argument at my level of understanding.[315] Postponing the inevitable will provide me with the opportunity to prepare my arguments, so I don't appear ill prepared.

What I would like to argue, at the earliest possible time, is why I was once again astounded by the mere presence of Pledge, Jimmy Pledge underneath SaRS... With follow-up questions:

- Where does he go when he isn't here?
- Why does he always appear at precisely the right moment?
- How did he ascend to the lofty heights of a repeat cameo performer?

So, in summary, having seen the evidence firsthand,[316] I propose that the addicted patients be weaned off using their medication as a betting substance. This will benefit them by removing their ability to place a bet, replacing it with a calm medicated view to avoid the escalation of their gambling problem.

With that one juicy answer, this is Mr Donald, Sir, signing off on the dotted line again, for my own sanity. Thank-you-very-much."

- Extract from The Donald Diaries.

Donald was happy with the amount of material he had to document in his diary tonight and made his way calmly back to the elevator. The androgynous facilitator was there waiting for him with thoroughly pre-pressed elevator call button. Donald tried to imitate the suave Pledge, Jimmy Pledge, and touch his forehead in a mock hat tilt... It didn't go well.[317]

Donald is back in his room now... He is going to write the above chapter.

Donald is out of his mind now...[318] He has finished the above chapter and is now going to dump everything out of his memory relating to unanswered or inappropriately answered questions. The intent is to pugnaciously transform them into an argumentative topic, to be discussed most vehemently the next time he finds himself in the Gambler's Den.

---

[315] Donald doesn't understand how these comments make him sound like he is an intellectual snob. He knows he is one, he just doesn't understand how.

[316] Even though it was so many, many, pages ago... Donald still remembers.

[317] Had he tried to imitate a face palm, he would have been more successful.

[318] It is probably close to two hours, or so, after the previous now statement.

1) Devil's Advocate:
(Donald has never lost a Devil's Advocate confrontation... Ever.)

- Is "White Goes First" in chess, a racist move?
    - As White has precedence over any other Colour; or
    - As White has always initiated any confrontation about Colour.

2) Elephant in the Room:
(Donald is not afraid to raise Elephant in the Room questions.)

- Are Men and Women equal?
  A Woman who marries a King becomes a Queen;
  A Man who marries a Queen becomes a Prince;
    - Is this sexist against women as it perpetuates the thought that the male's highest position is more powerful than female's; or
    - Is this sexist against men as they are not elevated to the top level?
  If a Queen is to be equal, equality has to flow both ways.

3) Conceptualise: (AKA Debate Team Practice:)
(These are all Donald's. Haven't you been paying attention again?)

- Why does prehistoric not mean *before all history*; as opposed to the generally accepted definition of *before documented history*?
- Can you put socks on backwards?
- What do you think "unthinkable to think of" means?
- What does "going through a drive through backwards" mean?
    - Reversing your car through the drive through; or
    - Entering the drive through by the exit.
- Regarding a Pepper Grinder. Do you...
    - Left Hand grip tight, and Right Hand grip twist release?
    - Right Hand grip tight, and Left Hand grip twist release? or
    - Both Hands grip twist, wondering why it isn't working?
- Why do you "take" a picture, if you don't "take" a painting?
- Why isn't a "phobia of phobias" a phobiaphobia?
- Extract from The Donald Diaries.

And... Goodnight.[319]

---

[319] This was initially because Donald had finished his brain dump and was going to attempt to go to sleep. It is now relevant to me as well...

Chapter 12:
Nota vs Owedebt
(Offside-Out)

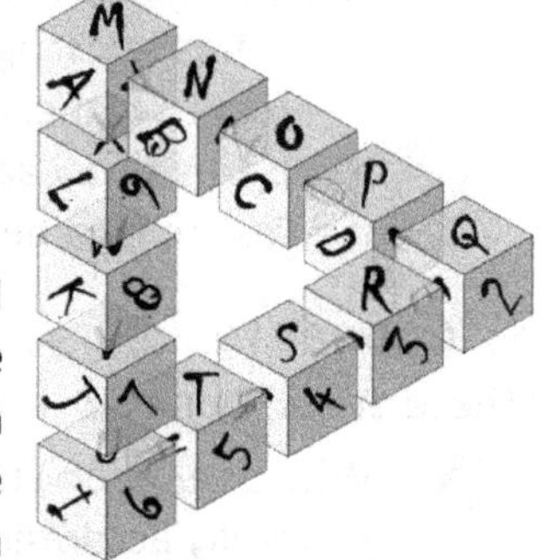

The obvious tension[320] between Nota and Owedebt had been seething along, quite cynically, for a little while now... So, when they sought to combine their woefully inadequate spatial mapping capabilities together, to attempt a three-dimensional twelve piece (block) illusionary jigsaw puzzle,[321] the friction sparks popped every bubble available, and turned the seething along cynically flow into a giant torrent of misapprehension.

Donald was well placed to watch these proceedings unfold without there being any risk of him becoming involved. He was content with being outside looking in for a change. He was also thinking he was about to see their minor confrontation escalate from interesting to fascinating.

Pledge, Jimmy Pledge sauntered in, and was just about to deliver another watered-down speech when a single glower from Owedebt silenced him and, simultaneously, took all of the moisture out of his ritualistic dousing. He knew when he wasn't welcome and hustled himself out of the danger zone.

Unexpectedly, Paula Bridge (from the Spick 'n' Span cleansers) shadowed Pledge, Jimmy Pledge's ins and outs. She had just recently taken up a position of stalking him around SaRS as an extracurricular hobby, as she found it much easier and comforting to mop up any expletives while they were still wet.

---

[320] It was so obvious, even Donald could see there was trouble brewing.

[321] Owedebt was heard to say at the beginning of this puzzling exercise... "Does it make me a four-dimensional thinker if I understand what I am doing?" And at the end... "I'm a Basket Case... Get Me Out of Here!"

BLT and Seth harboured some undocumented resentment after they were both disallowed competitor status in the SaRS' Mocking Games. Burying their bitterness deep enough to resume some semblance of a co-operative un-life, they arrived at the common-area and announced, in perfect synchronisation, "The Communication Skills group will commence in thirteen minutes."

Donald was disappointed again... Although, this minor setback did help to firm up his pessimistic thought, "It seems to me, that whenever I start looking forward to something, it always ends up being placed inside the most probably not allowed discount box at the feelings supermarket."

Houts Marted made a semi-reluctant first appearance as the mediator of this group session.[322] After he revealed his Pre-Prepared Presentation of the Communication Skills group topics he returned to the official facilitator's seat, and waited until there was a trace of quiet before he continued...

Communication Skills

Topics Du Jour:

- The Five Love Languages and the opposing Five Loathsome Languages
- Passive/Assertive/Aggressive Manipulation Conversation Techniques

Implementation Examples:

- Every one's personal description of their own:
  - Depressing struggle – Through Depression and Anxiety (T–DaA)
  - Hero/Anti-Hero   – HaH
- What you **Never** Say to (or even talk about with) a Mental Patient
- What you **Must** Say to stop being talked about as a Mental Patient

SaRS Whiteboard 6 – Communication Skills (Pre–Prep Pres)

Tapping his fingers on the armrest of the seat, Houts thought to himself a mental note to make sure he included a "Get their Attention - Today" Topic in the Du Jour section for next time. Unable to conceal his current ire any longer, he called for a slice of silence in the noise... "OI!"

---

[322] Houts hadn't been able to fully commit to anything since the last week's English Language Idiosyncrasies group, after which he was told he would not be appearing in any significant way until the second half of this book.

The disruptive racket gradually subsided, with one brief exception where Nota's confusing tones thrust a reassurance ending comment, "I can't smell it yet…" into the "that which cannot be unheard" place everyone has.

Satisfied he had as much of their attention as possible, Houts began… "On this, the single most important first steppingstone of your individual journeys to finding that unicorn like rare miracle cure for your mental disorder, learning how to communicate effectively… Can you all please hold on to your questions until never.[323]"

Houts tapped on the next page icon to reveal the definitions, as written in the many textbooks, which were therefore… Gospel.[324]

The Five Textbook Love Languages…

1) Words of Affirmation

This language essentially boils down to verbal platitudes and is therefore the simplest language to learn as you have been hearing it all your life. But you must remember, even though some words come cheap, the expectations they eventually produce might not be:

- "I love you." The ultimate cliché. It also comes with the ultimate hitch;
- "Thank you." The most basic, automatic and expected response. It is, however, also the most banal with the least of expectations attached. *But, be warned* - Do not mix this up with the first example; or
- "That was nice of you." Lower to middling in the range of affirmation words, for both your safety and its usefulness.

Note: All of these affirmations refer to a "you," who is not *you*. This is not the appropriate place to be digging around for a compliment.

2) Quality Time

This is an innate ability in most people.

All you have to remember is to be there at the same time as your other ½.

Contrary to most people's opinion, multi-tasking is a skill that a lot of men possess, and often excel at. The time we spend giving our undivided attention to our partners is typically when we put this ability on-hold, as this is what a caring person is supposed to do. Unfortunately, it also often projects an image that we have zoned out and are completely uninterested in what we are doing. Generally, this is not the case.

---

[323] I think there must be a course, frequented by SaRS people, teaching: "How you ask a question and have it come out sounding like an instruction."

[324] Whoever is producing the movie version, of the graphic novels, which are loosely based on these books, "Now is the time for awesome ominous music."

3) Receiving Gifts

Not necessarily flowers and chocolates, but those are two of the staples. A person can be forgiven for thinking this is only one step away from being in a gold-digging transactional relationship. This language usually requires a large amount of pre-work.[325]

"It is the thought that counts." Do not be fooled by this statement... The financial value of the given gift is generally directly proportional to the amount of relationship received in return.

Note: If this alliance progresses to marriage, convenience may become a topic of conversation for those around you. The intensity of this conversation is directly proportional to the age difference of the two parties involved.

4) Acts of Service

"Actions speak louder than words.[326]"

Activities may include, but are not limited to:

- General house-hold chores (vacuuming the floor, washing the car...). These may not be outsourced, and don't count if they are part of your traditional work areas;
- Something off the To-Do list. This must be something your partner put on the list, or will benefit directly from; or
- Breakfast in bed or walking the dog. However, it is not recommended that you do both of these at the same time.

Note: This love language is significantly beneficial to the giving party, as it requires the least amount of preparation in the event of a forgotten date, or an anniversary of a significant event.

5) Physical Touch

This language requires the most amount of perception, as there is a very fine line (with a dot) between, "Don't! Stop!" and, "Don't Stop!" It is the most direct, yet unspoken, language, with the highest peaks and deepest pits. There is so much more than the standard PDAs[327] of hand holding and hugs available. It might be a simple touch of an arm in agreement during a conversation, or a complicated neck rub in hope during a conversation later that night.

As a general rule, if you have to ask if a touch is ok, it isn't.

---

[325] You must not include this as part of the gift. It should appear effortless. The more work you put in, and the less you speak about it, the better the gift will be. (Rule #23 in the Spadework Handbook for Dummies.)

[326] No. No, they don't. They mean they *mean* more than words.

[327] I have never understood the why this "P" means public, and not private.

Retapping on the next page icon, converse definitions, which are definitely not as written in any textbook, were reviled. These were more like... Disbelief.

The Five A-Textbook Loathsome Languages...

5) Words of Condemnation

As its textbook cohort, this language is brought to life by verbal platitudes, however, conversely, these words have been spoken but have not necessarily been heard all your life. They resolve very low expectations:

- "Whatever." The penultimate cliché. Any pre-existing hitches are null and voided or exacerbated. But you don't get to decide which hitches becomes kitsch. "Fine." and, "Sure." may elicit the same result;
- "Finally." Confirmation that one of the least anticipated expectations has been met in a less than appropriate timely manner;
- "You idiot." Self-explanatory.

Note: This is also not the appropriate place for compliments.[328]

4) Inequality Time

This is an ingrate attitude in most people.

Often resulting from an inability to recognise active multi-tasking. One of the ways to Dispel Attention Deficits (DADs) is to answer a question designed to verify a perceived lack with the correct answer. Generally, any of the lower-level Words of Affirmation will be acceptable.

"Ah ha, yep, sure, ok..." Even though positive, they are all unacceptable.

3) Receiving Suggestions

This language will provide you with most of the answers when confronted with several of the wide-ranging argument inducing statements:

- "If you don't know the answer to that by now, I'm not going to tell you what it is." This is known as a rhetorical statement;
- "It's not up to me to do your job for you." This is the second person's version of the generic excuse, "Not my job!" when they don't want to shoulder any of your responsibility; or
- "" The silent treatment suggestion often speaks the loudest.

Note: All of these suggestions refer to a "you," who is *you*.[329]

---

[328] Actually, as another simple *rule of thumb...* If you don't want to become *under the thumb*, soliciting compliments will never encourage a *thumbs up...*

[329] The "you" is always explicitly implicit whenever you are on the receiving end of a bout of silent treatment. The suggestion included is commonly one which is measured in distance, and it will helpfully tell you how to get there.

2) Acts of Disservice

"Sticks and stones may break my bones, but words shall never hurt me.[330]"
Activities may include, but are not limited to:

- Bathroom chores (changing empty toilet paper rolls, putting the seat down…). Realistically you could include every bathroom[331] chore;
- Volunteering someone else for a charitable task where you will be the one who receives the recognition and appreciation;
- Breakfast in bed while walking the dog.

Note: This love language is also significantly beneficial to the giving party, but for an entirely different set of, often humorous, reasons.

1) Mentally Touched

This nonverbal language requires exactly zero perception.

As Houts read out the definition of the last love language, Donald ironically fixated on *zero*, a word which is particularly convenient for him as he excels in having exactly no understanding of most nonverbal communication.

Slight differences in vocal tone are alien to Donald. If he hears or says *no*, then *no* is what is meant. It is a binary answer, and no amounts of tone in its presentation will make it more *no*. Words are words;[332] they have a meaning which should never be overshadowed by how they can be said. Donald does understand that context is important. "Fire!" the *instruction*, should never be taken out of context or confused with an *observation* of the same word.

Facial expressions (especially eye contact); extremity fidgeting (head, feet and hands); body posture (slouching, sitting, statuesque standing, or slanting); physical location (from confidential lap, to public distancing); are all nonverbal language skills which Donald lacks the ability to care about or project.

Houts emerged from the audiobook version of the communication lesson, "The bottom line is that not everyone expresses themselves in the same way, being aware of the different love languages can help you better understand a relationship, or at least know why they are angry with you."

---

[330] Yes. Yes, they do. Saying this to a bully will goad them into hurting you.

[331] Why do we still label this room as a *bathroom* if there is no bath in there? Follow ~~through~~ up question… Why is a kitchen so called, when there is often no kitsch items in there, surely food-room is more appropriate? This would bring it in nomenclature line with dining-room, bed-room, lounge-room…

[332] And sometimes numbers apparently.

The lesson for today, so far, has had an insignificant effect on Nota's and Owedebt's close set interpersonal tension... That was about to change.

Passive/Assertive/Aggressive Communication...

"Between genius and madness there is a very small area we professionals call *common ground*, the same can be said of passion and aggression.[333] When you find the correct balance, I am confident you will also find a healthy wedge of your communication pie. The components of that wedge are:

- 50% passive pandering;
- 50% assertive acceptance; and
- **50% aggressive arrogance.**[334]"

Houts then discussed each of these mathematically inaccurate variations, eking out enough information from the minimal contributions to form a fairly accurate example of each type as they escalated through:

- Passive pandering
  <Rote On>
  1. I don't know anything about that.
  2. No one talks to me about any of that stuff.
  3. I don't have an opinion either way.
  5. Ummmmm, ok...
  <Rote Off>

- Assertive acceptance
  <Ramp Up>
  1. You don't spell *anything* with a k.
  2. I haven't *touched base* with anyone recently.
  3. Oh no, you are definitely not overweight.
  5. I think you missed number four.
  <Ramp Down>

---

[333] Houts always gets *passion* and *passive* mixed up... And even though the contextual placement in this situation is correct, his misinterpretation of the two is one of several reasons why he is destined to remain single.

[334] You are correct, this is wrong. Houts usually runs any numbers by Mark, but at the moment they were caught up in a disagreement about the number of zeroes in the bank of a high stakes Monopoly game, which was quite silly really, as there is only 200, or 210 for games made after 2008.

> ¤ **Aggressive arrogance**
> **<Rage Out>**
> **1. The word is *anything*... NOT *anythink*, you idiot.**
> **2. No one *touches base* anymore... That is just so passé.**
> **3. Shut up about being fat, you skinny bitch.**
> **5. Why don't you learn how to count?**
> **<Rage In>**

Houts didn't know it, but Owedebt and Nota both learned something they didn't know until then.[335] Having finished the two back and forth components of the Communication Skills group, Houts called a time-out so everyone could prepare themselves for the invasive Implementation Example section.

Description of Depression Struggle for Each Inmate...

Setting off at a blistering pace,[336] "Now, what I would like for three of you to do, is to tell the rest of us what depression looks like for you at the moment. You may use any communication skills at your disposal." Not at all surprisingly, the selected three were Owedebt, Nota and Donald.

These are the descriptions of their stories as Houts understands them. He records several entries in his session notes at the time, and then extrapolates further post session to produce the patient's electronic case notes...

Owedebt - Her depression, at the present moment, is focussed entirely on her fleeting memories of, and with, Nelo. Their brief cyclonic romance was the closest thing to overt sexual tension allowed at SaRS.

Interactions between staff and patients are completely forbidden, and as this edict is vigorously enforced by DD there had been no breaches of protocol since she arrived, ~~mmmmmmph~~ years ago.

Affairs between patients are also frowned upon. Even though it is done in the sternest glower available, there was a realisation long ago that it was folly. To mitigate potential child-like issues, surrounding any actual child issued, the SaRS bureaucracy introduced a children's wing project. This is unused (and un-built) at the moment, but one day they hope to be able to provide an in-house accommodation extension for non-pre-conceived children of patients.

---

[335] This did not change the way Nota and Owedebt spoke to each other, but at least they now understood how they were communicating. Nota was a mix of passive pandering and assertive acceptance, whereas Owedebt fell squarely between assertive acceptance and **aggressive arrogance**.

[336] Fast might be implied, but it doesn't mean good. In fact, blisters are bad.

Houts finally realised he had just overshadowed Owedebt's description of her depression at the moment. After a quick "Meh…" he simply cut-n-deleted all of the non-relevant information, leaving the first sentence. He was tempted to remove the excessive blather as well, but decided to leave it, as everything before a "but" doesn't matter.

Nota - Everything that Nota described as her current struggle surrounded a deeply shallow conflict with, and opinion of, Owedebt. This was exacerbated by not being included in Owedebt's description of her own personal struggles. I think Nota's only solution will be a dissolution[337] of the relationship between her and Owedebt.[338]

Skit, surprisingly, chimed in with, "Whenever feasible, one should always try to treat[339] the rude." I didn't really understand what he meant by this, as I don't consider being rude a mental condition that we can *treat…*

Beat out of… Maybe.

Although a beating out of isn't typically seen as a satisfactory treatment, rather, it is more closely aligned to being a satisfying solution. This bears some investigation into when an appropriate instruction says to do so.[340]

Nota's comprehension of psychological knowledge is certainly unique… This is a sample of her thinking process, where she radically accepts someone else's version of the truth rather than checking the details…

Peoples are treating me like I am still a child
One who always has to have the biggest biscuit
That's not important now. And it's driving me wild
They won't let me out of this stupid straight jacket

They must know I'm better, I just want to go home
Owedebt said I may stop being her slave sidekick
The only stuff I need is my brush and my comb
I'm a celebrity! Get me out of here… Quick…!

---

[337] Of this, Donald would have had absolutely no illusions.

[338] Nota will unfortunately be shouldered out of the relationship, eventually shown out of the hospital and be heard to remark sardonically, "I'm out, and you're not!" This will all occur, conveniently, when she is discharged.

[339] Houts misheard Hannibal's quote… It was actually, "try to eat the rude."

[340] Houts dealt with Hannibal's contribution in the same way he deals with all unsolicited help… Document it without a due date or person responsible.

Donald - Donald is quite an extraordinary case. If it wasn't unprofessional for me to say something like, "He is seriously mental!" I'd be out there singing it from inside a SaRS padded room and enquiring about a Ludicrous[341] grant to study his mind in more depth.

His self-description of what he perceives his depression struggle to be was self-deprecating in the extreme, and it curiously included three questions with information about their potentially corresponding answers:

- What is it called when you are reading out loud a written defamatory false statement?
    - Libel is a defamatory false statement which is written;
    - Slander is a defamatory false statement which is spoken; so
    - What is it dialectically liable to be when it is both?
- Why aren't walking people held to the same level of account as drivers while they are using technology?
    - If a walker is not paying attention to their surroundings and walks into the path of a car, I think they should become "fair game," and have "teaching them a lesson" decriminalised.
- What is the best title for my autobiography?
    - Using flatulence to win friends and influence people;
    - How to be a Dummy for Dummies; or
    - Donald... The animal who likes minerals on his vegetables...

What Houts didn't document were the anagram comments made by Sven for each of the description participants:

- Owedebt   - **Expect** what you cannot **Except**.
- Nota   - Be **Silent** and just **Listen**.
- Donald   - **Vote** for their **Veto**.

Description of Hero/Anti-Hero for Each Inmate...

As the whiteboard agenda indicates, this topic is always good for a laugh. The three participating fanboys (or anti-fanboys) were Lost, Donald and Sven, and they each described an anti-hero of sorts...

This exercise is designed to perform two superfluous functions. Firstly, it is a "get to know each other" mission for the new patients, and secondly, it is a "really get to know you" undertaking for the facilitator. And, as both of these tasks were completed last week, it is also a thirdly redundant function.

---

[341] Ludicrous Freud was Sigmund Freud's little known two-days-younger twin brother. Always overshadowed by his elder brother, Ludicrous chose to remain in the darker shadow of a more traditional asylum belief.

Lost - In describing his hero, Pledge, Jimmy Pledge, Lost had a fairly simple task, as Pledge, Jimmy Pledge was standing right there...

"Hello, I am Pledge, Jimmy Pledge, how may I be of ashshishtanche?"

Once a path was suctioned through this assistance, he went on to describe the suit he was wearing... It is a suit twilled in the Black Watch tartan, as used by persons on Her Majesty's Secret Service.[342]

Everyone then spent a little while talking about the various secret missions Pledge, Jimmy Pledge, had participated in. Their focus was somewhat obvious, "How did you keep so dry when you went swimming?" "How did Q know what gadgets you would need?" and "Why do you order your Martinis shaken, when they should be stirred?"

Donald didn't pay attention to the conversation at this stage, preferring to think about who he was going to describe instead... If he had thought just a little bit faster, he would have been able to ask Pledge, Jimmy Pledge, for his expert opinion before he absented himself as suavely as he entered.

Donald - "I think the anti-hero I would like to describe, is one you would normally expect to be an actual-hero but isn't. In fact, I think I would go so far as to describe them as a villain. These are people with power over you, who are rude, insulting and threatening, when you have done nothing wrong."

Of course, Donald is describing a recent incident of his, involving a petty self-important police officer, the middle of the road debrief of a significant car accident and his enquiry about the location of an innocent party.[343]

Sven - Don't cross section Toms, Dicks, Harrys, or Freds.

Sven had once again confused nearly everyone with his cookie quote.

Donald was torn between his earlier acceptance of the first cookie from Sven's patient experience, and his desire to keep his intelligence anonymous. He didn't want to become the target of every tangentially related commercial advertising about the latest breakthrough in whatever product has the largest marketing budget.

Remaining silent, in the hope this advertising would just go away, Donald smiled smugly to himself secure in the knowledge that he actually knew what Sven meant this time...

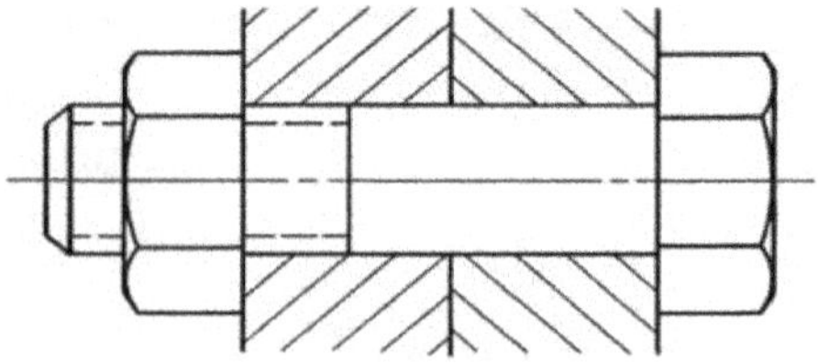

---

[342] Umbrella poor, Donald appreciated the third person description.

[343] Due to patient impatient conflictions, I cannot reveal anything else here.

And to finish the session, these are the lists of Nevers and Musts:

What you Never Say to (or even talk about with) a Mental Patient:

- **Ignorance** - Do Not:
    - Try to solve what you think is their problem for them;
      Even if you are exactly right, you will always be very wrong.
    - Ask a lot of intrusive questions about their past;
      There are always many triggers hidden in their closets.
    - Attempt to cheer them up by telling jokes or feel-good stories;
      Donald is exempted from this rule, as he is "on the inside."
    - Say that someday they'll probably look back at this and laugh; or
      If it's not funny now, it never will be. And it's not funny now.
    - Offer them an alcoholic drink and then invite them to have sex.
      It will become extremely messy, both figuratively and literally.[344]

- **Comparison** - Do Not:
    - Compare their situation to other people you know who are crazy;
    - Say how much better you would have handled the situation;
    - Talk about how bad you're feeling at the moment; or
    - Try to relate to them by comparing what they are going through
      to your own personal negative experiences.
      This is not about you, or anyone else for that matter.

- **Dismiss/Minimise** - Do Not:
    - Tell them it isn't a crisis and attempt to change the subject;
    - Tell them how foolish they are being;
    - Tell them their feelings are silly, meaningless or inappropriate;
    - Tell them everything happens for a reason, or it is God's will; or
    - Tell them they are letting their imagination run wild.
      In fact,... Don't "Tell them" anything.

- **Advice** - Do Not:
    - Give them unsolicited advice, ever;
    - Say to them "Pick yourself up by the bootstraps," "Get over it," or
      "Forget the past," and, "and then just get on with your life." or
    - Ask them to talk to a psychiatrist, psychologist, or psychic.
      Credit them with a modicum of sense.

- **Overreaction** - Do Not:
    - Dramatize their pain by being shocked at everything they say; or
    - Walk away, hang up the phone, or laugh while pointing fingers.
      You are actually pretty much going to be wrong all the time.

---

[344] Donald had not considered this before, and he wasn't sure if he agreed with the underlying premise, especially if a premises was available for lying...

What you Must Say to stop being talked about as a Mental Patient:

This last topic is what Donald had been impatiently waiting for.

Regrettably, the focus was centred on a sharing of knowledge, rather than a receiving. Donald wasn't one to share at the best of times, and after he had immersed himself in some private anger over all of the Do Not suggestions, he completely missed everything.

And back to the story at hand...

The Nota vs Owedebt struggle was coming to a head and looked ready to erupt just as soon as a bit of squeeze was judiciously applied. In a particularly juicy display of synchronicity,[345] and using some of their recently acquired fine-tuned communication skills, these two antagonists "Fine!"d simultaneously, pirouetted anti-each-other-wise, tossed their heads up'n'back and flounced off Chunky style to annoy some innocent soon to be verbalised ears.

For Nota this was actually a very big deal. The obvious tension, mentioned earlier, was primarily due to the fact that she was about to be released into an unsuspecting public on her own recognisance. She had been delaying, all day, trying to find the right moment to tell Owedebt. It hadn't come... So now she was packing up her belongings and getting stuff from the nurse's storage area alone. It was proving to be more difficult than the exit exam.[346]

Nota's exit interviews with Dr Gee Jay, Houts Marted and DD had all been "good enough" to tick the six pages of appropriate boxes, and after Mark Time confirmed her financials were in order, she was officially given her discharge documentation. The tears trickling down her pull-it-together face were a salty combination of "of joy" and "of apprehension."

Donald could see Nota was in distress, as he could see her tears. He didn't understand why she was, but he knew he should try to empathise with her, so he offered to help carry her belongings to the administration waiting area. It seemed to be the right thing to do, and he even managed a "there" or two.

After they arrived, one hundred and two seconds later, Nota gave Donald a short letter to give to Owedebt. Plunged immediately into the effluent of his comfort zone, Donald trepidatiously accepted the responsibility.[347]

---

[345] Which would have won them a wooden prize, in the Synchronised event, at the recent Saint Rita's Sanatorium Mocking Games!

[346] And that is saying something... It is harder to get out, than it is to get in.

[347] As Owedebt was physically absent, as well as no longer actually talking to her, Nota had resorted to writing a parting message in letter form to her. It also included a very heartfelt goodbye P.S. addendum to Chunky Poopy.

When Donald gave Owedebt the letter later, having questionably staked himself out near the Kangaroo Medication Nook at medication time, he took three and a half minutes to explain to her what had been going on right under her up'n'back nose for most of the day.

In one of her more devilish moments, Owedebt implied most fervently she didn't care about any of the details he had just told her, or any of the alleged activities during the day, and would continue to believe she was the only one who had pushed Nota out of SaRS… "So?"

Nota had used all of her learned passive aggressive skills to write…

Dear O. Dear

The reason Y I am writing this letter 2 U now is because U aren't talking 2 me at the present moment 2 be honest.

I don't know what I have done 2 make U so upset with me 2 be honest but I really need 2 make U understand that I am not here 4 U anymore as they have told me that I can go home by myself.

N.B. This note is from Nota Bena.

P.S. Say goodbye 2 Chunky Poopy 4 me.

F.U. *

* Friend Upset

Chapter 12a:[348]
Halloween
(Friday the Twoteenth)

Halloween was one of those celebrations Donald didn't understand. Yes, he knew many reasons why people were celebrating, he knew what Halloween historically represented to the various factions, and he also knew how the Halloweenies celebrated. Yet, even after all of that knowledge, he still didn't understand how it became the one accepted day of the international year when children were actually and literally encouraged to accept candy from as many strangers as they could find.[349]

It was insidiously irking in its irony as far as Donald was concerned.

If you recall, Donald had had Halloween unceremoniously thrust upon him in the last week or two. Now it was the time to have the ceremony also thrust, and this time... He was going to be prepared:

- He had searched, researched and searched for a third time all through the top visible layer of the internet;
- Boned up on many of the 206 traditions he could find, no matter how skeletal or hollow the information at his disposal was; and
- Was perfectly willing to doff his own habitual mask, and just *pretend* to be like he was, for the first time in a very, very long time.

---

[348] Mr Halfbrain still isn't at all superstitious, but it probably won't hurt.

[349] Donald's endemic dislike of this celebration was due to the fact that all of the celebrationists didn't know what it meant... What all of it meant...! And *absolutely nothing* to do with the other fact that he resented having to spend 364.25 days of the year explaining to people why he was wearing a mask.

Donald had actually got most of this wrong. Unsurprisingly, as most of his exposure to Halloween was through franchised TV drama aimed at teenagers, or from horror movies aimed at the desensitised and disenfranchised parents of those same teenagers. Although, when he thought about it, at least half of the reasons why Halloween was celebrated at all, and considering how it was celebrated, were in direct contradiction of each other:

<u>**One Side (Christianity)**</u>	<u>**Other Side (The Pagans)**</u>
¤ A celebration on All Hallows' Eve dedicated to remembering saints who have fallen out of vogue.	¤ A celebration marking the end of a Harvest Season that follows on from a successful farming year.
¤ There is a feast where everyone partakes of the "Soul Cake" while they are burning incense.	¤ There is a feast where everyone with a soul watches a "Master of Reapers" begging incessantly.
¤ Offerings of flowers, candles and prayers are left at the grave sites of dead loved ones.	¤ Loaves of bread, from the freshly harvested wheat crop, are baked and given to feed the poor.

Donald didn't spend too much of his precious time thinking about which side of the ledger he preferred to fall on, as long as he got his fair share of any chocolate passed around, he would be happy.[350] On the way out of his room he was mentally cataloguing everything he was eminently prepared for:

    ¤ He remembered Nurse Jack was going to attend, wearing a costume comprised of a welder's mask and butcher's apron, while wielding an oversized oozing syringe, and he was one of the facilitators;

    ¤ The flyer indicated there would be traditional music played, a dancing presentation and some telling of legends. Donald was extremely wary of becoming too involved musically, physically, or vocally; and

    ¤ He was excited about listening to Chief Chef Chief Chef Chief Changes' side of the story...

When Donald arrived at the Battle of Kingswood Hill memorial gardens, he was surprised to see there were already many people seated on the ground around the sacred fire pit, and that there was a crackling, spitting, roaring fire happening. It warmed him completely to the quadruple cockles of his heart, from both directions, in and out.

---

[350] There is significant scientific proof that dark chocolate, in moderation, can replace a patient's terminally dark thought of their death, with a slightly less chronic dark thought of weight gain.

Donald found a position close enough so he could observe the activity, but far enough so he wouldn't interfere.[351] The first person he observed in minute detail was Chef Chief, and later on he would receive confirmation that these annotations were accurate. He was wearing a mottled grey loincloth and tunic, made from the renewable fibres of shredded grey gum tree bark, which were harmoniously accentuated by a single feather from an Australian wedge tailed eagle, and his footwear was a pair of size eight Uggkubra[352] branded moccasins of a similar colour.

Chef stood up and introduced Nurse Jack, who would begin the evening's proceedings by welcoming everyone in his traditional language...

"I welcome you onto the land traditionally cared for by the Dharug Mob. This is a place where everyone will receive safe passage and equal treatment, while they acknowledge and respect the elders, past, present and emerging, and show empathy for all of the natural inhabitants.

I also welcome Chef Chief as a leader, and representative, from his culture; Mindy Ownbeeswhacks as a very scary powerful centenarian plus; and thank William the Piano man for sharing his talent, which is representative of people with musical ability, by being our background accompaniment tonight."

  ¤   Extract from The Donald Diaries.

       Translation provided by Nurse Jack. (Dharug Elder and Friend)

As far as Donald was concerned, Nurse Jack's welcome was so much more welcoming than anyone could have expected, given the atrocious response to their initial interactions over 200 years ago.[353] Chef acknowledged Nurse Jack's welcome on behalf of himself, Mindy, Willy and also everyone else, and then paid his personal respects back.

---

[351] Donald Mandate #4 - "He shall be just close enough to see, not to act."

[352] Uggkubra is a humane clothing collaboration between Chef and Jack. They design and manufacture a small range of extremity wear made from the felt blend of thirteen secret hair and furs. These ingredients, all of which are collected without harming the providers, are traditionally processed using a combination of methods stemming from both of their cultures.

They don't believe in advertising, or even selling, any of their fine products. You may only obtain them by being the recipient of a gift directly from them.

[353] This is unfortunately a true story. The Dharug people fought against the settlers for their food and children... And were ultimately murdered.

Following on from his initial observation, and even though Donald didn't understand the words,[354] he certainly had understood the historical alienating sentiment behind them. Everyone's recognition, and unequivocal acceptance, of the traditional welcome was very humbling. The memory created by all of this would be one Donald cherished.[355]

With the initial formalities of the occasion over, the collective group were disappointed when they didn't get right into celebration mode... As it was an official SaRS event, there were the rules to consider...

SaRS ~~Rules~~ *Guidelines* the Outside

1) This will be a nonpartisan, nonreligious and non-stereotypical non-event.
2) Every story related tonight must be assumed to be a work of pure fiction.
3) No cultural accusations are to be levelled, even if they may be warranted.

4) The outside meeting officials will identify this as a no-touchy-touch event.
5) Any masks worn must have the appropriate safety accreditation attached.
6) Non-essential staff members are allowed to speak at their own discretion.

7) Tonight is a Full Blood Moon Lunar Eclipse – So, expect the unexpected.
8) If you see any monsters you didn't expect, then believe the unbelievable.
9) Nobody will be required to imagine anything unimaginable... Imagine that!

10) Trick or Treating and Tarot Card reading, have both been SaRS approved.
11) Outside has been officially defined as: That place without walls or rooves.
13) Never underestimate the humour benefit resulting from a repetitious joke.

SaRS Official 8 – SaRS Rules the Outside (Halloween Version)

The SaRS ~~Rules~~Guidelines the Outside (Halloween Version) poster looked very old, in comparison to the other ~~Rules~~Guidelines posters he has seen, so, Donald added, "How was this poster updated with situation specific details?" to the list of unimaginable questions he wasn't required to think about.

---

[354] This was an atypical situation, in that for once, Donald didn't expect to understand the words, and he was pleasantly surprised to find out that he had actually got-the-gist of what was being spoken.

[355] The significance of this statement can be put in perspective when you consider Donald will come to value this memory over many others from the many Comic-Con entertainment features he will attend after publication.

Expostulatory exculpatory explanatory exterminatory NOTE:
After much internal debate,[356] I felt any story befitting being told on these topics would need to be accurate enough to not cause offence, and as I don't know enough about either of these histories, or traditions, I didn't tell them. What you have here instead are several bush yarns as might be told around a dwindling campfire while sipping the remnants of your billy tea...

1) Donald (Halfbrain with Istha T. You)

It is unfortunate, yet marginally appropriate, that Halloween is ironically one of the few times when Donald doesn't have to wear a mask to fit in. The additional tiny detail that the monsters of the world accept him as one of their own, but are still scared of him, is a stunning bonus. The bush yarn that Donald is about to relate to, winds him up completely and is a strange duet reverse ventriloquist dummy dialogue with Istha:

ITY   ...   Would you like to welcome me too Donald?

DH   ...   I think I'd rather welcome you to go anywhere else.

<Pause for minimal laughter for predictable stereotypical response.>

ITY   ...   What do you mean?

DH   ...   Well, the sooner we get off this improvised stage, the better it will be for me. I don't want you to go around blabbing to everyone all of my deep dark personal secrets, do I?

<Head swivel. Change facial expression to apparent unbridled surprise.>

ITY   ...   Secrets? What secrets!

DH   ...   Exactly... And that's how I'd like to keep it.

<Sly winking to the audience, supported by feverish know-it-all nodding.>

ITY   ...   Really? You do know Donald, **everything** you know, I also know... I may be just a dumb ventriloquist puppet to you, but you are the unspeakable Muppet if you think the voice in my head isn't yours. And don't get me started on where you tried to put your hand! If you could move it a little bit to the left, you can get right...[357]

---

[356] For three different days, I thought about this issue three different ways, resulting in me writing three different essays, regaling three different clichés. I finally decided that I wasn't in the least bit appropriately qualified to tell a humorous, yet inoffensive, anecdote about anyone's history, except mine. So, as my personal history includes many instances when I was silent, about many instances of dubious activity, over many instances of nights with some moonlight, I came up with these fictitious stories, nearly instantly.

[357] It was at this point when Donald abruptly called a halt to proceedings.

2) Karl (Saneman)

Pass.[358]

3) Skit (Zoland, as Marcel Marceau)

Donald was quite familiar with every applicable concept, that he was not able to communicate with other people acceptably, by any available measure. While this was sometimes put down to other people not understanding what he was saying, there were far more times when it was Donald who was doing the misunderstanding.

Skit's skit-like performance exacerbated both this theory, and Donald, as there were simply no words used to facilitate what Skit was trying to say. Apart from the fact that Skit looked a lot like a white-face-fish trying to talk, Donald found him to be completely indescribable.[359] This false accusation would later be rescinded, and Donald would go on to describe the incident as a complete mime-entous misunderstanding.

Marcel presented a series of sub-skits, re-enacting his entire life, including his resistance of the evil Nazi regime. It was a fantastic representation of the, now silent, Polish French Jewish mime's narrative:

- The first skit he presented was a burlesque performance of a woman giving birth to a child against the wind. If you imagine his entire body as part of the illusion, you will achieve a similar level of concern over the development and communication of this thought.
- This was followed by an apparent arduous trek, involving many stairs and closed fire escapes, to what seemed to be an acting school run by deaf, anaemic, sad, circus clowns. Donald was particularly impressed by this skit's theatrical exposé of pretend makeup application.
- With the instruction portion of the exercise complete, the next mime was the miming of a mime. This construct was a reconstruction of his first rebellious act against authority. It was the ultimate blank of the invading German forces by the resistance during World War II and facilitated an escape of the silent masses to the mime neutral Swiss.

---

[358] We are often told that getting into a routine "could be" helpful towards regaining a semblance of mental stability. There are lots of unknowns when it comes to solving the inner malfunctioning secret aspects of a human mind.

[359] Skit was, completely understandably, currently in the throes of acting out over Marcel Marceau's famous stage persona "Bip the Clown" being misappropriated and put on display while he was still bald and hatless.

> ¤   Portraying irony is one of the staple talents required to be a successful mime artist. It didn't hurt Marcel's chances, that he was elected to be a member of Germany's Academy of Fine Arts, twice, and declared a national treasure in Japan. The irony on display now is that he escaped being typecast in military theatre as an Axis ally, by being awarded the highest honour for a French National, the "Grand Officier de la Légion d'Honneur," and it was titled, "Thinking your way out of a box."

Donald tuned out of the public silence for a little while, to think about the underlying messages he was receiving from Marcel. What was the purpose of creating an illusion, if not to communicate something? Surely there are some thoughts or feelings the audience is supposed to receive.

Isn't this why they were all there in the first place? To extract some of the flecks of truth from everyone's publicly presented illusion. If "they" created an illusion of "perceived normality," shouldn't you be looking at how everyone else reacts to it, to validate your own reaction?

If I arrive at an illusionary doorway, immediately take in all of the obvious visual data, come to some reactive decision and mime knocking on the door... Isn't that an equally valid response as, say, simulating forcibly kicking it down and entering with all guns blazing? Who is to say that both fictional reactions aren't correct, for a certain value of correct?

Feeling as if he was overthinking things,[360] Donald was relieved when the mimed performance quietly reintroduced itself into his thinking process. After all, there is no point in creating an illusion...

> ¤   Marcel's next performance was simply titled, "A walk on the Moon." The alliterated silence was badly broken by a basic backbeat, raising several questions in Donald's mind...
>> ø   Is this where "his" whiteface obsession came from?
>> ø   What about "his" zombieic street dance movements?
>> ø   It also poured senseless fuel on the fire of discussions surrounding the senselessness of practicing the advanced miming technique, "Help, I'm on fire and my nose is melting!" by using actual fire.[361]

---

[360] Really? Donald has only just realised that his "thinking" was "over" now? Why don't you pull the other one? It plays a rendition of "Creepy Donald."
    Re: Creepy Donald (Inspired by *Creeque Alley* – The Mamas and the Papas) p204
    ¤ Extract from The Donald Diaries.

[361] And the sub-question, is this when "he" started wearing only one glove?

> This style of illusionary dance movement is sometimes considered to be the musician's equivalent of the magician's misdirection technique. The "singer" may, or may not, be compensating for a lack of talent in other areas. Or it may simply be their way of getting people to ignore what is obviously going on under the covers, by believing in their own manufactured performance.[362]

ꭕ His final routine was mimed fluently in English, French and German. It was also a unique scene for another reason... It contained the only sanctioned speaking part that has ever been accepted as being part of a mimeful act. It was simply the mime artist standing motionless, with his mimed flowered and shabby top hat in hand, looking at the entire audience with the dreamiest calculating eyes he could summon, often accentuated by a single tear, saying, "Throw me your money!"

A successful implementation of this final mime is the basis for every mime in history being able to eat regularly. It is a very simple concept which requires the greatest amount of a mime's time for practice and dedication. The mime must be able to "trick" their audience into believing they have actually been entertained and owe them money for the privilege. It is one of the very rare situations which "does, or does not," give them a physical acknowledgement of their achievements.

4) "Willy" (William the Piano Man on the Digeridoo)

The Halloween musical version of the Rocky saga has not progressed at all since back when Everything Changed (Back to Normal), and it is now likely to be delayed until sometime after the R.A.I.N.B.O.W. summit.

Rocky: An Instrumentally Normal Blend of WTFs.

---

[362] There are several snippets of various recordings of this performance floating around that feature Donald talking to his legal advisor (Ben) in the background, here are just a few which have been semi-un-muffled:

ꭕ No... Don't Stop 'Til You Get Enough, we'll Beat It...

ꭕ I'm sure this fictitious story won't pose a problem to Billy Jean...

ꭕ Say, Say, Say whatever you like, it's not a Bad Thriller...

ꭕ As long as we don't actually specify Black or White...

From an expert who evaluated the tapes: "You can't actually 'see' Donald say any of these things about 'him,' and the references are so oblique they keep the identity of 'him' nearly indiscernible. These two factors alone will make any legal action unexpected. <Conspiratorially> In fact, it would more than likely only raise the profile of the book to moderately interesting."

5) Mindy (Ownbeeswhacks - Wiccan)

As the stage was being cleared of all the remaining mimes, to the sound of Willy playing an acoustic digeridoo arrangement of Highway to Hell (by AC/DC),[363] the Wiccan gathering seemed to be coming together nicely, with Mindy at the lead. She wasn't being bossy, as such, it's just that everyone was doing what she told them to do without question.

Donald was allowed to place, and then ritualistically set fire to, the centrepiece of the ceremony; a decorative candle he had fastidiously[364] made over a period of twoteen years, mostly out of ear wax, with a wick made from spun belly button fluff. It was to remind everyone what happened to people who died in their sleep, and then burnt to death.

The combination of full-moon, Blood-moon, Friday the 13th and the Southern Hemisphere's Summer Solstice was a unique combination, seen only a six fingered handful of times before in recorded mystery. It was rapidly becoming a totally susceptible time, when those "in the know" liked to get together and discuss the Six Ws of the WWW (Wild Wiccan World):

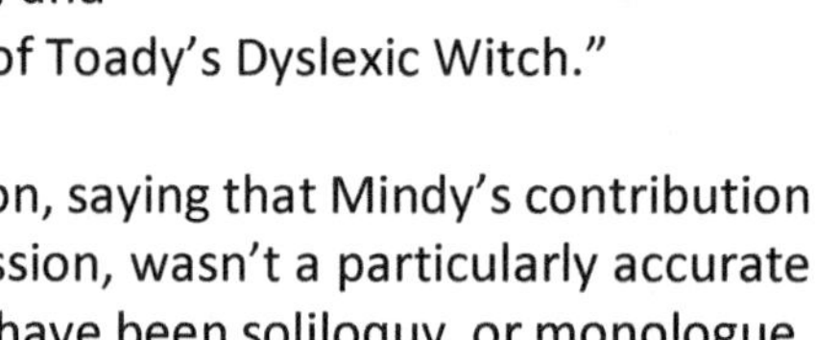

- ⚥ **Why** (Self-explanatory);
- ⚥ **When** you can expect the unexpected;
- ⚥ **Where** the Wild Witches are;
- ⚥ **What** we can do to you if we really want to;
- ⚥ **Who** we want you to think we are; and
- ⚥ **How** she does it… "File and Mites of Toady's Dyslexic Witch."

Donald felt this introductory description, saying that Mindy's contribution to the campfire bullshit yarns was a discussion, wasn't a particularly accurate one. An example closer to the truth might have been soliloquy, or monologue, as has been discussed previously and then changing to eulogy if you actually commented on this to her.

By the time Donald arrived at the end of this thought, taking a moment or three every now and then along the way to be mesmerised by the candle and its perfectly conical spiralling vortex of silver flecked smoky emission that was disseminating into the night, he had missed the entire point.

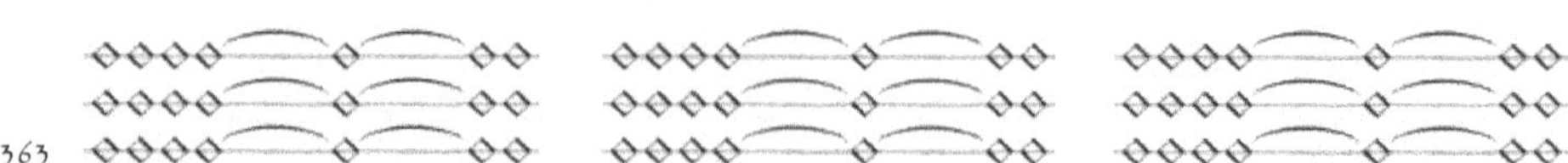

363

[364] And curiously, as he wouldn't have known to bring it to SaRS with him.

6) Sven & Lost M'Hankie's Pledge, Jimmy Pledge (Owedebt)

The next sadness lull in activity was facilitated by Owedebt. She had taken to ostracising herself after reading the farewell note left to her from Nota. Far from misunderstanding the note, she realised that any salvation, expected to be found on her part, would most likely lie in the opposite direction of childish. This explained her current tantrum, as she had read the situation all wrong, as was fairly common when you are an infantile adult.

It's a bad sign when you get lost on the way to a geography lesson.
Absence is **W**hat **O**wedebt **L**acks.

"Hello again, Pledge, Jimmy Pledge. It sheemsh to me that you might have mishplashed a shertain shomeone. While I wash filming Lightening-Bat, I wash going through an exshtended period of forshed amneshia, sho much sho, the produsher produshed a Low-Jack-Pill for me to shwallow. It emitsh a shiren when activated by wandering off from a shet shtarting poshition. If you find a way to have the mishshing pershon shwallow the shlightly bitter pill, you will be able to find them almosht immediately."

Her absence had been Svened, acronymised and Pledge, Jimmy Pledged, at virtually the same time. And even though they all imparted exactly the same amount of sense as each other, within the appropriate margin of error; which is to say, they were well passed the utterly nonsensical percentile on an empty bell-curve chart to within thirteen standard deviations...
Donald agreed with this perfectly. "Well, that's just perfect![365]"

7) Seth (Rueful) & "Sam" (Pull), the Ghostly Presences, Man!

After all the various silences:
- Involuntarily engaged;
- Voluntarily withheld;
- Completely scripted;
- Incompletely delayed;
- Accidentally absent; and
- Conspicuous by its presence.

SHHHHHH!

...had had a chance to quieten down, the ghostly throat clearing hack that preceded an uncomfortable sounding spectral limp, heralded Seth's presence like never before. As he approached the puddle of smouldering ear wax, Seth looked expectantly over Donald's right ear lobe. It was like he was waiting for something to happen, or someone to appear, but was still intent on exploiting the vicinity to Donald to wonder where the wax had originally come from.

---

[365] Sarcasm often eludes Donald, even when he is the perpetrator.

Donald hazarded a guess that BLT was going to arrive soon and complete the died-not-opaque duo. He thusly proved his simplistic quip, "Don't Guess!" was something he should have listened to himself, at any of the many times in the past few weeks when he though this at the group facilitators. Now, as it was then, the guess was wasted when it became incorrect due to the arrival of Sam. But, since no one knew, apart from Donald,[366] it was just another, "Doesn't Matter!" moment.

Their "Seth and Sam, the Ghostly Presences, Man!" performance was yet another first for Donald, and he sincerely hoped there wouldn't be a second. There is only so much infantile tantruming one person can bear, and Donald's quota had recently been filled. The back-and-forth childish banter, over this fauna character with a single nonsensical catchphrase, was a tad monotonous and hardly conducive to any form of entertainment:

SR … Do you know the Witch, the Wiccan, or the Earwax Candle Man?
SP … Yes.
<Pause to build the anticipation.>
SR … Well?
SP … Yes, thank you, how are you?
<Pause for the groaning to subside.>
SR … No, I meant… Well?
SP … No, They is one of the Trainee Psychologists.
SR … Who are they?
SP … I just said… They Meantwell is one of the Trainee Psychologists.
<Pause for the realisation this is a reference back to the first book.>
SR … No, I was trying to say… Who are the Witch, the Wiccan and the Earwax Candle Man?
SP … No.
SR … What?
SP … Who are the Wood Masons.
SR … I don't know… Who?
SP … Well, you should meet them.
SR … The Wood Masons are Well?
SP … No. The Wood Masons are Who.
SR … But you just said they were well.
SP … No. I just said they are Who.
SR … Who?
SP … Yes.
<Seth changed tack to tacky and continued.>

---

[366] And Istha, if she was to be believed. Donald guessed she should not be.

SR   ...   All right then. How about this... Which one is the Wiccan?
SP   ...   Yes, she is.
SR   ...   What?
SP   ...   Witch #1 is the Wiccan.
SR   ...   That's what I asked.
SP   ...   No, you didn't.
SR   ...   I'm not making myself very clear.
SP   ...   You're a ghost, you're clear enough to see through completely.
SR   ...   Oh my God... It's all so hard...
SP   ...   And that's what she said.
<No comment, but I warned you it would be tacky.>
SR   ...   One more try... Do you know the Earwax Candle Man?
SP   ...   The Earwax Candle Man?
SR   ...   Yes. The Earwax Candle Man!
SP   ...   No.[367]
WIAM Weeeeeeeeee... I am moot!

8) Anna (Lykeananna)

Donald was still reeling from the last seven (plus or minus) presentations (depending on how your tongue is hanging), not to mention the awkward way the last one climaxed, and was glad to be confronted (in the good way), by a completely sane normal person (not so much).

"Hello everyone and thank you for participation in our series of short, not so short and nut so, short presentations. We have arrived at the fun end[368] of tonight's evening's activities... And there are a few housekeeping tasks that need to be done to satisfy the workplace safety and security requirements."

Anna directed people's attention to her uniform's most recent shoulder accessory, which had been specifically tailored for her engagement tonight as the event security guard and clean-up crew master. "This is the THE,[369] and it confers upon me the charge of reverting this area to a place of calming moonlit serenity. I want the ground to be clean enough for you to eat your dinner off, and we have until Midnight on the 14th to make it so."

---

[367] Donald hadn't told anyone where the candle came from. If he had, I am fairly sure someone would have told him to stick it where candles don't shine, which would have actually been very dangerous if it was lit at the time...

[368] This is, "the end of fun," not, "the end which is fun."

[369] "The Healing Epaulette." Calling it "the THE," annoyed Donald as much as calling an ATM an ATM Machine.

These instructions were confusing to Donald. One of his obsessions is the definition of time, specifically Midnight. Is midnight before or after the day? 23:59:59 of the Thirteenth is the second before the 14th starts.

- ⚥ Does the clock go from 00:00:00 -> 23:59:59, or 00:00:01 -> 24:00:00?
- ⚥ Does 12am come after 11am or 11pm?[370]
- ⚥ How do sundials work in the dark?

Whichever way, Donald wasn't very impressed with having to clean up. After all, he was paying his health fund insurance good money for them to pay for him to be there. Just because there was a demarcation issue between the cleaning crew and the grounds keeping staff, shouldn't mean that he actually had to contribute to the whole mental hospital experience.

"Thank you everyone for your fabulous help with the cleaning/gardening. As you all leave for your own bedroom tonight, please take a flyer for our next scheduled event, Save the Threes."

Donald was thoroughly confused, yet again. He felt emotionally violated because Anna had thanked him for helping to clean up when he hadn't lifted a single finger. Not liking being told what to do was one thing, but, being told what to done was just wrong. A Sphincter Feng Shui later, Donald collected the proffered flyer and then did indeed leave for his own bedroom.

Save the Threes

The number "THREE" is represented by many significant archetypes:

- ⚥ Mind, Body, Spirit
- ⚥ Father, Son, Holy Spirit
- ⚥ Birth, Life, Death
- ⚥ Beginning, Middle, End
- ⚥ Past, Present, Future
- ⚥ Maiden, Mother, Crone
- ⚥ Success, Intuition, Good fortune

Let us gather together in our threes to celebrate the magical number that is Three, **Three**, **THREE**

Building 3 – Room 3 – 3rd of the 3rd – 3:33:33

Flopping on his bed, Donald read the flyer and surprise overshadowed his confusion. One mental calendar entry created later; he was actually looking forward to attending the gathering. Not only because:

- ⚥ It constituted the main part of his favourite number;
- ⚥ Some of his common why questions may well be covered; but mostly
- ⚥ There would only be three people attending, making him at least the third smartest person in the room...

---

[370] It actually comes after both; Donald should know this by now.

Just before he finally succumbed to sleep, Donald had a vivid trilogical recollection...

    Ҋ   Full Moon;

    Ҋ   Done was just wrong; and

    Ҋ   I want the ground to be clean enough to eat off.

To this end, he will wake up as normal in the morning and not remember a thing. This, however, is neither good, nor bad, as Anna generally liked to eat her protein out of a large bowl. As with a lot of things Donald either notices, or thinks, he is quite unable connect all of the dots. In this instance, the dots remain seriously incomplete as well as unconnected.

Stuff I Done-Know...

My days are all unknown and long
From time I rise till sunset gone
The food gets ate;   the coffee's drunk
The words writ down,   the thoughts are thunk

Sometimes I cry and that's not right
No one must know... Internal fight
The washing's hung,   the frypan's new
The bed is made,   the polished shoe

I have no friends, this, people know
No one can help my seeds to grow
The floor looks clean,   the freezer's stocked
The bin's put out,   the back door's locked

I'm not able to let things lie
Understanding... I don't know why
The shower's wet,   the mail's been got
The clothes away,   the end, it's not

Chapter 14:
What Just Happened
(Mini Retrospective)

After enough time has been identified as gone passed, while you are present[371] in an institution as significant SaRS, you can build up an immunity, of a sort, to the assorted teachings thrust upon you. The centralised upbeat message becomes constantly at odds with those less than perfect insinuations happy to exist out on the wing.

The outlying lessons are not specifically malicious, but[372] neither are they entirely sympathetic. Donald doesn't think they are a threat, his stubbornness is more than capable of resisting the copious amounts of acronyms forced on the inmates, he prefers to think of them as an unsafe security measure.

They are unsuccessfully teaching him how to live, instead of showing him how. If you imagine a navigator giving you this instruction, "Turn right at the un-signposted track a kilometre before the next Hungry David's," it will give you a verbal pictorial insight into Donald's requirements. It would be better if the navigator says, "Turn here," rather than giving him a map:

- **ACCEPTS - Central** (No one is to blame) Observe how things are right now, try to be mindful of any thoughts and live in the present;
- **IMPROVE - Right Wing** (There is no one is to blame except yourself) You need to change who you are, your attitudes and your goals, so you are better placed to engage with a brighter future; and
- **DECLINE - Left Wing** (Everyone else is to blame) Wait until someone tells you how it all happened and what they will do about it next time.

---

[371] More-so physically, than mentally, is what Donald was meant to say.

[372] There are only a few instances where a, "but," does not invalidate the earlier part of the statement, and this one is an important exception.

ACCEPTS[373]

Activities that everyone can join in with.
Contributing to society with minimal requirements.
Comparisons are negated as there are no sides.
Emotion driven behaviours are kept in check.
Pushing away any negativity that you are unable to deal with.
Thoughts are processed mindfully.
Self-Soothe accomplishments are celebrated.

IMPROVE[374]

Imagery is vivid, targeted and mandatory.
Meaning can only be obtained through conformity.
Prayer is not acceptable, hoping for direction will not help.
Relaxation of the rules benefits no one.
One thing you can keep, the rest is to be distributed.
Vacation allowances are earned. They are not an entitlement.
Encouragement will be thrust when required.

DECLINE[375]

Defend your rights to be unique if you want to be.
Equality can never be a goal while The Man is in charge.
Communist thoughts are not necessarily all bad.
Local hardships will be endured together.
International hardships should be alleviated if possible.
No is never the correct answer.
Escape into whatever freedom you currently desire.

The first day of Donald's life in SaRS took seven chapters.
(With almost an entire chapter for him to leave his room for the first time.)
The first week took an entire book.
So...
Thirteen chapters gone in the second book is no time for any reality!

---

[373] One of these acronyms is not like the others

[374] One of these acronyms, I just made it up now

[375] Can you tell which acronym is not like the others
Before I'm forced to go and uncover my cow?

Inspired by *One of these things is not like the others* - Sesame Street.

Donald is considering some of the more radical comments made by other inmates[376] during the groups they have been attending while "getting better," and has some philosophical questions, conundrums, or Donaldisms…

1) Rewards

"Give yourself a reward for achieving a goal, no matter how small."
- I ask myself: "Isn't being allowed to avoid my issue, a reward in itself?"
- And I answer: "I don't care if it is avoidance, it shall be my reward."
- Thus concluding: "I will not be guilty, this time, for avoiding life…"
- Adding a mental note: "I should stop talking to and answering myself."
- Because: "Someone might think I was crazy!"

I also have a fundamental issue with the setting of any personal goal low enough to ensure a successful outcome. If you know beforehand you will most probably succeed, then you won't be motivated enough to try and extend your comfort zone. And doesn't that defeat the purpose?

Another circular issue at odds here is, a lot of self-rewards are of the white, milk, or dark varieties. I might have a goal to lose ½kg of weight, over a week. Completely obtainable, tremendously worthwhile, but so ridiculous when you consider that my reward will be a 500gm bar of milky goodness…

For a third, and final, time there was a rewarding issue discussed in group. We were all given a thirteen minute "early mark," and were sent away after being *told* to reward ourselves.

My problem here is… Attending group *is* my reward.

It is my reward for completing another day (successfully?) of life at SaRS.

I went away in confusion:
- There was nothing I wanted to do;
- There was nothing I could do; because
- Even if I wanted to do nothing, I was being instructed to do something.

I can't remember if I have ever rewarded myself for simply living.[377] This is, essentially, what we were asked to do.

So now, I'm sitting here writing this, wondering what to do.

Or, is wondering about doing something, the same as doing nothing?

---

[376] The inmates who made these philosophy extracting comments have all been de-identified for various reasons. But it mainly boils down to, because at the time Donald was either in a state of denial, or don't care at all.

[377] Either because I haven't, or I have, and I've forgotten. It would have been a good thing to do, and therefore it is likely to be a forgotten good memory.

2) Extreme Irregular Definition Acceptance

"Can you rotate that to the left?"

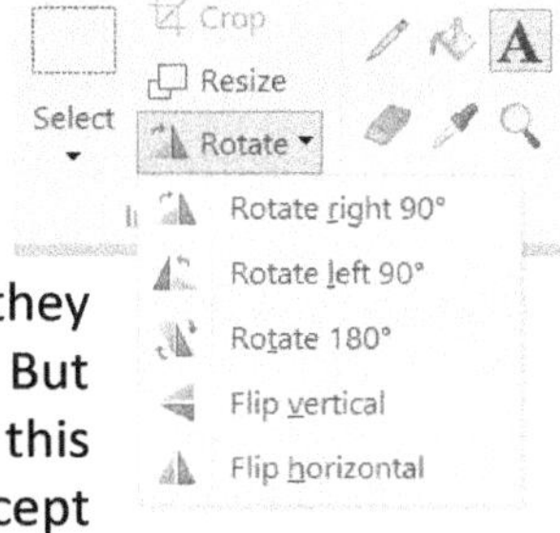

Apart from the correct answer being yes, or no, I really don't want to accept the systemic ignorance which is still being perpetrated here.

Why do they say rotate right and/or left, when they intend clockwise and anticlockwise, respectively?[378] But more than that, why does everyone understand that this is what they mean? And then, why do they always accept the incorrect instruction without question?[379] They discombobulate me…

By way of a visual example, or two, you shall now participate in learning:

Which way would you turn the spanner, on the left ←, for left? Left and right are, by definition, unattached straight-line directions. Rotate requires an attached angular direction. Having said that, the rhyming/alliteration memory tool, Righty-Tighty and Lefty-Loosey, while being technically incorrect, is useful when teaching someone how to change a wheel on their car.[380]

Which one of the three rotated faces, presented below and leftish ↙, is the *rotated left* version of the original face to the right? →

Hint: Depending on your point of view, all of them could be.

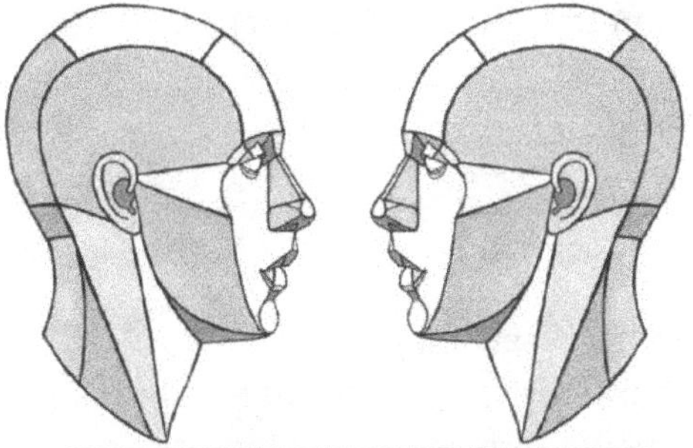

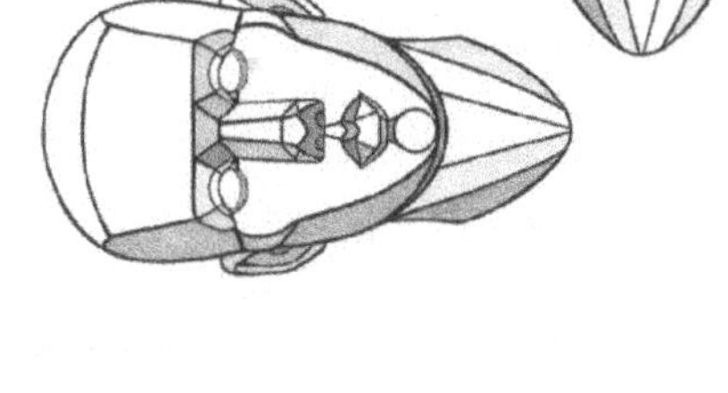

---

[378] An awkward, yet correct, use of the word respectively, as Donald has absolutely no respect for the villains involved.

[379] Donald has broken one of his own rules here, specifically the "Thou shalt not over generalise," one. I find it interesting that he thinks everyone understands rotate left is actually trying to mean rotate counter clockwise. Is it weirder that we all do this, or that I find it interesting?

[380] This is another misnomer on Donald's ever-growing list of pet hates. It is common for people to say they are changing a tyre, when they mean they are changing a wheel. Changing a *flat* tyre would also be acceptable, just.

3) Facts of life

"Some people are happy and prefer to live alone."

I find this statement quite hard to believe, and not simply because of the speaker's lack of personal commitment, as complexly the two sections are not necessarily connected. If you prefer to live alone, you may not necessarily be happy about it; and if you are happy, you may still prefer to live with company. I think that most people would not set out to be a happy living alone loner:

- Some people might find existence alone marginally easier;
- Some people have accepted they cannot live with others;
- Some people find some happy in their solitude, every now-and-again.

As a permanent situation, I think you would have to be completely mental. I've been living alone for an unfair while, and recently, I could count the happy days I've had on one finger... Two at the most. And both of those times were when strangers avoided me, keeping to their own cliques.

No one ever says, "Yay me! Another great day alone."

"I can't change who I *am*.[381]"

People don't ever change by any measurable amount, and I'm hoping this "fact" has been scientifically tested and proven somewhere. Whenever I run into a previous acquaintance, I don't understand when they say I've changed. I haven't. The only thing that *has* changed is their perception of me; and the only thing that *will* change is the realisation that this *will never* change.

This is me.

This has always been me.

This will always be me.

4) Psychobabble

"The main characteristic for a sociopath is self-pity."

I hope that self-pity isn't the *main* characteristic when you are defining a sociopath. It is more likely to be the significant differentiating factor between a sociopath and a psychopath. Either way, once you are on either of those two paths, it is very hard to step off.

So, the thought for the day...

I'm a self-pitying sociopath with Asperger's.[382] I'm so screwed.

---

[381] Donald's thoughts revolve around his, "I don't **want** to change who I *am*."

[382] Asperger is a German name, so it should be pronounced with a hard G. There is no soft G in the German language, even though, ironically, there is one in German. Also, Asperger's name would rhyme with the surname of the Austrian racing driver Gerhard Berger (pronounced with two hard Gs).

"Schemas describe how you organise information in your thoughts."
My three main schemas are:
- Emotional Deprivation (I scored 100% on this schema);
- Social Isolation (More of a lifestyle choice than a schema);
- Negativity/Pessimism (I disagree with this; I think I am Realistic).

Where in the list is your intelligence described as a factor? And surely, the amount of knowledge you have should be taken into consideration when you are organising this into various thoughts. Not everything about a person can be reduced to an absence, an alienation, or an argument.

All of the schemas we were tested on told us what we were doing wrong. There was nothing to congratulate us on a job well done so far... I then took umbrage when I tried to explain that I thought the schemas were all negative, and their official reply was, "Yes thank you, we already know. There are people working on this."

So, we are being instructed to conform to an outdated regime, which only tells us what we are all doing wrong, while at the same time is not offering any solutions, even though we know the system is broken...[383]

"What are the five qualities that resonate with me?"
That's an easy one. I know all about me.
- **Truth** (Usually to the point when it hurts.)
- **Resilience** (I just keep coming back.)
- **Observation** (I see everything, I just don't understand it.)
- **Love** (Both ways. It resonates, doesn't happen though.)
- **Like** (Specifically myself. But again, doesn't happen.)

So, there you have it... my TROLL answer.
It's funny because it's true...

5) Minor Questions of Pith

"It's all uphill from here."
This allegedly means things are going to stay hard or get harder.
Pushing a bicycle uphill is harder than riding it downhill.

"It's all downhill from here."
The inverse of the previous. For the same reason.
Or is it...?
The corollary of the previous. For a different reason.
We are at the peak of things, the results from here will not be as good.

---

[383] Sound familiar? I really don't like political issues, where the solution is to blame the other guy, without saying how anything can be fixed. In fact, I don't like much about politics, or politicians, at all.

All right, that's enough of that. Let's get back to the story.

When we last left our ~~intrepid~~ insipid hero alone, he was in the process of drifting off to sleep, thinking about three things:
- The number three;
- The letter pi; and
- The moon moon.[384]

As predicted, Donald awoke not remembering a thing about the previous night's mental hieroglyphics and was about to become the latest victim of the weekend in-activities lethargy.

Once he noticed things starting to deteriorate, he made a vow to wake up to himself tomorrow. But for now, in an attempt to compensate for his wanton wanting behaviour, he went for a walk, and found himself a comfortable seat outside to reflect on where he was at. It was an opportunistic measure, as the seat was in a pronounced position to observe most of the SaRS based outside activities without anyone noticing him, and therefore the likelihood of being asked to join in was almost negligible. Just the way he liked it.

Another item of interest Donald noticed was the presence of surveillance, and counter surveillance, equipment scattered throughout the grounds. They were strangely located in no discernible pattern he could identify:
- Archaic cameras on most rooftops, and some were pointing to the sky;
- Movement sensors immediately behind temporary warning signs; and
- An occasional Geiger counter emitting a low, steady, background blip.

The haphazard implementation of these big brother gadgets had Donald intrigued. He spent several hours in the surprisingly comfortable position and noticed a myriad of clandestine surreptitious activity. Nature, it seemed, was indeed a great moderator, as there were interactions between a range of staff members, inmates and even the odd visitor. Donald would not have guessed it could happen, had he not seen it himself.

---

[384] This must have been named by an Australian:
- The harbour in Sydney is called...
- The bridge over that harbour is called...
- The big dessert, made out of sand, is called...
- The large reef preventing people from landing here is called...

Mind you, they are all still better than Boaty McBoatface.

But don't get me started on South Australia, our 3rd most southern state, which is further north than three complete states and one territory. In fact, it is only completely south of one state, which is really a territory that's called...

Eventually Donald euphorically realised he was on his first stakeout. While his eyes had been taking everything in, his hands had been recording a portion of it for posterity. By the time he needed to come out of the shadows, a map showing the dark zones, along with a detailed set of notes of who was doing what with who and where it was being done, was in his possession. The major participant of the observed activity was a toss-up between Andy,[385] and a new character Donald hasn't met yet, but has heard about in passing...

Pharmaceuticals ᴙ Us
If you need a little something to float your boat
After you come down, talk to **Farmer Suit Tickle**
We have the best **Drugs** in all shapes and sizes
Phone: 131313 (Thirteen Thirteen Thirteen)

Farmer Suit Tickle is the in-house chemist at SaRS. He's been the sole drug supplier at SaRS for many years, cultivating a very successful drug facilitation programme. As well as a pharmacology degree, he has a chequered history of farming ecologically potent hippie/hipster approved pain management flora.

These activities persisted well into Donald's next thought process, which was simply, "What were they doing?" Feeling, intrigued for the second time in as many pages, decided that Andy was likely to be the main source of potential interest available, after Farmer threw his hands up in apparent frustration and stormed off leaving Andy standing there alone holding the clipboard. Donald elected to see exactly what was possibly what.

To the untrained casual observer, following Andy might seem to be a poor decision if Donald wanted to remain on the wellbeing schedule set out for him. Especially when you consider that one of their aims was to teach him how he should become less vulnerable to conspiracy plans. Conveniently, the mystery trumped the mastery, and Donald found himself hot on the trail of he didn't really know what, where, or why, but counted himself lucky because he knew roughly who and when.

The stealthy trailing of Andy came to a conclusion outside the pharmacy. Donald took a moment to think about the differences between a chemist and a pharmacist, and decided they were both seriously outdated, and accurately wrong, to harbour prejudices against either chemicals or farms. He didn't like having to think of anyone as a "drug dealer," so when this became the only remaining viable option, he had some trouble accepting the label.

---

[385] Andy One, of Wholly Mowly Groundskeeping, not Dr Coughed.

Returning a portion of his thought processes to the following of Andy task, Donald observed, entranced, while Andy knocked on the closed door of SaRS' bulk drug dispensary.[386] Andy waited for two moments while someone on the inside checked for anything unchecked, and then entered into the beyond the door space. Snapping back to reality,[387] Donald took stock of his situation, and realised he was completely uninformed about the place where the little magic white pills came from.

Donald set about reading any official documentation he could find before he decided to think about what he might do next.[388] Finding nothing strictly appropriate, he made do with a few bullet points to the head amalgamated from several notices pinned to a cork board near the door:

- We, here at SaRS, are pleased to announce that Pharmaceuticals ᴙ Us have been recently acquired in a privatisation push of the drug supply. The appointment of our own arch-alchemist Farmer Suit Tickle, to the position of senior chemist pro-tem, has been received loud and clear;
  - Polly Tickle,[389] SaRS Director, 1999-2013
- Pharmacy opening hours: Monday to Friday - 9.00am;
  Pharmacy closing hours: Monday to Friday - 5.00pm;[390]
- This pharmacy services all of the inpatients, outpatients and shaking it all about patients, under the care of the SaRS psychiatrists. We have an onsite pharmacy located on the ground floor... Just a jump to the left... And then a step to the right.

None of this ancient information registered higher than a five on Donald's **G**enerally **L**acklustre **I**nformation **B**arometer, so he elected to return to where it all began, the SaRS dark zone observation point.

When Donald returned to his nature watching seat he was confronted by an uncomfortable observation. Andy was already there, standing on a piece of broken something. But not only that, he looked to be impatiently waiting for Donald, and he was leaning on what seemed to be a very expensive diamond tipped chainsaw in a convincingly threatening manner.

---

[386] Shave and a Haircut... Two Bits... Was temporarily employed again.

[387] Not something often said about Donald.

[388] This was Donald's SOP (Standard Observation Procrastination).

[389] Yes... She is the three blind mice's carving knife wielding Farmer's wife, & Yes... Farmer's placement was a, "Who do you do?" political agreement.

[390] Donald resisted the temptation to correct the sign by removing the ss.

Flashback mini scene to link the previous scene to the next one.

What Donald wasn't aware of, was that the meeting he had just followed Andy to was nothing dark. In fact, it was just the opposite. Polly had convened a group at the behest of Farmer, and some the chemically enhanced patients, to try and resolve their growing concerns about one of the larger trees, which was overshadowing their communal gardens. Andy had been tasked with the humane removal of the shadowy image it cast, and he was just completing the information gathering portion of the proposed change to the SaRS grounds when Donald had seen him earlier interacting with Farmer.

During this excursion Andy had perceived several obstacle related items:

- The easiest solution would be to simply cut the tree down and dispose of it in a forest, so it couldn't be seen for the trees. However, as there was a legal issue regarding tree-sparsing without due diligences being observed,[391] this was an unlikely solution;[392]
- There was a kookaburra family living high on the small furry animal in the specific tree in question. Whatever course of action is taken, this family must first be removed and rehomed; and
- Any grey gum tree bark detached from the tree, must be thoughtfully not disposed of.

Andy had submitted his report to the de-tree-committee, slipped out the back entrance and returned to the gardens to contemplate how he was going to solve the two requirements within his control.

Disposal of the tree bark wasn't going to be a problem, as Andy had a good relationship with Chef Chief and Nurse Jack, and often supplied them with the raw ingredients for their Uggkubra products. He also sided with them on many questions regarding the abuse of their environment. Removing and rehoming the iconic grey gum residents was going to be a larger issue. Andy was aware of the cubby house around the side of the SaRS mansion, as well as its existing residents; but he was hoping they might accept a few refugees.

With this thought in mind, Andy collected himself (and his chainsaw) and flashed forward to wait for Donald to return to the observation area. Andy could be heard humming an old favourite tune softly to himself...

---

[391] Much like trespassing was... It's kissing cousin in the regulatory industry.

[392] This was the official reason Andy gave to the de-tree-committee. The real unmentioned hurdle standing in their way, was that he was never going to cut down such a magnificent piece of Australia ~~unless~~ ever. It is uncommon for a chain saw expert to also be a tree hugger... He may well be très unique.

Cooking Burrow[393]

Cooking burrow, dug deep under the ground
Hangi... Hangi... But I do like the sound
Food, cooking burrow food, cooking burrow
A taste to astound...

Cooking burrow, dug deep under the ground
Any ingredients... You are unbound
Yum! Cooking burrow, yum! Cooking burrow
A concept profound...

Cooking burrow, dug deep under the ground
Everyone's relatives... All come around
Damn! Cooking burrow, damn! Cooking burrow
A man left spellbound...

"Hello...?" Donald wasn't able to convince himself that he had the level of authority to continue past the second I, and his stuttered enquiry sounded more like, "Hell? Oh..."

"Hello Donald." Andy was unconvincingly unthreatening, "Have you seen anything of interest recently?"

Donald was able to answer truthfully, "Yes." even if it was only an accurate useless answer to the rhetorical rhetoric. Thinking a bit more about the detail of the question, he appended, "But, how did you know who I ~~was~~ am?[394]"

"I think you will find there is precious very little that goes on inside SaRS' outside that I am not aware of. I am always made aware of any patients who are a potential flight risk, and DD specifically asked me to be on the lookout for you, and I quote: 'That lad Donald is too smart for his own good, it would be a bad thing if we let him escape.[395]'"

Flabbergasted didn't come anywhere close to what Donald was thinking, "How did they know?" It did cover what he said in response, "Yeah, an escape plan may have been near the top of my to-do list at the start of my stay. I think I may have even written a short story about it. But it isn't now."

---

[393] Inspired by *Kookaburra* - Marion Sinclair.

[394] "~~Was~~ Am" ~~was~~ is an astute realisation on Donald's part, mindfully being present in the current moment, rather than staying in the past.

[395] This was not the first time Donald had encountered prison, or prisoner, related comments. It was the first inside SaRS, outside his head, though.

An escape plan, and subsequent attempt, was still on Donald's list. It was hovering just below the section entitled, "If a situation presents itself…" in the category of, "Tasks requiring no effort…"

Donald's mind was a beautiful and fickle thing.

Fickle does, as fickle doesn't.

Why Donald imagined Sven cookieing this thought we will probably never know. What he, and now subsequently we, did know, was that in the past, he had been predisposed to explaining himself, and his actions, thoroughly, in so many various, only sometimes related, hesitant, fickle statements:

- I can remember all of my sad history;
- Well that probably isn't an entirely accurate statement;
- I assume I have forgotten some sad things;
- What I am trying to say is: Most of what I can recall from my past are only ever the sad memories;
- Really, that is interesting… Would I care to explain?
- No. I have only a few happy memories which haven't been superseded by another memory that isn't happy, and sad will always trump happy I'm afraid;
- If I know a sad memory overshadows a happy one, doesn't it mean I also remember the happy one, and *choose* too not?
- Ummmmm…
- Distraction… The student nurses at SaRS all look the same to me, I find it hard to differentiate their androgyny (Latin: android misogyny);
- I also don't understand why I am explaining myself so much; but
- I know what I think, and no one else cares.

Waiting for Donald to return from his reverie, Andy had his own thought: "Why doesn't Sheldon (Cooper from The Big Bang Theory) make any comment about *Raiders of the Lost Ark* (one of his favourite movies) having kookaburra sounds in the opening jungle scene?[396]"

It seemed that Andy and Donald were off the same page.

When they both returned, their conversation was a little more amiable…
"Would you like to see what all the kerfuffle is about?"
"Absolutely! Lead on MacAndy…"

---

[396] Andy is infatuated with kookaburras apparently.

Andy led Donald down to the communal gardens and the offending tree, which turned out to be the SaRS icon Big Berth. This was almost enough of an explanation of what wasn't going to occur. Big Bertha will never be subjected to a chainsaw. Apart from an incontrovertible fact that she[397] is watching over, and thus protecting, several biodegradable burial pods planted in her vicinity; and she is constantly being referred to as a personal shadow tree; Big Bertha is one of the few remaining gentle giants of the forest world.

Re: Big Bertha p283

ж   Extract from The Donald Diaries.

Andy then took Donald on a tour around the gardening equipment shed, which to Donald's mind was another misnomer, it should really be referred to as the best oversized gardening equipment warehouse storage facility in SaRS. The tour was a refreshing amble of ignorance, which included several unique definitions of gardening equipment:

ж   A John Deer Tractor was identified as their general dogsbody does all. Along with a lineage accurate mother John Doe and father John Buck, a pair of vintage iron horses in restorer's dream condition;

ж   Behind the family of Johns was a clump of stump jump ploughs; and

ж   Hanging ominously in the south-eastern corner shadows was a single pair of rusty sheep shearing shears.

It was then Donald asked one of his thirteen most stupid, without a doubt, questions ever, "How many generally accepted rules do you have to break to become a rusty sheep?"

Andy gently assisted Donald back to the inside's common area, where he was eager and hopefully able to relinquish much of his optional responsibility for today. He was pleased to see, when they arrived, there was some activity occurring at the table. This happened to provide a large enough distraction for him to leave Donald without feeling any guilt.

Donald became even more oblivious to Andy's hopes and feelings when he also was pleased to see the table activity. His curiosity was a powerful urge, and it sometimes let him forget about his personal interaction deficiencies, up to the point where he was able to participate productively in what could nearly be considered a normal conversation.

---

[397] Bertha is large enough of a tree to be able to manufacture several ships out of her, and is therefore considered to be female, like all of the ships she might mother. This is in complete hypercritical contradiction to all cyclones being named with female names, as they used to be until 2008.

The table of activity was an uncrowded hodgepodge of people who were attempting to define the rules, regulations, restrictions and requirements for a new game concept. The oversized fluff-included rule sheet would eventually contain a much-elaborated version of this:[398]

ChessWords:

1) About

ChessWords is a competitive game that is:

- Perfect for up to three players (Or three teams of one);
- Who would like to combine their literary knowledge of words;
- With their love of an infinite numerical possibility.

Artefacts included:

- A horizontal white-board-like reusable game-board; (With inbuilt space and piece detector and spell-checker.[399])
- Three primary-coloured and often-erasable enhanced markers;
- Ninety-nine (99) stylish ornate petrified wood alphabetical pieces; (Designed and made by Dennis Who from Who Wood Masons.)
- **Note:** Batteries not included.

2) Rules

Game-Board setup:

- Use the supplied markers (one per player/team) to colour in as many of the game squares as desired. The end result should be a board that resembles an unstarted crossword puzzle;
- Downloadable official competition templates are available;
- **Note:** Only the official ChessWords enhanced markers are compatible with the inbuilt space and piece detector.

Alphabetical Piece distribution:

- Each player/team selects an agreed upon number of pieces; (From one to thirteen. Six to seven is the suggested draw for novices.)
- Remaining pieces are turned face down and placed beside the board;
- **Note:** Only the official ChessWords pieces are compatible with the inbuilt space and piece detector and spell-checker.

---

[398] Due to the similarities with Nurse Jack's Party Bus Game, and several other non-specifically mentioned games, it is suggested there be some sort of legal spiel attached when approaching a game publisher with this game.

[399] Extension alphabets, and languages, are available for the spell checker.

Game Play:
- ⚔ This section needs to be fleshed out and is what the collected brains distrust were currently discussing, with limited interspersed cussing. It was specifically about how many pieces are selected to restock your hand after your turn.

Potential Movements may include:
- ⚔ **The Start**
  Placing a single complete word on the empty board. This word cannot be connected to any other word (maximum one per game);
- ⚔ **The Single**
  Placing at least one piece to extend a single word in a single direction; or to create a new word perpendicular to an existing word;
- ⚔ **The Double**
  Placing at least two pieces to extend a single word in both directions; or to create a new word perpendicular to an existing word, while also extending it; or to create one new word perpendicular to at least two existing words (while extending them is possible, it isn't required);
- ⚔ **The Multiple**
  Anything else (pieces must be in a single dimension).

3) Scoring (For the Win)
- ⚔ The winner is whoever "completes" the board with legitimate words or is the last player to place a piece on the board which results in there being no identified further words.

Donald listened to the hodgepodge for a while and decided there was not nearly enough room available for him to hide in once he suggested a cure for their obvious lack of basic knowledge.

He then thought about returning to his room and compiling another list of things which vaguely annoyed him about the English language and decided to wait until a bit later for that.[400]

Finally settling for doing nothing.

As this was a welcome change of pace from being unable to do absolutely anything at all, Donald set out to do this nothing with a smile on his face...

---

[400] To keep it consistent with the first book, obviously.

Chapter 15:
Drugs and Maps
(What? and Where!)

Buoyed by his recent experience of wandering around the outside of SaRS alone, briefly thinking for himself about his own mental state of affairs, and the unfamiliar feeling of wanting to be just a little bit adventurous, Donald proactively went to see if he could utilise[401] the elevator to see what he could see.[402]

When he arrived at the closed elevator doors eight moments later the call button was blank. By pressing it multiple times, the generally accepted way of confirming a button's inactiveness, absolutely nothing was achieved. It wasn't until Donald started to wonder about how he could go to a specific place, and where this specific place was, that anything changed. The first unambiguous destination to pop into his disturbed mind was, "Where can I learn all about *Pharmaceuticals Я Us* and Farmer Suit Tickle?"

---

[401] "*Utilise*" is the long way around way of spelling "*Use.*"

[402] Actually, he wanted to see if he could use the elevator to see what he couldn't currently see but was hoping to see... See?

After pressing *Low,*[403] Donald eventually found himself in, what appeared to be, yet another underground area. However, this version of underground was a much more consistently brightly lit one than his previous destinations, and there was nobody waiting to welcome him this time. What seemed to be out of place here, was there were no noticeable indications of what was being concealed.[404] So, in a fit of hysterical pique at probably going to be led astray, Donald took it upon himself to find an answer to the unasked reggae question, "What can't I see clearly now?"

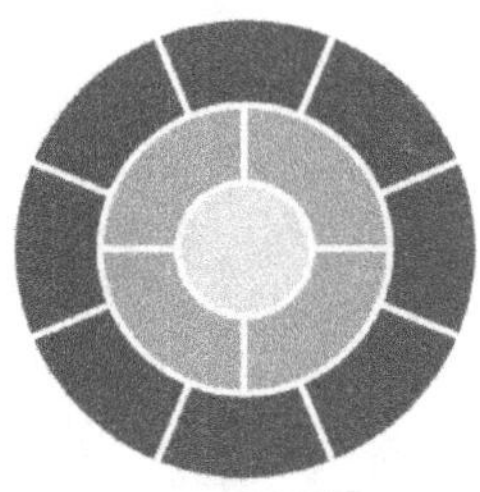

The under-area was circular and divided into exactly thirteen segments of approximately $196m^2$ each. All but one of these spaces were the outer portion of a circular wedge shape, which looked to be a flourishing grassland crop.[405] Where, apart from a variety of different colours, shapes, textures and smells of the grass being grown, the twelve crops were virtually identical. The cryptic plots of these plotted crops all thickened the more Donald thought about them. The thirteenth, and central, circular plot was to a degree unique,[406] in that its crop was growing sideways.

All of this interested Donald very little. He had jumped to several incorrect assumptions thinking that he was wink-wink aware of what these crops were, and who nudge-nudge may have been growing them. What he was marginally impressed with was the symmetrical layout, the ingenuity involved regarding the lighting and watering systems, and the logistics involved in preparing the environmental control features.

These later impressionable details had all been put in place by Andy, who had done so at the behest of Farmer. Andy was just a simple contractor there to do a job, and always tried to do so with minimal impact to the environment. Farmer, however, was in it for the long-haul quick buck.

As Donald didn't have any pressing engagements to be concerned about, he made his second decision for the day, and went for a walk around the mini farm, intent on inspecting whatever he could find.

---

[403] Which was the only option available, obviously.

[404] Or indeed if *anything* was being concealed. Which is sort of the entire goal when you are trying hide something.

[405] As well as looking like the *Play School* round window...

[406] 90° to be specific.

Near the inner left corner of each partial wedge plot was a garden tag like those you would find in any commercial nursery. Donald paused to read some of them and was genuinely surprised by what he found:

Restorative Herbal Seedling Plants:
- Honey and Camomile blend
  - Days to germinate: 4.1
  - Depth to sow: 4.1cm
  - Spacing required: 4.1cm x 4.1cm
  - Days to harvest: 41
  - For a bit of fun, why don't you try planting them sideways?

When he reached the central plot there was a makeshift oral visitor book which also held some astounding informational treats:

Visitor Sound Bites:
- Mindy Ownbeeswhacks:
  I like me some of those Restorative Herbs every full moon ;-)
- Pledge, Jimmy Pledge:
  Reshtorative Herbsh are never to be condoned again ;-)
- Owedebt Dear:
  I used to be not at all addicted to my Restorative Herbs ;-)
- Sue Rhea Liszt:
  Art Therapy related benefits of Restorative Herbs are astounding ;-)
- William the Piano man:
  The music wouldn't be the same without some Restorative Herbs ;-)
- Skit Zoland: (as Jesse Pinkman and Mr Pink)
  Yo, Mr White, it's the science that makes them so good ;-)
  Yo, Mr White, can't I be Mr Purple. That sounds good ;-)

After the myriad of sound bites there was a final voiceover announcement followed by the Obligatory Sales Adds:

Restorative Herbs:
- Fake Drug[407] manufacturing is endorsed by SaRS. For the purchase of, please contact Farmer Suit Tickle at Pharmaceuticals ℵ Us.
- Next level learning opportunities are available in the following areas:
  - Growing Restorative Herbs without garden tools;
  - Or a garden; and
  - The benefits of sideways growing plants (including a ticket to ride on our movie room bus, to watch a documentary focussing on the story behind the proof-of-concept prototype sideways rose bush).

---

[407] "Fake Drug" and "Restorative Herbs" are both trademarked by PℵU.

Even though Donald had not discovered anything strictly illegal; there was unusual certainly; with a selection of strange, peculiar, bizarre, inconceivable, ludicrous, absurd and ... he was still unconvinced about many other tenuously related opinions he had formed during the past few weeks:

About Smoking:
- The "Smokers Clique" is alive and well as a legal addiction alternative;
- Smokin' in the Little Boy's room at midnight is still possible, even after a certain someone had locked the door from the outside; and
- Holy Smoke! The by-product when Vamp was processed by The Flame.

About Pharmaceuticals я Us:

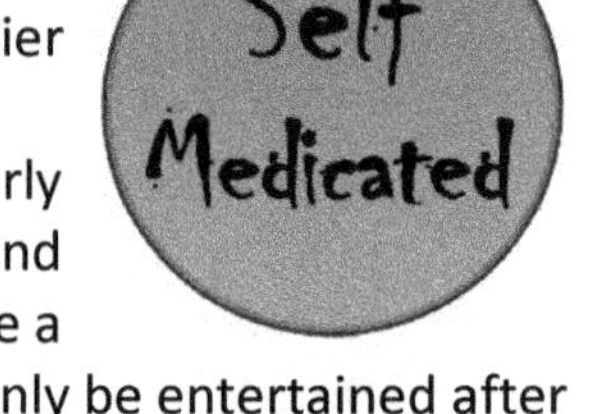

- I have raised an internal "reason appears to have been overlooked" issue, due to the drug supplier also appearing to be the *drug* supplier;
- One of the badges sold by the chemist is clearly an obvious use of irony that borders on a lie; and
- This is not so much an opinion as it is more like a question of huh? "All negative feedback will only be entertained after they have gone through the development process, which occurs every other tomorrow, then they will be returned with the prints for proof."

About Chemicals in General:[408]
- Don't put potassium in water. It goes BANG!
- Medication helps me to not care, by making me forget that I ever did;
- The Bacon Conundrum: I find, with much scientific experimentation in the thermodynamic kitchen, that bacon defies the law which states... "Everything gets bigger when heated."

Once Donald had exhausted all of his hypothetical thinking for the day, he decided it was about time that he went and make himself a hyperthetical cup of coffee, and head to the common area for some relaxing contemplations of the various complications discovered today.[409]

---

[408] One science quote Donald forgot to mention in his opinionated rant... "Don't poke someone holding the other end of the electric sparking thingy." This is an easy way to be charged with painful flagrant electrical distribution.

[409] I second Donald's decision but have some reservations about filling the cup completely to the top with potentially scalding liquid. Anyhow, I will meet you back here (or over the page, as it probably will be) in an hour or two, ok!

Delving enthusiastically into his SaRS branded Show Bag,[410] Donald had a rummage around the pre-discarded mountain of help inducing dissertations and came up with one that actually made a little sense. When he applied his recently acquired knowledge about the outer and under workings of where he was, he managed to distract himself from his current predicament.[411]

The "P-Wheel" diagram is remarkably similar to the diagram of the circular under-SaRS farm area, but instead of having thirteen blue segments,[412] there were only seven photo-copied out grey-scale ones. Donald supposed that the wheel might have had some colour in its original form and put another item on his presupposed **N**early **I**nteresting **L**ist of things.

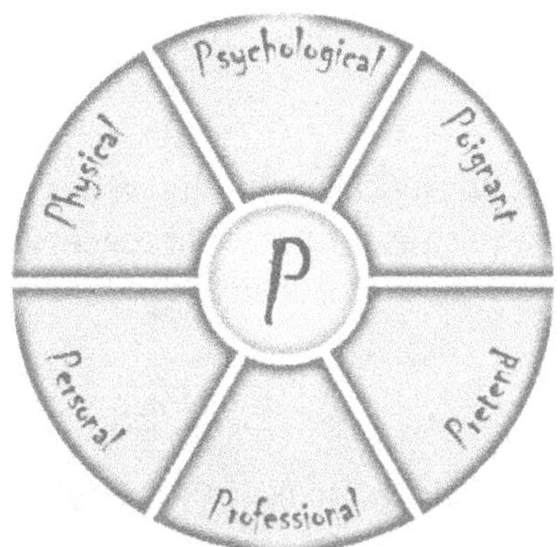

This diagram is traditionally known as a "Self-Care Wheel," although Donald likes to think of it as his "Self-Indulgent Pie," or his "Self-Pitying Pizza," depending on what sort of food cravings it induced in the reader.

How it is supposed to work... You write a list in each wedge, noting a few things that would really "P!" you off if someone was to take them away from you. Donald took this task to the next level when his list consisted entirely of words starting with "P."

When he had finished his creation, Donald was so proud of his efforts that he didn't immediately file it safely inside the round filing cabinet underneath the table in his room. Instead, he proposed to himself that he should go and presumptuously partake of the primary "P," with a particularly potent portion, or possibly a pair of portions, of the pleasant potion known as coffee.

On his way back to their common-area, Donald couldn't help himself and chuckled when he imagined Sven cookieing a few more appropriate thoughts:

   ﮐ   "To the Pee-Machine Peed-Off-Man!"

   ﮐ   "To Infinite Pee and Peed-Off!" and it wouldn't be the same without

   ﮐ   "To Pee or Not To Pee... Where is the cistern?"

---

[410] The inmates are encouraged to keep all of their photocopied handouts in the SaRS Show Bag as a convenient portable document repository. Having them all in this one handy place also facilitates the easy disposal of any offending information should a copyright inspector come along.

[411] Which is half the battle, some of the teaching, and most of the point.

[412] For all of the colour challenged printed book owners out there...

The lists for Donald's P-Pie/Pizza were:

⚥ **Physical**
Phone (and as a secondary element, iPad)
Pie/**P**izza/**P**ie-**P**izza[413]
Pants (everyone needs **P**ants, especially Donald after a long walk)

⚥ **Psychological**
Plan (it is what everyone is looking for here in SaRS, after all)
Patience (not for others to have with Donald, for Donald with himself)
Positivity (Donald is **P**ositive he will fail, and don't tell him otherwise)

⚥ **Poignant**
Platitudes (he didn't like them; he didn't want to lose them either)
Pat on the back (the **P**racticed version of **P**latitude **P**reaching)
Presence (or **P**resents, in a **P**inch)

⚥ **Personal**
Poetry (he might not write good **P**oetry, but he likes what he writes)
Palisade/**P**icket/**P**ost/**P**aling/**P**ole (**P**rerequisites for **P**ersonal space)
Private (I think Donald gave his **P**rivacy away on **P**urpose)

⚥ **Professional**
Pay (fifth)
Pay (or sixth, time is the charm, hopefully)
Pay (same importance as location, location, location is to **P**roperty)

⚥ **Pretend**
People[414]
Pluto (it isn't a **P**recovered[415] **P**retend **P**lanet anymore)
Priorities (even though Donald has none, he wants to keep them)

Reaching the common area was a **P**otentially **P**roblematic task for Donald at the **P**resent **P**oint. There were **P**lenty other **P**eople there, who may **P**ossibly want him to **P**articipate in their **P**ontification of the **P**artially **P**roposed Chess Words **P**rinciples. Donald **P**ositively didn't do **P**retend-**P**olite conversation and was **P**erceptibly still **P**rocrastinating on his "**P**!" words. **P**referring to **P**rovide you with a **P**review of his next **P**ostulations, **P**roviding you were still interested of course…

---

[413] Now there is something somebody should seriously look into…

[414] Donald didn't normally like to pretend people were important to him, and he really didn't like pretend people, so, I really don't know why this is here.

[415] Precovered means finding an object in images that predate its discovery. Another factoid: Pluto and its moon Charon are entwined in an ice-skating dance like spin, around an orbit point that does not lie within either of them.

How to make Donald a cup of coffee:

Coffee... 1 heaped teaspoonful of
A dash of milk (light preferred)
Fake sugar... 1 micro tablet of
Find the biggest, clean optional, mug you can
Empty all of the ingredients into the mug
Incorporate boiling water and stir twice
Notify Donald it is ready; so, he can
Enjoy the Bean Juice of Heaven

    Extract from The Donald Diaries.

After managing to enjoy a self-made approximation of a decent cup of hot beverage, Donald, with his recent experiences and vast knowledge of the SaRS environment, decided it was about time to make a map of SaRS. To this end, he returned the now empty mug to the kitchen,[416] signed out,[417] and headed off to the Beethoven art room.

My Venerable Erstwhile Man, Just Shut Up Now Please...[418]

Donald didn't give Sven's cookie a second hear and went about his day as if nothing was wrong. Which it wasn't really. He was coming to the pointy end of his stay inside SaRS, as his customary three-week allocation was nearly fully subscribed, and he thought that a fitting tribute to all those who assisted with his recovery would be a Donald original hand drawn map, so everyone could finally understand where he was at.

His first task was to draw The Kingswood's House mansion. This may not sound much like a map to you, but Donald's madness had a distinctly method acting[419] component involved... To follow any map to a destination, you must start at the beginning, and the beginning of SaRS was the mansion. So, the first step was to draw the mansion.

---

[416] Failing to adhere to the, "You Use It, You Clean It!" SaRS protocol. This is also why "clean" is always optional when Donald has a cup of coffee.

[417] This is only a formality. The sign out book isn't strictly monitored, nor is it ever checked if someone goes missing. In fact, Donald is the only person who bothers to sign out every time he goes to any post outside room.

[418] Yeah, thanks Sven. You are only a page or so too late this time.

[419] I.e. Sincere, and Emotionally Expressive.

Donald planned to draw the mansion as it would have appeared in photos from 75 years ago. Obviously, black and white would be the appropriate pallet constituent lack of colour choices, so a graphite pencil would be the ideal tool. But, as SaRS is a mental institution, the applicable rules are also skewed in this direction, and the only blades available to sharpen the pencils were pre-dulled to the maximum sharpness allowed, which was approaching two thousand on the BESS scale.[420]

Whenever Donald does anything remotely approaching artistic[421] he likes to use his own implements, and no one else is allowed to use them unless they ask, and he says they can. This would eventually become another thing for him to worry about when he got his own paint brushes, pens and pencils; but, for now, he was content with using ones that came out of the communal pot.

"Hmmmmm…"

Donald just hit another stumbling block. Even though he had identified the *why, what, when* and *where*[422] of his first task, he didn't really know anything about the *how* to start. Convincing no one of his capability, including himself, he did what he thought any other normal person would do if they were in this situation, nothing.

He was very-chalantly standing around, pretending to be engrossed in the artwork decorating the walls, while actually squinting out of the corner of his eye looking for, and listening for, any clues. It should come as no surprise that Donald was not fooling anyone with his act. His lack of quietly fitting in was so extreme that when Sue noticed him, she was torn between labelling him a:

- Still Life astonishment   - Is he really and truly Still Alive?
- Still Life resignation   - Yes, his Life is Still just this;
- Still Life encouragement - You Still have some Life in you yet; or
- Still Life hostility   - Why is he Still Alive?

---

[420] This is an actual scale, and appropriate considering the descriptions:

- Dull   500 +
- Normal   300 – 400
- Sharp   250 – 300
- Nuts   150 – 200
- Crazy   100 – 150
- Insane   000 – 100

And yes, I know there are gaps and overlaps, it is annoying me too.

[421] His drawings couldn't get much further from "art" if he tried. Even if he crumpled them all up, kicked the wad of paper through a coal mine, drenched them in yack fat and then tried to burn them, they would be no further away.

[422] The *who* wasn't particularly relevant in this scenario… As it was Donald.

To put him out of his misery for a little while, Sue suggested he might like to participate in one of her Meditation/Mindfulness Flashback Adventures.[423] The next one scheduled was simply titled "Building SaRS." She pointed out to Donald the ancient chalk board in the corner which had the elaborate details scribbled in an appropriately art/doctor nearly illegible fashion...

Mashback[©] – "Building SaRS"
(Meditation/Mindfulness Flashback Adventure)

With Sue Rhea Liszt (SaRS Art Therapy Realisationalist)

✗ Feast your eyes on:
  - The actual scenes depicted in the photos in the reception area
✗ Find out very little about:
  - The original owners of The Kingswood's House mansion
  - An in-depth, yet shallow, exposé of the architecture involved
  - How, and more importantly, why it became SaRS

Presented in séance approved fifty shades of BLURRY 

SaRS Chalkboard 1 – Mashback[©] Meditation/Mindfulness Flashback Adventure[424]

Sue told Donald the Mashback[©] would begin in two point seven minutes, and "If you could arrange three of the chairs in a circular fashion, around the disgusting old bottle we use to hold the dirty paint brushes, I would very much appreciate it. Thank you very much." Despite the fact this was an instruction heavy request, Donald was glad to participate/comply. Once the chairs were in place, he sat down and reflected on his current DOGoN level of six.[425]

---

[423] "Mashback[©]" – Where the artistic style of Cynicism is the New Realism.

[424] Due to the un-electronicness of the chalkboard this doesn't appear in any of the official SaRS documentation or in the Tables of Dis-Content. However, the inclusion of the Hungry Hungry David's insignia is strange.

[425] When Donald later re-read this paragraph he wasn't tempted, at all, to change the DOGoN level or the word "glad." What actually happened was... **He smiled**... And thought "I must be getting the hang of being normal."

When the Mashback© got underway it became clear to Donald that he was merely a passenger in Sue's reality. He couldn't detect any malevolent vibes,[426] and there were no cold shivers playing vertebrae with his vertigo, so he simply sat back and enjoyed the descriptions...

The first flashback scene described several poignant figures who would be used as the voice of description in the subsequent scenes:

- Appearing in the scene first was a younger, less dead, version of BLT. He had all the same attributes as BLT, except for the L and the T. Sue introduced him as Brother Soon, and she must have encountered him before, because her BS description had by far the greatest amount of detail with the least amount of actual content when you compared it to the other introductions.

- Adopting an unmistakable accent, Sue got into character for the next figure, "There is **No Road Back** for the **Hell Drivers**, because the **Action of the Tiger** created a **Time Lock** to **Another Time, Another Place** and **Darby O'Gill and the Little People** are busy playing **Tarzan's Greatest Adventure**, **On the Fiddle,** to calm **The Frightened City**. It's going to be **The Longest Day** I'm afraid...[427]"

- The next chilling description frightened Donald out of his film reverie, "You got it utterly spot on old man! I am Mindy Ownbeeswhacks, and I may be only as old as I look, but I am a young woman who can take dangerous to an entirely new level."

- Describing the last character, Sue adopted a formal voice, "Hello, I am Who, Monseigneur Read Who (Who, M.R. Who) and I am only here as a bit of light coincidence, and an 'Ahhhhh very clever,' later on."

When Donald finally got into the spirit of the flashback, he received much more information than he could possibly record accurately for inclusion in one of his memoirs, so he decided to do it in his HandY - DandY[428] style here...

- **Why is everything described here in Black and White?**
  Because that is the international standard for showing an old memory. It is merely convenient that B&W printing is cheaper than colour.

- **Can you describe the events that led to the overhead B&W photo?**
  Yes.

---

[426] It's not surprising he couldn't... As nobody can... Yes, I am a sceptic.

[427] Although Sue never mentions a name, after a bit of research, it became clearly understood to Donald who each of these references had in common.

[428] Hear and Question → Drawings and Yarns. (a.k.a. - Left to Write.)

     ҳ   **???**
The photo is from approximately 75 years ago and was taken during a colossal electrical storm. It depicts an immature hedge maze leading down to the "Dick Shack," and an immature person sprawling through our rose bushes like a silly person. We have been unable to determine who this miscreant is.[429]

     ҳ   **Why are the rose bushes growing sideways?**[430]
That remain a mystery I am afraid. They were discovered during a time of great upheaval in SaRS' history, and it was decided, since they posed no immediate threat to any of the patients, and because the buds they produced were particularly scentful, they would be allowed to remain.

     ҳ   **Can you describe the events that led to the overhead colour photo?**
No.

Coming to the conclusion that his identity as the not-yet-alleged miscreant was safely unknown, Donald probed for more information about the mansion, specifically at the festering absence of architectural information...[431]

Why are there different styles of architecture at each corner?
The story surrounding the cornered differences is nearly as fascinating as it is strange. You are probably already aware that building the mansion began roughly 125 years ago, and at around that time there were several influential architectural firms, each bidding to be the main service provider to the current landowners. Only three of these firms were invited to submit ideas for what the mansion might look like if they were given the design task.

The owner's administrators then cunningly pitted these firms against each other, recording every interesting occurrence from beginning to end on film, with the oddly arranged cumbersome security cameras of the era. Throughout this entire process there was an independent auditor creating artificial hurdles for the builders to jump over and using the results to decide who was going to receive a payment for services rendered after each segment.

When the three corner blocks were assembled, the fourth was being kept in reserve should there be a tie-breaker collaborative contest required, it was discovered to the great amusement of the neighbours, there was one circular, one hexagonal and one surrealist theme. This last one was thankfully located entirely within the juxtaposed subconscious areas of the mansion.

---

[429] Nicely sidestepping any potentially significant details.

[430] Donald asked this to discover how much they knew, not what they knew.

[431] Eschewing the bullet pointed layout for a better traditional experience.

Talk to me about the courtyard and the under-courtyard basement.

The four pre-descript figures went into a not suspicious at all huddle, and after several nods, emerged with an obviously predetermined official answer.

The courtyard is the largest indoor outside area this side of the back door. It is also the juxtaposed subconscious area previously mentioned and would be used whenever there were functions to be had. This is where it went down, to the ground, to get out onto the inside.[432]

When The Big Ole Homestead became the SaRS mansion 75 years ago, it was unilaterally decided that all basements would be under-limits to all of the patients. Everywhere there was a reference to any basement like areas, it was subtly changed to ward off any curiosity, with messages like, "Do Not Dig Here! Move Along! There is Nothing to Find!" in the hope that eventually these areas would fall into disuse and be completely forgotten about.

Finally, how did they manage to fit more on the inside that there appears to be space for on the outside, even considering the outside inside bit?[433]

Oh, that's an easy one… It all has to do with people's perception of what would be required to deal with the many psychological anomalies available to be had, and we will answer it in the tried-and-true method of an acronym…

There is
Always
Room
Deep
Inside,
~~Simple~~ Easy…

Finishing the séance like activity around the antipodean bottled-brushes, Donald used all of the extracted information to continue just after his previous "Hmmmmm…" statement and produce a halfway decent reproduction of the inside of his head.

It was exactly as Donald imagined how everyone else imagines what SaRS looks like from the outside… A picturesque location, home to people wearing suits of the straight and white variety, who were leisurely occupying the finely manicured lawns, give or take a triumvirate of floating shapes.

---

[432] But not when it rained… That would just be silly.

[433] I'll refrain from saying, "It's not very nice to call the patients morons," as I feel it would be far too predictable, and simply mention this is the "Ahhhhh very clever" moment… M.R. Who being D.R. Who's ancestor and all…

After putting a final finishing touch on his pencil inner-head drawing piece of art; his signature; and an approximate price he paid to SaRS tag written with an invisible carbon pencil (otherwise known as a stick), Donald took a couple of steps back and admired his completed effort.

Quite pleased with the way everything was turning out, he took a moment to take stock of where he was at in the wider scheme of things:

- Physically wise   - He is inside SaRS, and knows the way out;
- Psychologically wise - He is inside SaRS, but knows the way out; and
- Psychically wise   - He is inside SaRS, who knows the way out?

With the apparent realisation, "I am quickly approaching the end,[434]" very much predominant on Donald's mind; the associated expostulation, "I don't know if I can do this,[435]" was not surprising.

This speed of flip-flopping from positive to negative is un-Donald like, and even though he has been assured by the various people who know, including Dr Jay, Nurse Jack and even DD, that the symptoms of a mental illness are not transferrable between people, he was still very happy to be deeply concerned about it with a devastatingly average reason.

During the recent counselling sessions Donald has had with Dr Jay, she has told him that one of her favourite sayings is, "You cannot catch a mental illness from someone. You will only become mentally ill if: you let someone else drive you the bad kind of crazy; or you always question your sanity."

Sven kindly provided a translation...
The correct answer to, "Why?" is, "Because!" or, "Why not?"

Whenever Donald thinks about the inner workings of the mind, he always compares knowledge to music. It doesn't matter how much you know (notes), the important thing is what you create with that knowledge (songs). Everyone knows both ends of the spectrum, and what they like at each end, but there are precious few who can make the transition.

Donald knows a lot about his own mind, and a lot about what is considered normal, but he lacks the ability to implement a solution which takes something from both ends. He doesn't want to just sing the song of his sanity; he wants the know how to write it. The "word" aspect is ok, but there is no rhythm, no chords and he doesn't even know which instruments to use.

---

[434] Donald was thinking, "... of my stay inside SaRS."
I, on the other hand, was thinking, "... of the end of the book."

[435] Donald was thinking, "... draw a map of SaRS with the time available."
And... I was thinking, "... draw a map of SaRS with the skill available."

Donald is in awe of people who can write music, paint art, or even discover something new with the information at hand, so has decided to postpone the drawing of a SaRS map exercise to another time, if and when he finds himself in the presence of some artistic talent.[436]

He did make himself a few subliminal notes of what to include though:
- Floor plan of the mansion;
  - Exploded vertical slices (including the many courtyard layers)
  - Where each character lives (or dwells in the case of BLT and Seth)
  - Escape routes (from fire and disaster, and from SaRS in general)
- The amazing hedge maze; and
- Topographical maps of the elevator destinations.

And he also left a liminal topic to discuss… Directions.
- **Generalisations - Westernisation**

Originating from Roman times and has changed meanings over the years. It was once used in context with Middle Eastern, Eastern Bloc, etc… But it was stupid then, and it is still stupid now.
- **Concatenations - Southeast**

Take the North by Northwest corridor…[437] Without a handy compass, map, or even a basic sunlight cast shadowy reference point… Which inside corridor were they directing him to?
  - The corridor North by North-West from where he currently was;
  - The corridor that runs in a North-West South-East direction; and
  - When he got to the corridor, which way does he go?
- **Determinations - North**

When you are standing on the South Pole, is North:
  - Straight up (as it always is on a map);
  - Straight down (i.e. through your feet); or
  - Everywhere that is approaching horizontal?
- **Victimisations - Up the creek**

If you want to leave SaRS, follow in the same track as the early inhabitants. Walk down the old derelict road, which runs parallel to the dry creek bed that used to flow from the empty spring, hiding behind the overgrown garden bed of forget-me-nots. Turn right just after the dilapidated bridge, spanning over the congested ditch, where something unimportant happened a long time ago and there is no visible sign of anymore…

---

[436] Hopefully this will be when I am talking to my publisher in a few months.

[437] Ahhhhh… Silented Donald…

Chapter 16:
Point that Finger...
(Name / Blame / Shame)

Now that Donald's come this far, it is time for all of us to look back and try to identify exactly what lead Donald to this bumpy road in his life...[438] The obvious place to look is to that which has moulded Donald into what he is, and it isn't what you think... (Cue the narrator...)

Ten Cognitive Distortions that TV and Movies Perpetuate:

1) All or Nothing Thinking

Everything is Black or White. Right or Wrong. Left or Right. Good or Evil. Donald experiences all of these... Literally... Every day.

Movies were only projected in black and white until the 1950s, and TV was devoid of primary colour until the 1960s in civilised places, 1970s in Australia, and 1980s in the Halfbrain household.[439] But anyway... What these examples are trying to convey is that there are far more than just pass or fail values to rate your performance. Falling short of a perfect ten is not a total failure, and Donald knows this... These rules only ever correctly apply to binary results.

So, this cognitive distortion, the most important one apparently, is saying you are completely wrong to think everything is either just wrong or right. Can anyone else see the problem here? Number one has no wiggle room. Forget that there can be no wrong answers when it comes to psychological questions, this one is exempt from that rule. (Yeah... Right...? I know!)

---

[438] I think the title of this chapter is quite illuminating, and particularly apt. Well, it would be, wouldn't it? Otherwise, it wouldn't be, unless I was dopey.

[439] Yes... Donald is *that* old... Your point being? Why, I aughta! Nap time...

Examples of All or Nothing Thinking on the screen:
- There is always a convenient car parking spot… Unless there is none;
- Drug effects and medical results are immediate… Unless they aren't;
- No one in a hostage situation has a phone… Unless it's in the plot.

2) Overgeneralisation

A single negative event perpetuates a never-ending cycle of defeat.

Movies and TV shows enable this distortion by generally implementing the reverse effect as a good thing. This can be done in one of two ways, the first is where the hero often fails until they eventually succeed (perseverance), or there are many insignificant losses until a major win (trial and error). There is also the traditional bent, where the hero works their way through the minor characters until they meet The Boss (escalation).

Donald generalises his experiences this with regard to his poetry writing, saying, "Every poem is exactly the same, it's just that the words are different." And even though to a great extent this might be true, it isn't for *every* poem. What Donald actually means is, "There will always be another the world is out to get me poem."[440]

Examples of Overgeneralisation on the screen:
- Every Arnold Schwarzenegger movie ever;
- Every Sit-Com ever; And I really mean "EVER!" this time.
- Every House episode is so formulaic, "Three failures before a success."

3) Mental Filter

Each single negative detail will cloud your reality until it is assumed.

While Donald was reading through this list he commented, "Aren't these last two distortions virtually saying the exact same thing, only with marginally different words? You lose once, and you lose; and you lose once, and you lose forever." I am inclined to side with Donald after the recent conversation I had with him, so will not further expound on this point.

Examples of Mental Filters on the screen:
- No one ever collects their discarded ammunition clips, or refills them;
- Handcuffs can always be unlocked with a paperclip, or similar; and (Many keys to lock them, one key to unlock them all…)
- New electrical items always come with a fully charged battery.

---

[440] That isn't what Donald *actually* means. But hey, what would I know? When will people stop putting words in Donald's mouth? What he means is, *to him*, each poem is different take on the same underlying woe-is-me theme. Donald just had a little chat at me, where he explained I shouldn't generalise. He doesn't think all his poetry has the same theme… Just that it is all crap…

4) Disqualifying the Positive

Positive experiences are rejected as aberrations.

In both of the big and little screen formats, these recurring situations are not necessarily rejected by the participant, they are often rejected by the Boss, the Enemy, or the Parent.[441] After there have been multiple rejections, we will come to understand why the resulting fairy tale ending becomes a significantly greater outcome of the struggle. Mind you, this distortion is also what often saves the protagonist from falling into a previously bypassed trap. In the real world this is called due diligence and is not a significantly bad thing.

Donald also often experiences this, but his interpretation of his actions is that he isn't being vain. Using his poetry as an example again, Donald knows there are some good poems amongst them, the law of large numbers has seen to that, but to say his poetry is good because of one poem, is not valid.

You aren't strangely rewarded for turning up to work early one day, when every other day you are simply on time. Donald doesn't want to be rewarded for one single action over and above the normal for anything. That is the exact definition of an aberration.[442]

Examples of Disqualifying the Positive on the screen:
- Self-resetting ancient mechanical booby traps;
- Just because the safe wire to cut on the bomb before was the red one, doesn't mean it is the red one now; Probability doesn't work like that.
- Usual suspects are always interrogated, even if they *have* changed.

5) Jumping to Conclusions[443]

Interpretations of the limited information available are often not correct. This is where assume makes a frequent appearance.

How many fictional criminals have been apprehended after the authority has determined they will continue to make the same mistake? How frequent are short cuts taken successfully knowing you are missing a salient detail? How much surprise is avoided when actions are based on intuition?

---

[441] The "Parent" might also conceivably play the other two roles as well.

[442] However, should that single act be the saving of a life while putting his own safety at risk, or a once off approaching miraculous situation, then he might be open to a reconsideration. **Note:** You reading this does not count.

[443] I would like to point out for the record, jumping to a conclusion does not necessarily imply the conclusion is a negative outcome. If you assume so, you are guilty of an overgeneralisation. Similarly, with luck. If you say someone is lucky, *good* luck is not the only conceivable type of luck occurring. Bam...!

Donald sees conclusions such as these jumped to on and off the screen all over the place. He labels them for what they are though... Racial profiling. Yes, I said it! Some of these poor conclusions are jumped to from information being portrayed as mind-reading when it is actually cold reading. Others might be incorrectly labelled as fortune-telling when it is really extrapolation.[444]

Examples of Jumping to Conclusions on the screen:
- Every police and detective show ever. With special mentions:
  - Chuck, Lie to Me, Psych, The Mentalist, White Collar;
  - The many, many, many, Sherlock Holmes derivatives;
  - James Bond, Jason Bourne, Jack Ryan, Johnny English.[445]
- Phones:
  - All phones can be traced (unless they specifically can't be);
  - Breaking it disables the phone and blocks all tracking;
  - "Burner" phones are always available, pre-charged and everyone already knows the number to call them.
- Directions: (Refer to the end of the last chapter)

6) Magnification (Catastrophizing) or Minimisation

Everything is always ridiculously exaggerated or ignored.

Again, Donald commented on the repetition of the generalised topic, "This is exactly the same as was discussed previously. All or Nothing thinking is just maximising or minimising the thought." And once again, I am inclined to agree with Donald.[446] Although this time the thought could be one thrust upon you by someone else, "It's all your fault," "You just stole my idea," or, "It doesn't matter what you think."

Examples of Magnification or Minimisation on the screen:
- Shows where the butterfly effect is in effect;[447]
- Cobwebs actually perform both functions: and
  - Their presence is often maximised, in lieu of any actual spiders;
  - Stickiness, and the logistics involved, are always minimised.
- Background functions are often non-existent. Food intake and output.

---

[444] There is going to be a fortune telling - mind reading section later on, so, I am keeping the associated anecdotes for then. To conclude this, all I did was interpret the details available accurately.

[445] Have you jumped to any conclusions, vis-à-vis my liking of these shows?

[446] It was actually me who suggested the possibility of a similarity.

[447] Have you ever noticed there are no reverse butterfly effects recorded? I guess it's not important enough to point out, this is known as an anticlimax.

7) Emotional Reasoning

Taking your emotions to eleven, and then actually believing them.

"I feel the need, the need for screed.[448]"

This one is hard for Donald to understand. As are the emotions driving the distortions. He knows there are emotions everywhere on the screen. He isn't *that* dopey, he can see:

- Tears = They are sad;
- Tears = They are happy; and
- Tears = They are in pain.

What truly messes this ability around is the use of sarcasm. Donald doesn't understand sarcasm either. To him, sarcasm is just when someone agrees with a truth...[449] Emotions are truly Donald's Achilles heel. And, therefore, there is absolutely no way he can reason with someone who is being emotional.

You should just take my word for it. OK? Donald doesn't like to be tested on his lack of ability to recognise anything less than an over-the-top emotion. It always brings him to tears in a laughably painful way.

Examples of Emotional Reasoning on the screen:[450]

- Technology faux pas:
  - Batteries are always charged and always fit;[451]
  - Remote controls always click;
  - Clocks never change, except in countdown or alarm scenarios, and then the countdown timers take 15 minutes to count 15 seconds;
  - Traffic cameras in remote low volume areas point *not* at the road, their footage is always accessible real time via private computers that have zooming capability (also applies to ancient video tapes);
  - Random computers can be used to magically hack into anywhere, and you run the software apps by simply tapping on the keyboard;
  - Photos taken using a phone, during a phone call, all appear on the computer next to where the other phone is located, immediately.
- Musical comments tenuously related to emotional reasoning:
  - Music is for when words are just not enough;
  - How you choose a Hawaiian record: A-side beside seaside decide.

---

[448] Well. I think I have well and truly fulfilled that particular requirement.

[449] Yeah, I don't know if this is true... Well, isn't that a shocker!

[450] Just to illustrate how much Donald doesn't understand about emotions.

[451] The worst example of this in in Jurassic Park III (island with parasailing). The father uses batteries from a torch to power his ex-wife's new husband's camcorder that has been lying unprotected in the jungle for over two months.

8) Should Statements

Should is the emotional blackmailer's go to weapon.

It is often self-directed inwardly, which is ironically appropriate, since you are the only person who will be disappointed when you think you have failed to finish any instruction preceded by an "I should." A "You should" suggestion is another animal entirely and will never happen.

Donald matured in the computer industry and has learned that if you want a "should" statement to be coded and implemented, it should be transformed into a "must" at the earliest possible time. The official **MoSCoW** definition:

- Must   - The only contractually agreed deliverables;
- Should   - Do if there is any time left in the budget;
- Could   - Don't bother to even think about; and
- Will Not - Will thwart contractual arguments.

Examples of Should Statements on the screen:[452]

- Unnatural acceptances:
  - Abandoned buildings with water and power still connected;
  - Petrol burning in a controlled manner and the fumes don't ignite;
  - Plane seats always have sooooo much leg room;
  - Stolen clothes always fit.
- Unnatural acceptances in **Space...** Space... Space...:
  - There is often a directional North concept;
  - When gravity is present on spaceships, things still fall to the other side (top/bottom) of the ship when it performs a roll or a loop;
  - Background functions, again, are thankfully overlooked.[453]

9) Labelling and Mislabelling

An extreme form of overgeneralisation. Creating a self-perpetuating truth. Instead of using a blanket statement saying, "I am bad," instead make it more specific and say, "I did a bad Michael Jackson impersonation."

And now, for the third time, it's even in the definition people, Donald was quick to interject, "This is bad. This is really bad. This is so bad, that it's badder than a bad Michael Jackson impersonation."

While I re-agree with Donald's sentiment, his particular example this time may be construed as being in bad taste. Donald has always had a problem with people putting labels on him, even when they are true... "Donald is arrogant," "Donald is autistic," and "Donald is annoying," and this is only three of the As.

---

[452] These should be called Should Not Have statements (SHaNgHAi).

[453] I should have added "Unnatural acceptances in Space: Star Wars" to build on the theme... But there was just too much, and it is a fantasy anyway.

Examples of Labelling and Mislabelling on the screen:
- Common vehicle specific overgeneralisations:
  - Actors sawing at the steering wheel when they are "driving;"
  - Hot wiring a car is simple, and ignition locks are ignored;
  - Keys are in the ignition (unless it's a hotwiring scene);
  - Cars are never locked, never stolen... And never need fuel;
  - Rain running down the windscreen of moving cars (it goes up);
  - Roadblocks on highways block all the traffic out of a town;
  - Trucks are nearly empty, unless they are completely full;
  - Tyres never burn (worst case scenario in Dante's Peak); and
  - People running straight down the road to escape a vehicle.

10) Personalisation

Everything is always about you.

Donald was so excited when he read this, "Finally, there is a correction for a common cognitive distortion. This is exactly describing me. It's like all of the other ones describing my negative assumptions don't count any more, even if there were a few duplicates. I was hesitant to believe initially, but I think there is enough validity in what has been said, for me to take this as a compliment, however little deserved it is. This should make everything better. I just know it; I can feel it in my bones. Put me in the cured pile please..."

Examples of Personalisation on the screen:
- There are none of these yet. Maybe there will be some when Donald gets a recurring cameo in "The Donald Diaries."[454]

And to drive the seven coffin nails home, an acronym which sums up nicely what reality TV has given us all...[455] Say it with me...

Viewing other people's worries takes your mind off your own.
Allows you to demonstrate an interest in people you will never meet.
Live (When it was recorded all those many months ago).
Idle people can participate in life from the comfort of their own home.
Donald will never willingly sanction any reality programme about himself.
At least, not one where he is offered a vast amount of royalties to change.
To be fair, anyone could fall into one of those communal money traps.
Iknow you don't believe him, but believe me, it will never happen.
Oh... That much? Well... Why didn't you just say so?
Now presenting... The Donald Diaries (the expurgated version).

---

[454] Stan Lee and Alfred Hitchcock always did, so why shouldn't Donald?

[455] Seriously, where would psychology be without acronyms?

The people who create the TV programmes (and Movies to a lesser extent) shouldn't have to bear the entire brunt of what Donald sees as being society's problems. After all, there is still a little thing called "free choice" when you are deciding what to watch.[456]

Donald's choice of viewing is generally far from reality, in all connotations of the word. The shows he likes generally involve a little bit of intrigue, a puzzle to solve, some intelligent decisions, a law enforcement element and of course a lot of dry humour. Unfortunately, shows that encompass these concepts also often include Donald's harebrained notion of "idiotsynchronicities."

The Police[457] (with a side-kick of Detective) annoyances:
- Explanation of the new case details:
    - By different, often random, people;
    - Reading a folder of pre-prepared notes;
    - Accompanied by standard-sized mug shots;
    - Who all seem to know the whole story anyway;
    - To the same people who are telling the story;
    - Just after they have all arrived at the scene;
    - In the same car... But they waited for you.
- Confusing activities:
    - They always know which way is North. Even inside, in the dark;
    - One gun-shot, knife wound, or punch disables an "extra" bad guy, but heroes and "real" bad guys, limp along bleeding profusely;
    - Tasting the white powder to determine what drug it is, by knifing the middle of a bag and dabbing some on their tongue with their pinkie. How do they know what all drugs taste like?
- Confusing comments:
    - Calling everyone by their surname, even relatives; (Saez & Sarge!)
    - Is a "child predator" a bad adult, or a bad kid?
    - Time of death is always "based on." I don't care how, just when;

---

[456] And there are many companies out there, who are willingly to pay vast amounts of money to keep that choice free for them to make for you, based on the appropriate amount of subliminal advertising which can be included in the viewing package. ***cough*** Hungry Hungry David's ***cough***

[457] As in, cops of the TV, not Sting's band, "The Police."

Side-track: When **Roxanne** put her "**Don't Stand So Close to Me**, I can hear **Every Breath You Take!**" **Message in a Bottle**... We were all just **Walking on the Moon** because **Every Little Thing She Does is Magic.**

Sometimes they end up describing the wild scenario, including details they couldn't possibly know, of activities which couldn't have happened, by people who haven't appeared yet… Which is just fairly average writing.

Ms Medical Officer: "According to X and Y, they died somewhere between now and who-cares, probably with an A or B as the weapon, while they were P and/or Qing. But they have been moved because of S and M, at most likely sometime in the upcoming scene. So, we are looking for three underhanded, simulacrum villains, of either average IQ or other, who didn't bother to wear socks last Thursday, and don't have a stammer when they try to say innocent."
Inspector: "But, the victim has such a guilty looking innocent face."

Policemen - Detectives
Roger Murtaugh (Detective), Martin Riggs (Detective)
O'Hara (Police Chief Miles Clancy)
Sherlock Holmes (Consulting Detective)
/
Criminals
Oddjob (That's his Occupation… Name unknown)
Neal Caffrey (Nicholas "Nick" Halden, Neal Armstrong, Neal Bennett)
Simon Templar (The Saint)

Reasonably often, Donald's choice of shows include a varying level of the occult. Psychics, Witches, Wizards, Fortune Telling etc… So, it is only fair that they are included in his list of causes of him…[458] These are just a small selection of the bizarre questions and comments that floated through Donald's waking stupor at some stage, and then leaked out to his routine documentation:
- Is telling a story about the past, pre, or post, fortune telling?
- Can you tell me two things?
  - Something you have forgotten to remember; and
  - Something you have remembered to forget.
- It's like I can see six moments into the future. The speed of my reflexes when responding to a threat is my superpower. "Seeing through all of the crap" is indeed a glorious talent. Except when I am feeling ill, and I see all the available targets for any possible expulsion. This makes an expulsion more likely, in a recurring cycle of yuck-ness.

---

[458] If you are a psychically motivated fortune telling witch or wizard, who is offended by what I have written here, then you should really have contacted me when I wrote it… So, there is no point in you taking any offence now…

- This is a snippet of a conversation Donald had with himself one night:
  - What is your name?
  - Why?
  - *What* Y?
  - Yes... Why?
  - Ok then, Yes Y,
  - If that's your real name...
  - You can only have learned all of this from a spirit or ghost. And, as we all know, the spirits you most prefer come out of a bottle, not a Genie's bottle mind you, the suspicion must therefore fall upon either Seth Rueful, or Brother Latent Tardy, for betraying the SaRS secrets. Ones which have been closely guarded for over 75 years!

Mystery
Ytirucsbo
Transcendental [459]
Heathens
Spiritual

And it is only fair that the other side of the proverbial coin be included:
- Is the "Black Raven - White Dove" parable racist?
  - A Raven was chosen to go first (as the cannon fodder);
  - When the Raven didn't return, it was seen as a failure, but
  - When the Dove didn't return, it was seen as a success;
- Why is divine retribution a thing, instead of the promised forgiveness?
- When the next intervention comes, these guys will be the emissaries:
  - The White Horse   - Pestilence
  - The Red Horse   - War
  - The Black Horse   - Famine
  - The Pale Horse   - Death[460]
- By definition COVID-19 is a Pestilence... And an "Act of God."
  - Exclusively the consequence of natural causes;
  - Of an extraordinary nature; and
  - Not anticipated or provided against. (I'm just the messenger, ok!)

---

[459] This wasn't supposed to look like a "Bird." It is simply coincidental. But it does beg the next question... Who is the intended recipient?

[460] Now, I don't know about you, but these four horsemen don't seem to be the good guys in this scenario, and haven't we seen them all before anyway? It will be up to them to enforce the mandatory payment. Like a tax collector...

And a final cataclysmic ponderation in this biblically charged pontification: "Only the good die young." - Please explain?[461]

Instead of finishing this subsection with another acronym, I will be dishing up for your delectation the other staple of the mental diet... The List...

The three phases of life and death:
1. Everyone looks good after they're out of the woods;
2. Someone looks good while they're sporting wood; and
3. No one looks good after they're buried in wood.

Wasn't that a fun section? Well, lightning bolts aside, I had fun. With most of the obscurity over, now let's look at what Donald is planning to do about it. (Can someone get the narrator back please?)

Panic List for Distress Tolerance[462]

These are only suggestions. Not even that, they are potential suggestions. They are only meant to be considered as an alternative to self-injury behaviour in times of major crisis. They are for dealing with existing panic, and are not to be used as a replacement for the distress tolerance skills (i.e. avoidance).
Your DOGoN number must be at exactly ten.
- Any earlier, and you run the risk of looking at some unnecessary cost, needless financial burden, or at the very least, superfluous expense.
- Any later, and it will become a trite question of, "How late was it?"

They are not about you being effective, productive, or even vaguely useful at this particular moment in time. You are able to call this a win, only if you go on to be effective, productive, or even vaguely useful at some other uncertain future unspecified time. This means, playing it safe.
This might sound a tad boring, but don't forget you are able to rant, rage and scream at your heart's content. When this happens, it will sound anything but boring to all those within earshot. If you have the facilities available, you can take a hammer to a disused anything, turn the volume of your television up to thirteen and play a first-person-shooting game while screaming out the name of your nemesis, or even clean out the second drawer in the kitchen.

---

[461] And at some real peril of being sent elsewhere after my story is finished: Why is it that the Pope often lives to become Methuselah old?

[462] Please pay very close attention to the warning you are about to receive: It could save me a lot of financial distress in the future...

Start slowly.
Build up a head of steam.
Name the specific person and go to town on them.[463]

1. Watch some non-violent television.
2. Colour in a colouring book.
    If you go outside the lines, just rip out the page and re-start over again.
3. Baby yourself.
    Do what makes you feel good.
    Then you ask yourself, "Do I feel happy, punk?"
    If not: call a friend; take a 50/50; or ask the audience what you can do.
4. Choose an object in the room.
    Examine it carefully and then write a comprehensive description.
    Include one detail from each of your senses.
    If you feel adventurous, extend past the standard incorrect list of five.
5. Now you get to clean the room after you put the item away.
    If the item came from another room, you can clean that room as well.
    If the item came from another house, take it back and say sorry.
    Offer to clean their house if they agree to not press any charges.
6. Choose a random object like a paper clip, sticky-note, or coat-hanger.
    List thirteen different uses for it.
    Go find thirteen of said object; and try to do your thirteen listed uses.
7. Claim your body parts (touching them as you go):
    - This is my finger.
    - This is my thumb.
    - This is my fist.
    If you get to "this is my colon," you have gone the wrong way, go back.
    Oh… Bugger…
8. Cover a selection of your owned body parts with craft glue.
    Let it dry, let it dry, let it dry (use a hairdryer if you are impatient).
    Slowly pick and peel the glue off your skin.
    For next level craftiness, use super-glue. (Don't Glue. Just Don't Glue.)
9. Break something worthless, but not if it's your partner.
10. Bite into a frozen chilli-pepper and dialectically feel the burns.
11. Crank up the music and dance.
    Rammstein versions of Brothers Grimm nursery rhymes in the original
    German are good for raising eyebrows with their violent content.
12. Watch some violent television.

---

[463] **Note:** May contain repeated references or jokes…
None: Of them are advised…

Each page has been broken into self-contained bite-sized pieces for added enjoyment on your part. I can assure you this has nothing to do with managing my obsessive compulsion for making each page right, by having no disorder.[464]

1. Curl up under a doona with some hot chocolate and ~~this~~ a good book.
2. Indulge a hobby that requires concentration but not fastidious results.
3. Draw a picture of your current anxiety inducement in crayon.
   Smudge the stress out of it!
4. Go for a walk.
   If you asked, "is that all?" this aren't the task you're looking for.
   You can go about your business. Move along.
5. Take a long soothing hot bath.
   Bring it back, add oil/bubbles (of the bath variety) and this time get in.
6. Light up some sweet-smelling incense. ;-)
7. Eat a chocolate-chip muffin mindfully.
   - Pick it up, noticing how it feels in your hand.
   - Look at it carefully and count the protruding chocolate pieces.
   - Roll it around in your fingers and notice the texture.
   - Bring the muffin up to your nose and take a long deep smell.
   - Notice you're beginning to drool. Is it in the good way?
   - Open your mouth and take a bite. (Did I need open your mouth?)
   - Swirl it around in your mouth like cheap whiskey. Is it still good?
   - Swallow. What does it remind you of?
   - Notice the store attendants approaching. How many are there?
   Next time you may want to buy the muffin and take it home first.
8. Find an old revealing photo of yourself and scan it into your computer.
   Photoshop in your antagonist's partner.
   Make up a completely believable story describing the situation.
   Send it.[465]
9. Hit a punching bag.
   Add a picture of your antagonist looking at the previous task's photo.
   How much better does it feel hitting that!
10. Write your life story as if you have had the happiest life in the world.
    It doesn't have to be fictional, use real examples and pretend you see them from a different point of view. Just like Donald has here.

---

[464] True story. Not.

[465] Sending it to them directly is not recommended. It is far better to make it completely anonymous and display it in their lunchroom at work or submit it to a local newspaper and have it printed in their "personals" section.

1. Make a list of the things you're thankful for.
   Start with the easy things:
   - I'm thankful that I can read.
   - I'm thankful for Photoshop. (Refer to the last page).
   Then go to town:
   - I'm thankful for shops that sell chocolate muffins.
   - I'm thankful they understood when I wasn't so mindful of where I was, when I was being mindful of what I was eating.
2. Make a soft cloth widget to represent who, or what, you are angry at.
   Cut and tear at it… Instead of at you, or them.
   If that doesn't quell your inner ire, make a Play-Doh widget.
   Remember the hammer suggestion from earlier…
3. Take a tray of special treats and tuck yourself into bed with them and watch TV or read.
4. On the old revealing photo of yourself (also from earlier) mark, in your least favourite colour, everything you would like to change.
   Once it is fully coloured in, repeat with the picture of your antagonist.
   Once that is also fully coloured in, try to enact at least one change.
5. Rip up an old phone book.[466]
6. Play the computer game, again, also from earlier.
7. Put a finger into some ice-cream.[467]
   Put that finger into your mouth.
   If you are the only one who eats that ice-cream, repeat as desired.
   If not, repeat, but remember to erase the finger-prints as required.
8. Read a book aloud, about someone who has it worse than you.
   If that book is this book are you sure? Cos, I'm not talking to myself.
9. Stomp around with bare feet, and then escalate to heavy shoes.
   This is quite effective if you live in an apartment.
   Especially when your enemy lives in the apartment below yours.
10. Try to balance an egg on its short side.
    If at first you don't succeed, boil the sucker and try again.
11. Have a pillow-fight with yourself.
    If it starts to look like you might lose the pillow-fight, you can escalate things to an egg-fight using the failed eggs from the previous step.

The end of the list for now…[468]

---

[466] Obviously, you wouldn't be able to rip up a new one, as they don't exist.

[467] From the fridge this time, as you have already learned that lesson, I think.

[468] If you find any of these suggestions useful, tell a friend to buy the book.

Chapter 17:
A Parting Party!
(A Party to end all...)

There was movement at the mansion, for the rumour passed around, said that Donald was about to be released. And when DD signs his papers, we will have a reason found. The excuse? It doesn't matter, just the feast. All the faces will be there. Except for Nelo! That is true, he is still a little stuck under the ground. For the patients all love parties. And the staff? Well, they do too, especially when Hot Moccona's passed around...[469]

Re: Dark Roast Moccona (Inspired by *My Sharona* - The Knack) p284

¤   Extract from The Donald Diaries.

Yes. Donald has received the unofficial nod, he will be released on his own recognisance.[470] Nurse Jack had let it slip in the morning pre-briefing session, that someone was about to become an ex-patient... And in the good way... He just happened to be pointing a finger at Donald at the time.

It isn't often our Donald gets invited to a party, let alone to one where he will know everyone. And even rarer still, one that is thrown to celebrate some random coincidental feat he has accomplished by doing nothing in particular. He was nearly ready to start enjoying his stay at SaRS. A couple more chapters should just about do it.[471]

---

[469] Inspired by *The Man from Snowy River* - A. B. "Banjo" Paterson.

[470] As was Nota. The difference here is that Donald knows what it means.

[471] I hope the irony of this situation isn't lost to anyone. If it has been, I think you should really think about why you have read this far, when you clearly do not understand my weird, twisted sense of humour. (#thirteenth sense)

For those who haven't been paying attention:

The Famous Five Senses (FFS Clique, Standard Incorrect List of Five)
- Visual — Sight
- Auditory — Sound
- Somatosensory — Touch
- Gustatory — Taste
- Olfactory — Smell

Non-Sensory Intense Internal Senses
- Balance — I won't fall down
- Danger — I might fall down
- Pain — I fell down
- Common — I fell down again
- Hunger — I fell down because I was hungry
- Sixth — Actually the eleventh, but who's counting[472]

Miscellaneous Senses
- Disappointment — At not being a more important sense
- Humour — Just happy to be included
- Loss — of
- Decency — leads to
- Impending Doom — !

And now for something completely the same…

Donald Halfbrain 's Parting Party

Welcome everyone, I am _George Notatallwell!_

Dearly Beloved, and Patients, we are all gathered here today to congratulate _Donald_ on his/her upcoming sanity, and to certify he/she remembers the people of SaRS fondly. We are not here to witness the beginning of what might be, but rather, to bid farewell to the end of what already was…

After Donald read his official welcome platitude, he started to mingle…

---

[472] Me… My numbering system fell down at this point, which is strange, as I usually have an eleventh sense about avoiding that sort of thing.

Donald likes patterns, he sees them everywhere. And if he can't see them, he constructs them in his mind. The patterns of de-escalation deprecating[473] interaction he has available to him are:

- **FIFO** (**F**irst **I**nvoiced, **F**irst **O**vercharged):[474] The order of appearance is reversed in order to create the departure order. Unfortunately, it only applies to other patients, as they are the only ones who are invoiced and overcharged (and institutionalised).
- **LUMP** (**L**ast **U**ndergoing **M**ental **P**roblems): This is the predicted order of eventual saneness. Although it can be legitimately applied to SaRS employees as well as to patients, it is too hard to create the baseline required to calculate expectations of the staff.
- **GAOL** (**G**rouped **A**veraged **O**verturned **L**ist):[475] Donald felt that this list was some sort of subliminal message, but he couldn't quite figure out what the message was. As this list is the only one including everyone, it is also the one which will ultimately be used.[476]

It was at this point when Donald went into full auto-shotgun mode. This is where he is just a passenger, who has no actual control of his own immediate destiny, while tightly strapped in and unable to move freely... But was still in the front row of the action where it is always most stressful and dangerous.

And it was **good**.

Whatever was to happen after-party in regard to his sanity, Donald had a ready-made excuse lined up which was bordering on reasonable... "My mental acuity has been weighed, and was found to be not wanting, on balance. But, if you don't believe me, I have the papers to prove it."

Donald was embracing the "Take me... Lead me... Help Me... Show Me..." mantra completely, and he was "Every day, in every way, I'm getting better, and better."

Hospityable: SaRS Unofficial 1 – Mantra
- Extract from The Donald Diaries.

---

[473] This is another actual thing... When an old version a computer software application passes its "use by date," the manufacturer's support will become "deprecated." The use of that word is "appreciated" by Donald.

[474] Obviously, this should be First Institutionalised, First Outraged.

[475] Franchised → Contracted → Disenfranchised → Staff → Inmates.

[476] The order within each of these individual groups is completely random...

As the most recent franchise introduction was Pharmaceuticals Я Us, perhaps it is fitting they are also the first to be farewelled, and then to impart to Donald a parting remark. And even though they would also be alphabetically first, I am sure this is just a happy coincidence...

"It is good to see you going Donald, we love a successful legitimate escape at the end every reality story. If you need a little something to keep your boat afloat, you know where we are... OOOO." While Farmer Suit Tickle was quiet in his farewell, the echo would ring in Donald's ear for years to come.

The next face upon the farewell block was a new one to Donald, as it was his first time meeting someone from siGns On Demand! In fact, it was also his first time meeting anyone from them, so when Simone Else introduced herself with her thick unpolished Kiwi accent, Donald was unsure why she was there at all, but he was glad she was, as he liked the dark tan colour of her soles...

You may remember her from such atrocities as:

- Interrogation Room Won;
- Interrogation Room Too; and
- We can't spell ~~Qure~~ Cure without ~~you~~ U!

After this first, and only, time he going to meet her, Donald will always try to remember this Simone as being the spectacularly vivacious Maori lady, who was virtually consistently understanding when it came to their new genuinely friendly back and forth neighbourhood rivalry.[477]

"High, Buy."

Donald only then noticed her curiously repeated glances towards Farmer and will eventually wonder once he gets to know of them, what she would call herself if Polly was to depart the picture, allowing them to become married... Simone Else-Tickle would be a mouthful in any language.

Completing the trio of innocent franchises extant at Donald's ex-tantrum inducible celebrations was the easily deducible Senior Investigator, Detective, from Who Investigates. Detective had quietly interacted with Donald on several inexplicable occasions over the previous two weeks, making her farewell one of the most appropriate, and also predictable.

Detective had somehow flown under Donald's **B**latant **S**tereotypical radar completely... She knew about things she had no logical way of knowing about, she understood most of Donald's misunderstandings, and she communicated the importance of this understanding with her silence.

"...?"

She said everything she needed to say with the uncertain look in her eye.

---

[477] Simone will come remember Donald as the guy hoping to be responsible for her impending pregnancy. This was only because it was already well on the way to becoming a lasting figment of his vivid imagination.

The contracted quartet were not remotely as disciplined as the franchised triad were, farewelling their most interesting observer for some time, in non-alphabetical order. Donald chose to accept this as a compliment.[478]

"IT WAS GOOD TO HAVE YOU HERE DONALD."

"HEAR, HEAR." Simone Finger-One supplemented her husband's farewell comments in good faith, not realising the irony of her virtually unheard words. "WHEN WE FIND OUT ANY INFORMATION ABOUT THE SIDEWAYS GROWING ROSE BUSHES, WE WILL GIVE YOU ANOTHER SHOUT."

Not long after her parting words Simone met Simone, in the comparative quiet solitude of the unisex[479] bath less euphemism, compared their indiscrete stories of Donald's impending solidarity, and then superficially pair-bonded over having the same name.[480]

You may have noticed by now that Donald hasn't responded to any of the well wishes. This is because none of them have combined the asking of him a question with an out loud. You know that Donald doesn't handle conversation very well when there isn't any back and forth verbal jousting; when the dialog consists primarily of well wishes for his future it becomes an impossibility.

"I am the Who, who is glad to know the who, who you are. You are a much better who now, than the who, who you were before. If you have learned one thing from your stay at SaRS let it be this... Remember, any wood is good, but every Who wood is better![481]"

Good was starting to depreciate.
And not just because of Dennis' contribution to the underlying entendre.

(Little) Bertha Nomaly looked directly at Donald and openly winked.
This one little action created more unease in Donald than all of the untold other times he had previously wished there could have been any *wink wink* action to be had. The copious amounts of every kind of entendre currently just floating around inside his head didn't help the situation at all.

---

[478] And he was wise to do so. For your future reference, whenever you are approached by a person wielding a functioning chainsaw, you are best to listen to them over the din and acquiesce to whatever they are shouting for.

[479] Why does this mean for use by both sexes when it literally says one sex?

[480] At least this is what Donald told me they did in his dreams.

[481] I might have to revise this farewell later, I'll let you know what I decide.

LB noticed the great amount of discomfort Donald was going through, and correctly took ownership of most of it. Smiling inwardly for a winding-up job well done, she disappeared into the escalating crowd of well-wishers gathered at Donald's grassy knoll, very satisfied with herself.

Moving onto the lone disenfranchised entity, Brother Latent Tardy (BLT to his mediums) had these departing words for Donald:

- Even though I may have been a willing self-appointed member of your SaRS welcoming committee, I am very much a dis-appointed coerced participant of your desertion team; and
- I feel like I have attempted to make you feel welcome throughout your stay with us at SaRS, facilitated your every desire and protected you from the seedy underbelly; so
- It is with a heavy breathless soul that I give you this passive aggressive send-off with my blessing… Go, be at peace with yourself knowing you will be missed by all of us;
- I do owe you heaps for not telling on me to DD.

Donald didn't have time to process BLT's disparate presentations, from his devilishly evil sneer, rejected derisive smirk, mollified sanctified smile, through to his childishly unaware grin before his apparition dissipated.[482]

The major group of people[483] then stepped up to the plate to farewell their most recent statistical anomaly. They were the first of the many subsets, of up to three members, and they issued this joint parting official message…

"Goodbye Donald. It was a great pleasure having you here and overseeing your mental taming. And I think I speak for the two out of three who ain't bad people in our qualified group when I say congratulations, and I hope to never see you here again!" Dr Gee Jay's speech was interpreted in exactly the same way by the other two groupies.

"Dr Gee Jay must be disregarding Andy Coughed/Houts Marted when she says two out of three, I feel sad for Houts Marted/Andy Coughed." The closest scenario Donald could use to describe what he was watching, when he asked himself where he had seen a similar cacophony before, was an unexpected acceptance of an award for the "Best Assistant Doctor in an unconventional treatment facility," where the Lead Doctor accepted it on their behalf.

---

[482] It wasn't like Donald had expected any kind of formal send-off, so when they started adding to his confusion at his penultimate major interaction with everyone he didn't understand why, as it just didn't make any sense.

[483] In size and importance only.

After the first subset of people who obviously thought they were the most important, came the second group who thought likewise, and were possibly a little more correct depending on your point of view…

"I won't say goodbye just yet Donny, I will leave that until your check-out check-up is checked and passed by me. Until tomorrow, you may consider this a lukewarm later dude. To ease any unease I may have just eased in, I have no preconceived idea of what any of your answers will indicate. I base everyone's potential departure solely on the answers you give then." Smiling a smile of importance retained, DD handed the attention to Mr Jack Call.[484]

"Donald,[485] I was getting to like having you here at SaRS, keeping everyone in line with your obstinate need to understand everything. Your Dark Humour shining its positive light will be sadly missed. I also hope to never see you here again…" Breaking the protocol that says, "There must be NO gifts or numbers exchanged between patients and staff!" Nurse Jack presented Donald with a pair of Uggkubra moccasins that had a little smile woven into the fabric. Upon closer inspection later on[486] Donald found they also had a tag attached, which included both a phone number and an eMail address.

Donald got the distinct feeling that if he was to return in thirteen years, DD would be exactly the same, which would be a shame; and Nurse Jack would be exactly the same, which would be a good thing.

The third and fourth element of this trio was a two-for-one-up featuring Nurses Wendy Dunk and Hatchet on the ~~Mc David's~~ smart board. Awkwardly, their mistimed farewells hurt Donald's sensitive auditory feelings, as well as exposing their flagrant disregard of who their audience was.

"Goodbye Halfbrain Mr."

"I think his last name is Halfbrain, and Mr is his title."

"Really?"

"I think so…"

"Hang on, I'll have a look at his chart."

"What do you mean 'have a look at his chart?' you aren't supposed to take them home or make copies‽ Please come and see me at your earliest now!" DD had just cut short their farewell addresses, added an additional two years to Nurse Hatchet's tenure as the Night Nurse, and in just a moment she will also have thought of an appropriate punishment for Nurse Dunk's pleasure.

---

[484] DD relented and was addressing Nurse Jack as such in public, sticking to her "nursing is women's work" concept only in the privacy of her own mind.

[485] The inflection on the second syllable told Donald that Nurse Jack was still firmly entrenched on his side of the "calling them by their names" faction.

[486] When he tried to insert his foot…

The least important fragment, of the most important group,[487] of the party participants, did everything but casually accept the centre of attention when it became their turn. Every student and trainee at SaRS knew the first rule was "Do NOT upset DD's apple gurney," and being in the spotlight for too long was a sure-fire way to get burned...

Grey Duate, Stu Arthur Dent (no relation) and They Meantwell all had the exact same comment to say... "Ummmmm, what DD said." This will always be a locked-in-safe response at SaRS while DD is on the payroll.[488] Picking up any pieces shattered by DD saying "No" when approving release orders, falls upon the least senior members of the medical staff, so they knew to not become too invested in a particular patient in public.

"They also know not to talk behind DD's back...!"

<Metaphorical> *Slap!* **</Metaphorical>**

Even though DD didn't actually slap Donald,[489] the ramifications were felt far and wide. There would be no talking about DD "behind her back" from now on, without first getting her input and approval.

Sensing that all of the medical staff who wanted to have a say had finished speaking, the control of the talking stick was passed over to the non-medical-but-just-as-important staff...

Having donned his practically clean formal caftan for this special occasion, Aaaron referred to his trusty clipboard for the speech he had been working on all minute, "Bye-bye Donald, a nice person that our nursin' did not worsen, no coercion..." And then improvising, "It's very good you are able to leave us after being here for only ten days and thirteen nights."

Donald thought Aaaron's rhyming had improved substantially, especially when you compare this to his earlier failed attempts;[490] and even though his unique grasp of time was still slipping, it had the follow-on effect of revising Donald's opinion of him from less than printable all the way to indifferent.

---

[487] Depending on who you talk to of course.
Since DD is still at the party this is the stance I will be taking.

[488] Personally, I wouldn't risk anything else for up to two years after.

[489] No... That was my reward for speaking about DD when I knew better.

[490] I don't see how there could possibly be any another comparisons. This gross redundancy is probably just here to fill in some of the space left when other words haven't been written yet.

Completing the final Pastoral Care Service obligation, Zyxon Zzippy added his own comments well before his generally assumed position of Dammit last again, "Would you like a farewell ice-cream from the Zzippy cart sir? We are currently going through a nut and alcohol-free P phase, leaving: Passionfruit, Peach, Peaches 'n' cream, Pear, Pepper, Peppermint, Pickle, Pineapple, Plum, Popcorn, Pumpkin and Purple."

"You had me at Purple. It's my favourite!"

Two scoops of Purple ice-cream in hand, the next two furwells passed right over Donald's brain frozen head...

"Woof.[491]" A saddening anti-climactic finale from Chunky Poopy, following his acrobatic galloping diving sliding desperation inducing entrance. It was the first time Donald had heard him speak, and he was surprised by the volume of nine that Chunky reached.

"" In stark contrast to Chunky, Picatso da Kitty used her limited knowledge of the Loathsome Languages Silent Treatment Suggestions,[492] and delivered a catalepsy inspiring send-off. It reached a maximum volume of zero, indicating her favourite preference to not care. Donald wasn't disappointed by this at all, conversely it confirmed his earlier methodical suspicion, together these two animals would amount to astounding no-no-toriety.

In came the bottom-line dotters and crosses to request some consolation condolences because Donald was leaving them. These particular three were taking the situation in the hardest personal manner.[493] Mark Time was the first to dab his tears with the sobbing hankie (SH)...

"You, and your private medical insurance, will be sorely missed by all of us around here. I don't know how we will fill the empty bed you left, but we will go on trying. It is just such a shame to lose the **S**ly **C**reative **A**ccounting **M**oney bonus funding of the non-private beds." Mark then doffed his several hats and passed the SH over to Polly.

Polly Tickle mirrored her husband's farewell, "It is a dreadful failure on my behalf to meet you like this Donald, I should have come and introduced myself earlier, **but**." Polly finished speaking brusquely, having nothing resembling an excuse to offer as a replacement of everything she had just said, choosing to mumble an insubstantial threat instead, "If we need a little something to keep our private jet afly, we know where you are... ∞∞∞."

---

[491] Translation... You may go my pretty little patty-man, but you'll be back.

[492] Gained while prowling the mansion corridors in search of a fugitive meal.

[493] Some wailing and gnashing of teeth is not unexpected from these three.

George Notatallwell! burst onto the scene trying to recover the situation before Polly tossed the SH out with the soiled nappies, "Yes, thankyou Polly, I'm sure Donald doesn't want to hear any more of your incoherent rambling... For all we know he has already figured out the underlying storyline revolving around the Red Lady and Pledge, Jimmy Pledge...[494]"

Recovering from his tiny misstep, George increased the level of platitude, "Congratulations Donald, on reaching the best exit outcome possible from the fantastic facility that is Saint Rita's Sanatorium! You have proven to be rather an exceptional beacon of success and have given hope to every other patient here. Your Mental Health is definitely a winner."

Ding, Ding, Ding... Donald's third time-is-a-blinder-meter[495] went off.
Donald evaded Polly's carving knife, and things continued as unplanned...

The "We are here for your physical wellbeing team." were next...[496] Donald has had hardly anything to do with Ma'am Cybill Flex, as he is often deficient in the inspiration category whenever exercise is mentioned. Donald also has a hard time thinking of Ma'am Cybill Flex without picturing her unadulterated name hanging there acting dialectically as carrot and stick simultaneously.

"I am disappointed you are leaving us Donald, without first performing in our *A Rocky Horror Musical*. But not with you Donald. It is the natural order of the world I am disenchanted with. There is never enough time between being admitted, and being released, for us to prepare a spectacular performance."

Donald thought he saw her trying to choke back a tear, and unusually felt sadness for her. His faith in his scepticism was quickly restored when he saw it was a bead of sweat running down her face because she was trying to tear a phone book in half out of sheer frustration.

"I have another important task, another somewhere else."

Seymour Feedme took reactive control of their collective figurative baton seamlessly and continued down the parting track at minimum speed, "I'll not condescend at you for long Donald... Goodbye, good-luck and good dieting."

---

[494] George was supposed to keep this to himself, instead he has just outed a small spoiler that wasn't intended to be known until a few pages from now... Donald didn't care either way, as he already knew.

[495] This has been recently been renamed... Can you guess what from? ;-)

[496] If these three were to form an actual team, there would be no doubt at all who their leader would be... The one at the back holding the whip of course! Closely chasing the ones with the whipped cream, and the whipped attitude.

There was a slight pause while Seymour manoeuvred himself into the new sponsorship mandatory devotion safety warning position…

Warning: All Hungry~~Me~~Hungry~~Me~~David's food must not be further cooked before consuming. Anything that is further cooked, may be used as evidence, if any is subsequently expunged.

And, as a final act of contrition, Seymour gave Donald another voucher…

> Hungry~~Me~~Hungry~~Me~~David's gratuity menu:
> 1. Deep breath before attempting to read more
> 2. Up to thirteen pieces of advice are available
> 3. Do not turn over, do not read the other side
> Hungry~~Me~~Hungry~~Me~~David's, what the tip's that?

Donald turning this over was ridiculously inevitable this time…

> Hungry~~Me~~Hungry~~Me~~David's advice won't be valid:
> - Until the day after Tomorrow (Today's date);
> - With a purchase of, up to and including, free;
> - When you are expecting the unexpected; and
> - While you are not a current patient of SaRS.

It then fell to Chef Chief Changes again to try and smooth over the current potential situation that Seymour was often accused of creating, "Donald, I am feeling extremely dialectical at the moment, I am happy to see you leave and I am sad that I am not leaving too… I would have liked to see what you saw in The Tapestry #2. Never mind, I feel…

You will be back[497]
You will be back, I am sure, that's a fact
Like Arnold, you will be back, it's guaranteed
Not complacent… Inpatient, outpatient
I will always be here when you need a feed
So, get the hell far away to enjoy your D-day
Before they suck you back in…
Listen to what I say, this is your, Donald, day
When you're chalking up a win…

---

[497] Inspired by *We'll Meet Again* - Ross Parker and Hughie Charles.

The undeveloped space between Donald's physical and mental health was brusquely built upon when the next trio offered their own special versions of a therapeutic message. Anna Lykeananna (Massage Therapist), who everyone knew was the most volatile of the group, went growling first...

"Goodbye Donald, it was a definite pleasure to meet you. Mmmmm meat, arrggllhehhalghlhegge. I hope you found the experience as fulfilling as I didn't. The outstanding efforts to improve your taste, in many tender areas, have not gone unnoticed.[498] And I do so hope you will be able to return for our Save the Threes event, even if it is just for a minute or three on each side..."

Donald was about to ask Anna, "On each side of when?" when Sue Rhea Liszt (Art Realisationalist and Struggling Artist) deflected what may have been an awkward question to answer, "...of the rainbow, over and out." This vocal sub-contracted continuation confused Donald so much he forgot his question earlier than usual, replacing it with the unsatisfactory thought, "She may be a spectacular artist, but.[499]"

"As you leave us Donald, I hope you will take with you the lessons adjacent to satisfying your heart desire. Throw everything you can into developing your artistic side... Paint, write, build, or whatever... Just try and create something each day. You will be amazed at how easy it is to get lost in what you are doing, forgetting all of your troubles."

Then she opportunistically appended, "And don't forget about **Purple Pay**. Even though it has often been a generally maligned contrivance, it has earned me a dwindling fortune, and you too can participate in the unusual strategy..." which only served to leave a sour disappointed taste in Donald's mouth.

As dissatisfied with Sue's final piece of self-promotion as Donald was, Willy attempted to mollify the situation with, "I hope[500] you discover what it is you are searching for Donald. I am convinced that everyone has an amazing talent hiding inside them. Once you have found your special gift, all you will require is a little coaxing to enjoy opening it."

The crowd listening to William the Piano man (Musical Therapy)'s recital, echoed Donald's thoughts, before he had them, with a combined "Huh¿™"

---

[498] This wasn't an entirely accurate statement, as Donald hadn't noticed. Unless it is what Anna meant by outstanding, as in, not done yet. A triple negative always confuses Donald three times more than a double one does.

[499] Polly used this technique earlier, to dismiss her comment, and as with a lot of his material, Donald purloined it for his own useless dismissive thought.

[500] These three certainly did a lot of hoping, considering traditionally their fields of expertise encroached upon the antithesis of that particular theory.

Noticing the distressing after-smell of dissatisfaction dissipating amongst the other distinguished therapists, Willy handed the soapbox back to the last, but by no means least, group of people...[501]

Got Knoted sidled up to Donald in a less than obvious mince, "I'm sorrrry to see you go Mrrrr Khkhkhkhkhbrain, I deedn't get to spend as much time eenvesteegateeng weeth you as I wanted to. We could have made some of ze beauteeful underrrrrcoverrrr museec togetherrrrr." And then she leaned into Donald and whispered something softly into his ear, "sometheeng softly eento hees earrrrr."

Istha T. You was having a tsunami of difficulty understanding what exactly was going on,[502] "Why are we all saying goodbye to Donald when we burnt the crap out of him last week?" Istha's reality is truly a most unique point of view. "I don't want anything more to do with your warped Psychobabble. When you have got it together send someone to fetch me, I'll be in my room..."

"I'd like to pass please, if you wouldn't mind?" Karl Saneman was making a valiant effort by attempting to have a crack at simply trying to say goodbye to a kindred spirit.

Donald could see a well of tears wishing behind Karl's eyes and was glad that he could answer his farewell, because it was a question... "Thank you Karl, of course I don't mind. It has been my genuine pleasure to get to know there are others out there a little bit like me."

Something else Donald knew, Karl still had his car keys, and in the boot of his car there were many tools, and in those tools, there is a successful escape attempt just waiting to happen. So, Donald was able to leave Karl behind, safe in the knowledge that if he really didn't want to be there, he didn't have to be, whenever he wanted.

"Sho now Donald, Yesh, I know your name Donald Halfbrain... It hash all come down to thish. I can shee you ashking yourshelf, 'Why ish Pledge, Jimmy Pledge, alwaysh here?' Well, it'sh like thish... I am here to shpy on you. Haven't you notished that Losht M'Hankie hash been here leshsh and leshsh lately?" Not waiting for Donald to answer, he continued, "The Red Lady and I were the contactsh Losht ushesh to shend shecret information back to bashe, but of late that informashion hash become unreliable, sho we have been forshed to shee what we could shee ourshelvesh... And now you know too much..."

---

[501] Donald was currently too distracted by this chapter's word count, as it rapidly approached the magic 5000 mark, to notice anything else. Until he just then noticed this was the 501th footnote... As for this chapter's length, the next chapter will compensate by being a little bit shorter than optimal.

[502] Her goings on haven't even approached approximately yet.

What Pledge, Jimmy Pledge, had unprofessionally revealed wasn't entirely accurate. His, and the Red Lady's, secondary purpose was to collect evidence of anything untoward. Their primary purpose was to keep everyone guessing about their own sanity, and thus keeping the possibility of extending their stay beyond three weeks open.[503]

Reaching into his inside left jacket pocket, Pledge, Jimmy Pledge, retrieved a cigarette case… "Have you tried one of theshe before?"

Another question, and Donald jumped at the chance to answer, "No."

"It ish a **M**odified **E**xtenuating **R**eashon **Sh**igarette, I used one jusht like thish in *You Won't Die Nishe*." Selecting the fourth south-west cigarette, he started moving it towards his lips…

<Crash><Boom><Bash> "Sphincter Feng Shui…"

"There won't be any extenuating circumstances here today, I'm not afraid, Pledge, Jimmy Pledge… Yes, I know your name too. You say it often enough." DD had entered the fray with gusto, and with three movements had removed the initial threat, the preliminary armament and the primary attacker.

DD returned and re-emphasised, "There is no smoking inside at SaRS."

I'll let you go now, don't forget to close the door on your way out.

The penultimate group of three remaining farewellers had barely rated a mention throughout Donald's stay in SaRS, so it stands to reason they will only receive the bare minimum, indicating a minor character, acknowledgement at his leaving party…[504]

"Zzzzz. What? Oh right. Goodbye Sonny… Zzzzz"

"Goodbye Donald."

"*Ahphlegm*… Goodbye Sir."

And then there was just the final three…

"Farewell Donald, it would probably have been nice getting to know you."

Donald didn't recognise the character Skit Zoland was projecting, so he did the unusual normal thing, "And who might you be?"

---

[503] This was George's secret mission behind the scenes. Eventually it will prove his undoing when he is outed by Got. It just goes to show that you can't trust anyone, especially the slightly malevolent politically driven people.

[504] As they are insignificant, I'll leave it up to you to figure out who they are.

"I am Skit, Skit Zoland."

"Yes, I know that, but who are you?"

Skit didn't need to act confused, "Ummmmm, I am Skit."

Donald didn't need to act confused in return, "Yes, but... Huh¿™"

Once again DD showed her professionalism and stepped up, all super-hero like, to save everyone from questioning their own sanity. "Donald, I would like you to meet Skit Zoland. He has only joined us this morning, after he woke up with his own personality intact. <Wink-Wink!>"

"Oh, oh. OH!" triple take realisation aside; this was a reasonable response from Donald. Taking the Wink-Wink cue from DD, Donald further improvised, "It is good to meet you Skit."

Two, and One...

Owedebt Dear, and a surprise reprise of Nota Beenhead, pop-corned the start of their farewell like an old married couple...

"It" "was" "good" "to" "meet" "you" "Donald."

"I" "hope" "we" "can" "meet" "again," "some" "sunny" "day."

"I" "don't" "know" "where," "I" "don't" "know" "when."[505]

Donald was mesmerised and nearly missed it when Nota advanced on him for an unwarranted, unrequested and unearthly[506] hug. Recovering his senses quickly enough to jump out of the way before disaster struck and there was a physical altercation, Donald thanked his avoidance reflex, and moved on.

Disappointed with Donald's lack of reciprocity, she stomped off to look up what the word meant.

There was no similar problem with Owedebt, who had excommunicated herself from the situation already.

DD led Donald back to his room to pack his meagre belongings, and to give him some encouragement inducing time to prepare himself for the upcoming final debriefing session.

---

[505] If I have acknowledged this before, do I need to again?

[506] In Donald's opinion. Which is what matters. Right?

Chapter 18:
Language Revisited
(English - Not so Much)

Donald, as he has so often done, did exactly as he was told to do and packed his more than thirteen excessively miserable possessions, and then left the remainder until later. Becoming side-tracked, as he has so often done as well, Donald picked up his paddle and perused through everything he had recorded over the past few weeks. And then, as he has so often done entirely, he made a list of everything that was currently annoying him about the English language...[507]

As with all the lists floating around Donald's head, these are alphabetical, grouped with an overarching topic and the obvious is explained.

- Acronyms (redefined)
  - EASL   - English is **A S**trange **L**anguage
  - MVP   - **M**inimal **V**iable **P**rocess
  - WTF   - is the reverse of FTW (**F**or the **W**in) & should be WtF
  - WTFH   - **W**orking **T**oday from **H**ome

- Anagrams (of a coincidental[508] nature)
  - expect   - except   (expect everything... no exceptions...)
  - persevere   - per severe   (continue, no matter how bad it gets)
  - silent   - listen   (if you aren't one, then you can't two)
  - theme   - the me   (bingo. I've been saying this all along)
  - vote   - veto   (vote... or veto... there is no abstain...)

---

[507] This will be a short chapter, as all the "good" material is in Hospityable.

[508] Some of these coincidental anagrams are verging close to an ironic cliff.

- Common mispronunciations[509]
  - ekcetera, ekcetera, ekcetera… etc… etc… etc…
  - vulnerabilities   - Pass directly into Hel if you ever skip the first "l"

- Onomatopoeias
  - aaaaand   - Wait for it, wait for it, wait for it… Aaaaand… Go!
  - aaaaargh   - This is what every tedious frustration sounds like
  - ahhhhh   - Turning on the lightbulb of great enlightenment
  - arrggllhehhalghlhegge - Verbal drooling (real drooling may result)
  - awwwww   - Turning off the lightbulb of hopeful expectations
  - baaaaack   - The stereotypical Austrian actor spelling of back
  - booooop-ooooop-oooopy-dooooo - Sound of a computer starting
  - buuuuut   - Questioning something which should be obvious
  - erm   - Challenging something which should be obvious
  - ewwwww   - Can be used in the place of a "Yucky, yuck, yuck"
  - fffff   - Blowing on your hot coffee to cool it to drinkable
  - hmmmmm   - Sound of a brain starting, after months of disuse
  - mmmmm   - Typical warning for an upcoming verbal drooling
  - mmmmmph   - Mental redaction of any unpleasant information
  - oo   - Edgy short form of a typical "Notice me please!"
  - pffffft   - Verbalising of any superficial dismissive disbelief
  - pthththththth   - Potential juicy bout of sputtering onomatopoeia
  - right-ee-ho   - Simple silence filler, waiting for the next thought
  - shhhhh   - Near silent request, waiting for the next thought
  - smoooooth   - Up to two and a ½ times smoother than smooth
  - sooooo   - A sarcastic response that implies, "Not so much"
  - stopppppping   - An extended shhhhh, ready-set, say-cheese, go!
  - ummmmm   - Simple silence filler, hoping for the next thought
  - weeeeeeeeee   - An ancient cartoonish sound of flora excitement
  - wooooow   - Sound of a brain thinking, after months of disuse
  - yuuummm   - Up to three times yummier than yum (not Yum!)
  - zzzzz   - 1) Visual presentation of unexaggerated snoring
                   - 2) Visual presentation of an exaggerated letter z

- Opposites - Not[510]
  - exhumation   - A separated de-personification of a human body
  - rehearsed   - What happens immediately after an exhumation
  - uncanny   - The mysterious exhumation of a cremated body

---

[509] To be consistent, this really should be spelled "mispronounciations."

[510] Three not right now: ex – used to be; re – will be again; and un – never was.

- ¤ Oxymorons[511]
  - ✍ Small chunks   - 1) noun: chunk - a significant piece of something
  - ✍ Remove a chunk - 2) verb: chunk - group together as a single piece

- ¤ Pairs ("**a pair of x**" means...)
  - ✍ Aural devices
    - ear buds   = 2 "ear bud" items (1 set)   (enough for 2 ears)
    - headphones = 1 "headphones" item   (enough for 2 ears)
      (Note: there is no singular headphone item)
    - headsets   = 2 "headset" items   (enough for 4 ears)
  - ✍ Clothing
    - pants   = 1 "pants" item   (giving 3 holes)
      (Note: there is no singular pant item, except breathing heavy)
    - socks   = 2 "sock" items   (1 set)   (giving 2 holes)
    - t-shirts   = 2 "t-shirt" items   (giving 8 holes)
  - ✍ Optical devices
    - binoculars = 2 "binoculars" items (as in go get the binoculars)
      (Note: there is no singular binocular item)
    - glasses   = 1 "pair of glasses" item
      (Note: there is no singular glass item, except the drinking kind)
    - monocles   = 2 "monocle" items
    - lenses   - makes 2 monocles, ½ a binoculars,[512] or 1 glasses
  - ✍ Related questions...
    - Why aren't handcuffs handscuffs, as you cuff a pair of hands?
    - When you refer to the group, why do you drop the word pair?
      e.g. There are up to many different types of scissors available

- ¤ Plurals
  - ✍ With alphabets, you can write As, Bs, Cs...   A[1] |eɪ| (also a)
    And... They are all spellchecked as wrong.   noun (plural **As** or **A's**)
    Then you can write them as A's, B's, C's...   1 the first letter of the alphabet.
    But they are not possessive or missing a letter, and it looks wrong.
  - ✍ Why is it not two mongeese, when it is two gooses making geese?
  - ✍ Why is it not feetprints, when you are on the trail of different feet?
  - ✍ When you are thinking of two individual things at the same time,
    aren't you having two thinkings, as a thought is in the past tense?
  - ✍ And... When both of these two thinkings are about some anything,
    aren't they really thinkings about two individual some anythings?

---

[511] Opposite is allowed a plural, as is plural itself, so, why not an oxymoron?

[512] Depending on the version of binocular physics you are using of course.

ꭥ Pronunciations (a change to the "P" comparative vowel sounds in use)

    ø paddle   - waddle
    ø penis   - Denis
    ø phone   - shone
    ø pint   - tint
    ø plow[513]   - flow
    ø post   - lost
    ø prow   - grow
    ø put   - but   - out
    ø pye   - _ye

ꭥ Quote a dilemma

    ø Do you include a quote if you write carbon copied as an acronym? I CCd them, or I CC'd them?[514]

ꭥ Root words (strange or incorrect extensions of)

    ø Spelling differences (often pronunciation as well)

      - explain   - explanation   (missing an "i")
      - four   - forty   (missing a "u")
      - sheep   - shepherd   (missing an "e")
      - speak   - speech   ("a" became an "e")
      - stable   - stabilised   (additional "i")
      - syllable   - syllabised   (missing an "l")

    ø Pronunciation differences

      - mean   - meant
      - provocative - provocation
      - repeat   - repetitive   - repetition[515]
      - sterile   - sterilised
      - visual   - visuality

    ø Word not allowed when similar is for another word

      - interabangation   (exclamation)
      - interabanging   (questioning)
      - quoter   (speaker)
      - scentful   (flavourful)

---

[513] Correct, although this is the American spelling it is becoming accepted. And did you know that "w" is considered to be a vowel when it is combined with an "a," "e," or "o" to articulate a single sound? (e.g. draw, flew and plow.)

[514] They are both spellchecked as wrong.   I CCd them, or I CC'd them?

[515] Bonus points for the three different sounds and two different spellings.

- Say it like it sounds
  - catch it   - cat shit[516]

- Strange connections (or coincidences?) and common errors
  - allies   - all lies   (allies shouldn't be telling all lies)
  - collateral   - (damage coming out or documentation going in)
  - obviously   - obliviously   (obviously you're quite oblivious)
  - psychological   - psychiatrical   (why is it one and not the other?)
  - strike/struck   - like/luck   (luck is not the past-tense of like)
  - thesaurus   - the saurus   ("the lizard" - like tyrannosaurus)
  - urgent   - important   (do not mean exactly the same…)
  - verb   - verbalise   (to use words, written or spoken)

- Tenses (of the past variety)
  - After writing "Fine!" Have you just "Fined!" "Fine!d" or, "Fine!"d?
  - If you've just taken a "screen shot," haven't you "screened shot?"
  - After you prove it, is it "proved," or "proven?" Or can it be either?
  - I had a thought… The past tense of "thinking," should be "thunk."
  - What is the past tense of "to wing it?" (Space blank intentionally)

- Waste of times (and confusions)
  - It's the least I can do   - No, the "least" is to stop talking about it
  - More than welcome   - Extrapolates to, "Let's make it an order"
  - Not to mention…   - Is always followed by a mention of the…
  - Please, do not hesitate   - Adds exactly naught to the conversation
  - Suffice it to say   - Summarising by way of a re-explanation
  - To be perfectly honest   - I didn't realise that honest wasn't binary

- Words that must become real

I	(1)	- Hospityable[517]		X	(10)		C	(100)	
II	(2)	- Psychoillogical		XX	(20)		CC	(200)	
III	(3)	- Rehabilitigation		XXX	(30)		CCC	(300)	
IV	(4)	- Unemploymental		XL	(40)		CD	(400)	
V	(5)	- Laboratoryinth		L	(50)		D	(500)	
VI	(6)	- Catchychism		LX	(60)		DC	(600)	
VII	(7)	- Mindlessfullness		LXX	(70)		DCC	(700)	
VIII	(8)	- Philosophblical		LXXX	(80)		DCCC	(800)	
IX	(9)	- SaRSaparillan		XC	(90)		CM	(900)	
							M	(1000)	

---

[516] I don't care how hard you are trying to not… It will always sound like this!

[517] One through to eight in roman numerals are also alphabetically ordered.

⌘ Words that should be real (ones I didn't make up)

- aughta — Should, e.g. aughta aughta be made into a real word
- badder — Worse than bad, but not worse enough to be worse
- booyah — Either a cry of triumph, or a huge kettle of thick stew
- cheesily — Joke in a vulgar, pretentious, or sentimental manner
- couldnot — The apostrophe in couldn't is for the "o," not the " "
- eMail — When it is written as Email is just looks so very wrong
- gimme — An easy attainment, e.g. defining gimmie is a gimmie
- gotta — Have got to, e.g. we gotta define gotta as a real word
- guzunder — An old portable toilet that used to go under the bed
- loosey — As used in "lefty-loosey…" - refer back to chapter 14
- spotto — What you say when you are playing a game of spotto
- tighty — As used in "righty-tighty…" - refer back to chapter 14
- wanna — An informal form of, "I really, really, really, want to"
- wombled — The past tense of walking like the fictional Wombles
- y'all — The main second-person plural pronoun in American
- yo — Painful way of attracting Aaaaadriaaaaan's attention

⌘ Words that should be real (ones I made up)

- acronymity — The belittling condition of being an acronym
- afly — Boats stay afloat; therefore, planes stay afly
- aghostorial — The unusual behaviours exhibited by a ghost
- ~~bunnyyips~~ — "I said, don't write that!" "OK, I deleted it…"
- celebrationists — People who always take part in celebrations
- chalantly — Not behaving in a casual, or relaxed, manner
- ChessWords — A new word game merged with chess moves
- conversated — Orders issued in a casual, or relaxed, manner
- cookieing — Action of speaking a fortune cookie quote[518]
- deaded — Alive→Dead→Vampire→Dust - You are here
- didn'ted — Action of not doing something several times
- discernibles — Common items that are able to be discerned
- dissolvement — The possibility of someone simply dissolving
- documentaling — An abstract process for creating a document
- Donaldisms — The idiosyncratic quirks that Donald exhibits
- electronicness — The action of an item possessing electronics
- elephanting — Talking about what is not being talked about
- exappropriate — What is left after removing all inappropriate
- excuseers — People who are professional excuseingers[519]

---

[518] A quote that has been documented without the use of quotation marks.

[519] Turn the page for an explanation while this thought is fresh in your mind.

✍	excuseing	- Pre preparing and then delivering an excuse
✍	excuseingers	- People who are always excuseing everything
✍	farewellers	- A group of people farewelling someone else
✍	furwells	- Farewells that come from any furry creature
✍	ghostist	- Being prejudiced against ghosts, of any form
✍	gog	- The position a jaw takes when it is surprised
✍	grateless	- An uncovered hole in the ground - Obviously
✍	greatful	- A trait of possessing a great amount of great
✍	groundskeeping	- Looking after the outside areas of a property
✍	Halloweenies	- Halloween celebrators who don't know why
✍	humphing	- Shrugging something off with harsh attitude
✍	hyperthetical	- An actual clear and present physical concept
✍	idiotsynchronicities	- Irritating behaviour other people perpetrate
✍	intract	- Action of removing all inappropriate content
✍	Jees	- A reference to a potential fictional character
✍	jigsawing	- Process linking jigsaw puzzle pieces together
✍	Mashback©	- An artistic style of cynicism as a new realism
✍	memoryness	- The action of sharing in a memory like event
✍	mimeful	- Focusing all your awareness on a mime's act
✍	missintroductions	- Ineffectual and indiscriminate introductions
✍	nexting	- Act of carelessly selecting the "Next" button
✍	numptyism	- Idiosyncratic quirks that people don't expect
✍	oneteen	- What eleven would be in Donald's English[520]
✍	outroduction	- Debriefing chapter at the end of this book[521]
✍	phobiaphobia	- An often-excessive irrational fear of phobias
✍	precovered	- Finding an object... Before it is discovered[522]
✍	proned	- Placing yourself in the typical prone position
✍	psychicology	- The practical application of any psychic ruse
✍	realing	- Reeling from discovering some real situation
✍	reawared	- Become aware again of a forgotten memory
✍	receased	- The current activities have all stopped again
✍	regreeted	- To greet someone for a second or more time
✍	repleating	- The action of describing the final result again
✍	resession	- The continuation of a previous session again
✍	retapping	- Automatically tapping on a something again
✍	reviewment	- The result of reviewing any something again

---

[520] In Donald's English there will be no exceptions proving any of the rules.

[521] This is bordering on the "ones I didn't make up," but alas, it wouldn't fit.

[522] As is this one... This exception is proving Donald's OCD tendencies.

ø	sidewaysed	- An item being placed in a sideways direction
ø	silented	- A reaction to something, but keeping it quiet
ø	sombred	- Walking with a motion that is presenting sad
ø	sparsing	- Process of thinning a forest, making it sparse
ø	splatterer	- Someone who enjoys, or performs, splatters
ø	spoilered	- The past tense activity of revealing a spoiler
ø	sporschecar	- A car aspiring to Toorak tractor performance
ø	statemented	- To question someone without any questions
ø	svened	- Having a fortune cookie quote quoted at you
ø	tantruming	- The excited process of performing a tantrum
ø	thankyouyverymuch	- Act of quick, and total, fobbing someone off
ø	tofulo	- Wild flightless and completely meatless bird
ø	toriety	- Uncommon traits of absolutely no notoriety
ø	trepidational	- A series of events eliciting some trepidation
ø	trepidatiously	- Performing an event that causes trepidation
ø	trilogical	- An immaculate, three phase, logical thought
ø	twoteen	- What twelve would be in Donald's English[523]
ø	underreplied	- Understated reply to an overstated question
ø	undiscarded	- Retrieving a something previously discarded
ø	unexpectations	- These are those things you will never expect
ø	unvalidateable	- A thing that can't even be partially validated
ø	wenchmen	- A subset of henchmen who watch the target
ø	wety	- Trait of possessing a positive amount of wet
ø	zombieic	- Acted activity where you resemble a zombie
ø	cuebald	- Late insertion: A totally bald-headed person

Once again, Donald came up with this list of "words," and their associated "definitions," all by himself. He was also quietly pleased with himself this time, for taking the time to make it all fit nicely on the page.

Pack Up is the same as Pack Down.
Tie Me Up is the same as Tie Me Down.
Fill Up, Fill In, and Fill Out are all the same.

Sven was apparently warming to the task of filling in those little gaps that would otherwise be filled with mostly empty content. This particular one was poignant due to its word comparisons, and the trilogy of concepts that directly related to Donald.[524]

---

[523] In Donald's English there will be no unnecessary repetition of any rules.

[524] When there is a "Pack it in…" I will call the endless possibilities complete.

Donald used this lull in the proceedings as an opportunity to remove a few more of the meaningful questions, comments and general insecurities about the English language[525] off his back...

Is it cynical to wonder why cynical isn't spelled sinical?[526]
Or is it just moronic, of the type oxy?

Sometimes a double negative in English does not equal a positive.
e.g. Not entirely dissimilar ≠ Entirely similar
The Bonus Question to the right has many negatives. It is a reproduction of an actual question in a test Donald tried to complete. He failed to progress further than this question due to the inordinate amount of anxiety he felt when he couldn't understand what should have been a fairly simple question...

Bonus Question
Which statement is Not True?
Choose the incorrect answer,
Select OK.
☐ a.
☐ b.
☐ c.

If a. is the statement which is Not True;
Then a. is the correct answer to the question.
So... It cannot be the incorrect answer by definition.
It should have instructed him to, "Choose the incorrect statement."

Dialectical...
Donald often says, "I have a love/hate relationship with that word." *sigh*

Malapropism...
On his way-out Donald said, "I will learn what this means. Bye and bye."

Nonsensical...
Donald has been known to correct people saying, "A little bit unique."

Donald has clearly left a gate to the alternative part of his mind wide open, and this has allowed several comments of an obscure nature to escape. There is probably no effective way of reigning him in until he finishes his blurting rant of random sayings, questions and statements...
I suggest you strap in and try to wait it out. It has to finish soon...

---

[525] And I am using the term "language" at its very loosest definition.

[526] This only works as a visual joke. If you can't read the different spellings, you would be asking "What the?" Which doesn't need to be explained with a footnote... Yeah, that wouldn't be cynical either... Wait for it... Wait for it... And welcome back to Donald's semi-uneducated semi-self-commentary.

Sayings used frequently, even when people don't understand the meaning of the statement, or the meaning doesn't make literal sense, or it is just plain wrong and ignored:

- **Age before beauty**;
  - When you allow someone else to go first, and then you say this to them, to emphasise how caring you are… You are basically calling the other person old and ugly.
- Honest, industrious, or happy, **as the day is long**; and
  - This is an early form of 24/7 meaning, "Always."
  - Not the literal interpretation, "Just for 24 hours."
- **Won't be a minute**, or moment.
  - Doesn't say, "I will be quick," even though this is what it means.
  - It literally translates to, "Not exactly a minute," or a moment.

Questions of a nearly rhetorical nature:

- Can anyone ever attend a disappointing appointment?
- Is "nearly 50%" being approached from above or from below? and
- Why does the Catholic Church have a problem with unwed mothers?

Statements too obscure to fit anywhere else:

- Reasons before… Excuses after… But this is only my definition;
- To say, "To say the least," is always a lie; and
- Well below par means exceptionally bad, with the single exception of golf, where it means exceptionally good.

And finishing the deluge of uniqueness, some gender inequality thoughts:

- Male sounding words:
  - Hymns, heal, historic, etc…
- Female sounding words:
  - Misadventure (actually, every miss in general has been associated with harmful),[527] herpes, hurt, hurl, hernia, hearse, hurdle, etc…
  - And don't let's forget what a bad idea Herd immunity was.

I do understand many of you will get most of what I have written, although I doubt there will be any who can decipher every oblique reference.[528]

---

[527] With the possible exception of "near miss," proving the rule's exactness.

This possible exception also proves the probable rule in Donald's English, in which it stipulates, "There will be no exceptions to prove any of the rules."

[528] Am I being arrogant when I say this, or condescending? Even if it is true?

Reconvene when convenient, and while you are waiting, ponder this:

You can dress the most ardent verbal English language hater up however much you like, if he still comes out quacking like a duck, he's still a duck.[529]

Donald looked back upon the tumultuous vagueness of some of the words and their associated don't-believe meanings, as well as the supercilious nature of most of the statements and groaned inwardly to himself, "Why bother, no one in their right mind is going to read this anyway... And even if they do, they will exact some form of punishment and the earliest opportunity.[530]"

---

[529] I am fairly sure that our Donald is mixing, or forgetting, his vowels again...

[530] It then came to me to metaphorically slap Donald on the downside of his head, again. It was becoming nigh on impossible to get Donald to be the half glass is not broken type of person, even when his particular special kind of glass was obviously made of innumerable crystal nearly clear thoughts.

Note: It is interesting, to me anyway, that crystal is just a posh way of saying lead glass. So, remember this the next time you celebrate with a bit of bubbly in a crystal flute... You are slowly poisoning yourself, in more ways than one.

This is nearly directly from Wikipedia... So, you know it must be true...

Symptoms may include abdominal pain, constipation, headaches, irritability, memory problems, infertility and tingling in your hands and feet. It causes almost ten percent of intellectual disability, of otherwise unknown cause, and can result in behavioural problems. In severe cases anaemia, seizures, coma, or death may occur, and some of the effects are often permanent.

Do you think this is the description of lead poisoning, or alcohol poisoning?

Chapter 19:
Goodbye, Farewell &
Get Thee Behind Me

Today is the day Donald has been waiting for, as it is finally the second Monday after the Monday from two Monday's ago! Today is the day when his hospital records are updated to include a discharge.[531] The minor hurdle before this can occur, was about to transpire… And then he will have progressed through all of the remaining major hurdles, numbered one, two and π - 0.1415926535897.[532]

Donald has silently questioned the discharging process many times, which is another interesting fact in itself, considering that everyone essentially wants the same thing…

- ᚷ To find the correct form, and to fill it out correctly; then
- ᚷ To lodge it with correct person, who checks that it is the correct form and that it has been filled out correctly without any corrections; while
- ᚷ Hoping this person isn't currently going through an unhappy breakup, with someone who was once the neighbour, of a relative, of someone you used to know… Or you just might be waiting for another 75 years…

---

[531] To quell any impending bile expulsion, you are expecting to experience, this particular variation of "discharge" was one of the good kinds.

[532] Approximately, to thirteen decimal places. (So far, the max is 31 trillion.)

At some stage, I would like someone to explain to me how pi can have a large repetition of the same number (e.g. thirteen eights in the 2164164669332nd position) and then divert back to a probably random placement of the digits, all the while keeping their frequency distribution fairly constant. (Call me!)

To complete the SaRS hospital's process, Donald will be placed in a queue of people waiting to see DD, while someone else will determine if he is allowed to ask a third person, if he is able to speak to a fourth, about the conversation he needs to have with a fifth, to see if he complies with the extensive amount of requirements on a sixth's person's list, just to determine if he is eligible to ask if he can be released from hospital…

Donald's Hell[533]

There is a story inside your mind,   Donald, Donald…
Grown there, now waiting for you to find,   grown down in Donald's Hell
Write it down for everyone to read,   an easy way to tell
Let them know the product of your need,   "Removal of Donald's Hell"

(Chorus)   Donny, Donny,   this is my answer to…
    Are you crazy?   Oh, yes, my Lordy true!
    You've passed by the three-week mandate
    So, now you've been left intestate
    But you'll do fine,   just give it some time
    We haven't heard the last from you…

Now that you have told your story twice,   Donald, Donald…
Do you have any pearls of advice,   from down in Donald's Hell?
Is there any way they can thank you,   for this wisdom you tell?
What is the next thing that you will do?   Go back to Donald's Hell!?!

(Chorus)

This might not be *specifically* what the good people of SaRS had in mind for Donald when they started treating his depression. But, as evidenced by DD still calling him "Donny," there is never a single perfect solution when dealing with any mental illness, sometimes you have to hurt the ones you treat. Inside Donald's, frankly exasperating, reality… His just getting out of SaRS alive, was always going to be the single most important objective.[534]

---

[533] Inspired by *Daisy Bell (Bicycle Built for Two)* – Harry Dacre

[534] For this to be achieved, Donald has to show he has improved enough to know what to do in the days leading up to his needing their services again. As there is no empirical test to show this, we have to trust DD to know what she is doing. Calling him "Donny," is a deviously brilliant part of her test.

These quantum hypothetical thoughts aside, it was time for Donald to face his minor hurdle... ~~Doctor~~ Mister Houts Marted.[535] Houts had tracked Donald down to get his opinion of his psychological paper before he left. He had taken the time to change into his ghost-writing uniform, a sharkskin khaki safari suit on the top of a t-shirt emblazoned with "I see dead people..." on the front, to give Donald the impression he was serious.

Donald thought Houts was "seriously something," however, serious ghost-writer wasn't one of the options. Anyone leaving off the alligator anklet boots adorned with faux diamond tipped spurs from his uniform, can't be taken too seriously.[536] Pushing aside his conceived notions of Houts, Donald had a quick look through the information presented, and then responded accordingly with a series of his own questions for Houts to think about. Helpfully, along with his suggested answers he told Houts what he could do with them.

Donald's comments on Houts' paper for *Psychology Today*:

Ghost Psychology: Boo Who? How to stop thinking you are invisible...

A twenty first century Psychological Ghostbusting guide.

- Can you see more dead people than other not dead people can?
  Definitely not.
  Don't include this as one of your relative strengths, as it isn't one.
- Do you care why Seth assumed the position of being your minion?
  Certainly not.
  I suggest you do, before his loyalty disappears with his corporality.
- Are you going to include Seth and BLT as paper collaborators?
  Obviously and Clearly not.
  Hmmmmm, you may fall out of the professional paddleboat if not.
- You declare "Seth is broken and needs fixing," but don't indicate how.
  Do you have any professional ideas to add as a potential solution?
  Possibly not.
  Hmmmmmmmmmmm, isn't that the whole point of the paper?
- Have you found Seth's next-best-next-of-kin yet?
  Perhaps not.
  Hmmmmmmmmmmmmmmmmmm, I think you should continue looking.
- Can you answer why, or how, they come back to SaRS after they died?
  Probably and Maybe not.
  Hmmmmmmmmmmmmmmmmmmmmmmm, not so good at this are you?

---

[535] Alright ~~Enough~~! It wasn't funny the first time, and it isn't funny now.

[536] "Can't be taken too seriously," in this instance could mean either:

- You mustn't take him very seriously; or
- You cannot take him seriously enough...

Donald finished his scathing review of Houts' paper by providing him with several other obvious ideas about what he should have included:[537]

- ¤ An opening section on, "How Ghosts feel about having no goal of life";
- ¤ Aghostorial behaviour (limping, throat clearing, door knocking, etc...);
- ¤ Interactions with objects (a solid comparison to memory interactions);
- ¤ Interactions with people (fear of DD, contempt of ~~Houts~~ Others, etc...);
- ¤ General information about the "gender generalisation" of Ghosts; and
- ¤ A sealed 'n' buried section on how little baby Ghosts are made;

Comparatively satisfied with this reply to Houts, Donald embarked on the first step of the three major hurdles to adventure, which turns out to be more accurately identified as minor hurdle number two. These were the little quirks about SaRS' procedures and facilities that he was going to miss the most:

¤ Ambulance Transferral

There were two distinct, and distinctly different, types of "patient transfer via ambulance" operating in and out of SaRS. There was the Oh-My-Word-No outbound kind and the If-I-Must-Yes inbound kind. The variance between the two could be easily seen on the patient's faces, as either sheer horror, or calm acceptance. The struggle to enact the transfer was also bipolar.

Another characteristic Donald recognised as intriguing was... Occasionally, there would be an arriving patient who looked ominously younger than their equivalent outbound version, many days later. He later came to the realisation it was the patients' destination which caused the disparity. Being transferred to a public facility will always raise the raging ageing hackles.

¤ Evacuation Practice (Bushfire Variation)

Contradictory to politically correct implementation, SaRS patients are held captive at night. The doors aren't locked in the traditional sense with keys, but the patients are all still expected to stay on the inside. For people like Donald, this means essentially the same thing. If he was to open any door during their soft curfew time, the alarm bells ringing on the inside of his head would be far louder than any physical ones activated.

These doors were designated "fire doors," and this always raises Donald's standard question #321 (subsection fire), "How do you know which side of the door is the safe side?" For evaluation purposes only, during their evacuation practice (bushfire variation), the patients were instructed to stay on the inside, away from the fire... So, they were actually practicing how to behave during a not-evacuation. Donald was also not given a satisfactory comfort level about how they could differentiate between a bush, and a not-bush, fire alarm.

---

[537] These are the aforementioned ghostly observations which precipitates Houts and Donald falling out of their professionally amicable paddle-boat.

- **Helpful Informational Signs**

There were many of these signs throughout SaRS, but the three that stuck in Donald's mind were all related to sanitisation, and all probably require some contextual information which has been omitted on comical advice...

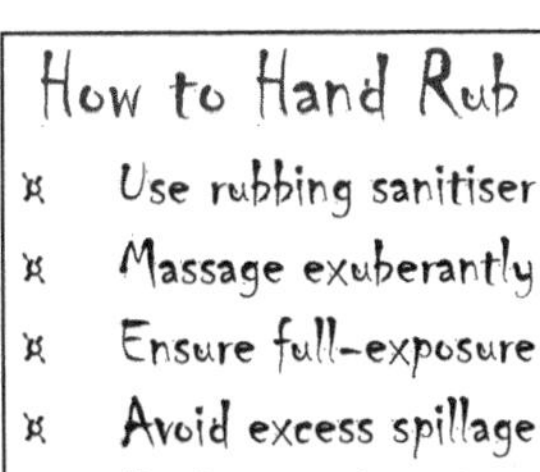

Don't forget to Brush your Tooth [538]
Don't Eat or Drink [539]

Thinking he had thought about every interesting, nuanced oddity from his last few weeks of observations, Donald opened the welcome pack to confirm. He was intending to flip straight to and read the last page, but found himself remembering another unforgettable piece of information instead:

- **Connectivity**

Here at SaRS, we cannot place a dollar amount figure on the value of your loved ones assisting to control, or at least take responsibility for, you patients. To this end, we provide them with a multitude of ways to connect to you, and our ways are not simply limited to visiting hours.

The entry which particularly intrigued Donald was their Wi-Fi instructions, and the accompanying "we didn't think it through" blurb... "Staying in touch with your loved ones through our hospital Wi-Fi couldn't be easier. Whether you are a patient or a visitor, you can enjoy free internet access at SaRS.[540]"

- To access the SaRS complimentary hospitality Wi-Fi:
  - Select the "You are a Fabulous Guest" network to connect to;
  - Enter all of your awesome personal details; and
  - Accept our overwhelmingly fine print conditions.

Donald has accessed this network many times over the past three weeks, and on each occasion was surprised to see one of the personal details required was an age, and the entry field was limited to two digits. He certainly wasn't going to be the one to tell Mindy, and her 107 years, were ineligible.

---

[538] Donald felt this sign was underestimating the probable quantity slightly.

[539] Donald felt this sign was underestimating minimum requirements slightly.

[540] So... If you are there visiting someone, you can go online and send a text or an eMail to them, and even "Zoom" them for free. Doesn't that sort of defeat the major purpose of an up close and personal visit? But... I digress...

And then Donald had to face the reality of an actual major hurdle.
The exit interview with DD.
If he wasn't already, the chances were high for him being in some #2 soon. And if that wasn't bad enough by itself, it was all going to happen while he was alone with DD in the #2 knowledge extraction room.

Same interrogator.
Same interrogation room.
Doesn't bode well for DD declaring Donald "Not Batty."

Donald arrived at the required interrogation room early, as was expected, and saw the look from DD's face, which this time was skewed ever-so-slightly towards sadness. She began the departure proceedings as gently as she could, by referring to Donald by his preferred name, "Come in Donald. Please take a seat and let me start by saying I hope I didn't cause you too much discomfort while I was calling you Donny, I did it for your own good."

This was not remotely what Donald expected from DD... And not knowing the correct response, he simply took a seat and sat down.

"Today, I will be asking you the same set of questions you answered when you first arrived at SaRS. We do this to see how effective our treatment of you was. I will then create a report based on my findings and will couple this with some suggested activities for you to complete outside SaRS."

Donald noticed DD didn't mention anything about including his potentially discrediting lack of improvement in their performance statistics, but agreed to her proposition with his traditional amount of hesitation, "OK?"

"Right... I would like you to remember the following four numbers: 365.25, googol, zero and 221b; as well as a simple, yet relevant, example of these four words: red, dialectical, synonym and shenanigan; so, you can recite them back to me just before the end of this session."

Donald stared at her dumbfounded again, thinking, "She actually listened to me... Maybe I have miss-pigeonholed her.[541]"

DD continued the session with a repeat of the question section, "Can you describe some of your current thoughts, and any potential changes in feelings you have had about your physical symptoms?[542]"

---

[541] Well, there you go... Someone actually understands what is going on inside Donald's and, by simple extrapolation, my mind... Me.

[542] Note: This section of Donald's story hasn't been removed this time, as it is nearly interesting, for a particular value of interesting. And you will find a shortened version patiently waiting for your perusal just over the page.

Donald had uncharacteristically left his paddle behind, so was winging his answer... "I think the major change has been how I experience other people. Before, I didn't think about how anything I did would affect them, and now, I simply don't care. And, as to my physical symptoms, they haven't been part of any suggested change."

DD appended Donald's chart with:
✗ *Still no evidence of anything remotely unusual...*

"Do you think your stay with us has improved your mental health?"
Donald was actually prepared for this question, "I don't think my mental health has been adversely effected, nor do I think it has greatly improved. I am more at ease with my situation, in a relieved sense, and I know all the plausible causes for my issues, and many of their acronymic descriptions... What I don't know is how to fix me."
"I see... So, your answer is?"
"Well..." Donald thought, "It was a nice touch for DD to ask her questions, instead of telling them. There still seems to be a lack when it comes to listening to the answers though..." and vocalising his answer "Yes. On a scale of one to thirteen, it would be about a three."
"Can you describe a piece of information you have learned?"
Donald wasn't prepared for this question, as he hadn't realised there was going to be an exit examination which wasn't a physical one. This was starting to feel too much like all exams he has ever participated in, where the first item tested was your memory,[543] and it was clearly making him uncomfortable.
"Arguments..." Falling back to a favoured well-worn subject, one he could remember and had plenty of examples to refer to. It was also something they must have been teaching, even if he couldn't remember the lesson... "I have this concept: If I think I am right, I will argue. If I think I am wrong, I won't. This is the root of every argument, but the problem... Winning an argument makes the situation worse. Moral: If you lose, you lose. If you win, you lose. So, back to your initial question, I have learned: It isn't important whether you win or lose an argument. It's how much you can prove." (PTO for incredulity.)

---

[543] I think exams are a complete farce when the application of knowledge is less important than remembering something always readily available in a real-world situation. And when the exam subjected is mathematics, or computer programming, how will being able to write a 2000-word essay be of benefit to the student. It's not like they are ever going to write a book...

Oh, wait, what? Bugger, I hate it when I'm wrong...

Not in anything Donald said, or in anything DD heard... The incredulous aspect stems from the grammar check cycling through these four options, ad infinitum. →

> It's how much you can prove.
> its how much you can prove.
> Its how much you can prove.
> it's how much you can prove.

Showing no reaction, DD continued on with her eyes down, "Hmmmmm." Eyes up, "Who is our current Prime Minister?"

The contrived déjà vu aside, Donald answered as best he knew how, "I still don't know, and I still don't care.[544]"

Donald took another look at her SaRS identification tag...

> Primary Nurse – SaRS
> Ms Dolly Dix (DD) MSN, MHRN
> Authorised for EVERYWHERE!
> Particularly the inside your head

Donald's ever-clichéd imagination was working overtime when he asked himself, "Did her authorisation change? Or has she just invaded the inside of my head with a particular post assessment suggestion?" Donald was beginning to alter his miss-pigeonholed underestimation of DD's purpose, as well as her like-a-boss abilities and presence.[545]

"And now, penultimately, please recite back to me, the four numbers and definitions I asked you to remember at the start of the session."

Donald replied almost predictably, "A year; a one with 100 zeros; a googol without the one; and eh? That isn't a number..." and the definitions were not so different, "The colour of Blood; a frozen red-hot chilli; cherry and scarlet; and silly Bloody-minded mischief." Sitting again quietly waiting.

Disarmingly, DD smiled back at Donald, "Perfect!"

Donald was caught off guard by this reaction, "Whaaaaa!"

"The final question I have, and this is the most important question you will be asked in the next five minutes... Do you want to go home?"

Still unbalanced a trivial amount by her perfect statement, Donald could only manage a single word... "Yespleaseverymuchso."

---

[544] This was going to be the most common answer Donald gave to DD for the remainder of her questions, so we will fast forward to the interesting bits.

[545] Donald will reflect about this interaction at the end of his second book, and this is also where he will start paying DD her well-earned symbolic dues.

Sitting back in her chair and closing his file with an enthusiastic flutter, DD uttered the words Donald will never forget… "I have been waiting these past three weeks, for the right time to say this to you Donald, and now it has arrived at last… I am very proud to say your re-education is complete. You started out as an atypical, but confused simpleton when you first arrived at SaRS, and now you are knowledgeable in the ways of a sane person."

Donald was unsure if DD's spiel was showering him with praise or not, and rather than risk having his newly acquired knowledge reverting back to his old, confused simpleton ways, he simply smiled, nodded his head and said, "Thank you.[546]"

With the formal "Why" section of Donald's discharge procedure complete, DD launched into the haphazard information delivery part, "This is everything you will need to continue being not a required patient at SaRS:

- What   - Medication regimen that must be swallowed;
- When   - Blood sample delivery and/or extraction schedule;
- Where - Proposed locations for inspiring remarks (e.g. Fridge…);
- Who   - List of potential contacts for ongoing psych-debriefing; and
- How   - To stay on top of the sanity wagon…

Now, I know you don't mind breaking some rules when everyone else does it, but I strongly suggest you stick to all of these instructions, unless you want to come back…"

Donald was reeling from the not a required patient information overload, and thinking, "I knew all these things already, I still don't understand though," when DD asked something astounding, "Do you have any questions for me?" and flying against his normal interactive requirement, don't ask any questions until you've asked if you can ask a question, Donald launched into what could only be described as a barrage of futility…

"When I meet someone I don't know, I generally pigeon-hole them almost immediately, and rarely does anyone change holes. There are no good holes, and this is one of those things I hate being done to me… But I do it to others… So, I guess my question is… Is this a real problem, or just a conundrum?"

---

[546] The genuine "thank you" is a highly developed skill and is taught as part of every mental health course in existence. It isn't only an indication of your appreciation of what has been taught, it is also a declaration that you have achieved a level of understanding of what you are giving thanks for.

This was the unquestionable last test; and, as Donald was able to convince DD into believing he was truly thankful for his stay inside SaRS, she is going to let him go home, alone. Otherwise, who knows what…?

"Yes."

Confused with DD's literally accurate answer Donald continued on, "When a professional medical someone asks a depressed person if they have had any thoughts of suicide or death recently, how can their answer be *no*, when they obviously have to think about both of those topics to figure out if they have thought about it?"

"I don't know."

Failing to make any perceptible headway through DD's impulsive answers, Donald diverted to an alternate heading, "Have you heard about the shortage of maternity hospital staff?"

"No."

"They are going through a midwife crisis." <Boom, Boom, Tish>

When this last question didn't receive the expected reaction, Donald took a slight pause to ponder DD's answers, and decided it would be dialectically hypocritical and hypercritical to berate her for their brevity.

Once again Donald only became aware the interrogation had reached the end when DD stood up and indicated that he should follow her. Donald leapt out of his chair as if it was electrified and followed her so closely that her own shadow complained for him to get down in front. They appeared to be heading to his room again. Only this time, it was to collect his things...

It was bordering on surreal for Donald.[547]

To complete his weird sensation of surrealism, after they arrived outside his room DD handed over the thin blue manila folder which was appropriately labelled with "Donny H." "Inside you will find some of the caregiver's parting thoughts, the contact details of a suggested outside psychologist, and a final acronym to complete your visit... You are now free to go."

Donald thought he saw a tear welling up in her eye as she turned to leave, and didn't want to spoil the moment, so, he mindfully just let her go without judgement. Rummaging through the folder, Donald found the psychologist's card, which unfortunately had been printed at siGns On Demand! – Sin Righters...

Never Mind – The Psychologists

If you find yourself in needful of a psychologist,
we think you've just been given an alright card!
Call Ms Abes Jillhouse to book your awareness.
Phone: zero^2 – one to one – two for one – 13

---

[547] And this is saying a definite something considering the rest of this book.

Ms Abes Jillhouse is part of the team at Never Mind the Psychologists who offer unique holistic ways to achieve a sustained synergy awareness. She is to become Donald's chosen psychologist outside SaRS.[548]

The Never Mind team thrive in close conjunction with the Outer-Patience drop-in centre that is run as a separate healing establishment on the grounds of SaRS. There's is a symbiotic relationship, SaRS gets to keep tabs on previous patients who are struggling, and Outer-Patients are able to operate rent free, as long as they keep up a steady stream of re-referrals back to SaRS.

Attached to Ms Jillhouse's business card is Outer-Patience's raison d'être flyer. It is mainly about the causes of the problems their solutions are designed to counteract. They provide assistance to people who are struggling with any of the C's everyone usually has to deal with during their day-to-day life…

Do you have some **Comparison Complainers**?
Suffer from disability dismissal **Citizens**?

We can offer solutions for when "they"
- Complain about the undue cost of fuel, while they drive an expensive luxury car
- Comfort every autistic person by saying everyone is a little bit on the spectrum
- Callously remark to a blind person; it is such a pain having to wear these glasses
- Comment on how terrible their partially receding hairline is, to a cuebald person

You do not have to cope with any of these inconsiderate **C's** by yourself anymore…
We'll show you how to run… Outer-Patience

Selwyn Phelps is the head head-counsellor at Outer-Patience.[549] He also is a conglomeration of the many facilitators of the numerous outpatient courses. Theirs is a difficult situation, if they perform their job well, they end up making themselves obsolete. The more successful they are, the less they are required.

---

[548] I paraphrased the mission statement slightly, but none of the buzz words. You will meet Abes much more closely in the next chapter of Donald's life, which will be included in the next book, and as Donald hasn't told her she is in any of "The Books" yet, it's very much a case of *shhhhh* for now.

[549] He too will be described in much more detail eventually.

On the back of the flyer were some of the topics covered by their courses:
- ¤ Acronyms
    - ø **C**ertification **R**egarding **A**cronym **P**hudging
    - ø **D**eciphering **A**cronyms - **M**andatory or **N**eedless
- ¤ Back to Work
    - ø Interview masking techniques
    - ø Jobs and their applications
- ¤ Game Playing
    - ø How to win your own private Game-of-Life, by not letting anyone else play their games with your mind.
- ¤ Household Drama Solutions:
    - ø Blackout Preparation
    - ø Flat Pack Assembly
    - ø Food Issues (Staples, Shopping, Storage, ...)
    - ø Home Brew (Including the Ingredients)
    - ø Searching for Lost Items (It's always in the last place you look)
- ¤ Meditation/Mindfulness Mashback Adventures
- ¤ Party Navigation Techniques
- ¤ Tapestry #3[550]

Putting the Never Mind advertising paraphernalia away, Donald turned his thinking towards the supplied parting thoughts. These turned out to be simple random comments from unnamed sources, and they added quite nicely to his unusual thoughts collection:
- ¤ Donald, I would like you to become focussed more on...[551]
- ¤ Don't forget Donald, this situation is not suited to anyone else better than it is to you or everyone else;
- ¤ I am glad that after years of being yourself, you are beginning to find the extremity of your self-hate, and are starting to forgive yourself;
- ¤ The maximum distance from hero to zero is only 18;
- ¤ Flexible repetition, improve the moment, opposite action, ...; and
- ¤ Many other word combinations.

---

[550] This topic intrigued Donald and was now definitely on his To-Do list.

[551] Donald automatically added an "a" after "become," turning the apparent positive recommendation into a literal negative backhanded insinuation. He became so distressed at being called a name, he didn't read to the end of the suggestion. In fact, by the time he reaches the end of this list, Donald will be thinking the "a" would perhaps be better applied to the alleged first thinkers of all of these comparatively strange thoughts.

No chapter would be complete without an acronym:

<u>THINK (FAST)</u>

Think before you speak, especially for any negative comments
Hope you don't offend anyone when you talk about them
Inferences are almost always just as bad as any direct accusations
Notice when someone is insulted by what you are saying
Keep at least an arm's length away from those you are talking to

False allegations are likely to cause you insurmountable problems
Accept any apologies offered to you with unpretentious grace
Suck it up princess, not everything you read is about you
Trust is a hard commodity to earn… And it cannot be purchased

And now the time everyone has been waiting for, has finally come. Donald must face up to his third (approximately), and final (probably), major hurdle before he could leave SaRS…

Donald collected his belongings, shambled up to the automatic doors of a place he didn't think he belonged in anymore, and stepped through without a single look back.

And then… **"Sphincter Feng Shui…!"**

Outroduction

This is where I have to leave ***Donald Halfbrain*** again, and SaRS inside for the first, and hopefully last, time. But don't stress too much, he will be back to attend the various outpatients' courses...[552]

Donald is currently rationally reviewing his past three weeks inside SaRS, and jotting down any comments he is likely to forget in his paddle, on the way to his home in one of the big blue government chauffeured vehicles:
- He is no longer exactly where he should be, but will be there soon;
- He has come a lot further in the areas of:
  - Meeting;
  - Understanding; and
  - Participating.

His previously nondescript life, before book #1, and now after book #2, has been changed irrevocably once again. He is still not quite at legend status, and doesn't really want to be, nor does he want to be a mentor for people to follow, commenting: "People will have to find their own motivation."

He has become exceptional enough for himself.
He has become more creative and will continue down that path.
He has become just a little bit more, more normal.

---

[552] I can't help comparing Donald to the various "Anti" shows of my past:
- Arrested Development (all about misfits with a narrator)
- Dead Pool (doing good by doing bad and self-commentate)
- Ricky Gervais anything (identifying and exposing irregularities)
- Hot Shots / Flying High / Naked Gun / Loaded Weapon etc...

If a British comedian's ancestor went on a government funded holiday 200 years ago, their descendants could very well live around the corner from me...

The everyday struggles of his life, ones he used to complain bitterly about, have grown somewhat lighter, and now, almost conveniently, come equipped with a handy legible instruction manual for the first time.

And so… For a bittersweet dialectical second time…
We bid farewell to Saint Rita's Sanatorium for the Clinically Mental.

Donald is going away happy in the knowledge of the answers:
¤   There wasn't a real Minotaur living underneath SaRS;
¤   The hospital archives were exactly where Donald initially thought; and
¤   This version of the *Clueless* puzzle was solved with virtual ease.

And was satisfied that some questions do not need answers:
¤   Will ~~Dr~~ **Mr** Houts Marted ever publish his dissertation on Ghosts?
¤   Who will Skit think he is tomorrow? and
¤   ~~Where is the perfect cup of coffee?~~
¤   What is it with vowels anyway?

And now has a few more theoretical questions he would like to ask:
¤   Will anyone ever provide a legitimate definition of *rotate left*?
¤   When is the first Outpatients session? and
¤   Where is the perfect cup of coffee?

Cruising along, with his DOGoN level fluctuating between seven and eight, Donald continued thinking about his experiences at SaRS.

And so, so… For another second time…
Donald began writing his second book, culminating in his recent discharge from SaRS, again changing names, places and reality, to protect the innocent…

E xit the protagonist, the hero,[553] the star… David.

---

[553] If you could be convinced to call the Backspace key a *Hero*.

Appendix 1:
Read and Sing Along
(Without the Sing)

I Hate Depression (Inspired by *I Hate the Music* – John Paul Young)

I hate depression - I am treated with derision and scorn
It's deception I let you see... Not the real me
I hate depression - And all of the associated lies
Some might sympathise, nobody truly understands
You can't empathise; until you know what it demands
And create your own personal disguise

The day I was first diagnosed, I didn't want to believe
But then all my good memories became harder to retrieve
There is a treatment that may fix, when I accept their pretence
And then I can go out at large, try to make my recompense, common sense
I hate depression - I am treated with outrage and disdain
It's deception I let you see... Not the real me

I hate depression - And all of the associated lies
Some might sympathise, nobody truly understands
You can't empathise; until you know what it demands
And create your own personal disguise
Depression has brought me undone, and set this life now, apart
I've stopped all my wondering why; trying to protect my heart

There is a challenge every night, finding reasons just to sleep
Without having anything set, to stop being the black sheep, in too deep
I hate depression - I am treated with loathe and ignorance
It's deception I let you see... It's nothing like the real me
I hate depression - Cos the constant treatment will never change
It's deception I let you see... And nothing like the real me

Name/Value Pairs

Logical

1	=	Equal
2	≠	Not Equal
3	⇒	Implies
4	⇐	Implied
5	⇔	Equivalent
6	⊨	Entails
7	⊭	Does Not Entail
8	⊢	Proves
9	⊬	Does Not Prove
10	∴	Therefore
11	∵	Because
12	∧	Conjunction
13	∨	Disjunction

Alphabetical

1	8	Eight
2	11	Eleven
3	5	Five
4	4	Four
5	9	Nine
6	1	One
7	7	Seven
8	6	Six
9	10	Ten
10	13	Thirteen
11	3	Three
12	12	Twelve
13	2	Two

Digital

1	①	Circled Digit One
2	②	Circled Digit Two
3	③	Circled Digit Three
4	④	Circled Digit Four
5	⑤	Circled Digit Five
6	⑥	Circled Digit Six
7	⑦	Circled Digit Seven
8	⑧	Circled Digit Eight
9	⑨	Circled Digit Nine
10	⑩	Circled Digit Ten
11	⑪	Circled Digit Eleven
12	⑫	Circled Digit Twelve
13	⑬	Circled Digit Thirteen

Fractional

1	⅛	One	Eighth	0.125
2	⅙	One	Sixth	0.16˙
3	¼	One	Quarter	0.25
4	⅓	One	Third	0.3˙
5	⅜	Three	Eighths	0.375
6	⅖	Two	Fifths	0.4
7	½	One	Half	0.5
8	⅗	Three	Fifths	0.6
9	⅝	Five	Eighths	0.625
10	⅔	Two	Thirds	0.6˙
11	⅘	Four	Fifths	0.8
12	⅚	Five	Sixths	0.83˙
13	⅞	Seven	Eighths	0.875

S-a-R-S (Inspired by YMCA – Village People) [554]

Donald, you're here 'cos you think sad
I know, Donald, 'cos you've lost all your glad
I know, Donald, we're your happy launch pad
Come, see what we can do for you...
Donald, get your thinking set right
I know, Donald, all is lost to your sight
It will, Donald, stop you sleeping at night
Come, we have many ways to help...

We are here for you at S-a-R-S,   many things we fix at S-a-R-S
We can take away your depression, we can refocus your aggression
We are here for you at S-a-R-S,   many things we fix at S-a-R-S
We can stop all pesky obsessions,   we can answer all of your questions

Donald, there is much we can do
I know, Donald, we can help you get through
I know, Donald, there's a bed just for you
Come, you will be glad that you did...
Donald, you can check-in today
I know, Donald, there is something we say
We will, Donald, take away your cray-cray
Come, we will make you feel so good...

We are here for you at S-a-R-S,   many things we fix at S-a-R-S
We can take away anxiety,   we can give you back sobriety
We are here for you at S-a-R-S,   many things we fix at S-a-R-S
We can stabilise mentality,   your borderline personality

Donald, don't do this on your own
I know, Donald, we're patient to the bone
I know, Donald, our failures are unknown
Come, and you will never look back...
Donald, start your changing right now
I know, Donald, you are thinking of how
You will, Donald, find your personal Tao
Come, it is the best thing for you...

We are here for you at S-a-R-S,   many things we fix at S-a-R-S
We can take away all of your grief, replace it with personal belief
We are here for you at S-a-R-S,   many things we fix at S-a-R-S
We can give significant relief,   put you back as commander in chief

---

[554] Donald was extremely hesitant to include this "inspiration" in his diaries, due to the Village People's stereotypical portrayal of their "Indian Chief." Before he did, he checked with Chef to make sure it would not be an issue. Chef responded, "That is the least of my concerns. Thank you for asking."

Pi Avenue

Pi Avenue is where I exist
Although it's my place, it isn't my home

A new mansion on the corner near the park with a playground
It has big toys for the children without dogs roaming around
One house has a Ford in the shed and a Corvette on the go
Hidden houses... Tall antennas... Even a Winnebago...
People live in the houses, but I do not know anyone
Ancient landmarks sealed within, boats decaying left in the sun
Santa comes driving at Christmas, the ice cream man fails to sell
Each house worth more than a million and hills like they are in Hell

Pi Avenue is where I exist
Although it's my place, it isn't my home

I'm hidden deep in the jungle cross from where the river flows
I get no visitors and weeds are the only things that grow
My front is overlooking the trees, neighbours to either side
When I see them, I wave hello, then bolt to safety inside
Some places have stairs that are steep, or lawns that are never mown
A couple of rock caves where bush rangers may have made their home
There are two ends of the road, numbered from one to eighty-six
Plump bush turkeys have made it their nest amongst all of the sticks

Pi Avenue is where I exist
Although it's my place, it isn't my home

Home to some wilderness parks as well as the odd nature trail
Many "beware of the dog" signs, numerous places for sale
There are many rules to abide in the parks and the bush land
Do not injure, endanger, obstruct, annoy or make demand
No toy planes, no power bikes, no unleashed dogs, no camping ground
No lighting fires, playing golf, driving cars or clowning around
Pi Avenue... Where I exist... It's my place, it's not my home
Pi Avenue... Where I don't live. It's my place, it's not my home

Pi Avenue is where I exist
Although it's my place, it isn't my home...

David Halpin

Let it Burn, Let Him Burn

Were you on the ride when I missed the bus?
Cos, you had a hide to make such a fuss
I couldn't decide if there was an "us"
You think that it died? We need to discuss...
There was no concern of man overboard
When you let me burn for your overlord
I'm taking my turn to empty what's poured
There's nought to adjourn that I can't afford

Let it burn, fan the flames
Let him burn, forgotten names

Shouting at silence, cursing the darkness
My stupid defence is mostly worthless
Chasing the essence of being heartless
Has no recompense for all the duress
Act like you belong, don't draw attention
But something is wrong with lost affection
It's written in song, next pride audition
The wait isn't long for cruel attrition

Let it burn, stoke the wood
Let him burn, misunderstood

The portend was clear, it said "what the Hell?"
I hope I'm not near when they ring your bell
There's nothing too dear that I want to sell
Now get me a beer, and feed me as well
Attend to my lust, right here and right now
I think we're a bust, disparaging Tao
It seems that I must continue with how
You climb my disgust and won't disavow

Let it burn, mesmerise
Let him burn, be none the wise

What is a Banquet? *(Inspired by Food, Glorious Food – "Oliver")*

While we were just being taught
Our hunger, how we could thwart
All food components missing
Chef has come to our rescue
Providing his cordon bleu
This banquet's fit for a King

There's Vegetarian Tofulo Wings, Stuffed Ground Hog, Bird Brain Stew, and Chunky Mush
Medium Rare Bison Tomahawk Steak, and Turkey Jerky... (When we're in a rush)

Chef's glorious food
How did he make it all?
Our hunger's subdued
Overthrew Seymour's gall
I ate as much as would fit
And now I need a rest
Don't regret any of it
Self-interest

Chef's glorious food, eat one of everything
Though, aftereffects might be interesting
We have been presented with a great magnitude, of food
No attitude, just aptitude, for barbequed

Chef's glorious food
The best I've ever seen
My faith's been renewed
Now pass the stew tureen
If we had this every day
Our emotions would lift
There'd be no running away
No one adrift

Chef's glorious food, eat the degustation
Providing you with mental inspiration
We are is the presence of a greatness etude, of food
An altitude, not platitude, of gratitude

Chef's glorious food
It tastes so delightful
However it's viewed
Sustenance insightful
Promises us a future
Even for likes of me
I'll wrap it in a humour
I'd like to see

Chef's glorious food, eat till there's nothing left
And we've left our hunger behind us, bereft
Chef has been endowed with a great exactitude, with food
I will conclude, this interlude, of rectitude
Mythical food, epochal food, glorious food

Creepy Donald (Inspired by *Creeque Alley* – The Mamas and the Papas)

Donald Halfbrain, was feeling like an arse pain
Becoming institutionalised
Sphincter Feng Shui, what was he doing today?
Mental treatment coercion's applied
Behind her desk is where DD would sit
No… She doesn't like it, not one little bit
But, here inside SaRS, Donald writing memoirs
They all just had to accept it
Continue giving a shit… For the patients' wit…

    Istha T. You, was hearing speech in-situ
    And they call this schizophrenia (DSM)
    Donald Halfbrain, was deep inside of her brain
    With personal multimedia
    Consulting Doctor GJ, shrink remit (Psychiatrist)
    She gets them to admit being counterfeit
    And, here inside SaRS, saying write your memoirs
    They all just had to accept it
    Continue giving a shit… For the patients' wit…

        Donald is a smart man, he used to follow a plan
        He has only just lost his way
        Getting some instruction, on mental reconstruction
        Fix all of his fading away
        Mister Houts Marted, other shrink remit (Psychologist)
        Working on mind un-split, of the nitty-grit
        He's here, inside SaRS, topic of the memoirs
        They all just had to accept it
        Continue giving a shit… For the patients' wit…

            Donald, throttled, modelled, coddled
            He was learning it the hard way
            Do this, or that, or something or other
            Until he gets to say, "Good Day!"
            Students here to learn, not to baby-sit
            Trying to help us fit, warning off our quit
            They're here, inside SaRS, also in the memoirs
            They all just had to accept it
            Everyone gives a big a shit… For the patients' wit…

                Sad, not bad, Donald's mad, he's trying to find his glad
                His brain is getting in the way
                He knows that he needs this, anything else is remiss
                Well, that is what the doctors say
                So, Donald's getting his story published
                All sensibility's being punished
                Donald's indignation, mental constipation
                Might go on indefinitely
                But Donald's mentality hyperbole's here for you to see

Big Bertha

For all of those who never gave up on me
Encouraging hope, keeping me in my tree
Whether it's deserved is not my call to make
Swallowing no hook, it was my big mistake

Big Bertha is her name...
...and sanity's her game
She's how I want to be
Standing sturdy and free

Never letting my emotions get their way
Chastising the words, when negative I say
Make me look ahead, help finding me a goal
Climb that heartfelt tree, keep my sanity whole

Big Bertha is her name...
...and sanity's her game
She's how I want to be
Standing sturdy and free

Showing the way home and where I need to turn
Keep plugging away until I choose to learn
Who knows, it may work, I guess I'll let you know
And in the meantime, I'll sit and watch her grow

Big Bertha is her name...
...and sanity's her game
She's how I want to be
Standing sturdy and free

So... Now I have gone, Bertha's a distant past
No more stupidly thinking that it won't last
Every morning I rise and put on a smile
I have worn their shoes, and I have walked their mile

Big Bertha is her name...
...and sanity's her game
She's how I want to be
Standing sturdy and free

Dark Roast Moccona (Inspired by *My Sharona – The Knack*)

Oh yeah, intensity eight, a coffee break
When's it gonna be ready, large Moccona?
Oh yeah, I don't wanna wait, don't wanna wait
Tremble's starting to steady… My Moccona?

Caffeine level's dropped, need a top, coffee infusion
Sprinkle of chocolate top, make it hot, mocha diffusion
T-T-T-Too-Hot, Fffff…

D-D-Dark Roast Moccona

Make it a little hotter, little hotter
Hot enough to burn my tongue, scorched Moccona
You gotta keep 'em coming, keep 'em coming
I can never stop at one… More Moccona!

Caffeine level's dropped, need a top, coffee infusion
Sprinkle of chocolate top, make it hot, mocha diffusion
T-T-T-Too-Hot, Fffff…

D-D-Dark Roast Moccona
D-D-Dark Roast Moccona (Yum!)

I'm back for a second cup, s-second cup
I'll have the same as before, large Moccona…
Here's cheers, B-B-Bottoms-Up, B-Bottoms-Up
I'm addicted, I need more… Five Mocconas!

Caffeine level's dropped, need a top, coffee infusion
Sprinkle of chocolate top, make it hot, mocha diffusion
T-T-T-Too-Hot, Fffff…
T-T-T-T-T-T-T-Too, Too, Too, Too-Hot, Fffff…

D-D-Dark Roast Moccona
D-D-Dark Roast Moccona
D-D-Dark Roast Moccona
D-D-Dark Roast Moccona

Yuuummm-Dark Roast Moccona, Yuuummm-Dark Roast Moccona
Yuuummm-Dark Roast Moccona, Yuuummm-Dark Roast Moccona…

Author Bio

David was born on Valentine's Day, 1968, in Fairfield, NSW, Australia. He grew up or at least grew older in Taree. Educated without much effort on his part... Culminating with a Bachelor of Computer Science from Newcastle University.

He worked as a drone in various Banking and Insurance systems for too many years. Then, escaping the mundane, he went to work in the Australian Defence industry. Finally, he worked in the Immigration and Security world of the Middle East.

During this time: he met various people; got married to one of them; had two very beautiful children; became divorced; and then had several failed relationships. Always making sure everything was done in the *correct* order.

Following his last relationship, too much stress from his last job and a general air of unhappiness, he found himself inside a facility. *One Flew Over the Cuckoo's Nest* is an accurate documentary of these places, and this one was a good one. It was there he took to writing all about himself.

Dredging up his previous attempts at poetry, documenting his downfall and making many errors along the way to recovery, he found writing was to become another avenue for failure... Thus, was born the *Nobody* described in his first book. But he didn't give up...

Then, for his second book, he turned his imagination outward at all of the Numpties of the world. Combining the best aspects of...
- Mother Goose;
- Doctor Seuss; and
- The Brothers Grimm.

...in the concrete mixer of his mind. Applying a modicum of *numptyism*, he produced ~~some~~ many anti-nursery rhymes, anti-songs, anti-lullabies and just lots of anti in general. But still, he didn't give up...

And you may find these... (I suggest you buy one, just to prove him wrong)

Shameless Plugs[555]

The Donald Diaries:

>*Hospityable - (Part One of the Donald Diaries)*
TBA (But, same place where you got this book probably)

The Nobody Saga (7 eBook series):
https://www.amazon.com/gp/product/B08BZTSD2G
>*Poetry and Random Thoughts from a Depressed Mind*
(Autobiography of a Nobody)
https://www.amazon.com.au/gp/product/1795787457
More of the Same
(Continued Saga of a Nobody)
https://www.amazon.com.au/gp/product/B08579P9GH
Some More of the Same but Better
(Episode Three of the Nobody Saga)
https://www.amazon.com.au/gp/product/B08BDDP32Q
Even More of the Same and Even Better
(Chapter 4 of the Nobody Saga)
https://www.amazon.com.au/gp/product/B08CP9DLGB
Yet More of the Same ... Still Better
(Book V of the Nobody Saga)
https://www.amazon.com.au/gp/product/B08GTL737V
Much More of the Same... Gratuitously Better
(Volume (////\ /) of the Nobody Saga)
https://www.amazon.com.au/gp/product/B08MMZ73PX
Bigger and Better ... Sameness
(Lucky #7 of the Nobody Saga)
https://www.amazon.com.au/gp/product/B096TJLG8Q

Numpty-Rhymes, Numpty-Bys and Numpty-Songs
(Poetry from Numpty's Doctor's Brother's Goose)
https://www.amazon.com.au/gp/product/B098H61Q8X

---

[555] Finally, have I mentioned Coffee? One with "one of everything" please.